Charisma's Turn

Also by Monique Couvson (as Monique W. Morris)

*Sing a Rhythm, Dance a Blues: Liberatory Education
for Black and Brown Girls*

Pushout: The Criminalization of Black Girls in Schools

*Black Stats: African Americans by the Numbers
in the Twenty-First Century*

Too Beautiful for Words: A Novel

*Cultivating Joyful Learning Spaces for Black Girls:
Insights into Interrupting School Pushout*

CHARISMA'S TURN

A Graphic Novel

MONIQUE COUVSON

ILLUSTRATED BY
AMANDA JONES

THE
NEW
PRESS

NEW YORK
LONDON

Requests for permission to reproduce selections from this book should be made through our website: https://thenewpress.com/contact.

Published in the United States by The New Press, New York, 2023
Distributed by Two Rivers Distribution

ISBN 978-1-62097-401-8 (hc)
ISBN 978-1-62097-402-5 (ebook)
CIP data is available

The New Press publishes books that promote and enrich public discussion and understanding of the issues vital to our democracy and to a more equitable world. These books are made possible by the enthusiasm of our readers; the support of a committed group of donors, large and small; the collaboration of our many partners in the independent media and the not-for-profit sector; booksellers, who often hand-sell New Press books; librarians; and above all by our authors.

www.thenewpress.com

This book was made possible, in part, by a generous grant from Art for Justice Fund, a sponsored project of Rockefeller Philanthropy Advisors

Book design and composition by Bookbright Media
This book was set in Palatino and Brandon Grotesque

Printed in the United States of America

10 9 8 7 6 5 4 3 2

For Nikki Giovanni,
whose revolutionary dreams continue to protect the yolk

Foreword

I will not mince words. I am raising revolutionaries.

Over twenty-five years working with middle school students, I have had boots on the ground, creating spaces for young people to discover the power of their voices.

Since stepping into my first classroom in East New York, Brooklyn, I have insisted that my students identify inequities, address them, and move us forward. In this way, I wound up cultivating a curriculum that introduced young people to their ability to be change agents. This was before pedagogical debate, misinterpreted terms, and new framing for the sankofa tradition of combining innovation and hard-won wisdom.

It happened organically as I shaped black construction paper into the forty-one bullets that unjustly killed Amadou Diallo and created a timeline in the back of my classroom for my eighth-graders to follow the case of the African vendor who held up a wallet that was mistaken for a weapon. My students collected articles, watched the evening news, and reported from the streets as we waited for justice.

Little did we know that many years later we would don hoodies for Trayvon and grow disheartened as a litany of hashtagged names became vigils for brothas and sistas lost to racial violence. From my new home in Atlanta, I would begin to feel despondent. I would question if

I had it in me to keep watch over the next generation of activists. With each name, each heartache, and each soul lost, the demand that our humanity be respected began to feel almost futile—but then my children answered.

The children I had taught to speak loudly and freely, through their hearts, through their art, and through their calling took up the mantle. I realized that from the first piece of chalk I held at summer programs and storefront after-school programs and theater programs, I had introduced the *Last Poets*, opened mics and set the stage for them to use personal narrative as salve and fortification. Their purpose was rooted in their story.

So I recognized Charisma immediately.
Knew that bravado intimately
Could see through the furrowed brow
Could feel past the sneered facade
Could hear the longing between the lines
Her flying fists didn't faze me
Because I taught where I went to school
Knew how genius was missed because latch key responsibility took precedence
Knew how brilliance might not show up the way people needed, wanted or quantified
Knew balled fists slammed checked boxes that said nothing about how we saw ourselves
Knew we wanted to be called smart then dared to show it so I taught Toni's missing marigolds, serenaded my children with strange fruit, climbed the fence beside Zora, reached for dreams with Langston, watched from windows with Cisneros, and lit a fire with James while Nikki doled out black feeling, black talk, and black judgment.
I would consequently hear, "What grade do you teach?!" when they

saw the collection of elders and ancestors I gathered, but I taught children who faced ups and downs beyond their years with valor and conviction.

These were no shrinking violets.

They were already hustling for the come up and striving to bring friends and family with them. My work was urgent and I couldn't have them wait until college to meet the authors that could show them how to fend for self and create the lives they wanted.

So I knew Charisma would appreciate wisdom.

I knew she would welcome the opportunity to show the side of her no one expected. Or maybe she didn't think people could see because she spat a protective "Well?!" at someone who caught a glimpse behind the mask and they backed off.

But I knew that sista too.

The one who would ride for family. Whose girl trusted her without question. Who repped her 'hood to the fullest. Who loved afternoons in the park. Who danced to classics blasted during Saturday cleaning. Who was mesmerized by perfect double dutch arcs whipping through the air. The sista people believed in because they peeped how she moved when she believed her own light.

And that is the vital work that should be happening in and outside of classrooms everywhere.

Empowering the light.

How else do we move forward? How else to humanize us? How else to connect us if not through the light in our next generation of scholars and inventors and creatives found within these pages where Toni is advising? Betty is sanginnn and double dutch ropes hiss through the air tapping out a redemption song for an unlikely heroine who might have been dismissed if not for the opportunity to discover the super-power embedded in her story.

How many of our heroines need us to readjust our gaze?

Need us at the ready with a word and water when she has caught her breath, the anger has abated and she is ready to attack the problem out loud? A tentative whisper turned emphatic as she grows confident in the power of her voice.

The rope these bars
Her feet these notes
Jingling bracelets
Punctuation marks

She finds her rhythm
And I listen closely
Turning the rope
Just fast enough
To create steady arcs to frame her movement
Just slow enough
To give her an entry point

It's Charisma's turn
And I suggest you make way
Because she's definitely got next.

—Susan Arauz Barnes

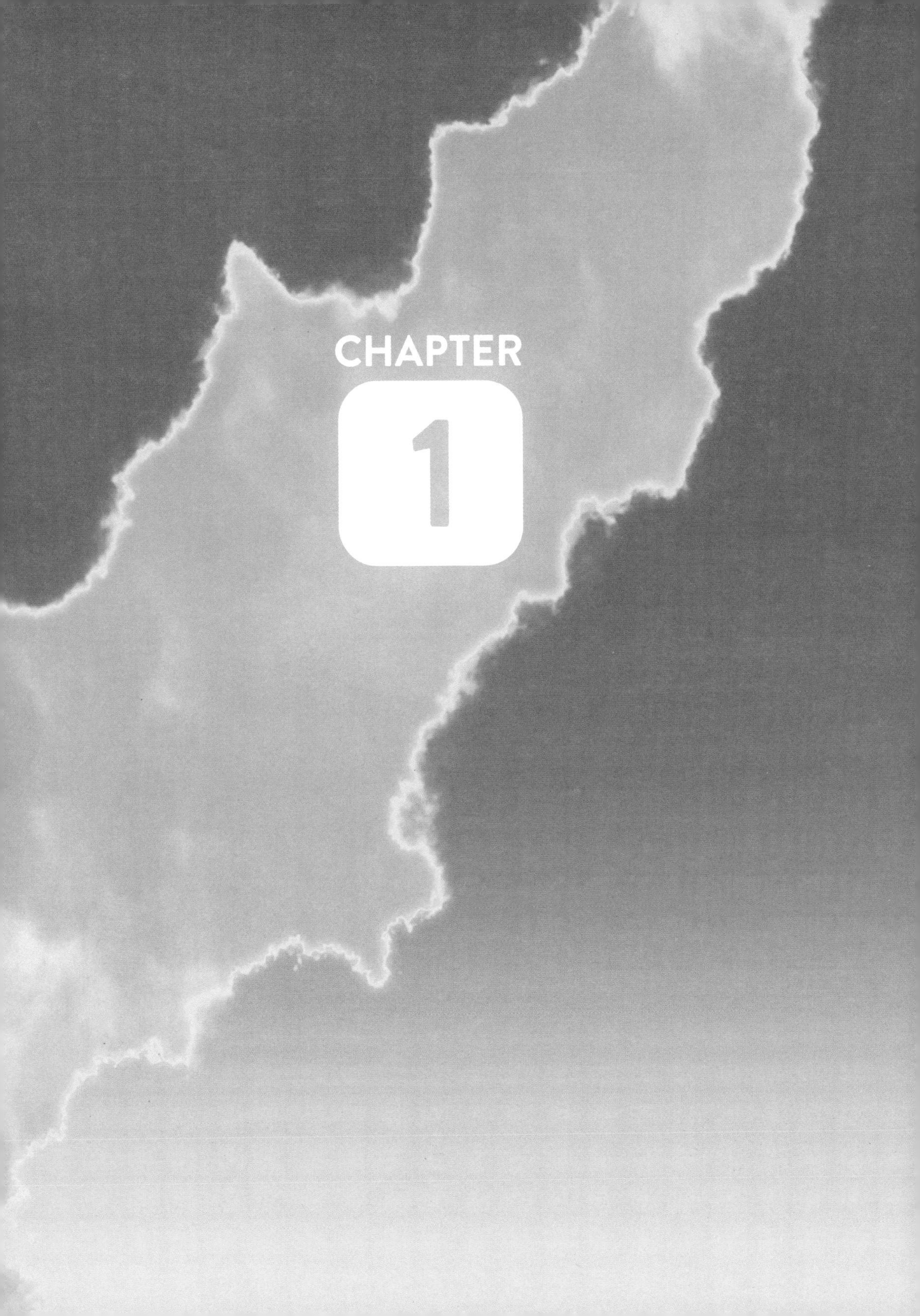

CHAPTER 1

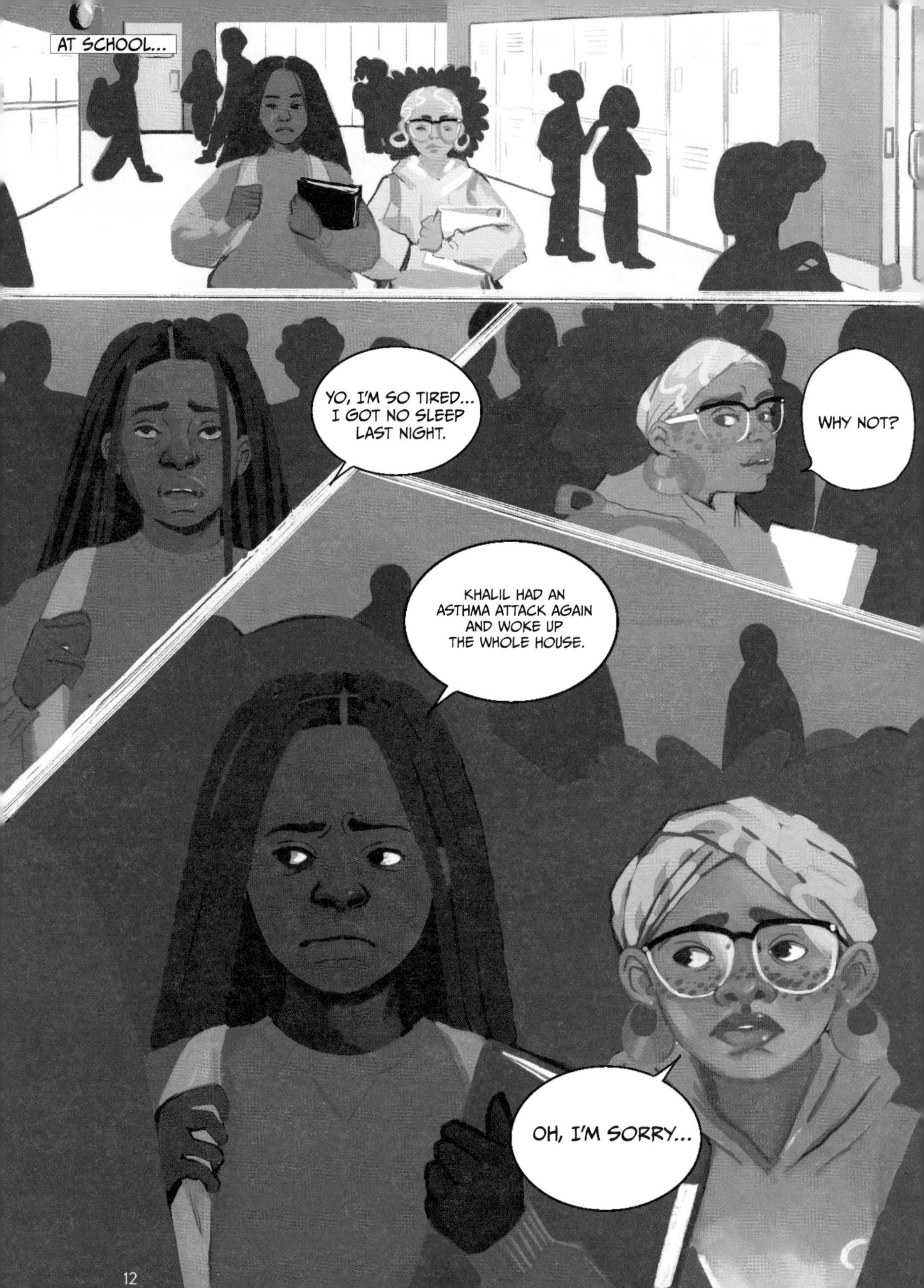
AT SCHOOL...
YO, I'M SO TIRED... I GOT NO SLEEP LAST NIGHT.
WHY NOT?
KHALIL HAD AN ASTHMA ATTACK AGAIN AND WOKE UP THE WHOLE HOUSE.
OH, I'M SORRY...

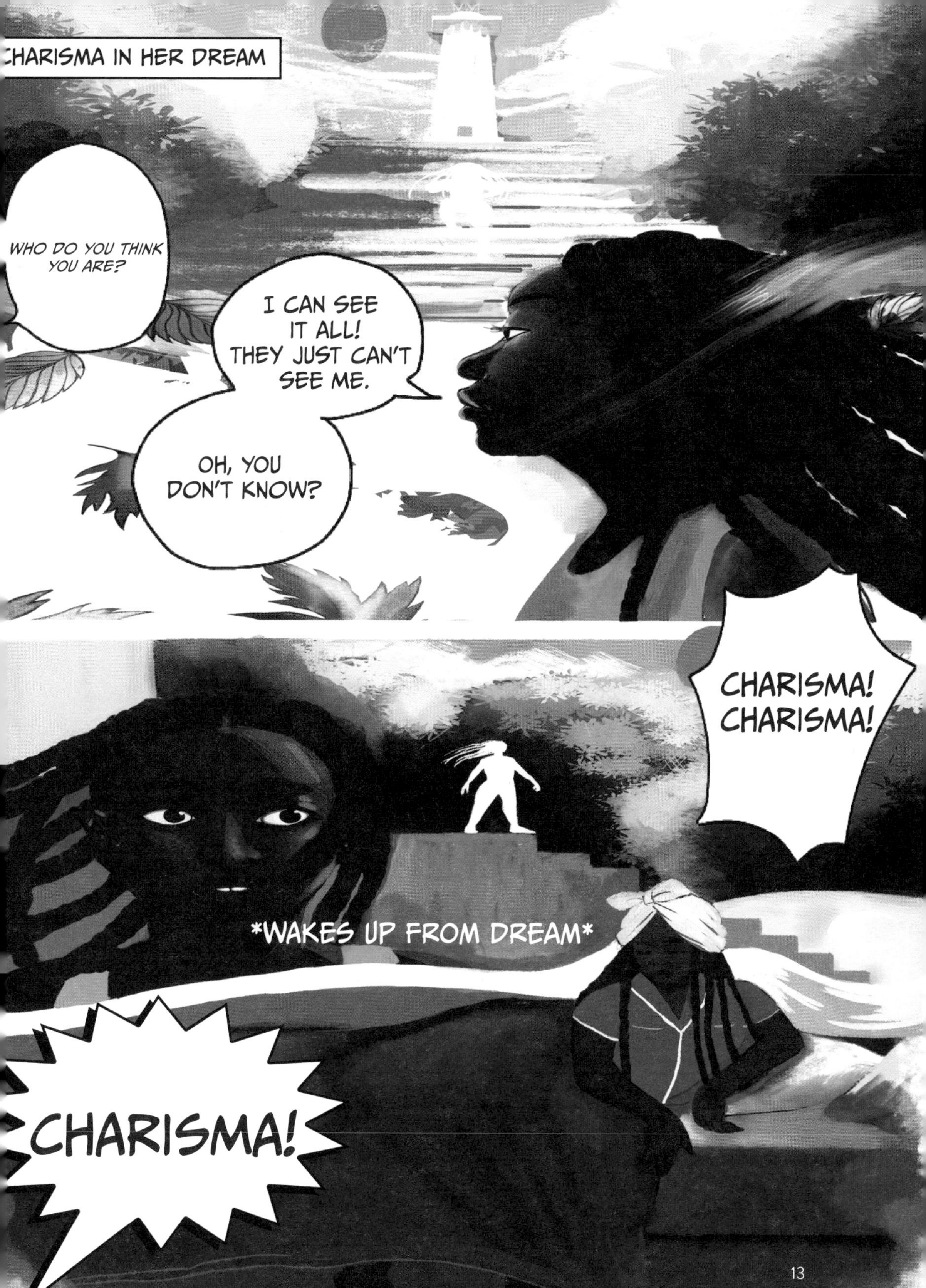
CHARISMA IN HER DREAM
WHO DO YOU THINK YOU ARE?
I CAN SEE IT ALL! THEY JUST CAN'T SEE ME.
OH, YOU DON'T KNOW?
CHARISMA! CHARISMA!
WAKES UP FROM DREAM
CHARISMA!

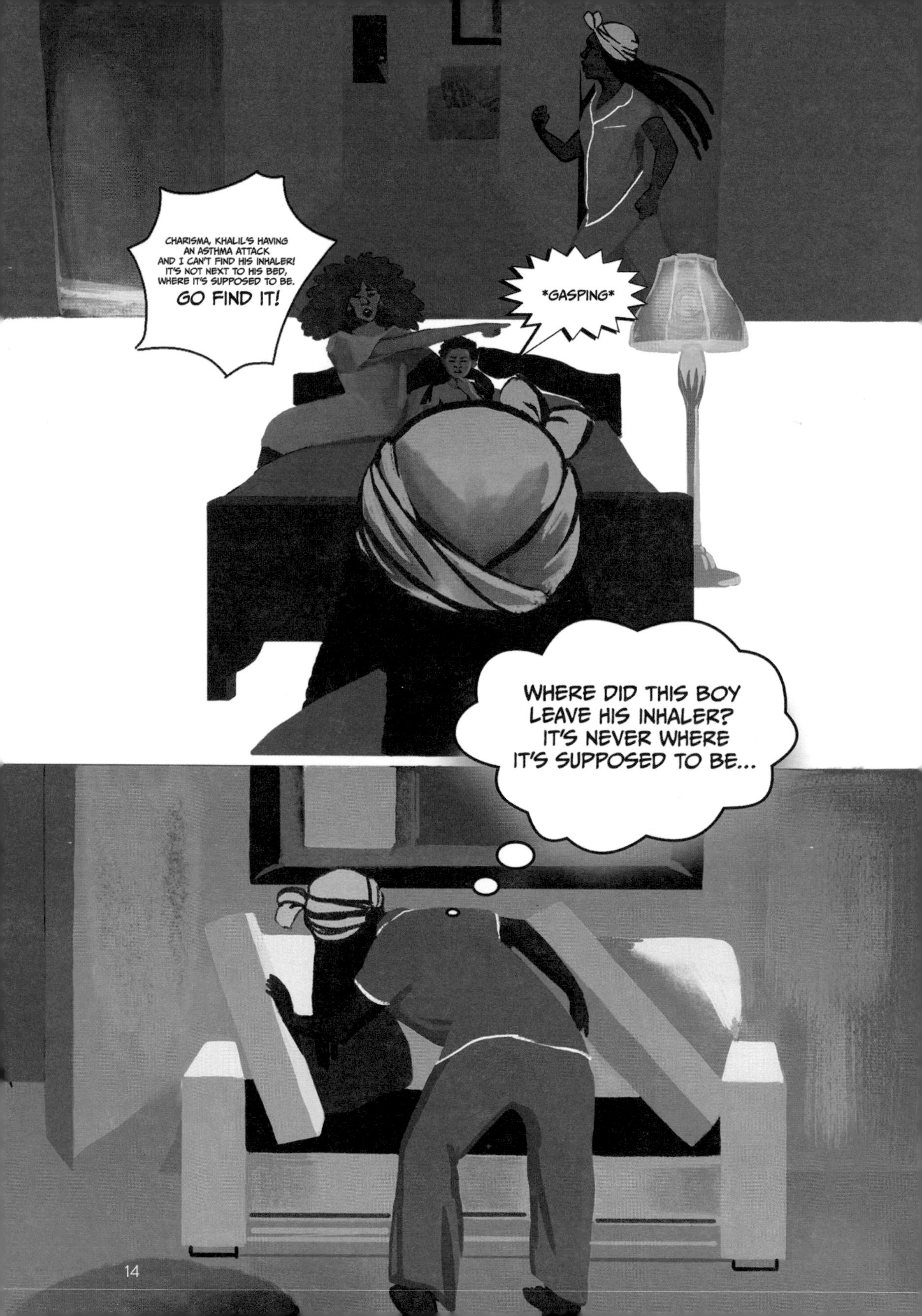
CHARISMA, KHALIL'S HAVING AN ASTHMA ATTACK AND I CAN'T FIND HIS INHALER! IT'S NOT NEXT TO HIS BED, WHERE IT'S SUPPOSED TO BE. GO FIND IT!
GASPING
WHERE DID THIS BOY LEAVE HIS INHALER? IT'S NEVER WHERE IT'S SUPPOSED TO BE...

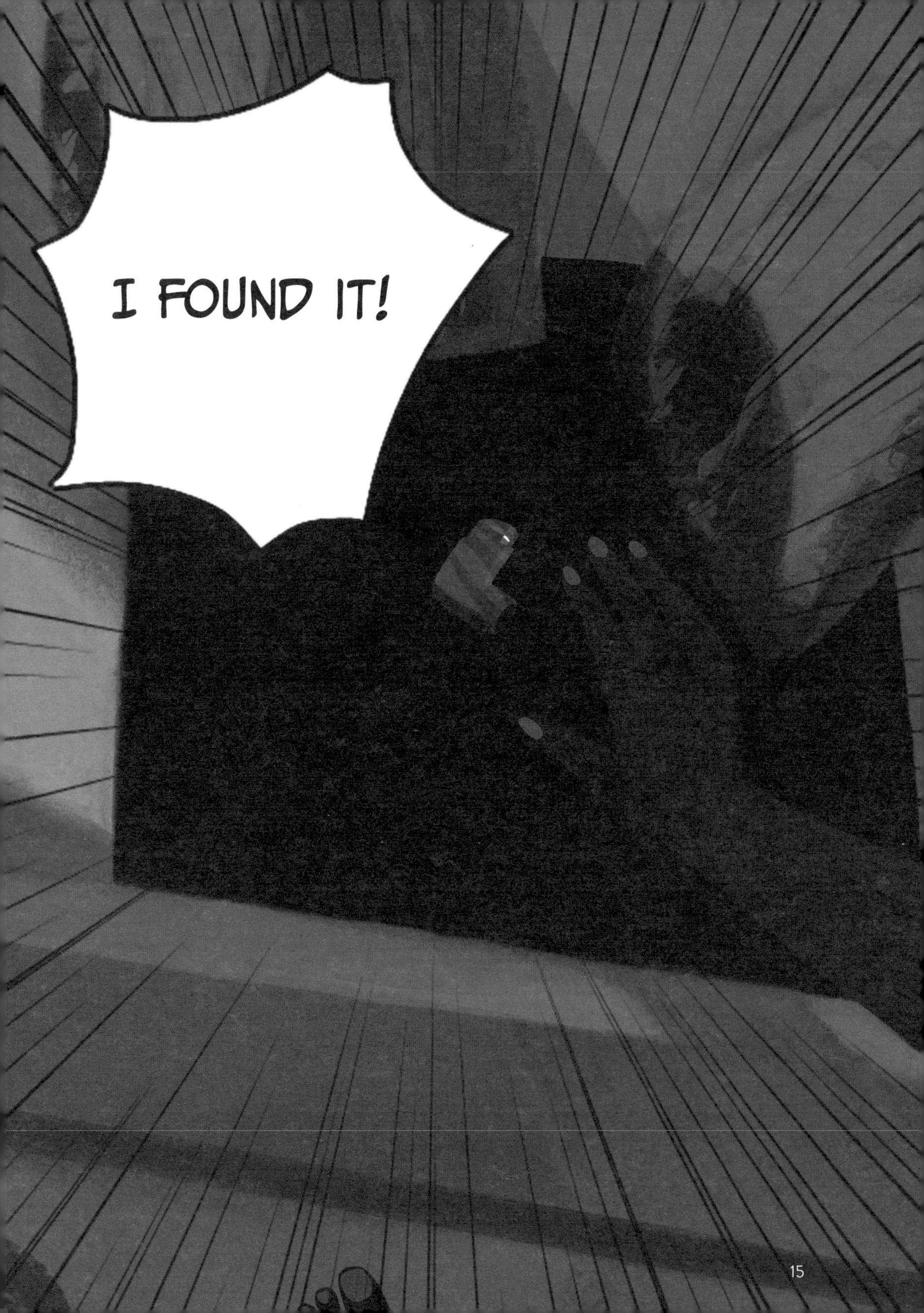
I FOUND IT!

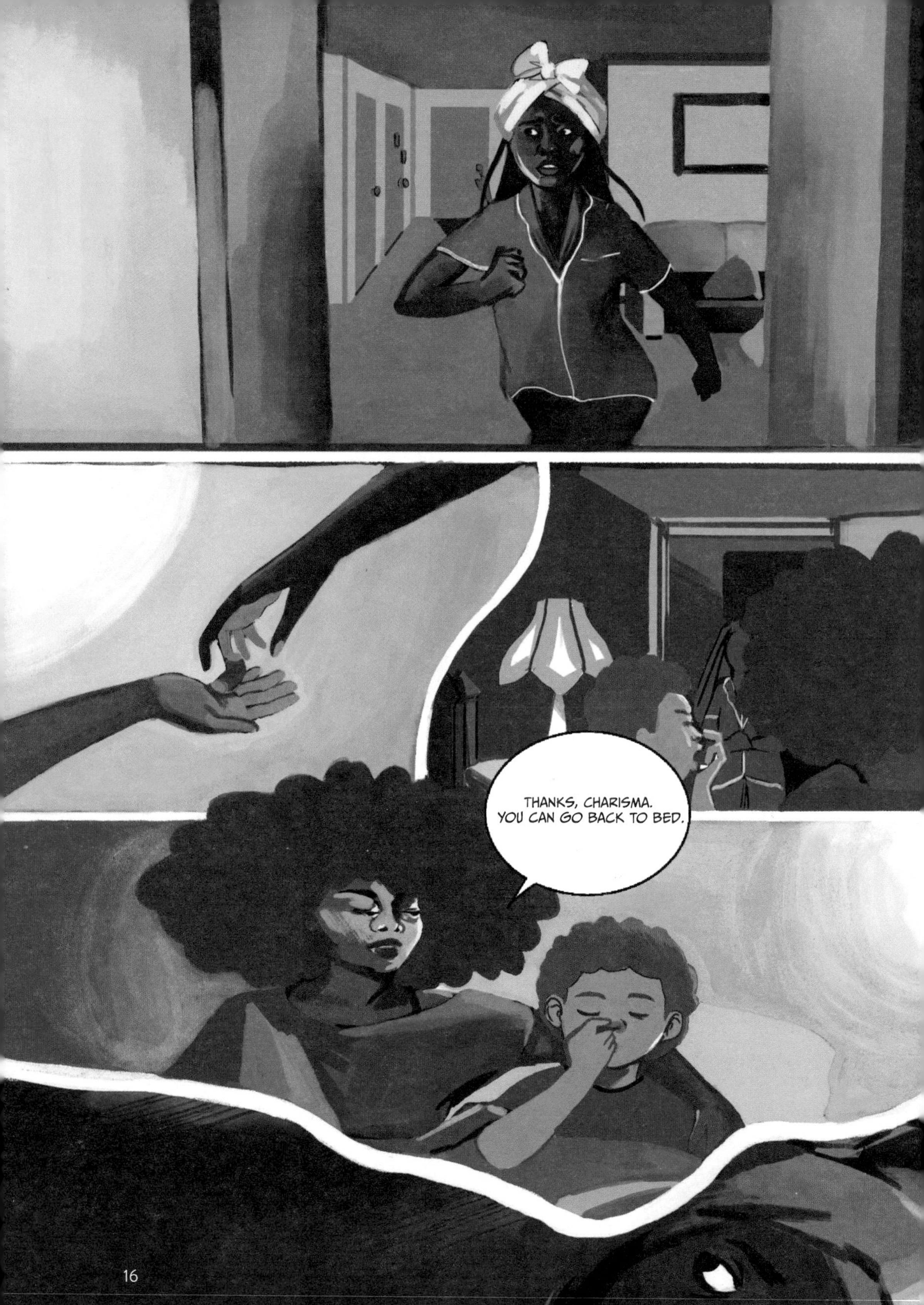
THANKS, CHARISMA.
YOU CAN GO BACK TO BED.

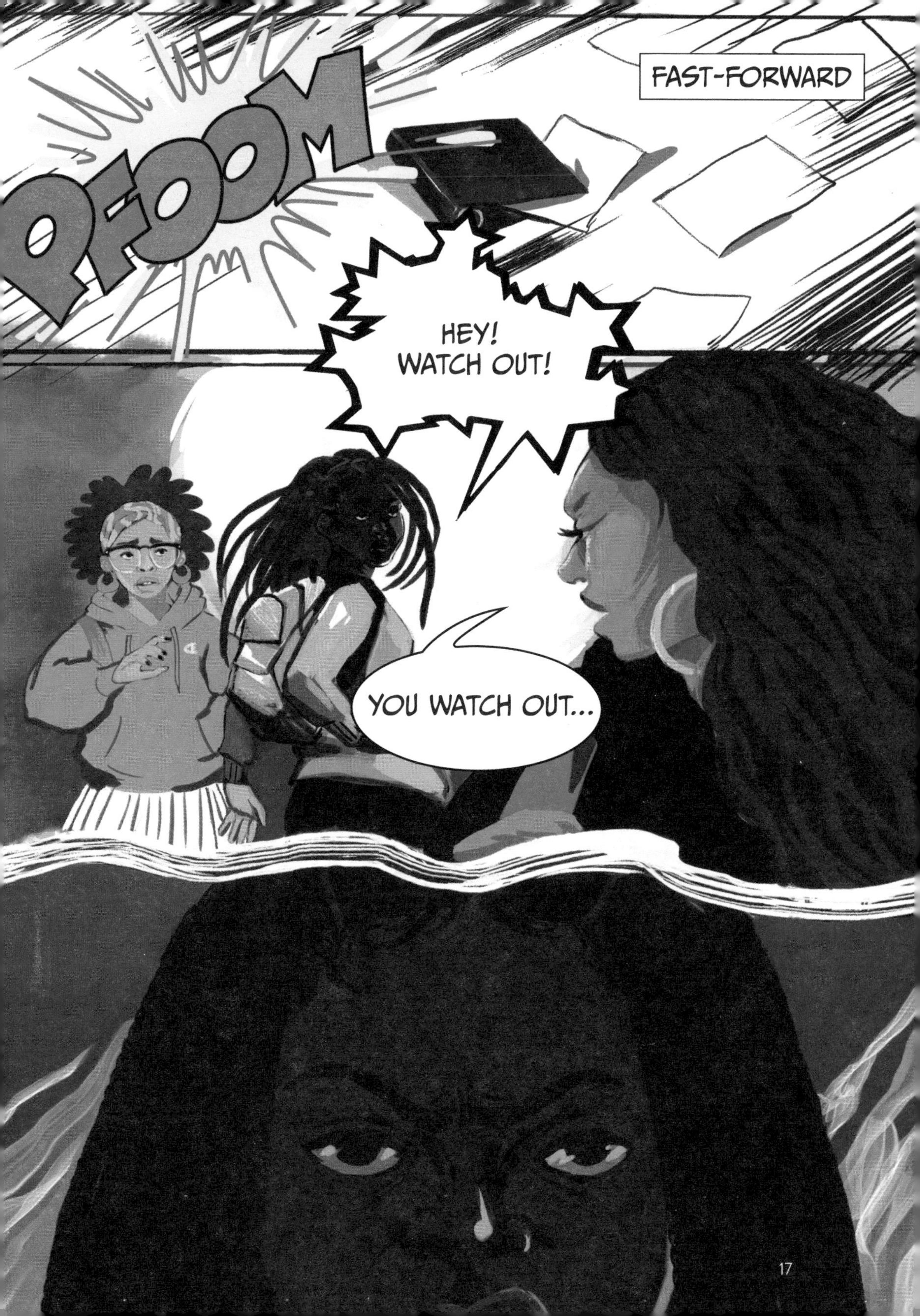
PFOOM
FAST-FORWARD
HEY! WATCH OUT!
YOU WATCH OUT...

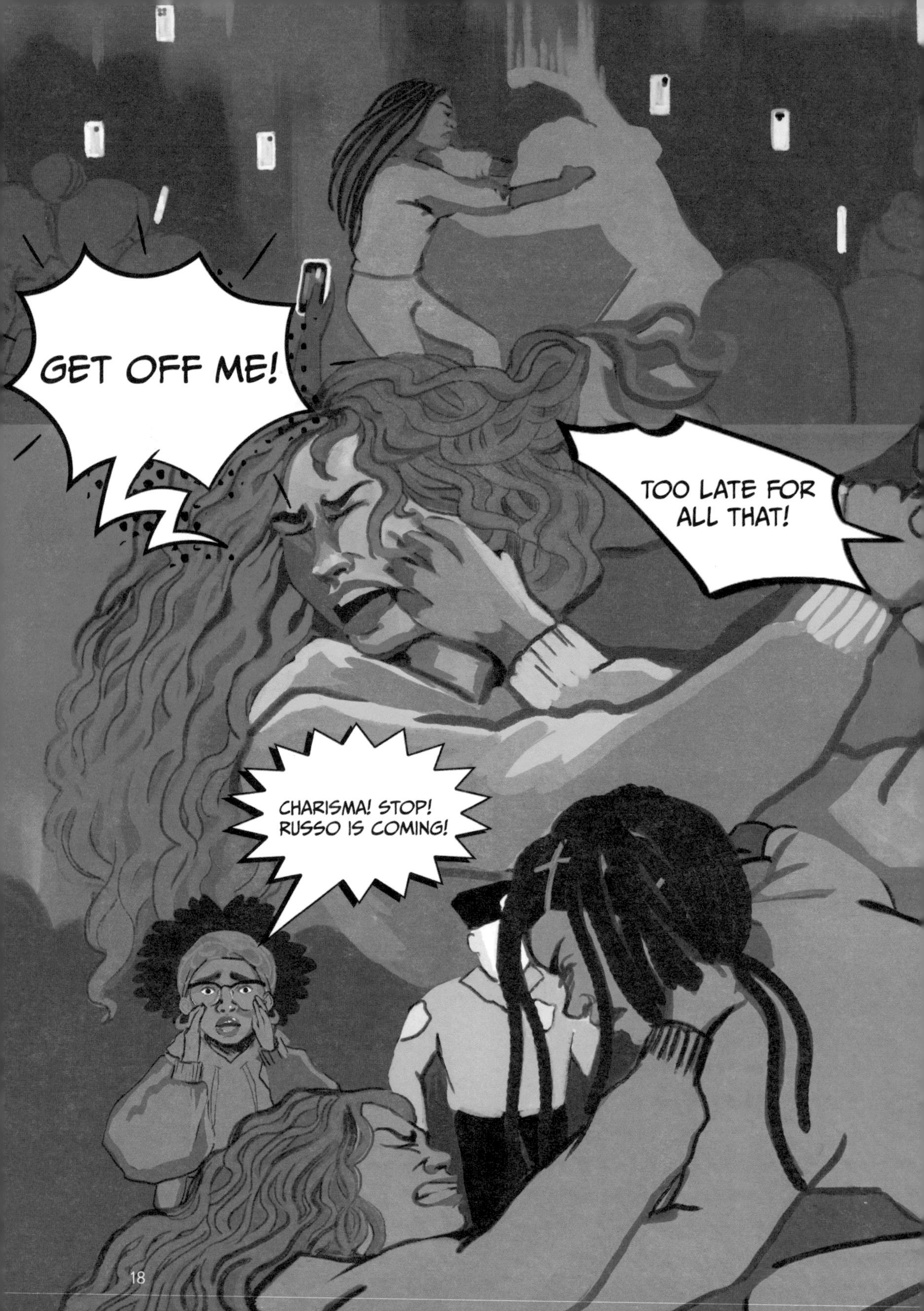
GET OFF ME!
TOO LATE FOR ALL THAT!
CHARISMA! STOP! RUSSO IS COMING!

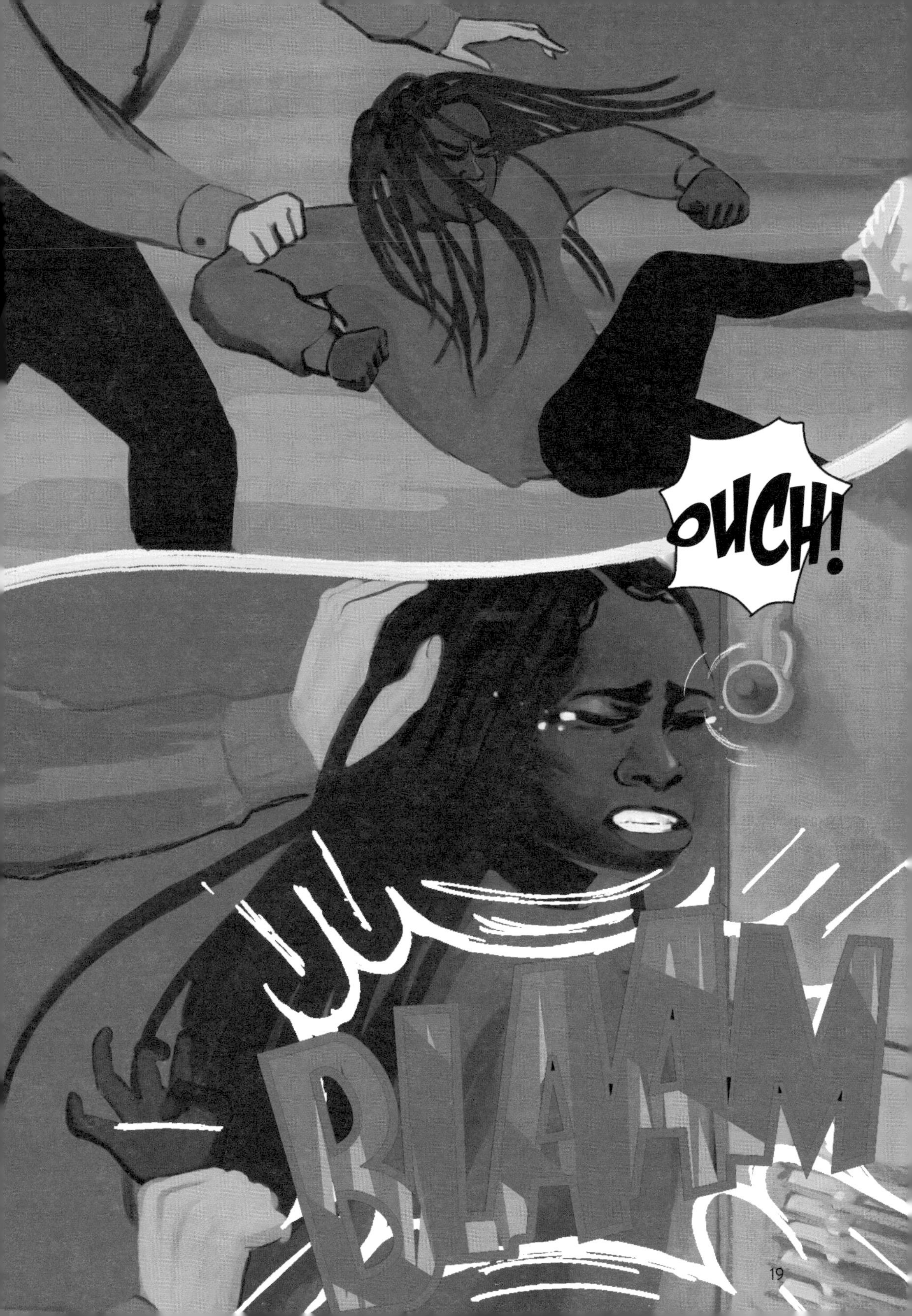
OUCH!
BLAAAM

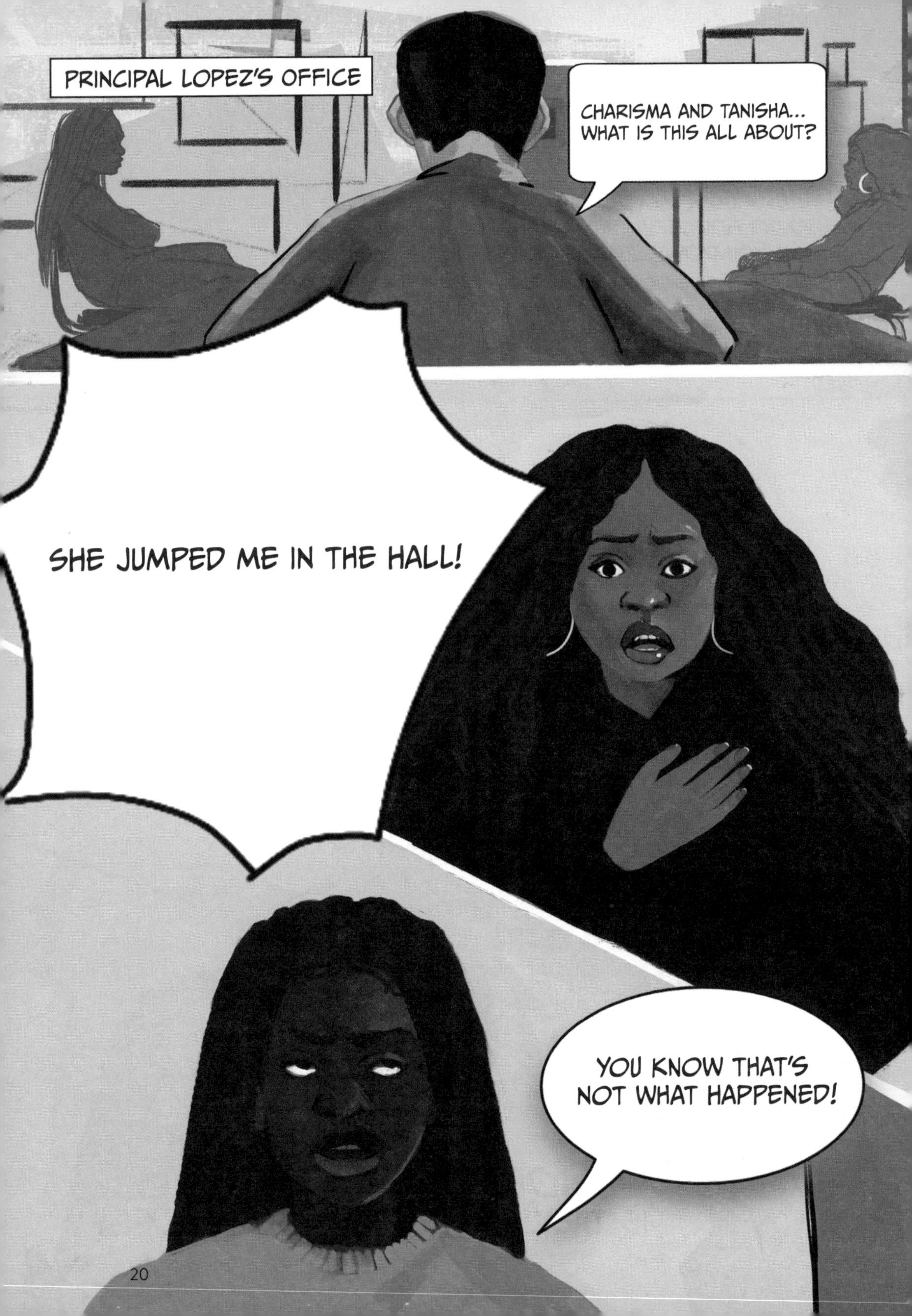
PRINCIPAL LOPEZ'S OFFICE
CHARISMA AND TANISHA... WHAT IS THIS ALL ABOUT?
SHE JUMPED ME IN THE HALL!
YOU KNOW THAT'S NOT WHAT HAPPENED!

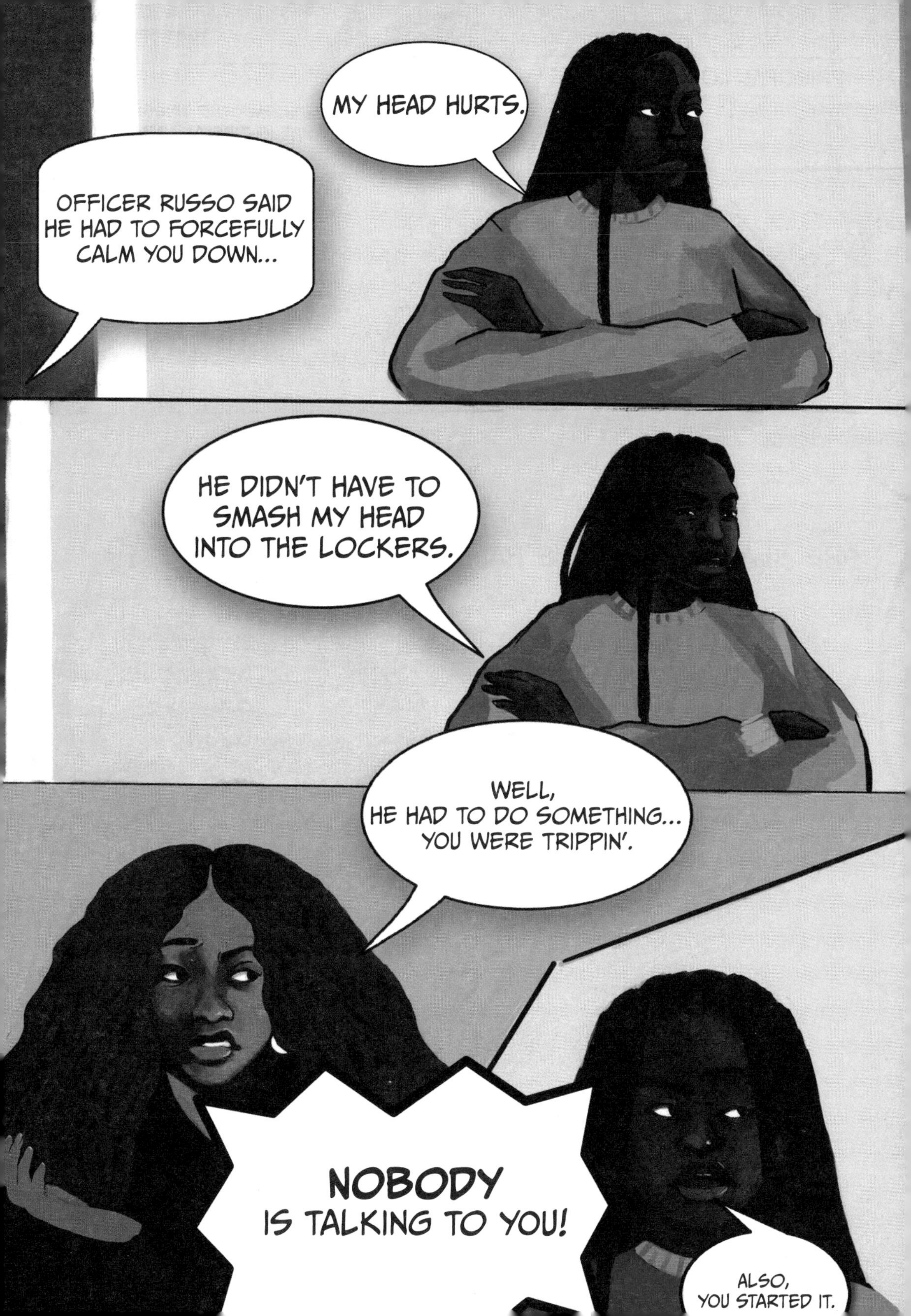
MY HEAD HURTS.
OFFICER RUSSO SAID HE HAD TO FORCEFULLY CALM YOU DOWN...
HE DIDN'T HAVE TO SMASH MY HEAD INTO THE LOCKERS.
WELL, HE HAD TO DO SOMETHING... YOU WERE TRIPPIN'.
NOBODY IS TALKING TO YOU!
ALSO, YOU STARTED IT.

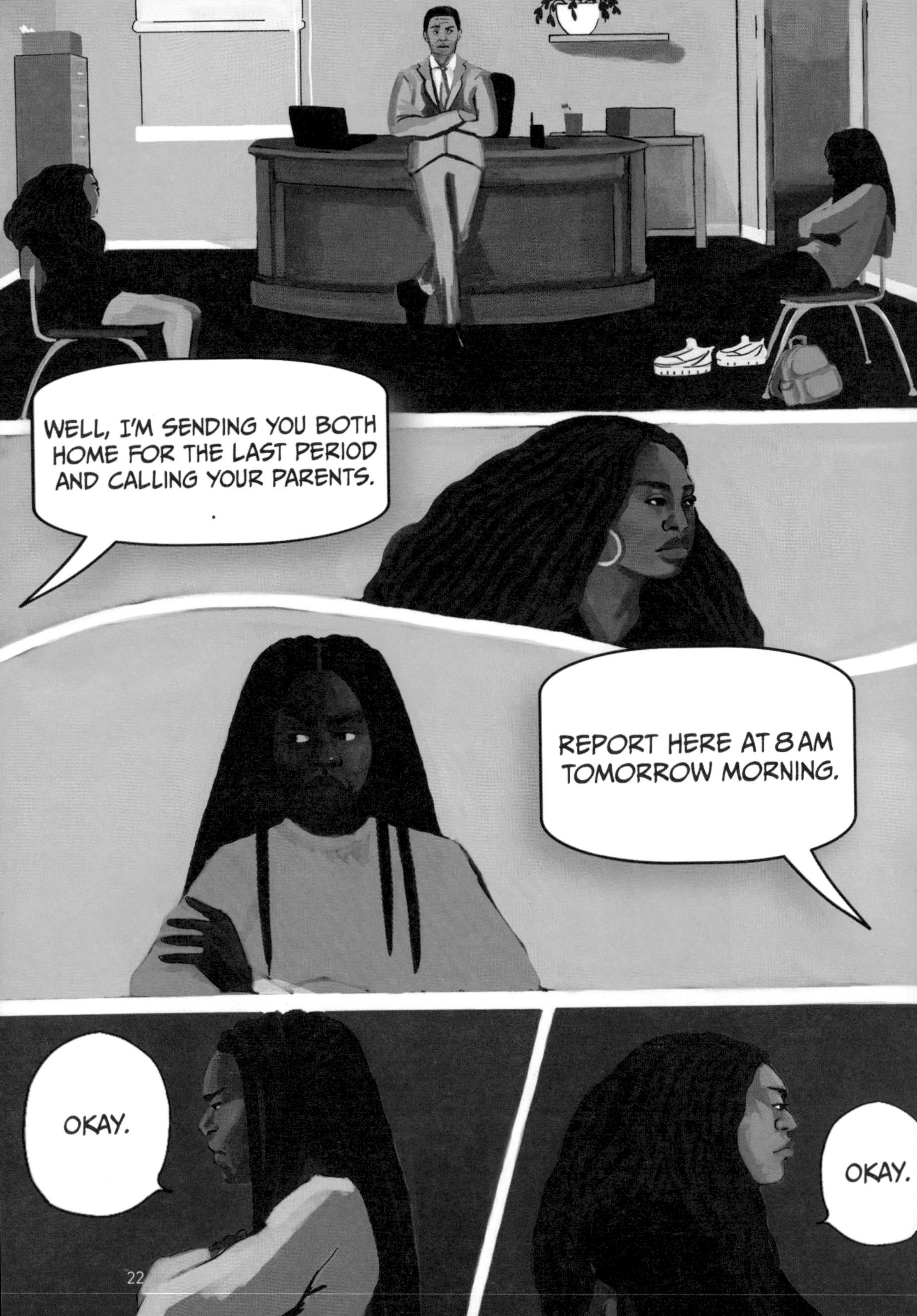
WELL, I'M SENDING YOU BOTH HOME FOR THE LAST PERIOD AND CALLING YOUR PARENTS.
REPORT HERE AT 8 AM TOMORROW MORNING.
OKAY.
OKAY.

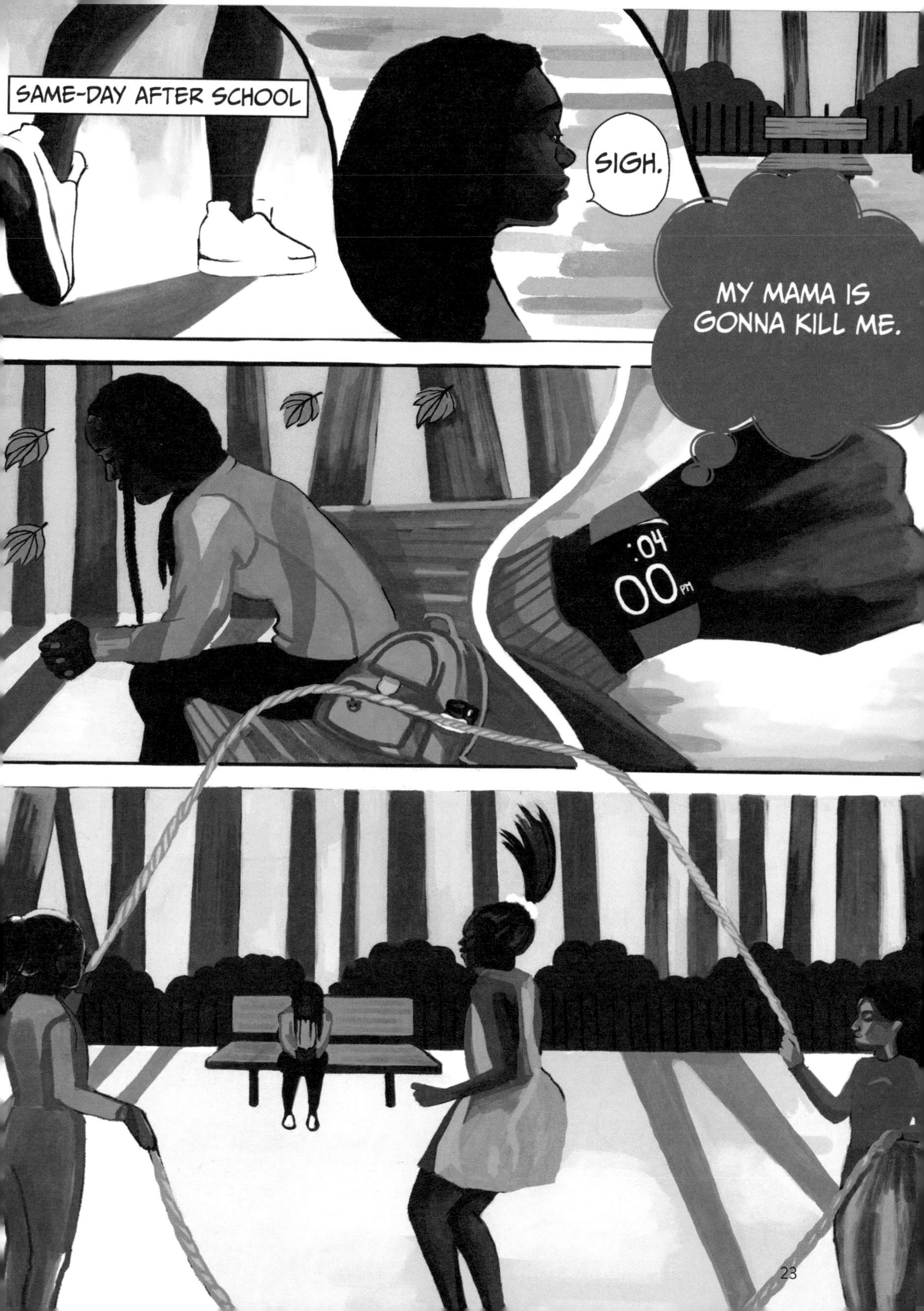
SAME-DAY AFTER SCHOOL
SIGH.
MY MAMA IS GONNA KILL ME.

CHAPTER 2

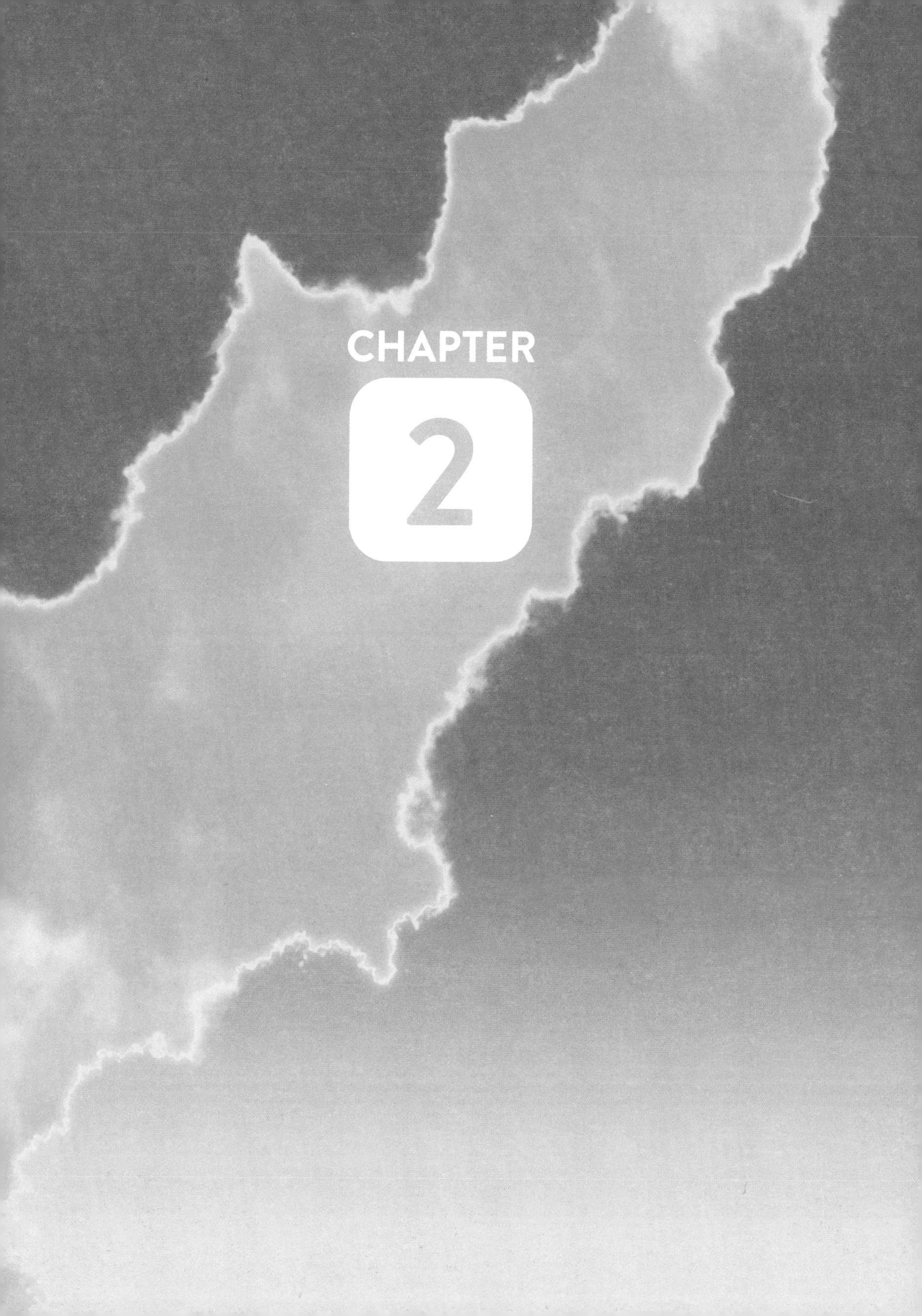

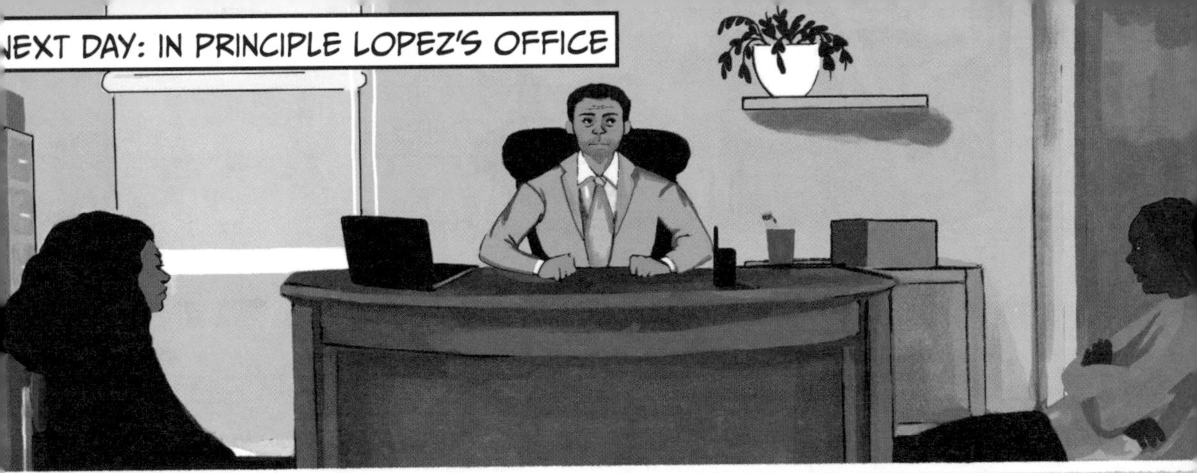
NEXT DAY: IN PRINCIPLE LOPEZ'S OFFICE

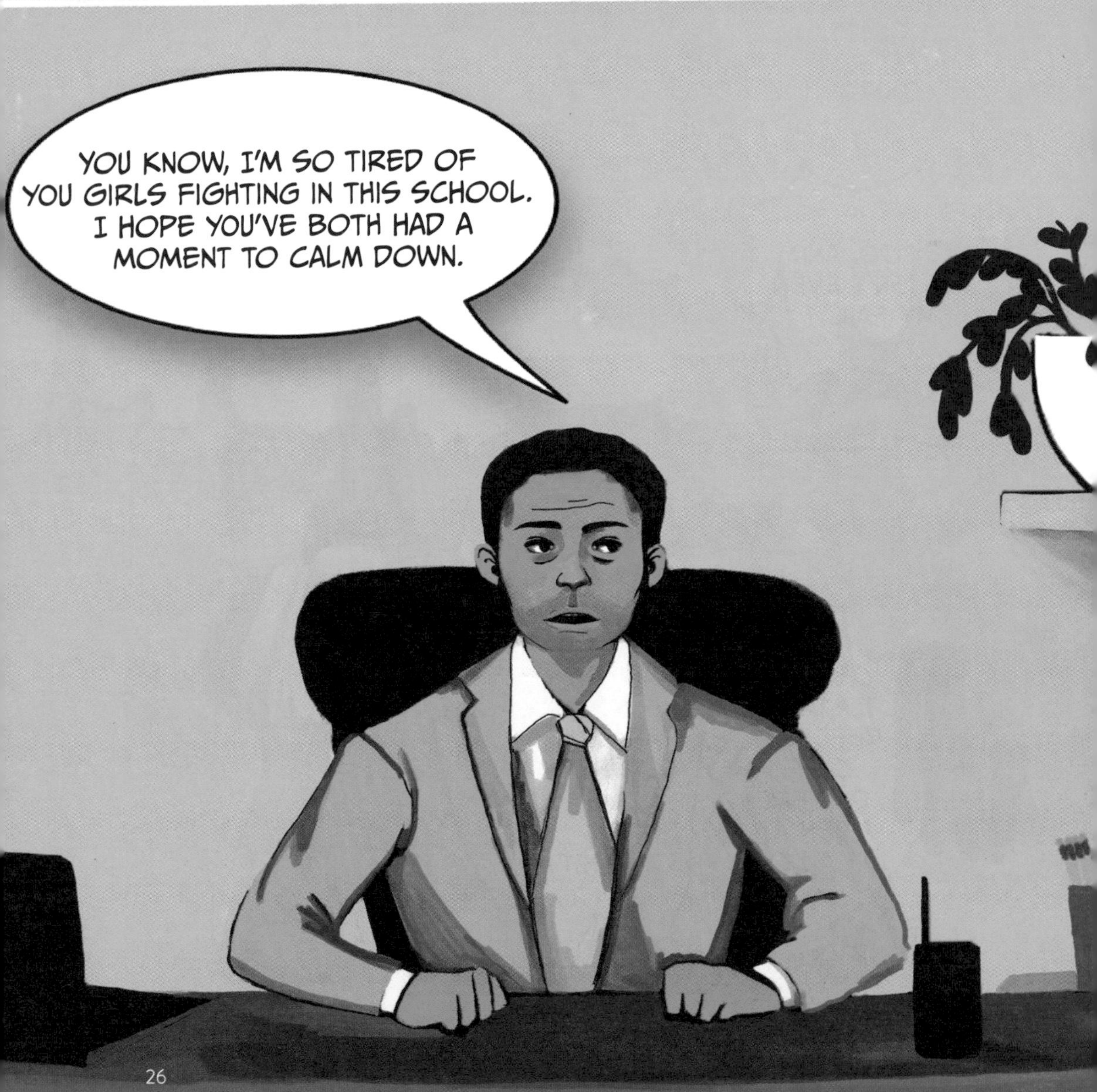
YOU KNOW, I'M SO TIRED OF YOU GIRLS FIGHTING IN THIS SCHOOL. I HOPE YOU'VE BOTH HAD A MOMENT TO CALM DOWN.

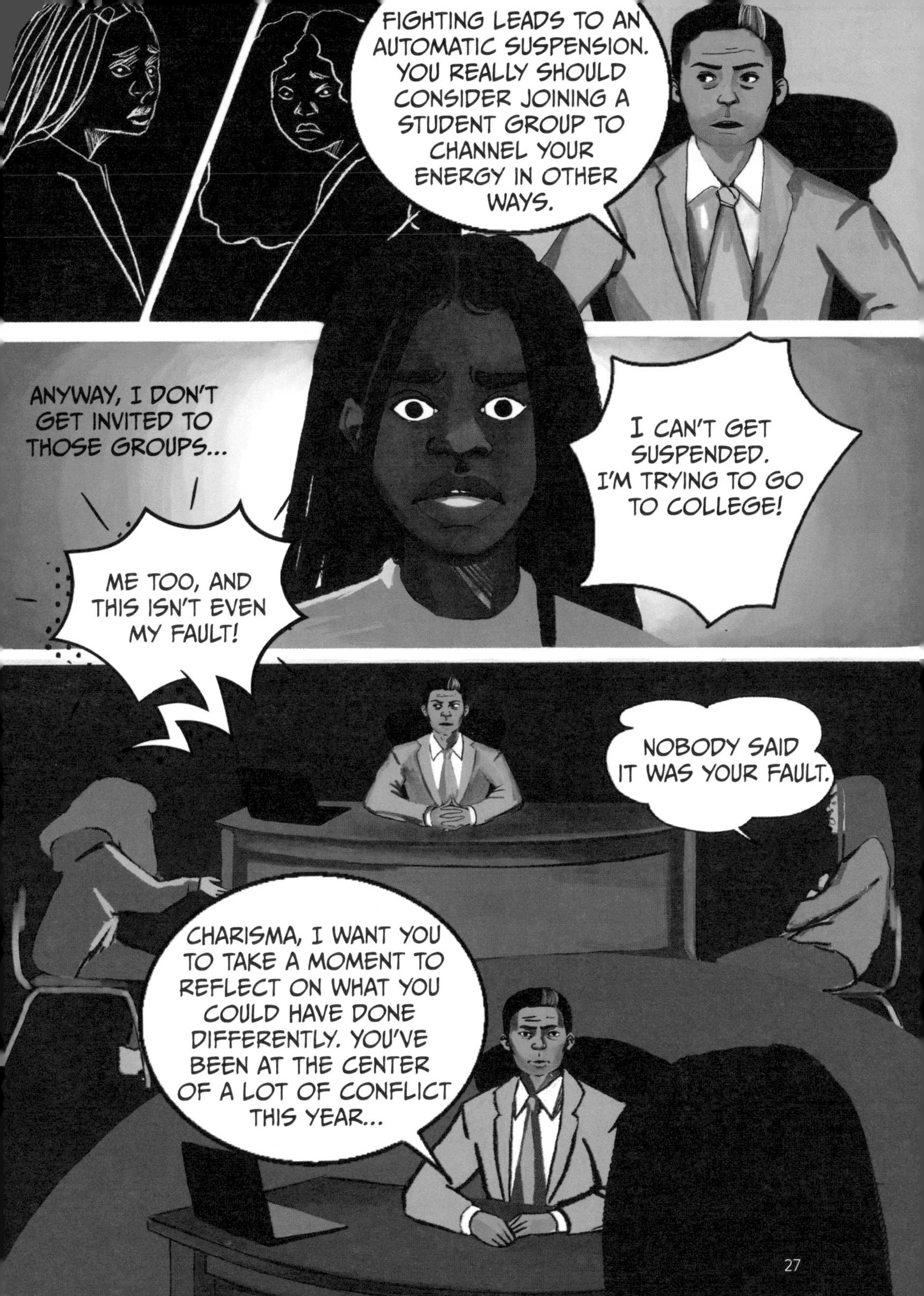
FIGHTING LEADS TO AN AUTOMATIC SUSPENSION. YOU REALLY SHOULD CONSIDER JOINING A STUDENT GROUP TO CHANNEL YOUR ENERGY IN OTHER WAYS.
ANYWAY, I DON'T GET INVITED TO THOSE GROUPS...
I CAN'T GET SUSPENDED. I'M TRYING TO GO TO COLLEGE!
ME TOO, AND THIS ISN'T EVEN MY FAULT!
NOBODY SAID IT WAS YOUR FAULT.
CHARISMA, I WANT YOU TO TAKE A MOMENT TO REFLECT ON WHAT YOU COULD HAVE DONE DIFFERENTLY. YOU'VE BEEN AT THE CENTER OF A LOT OF CONFLICT THIS YEAR...

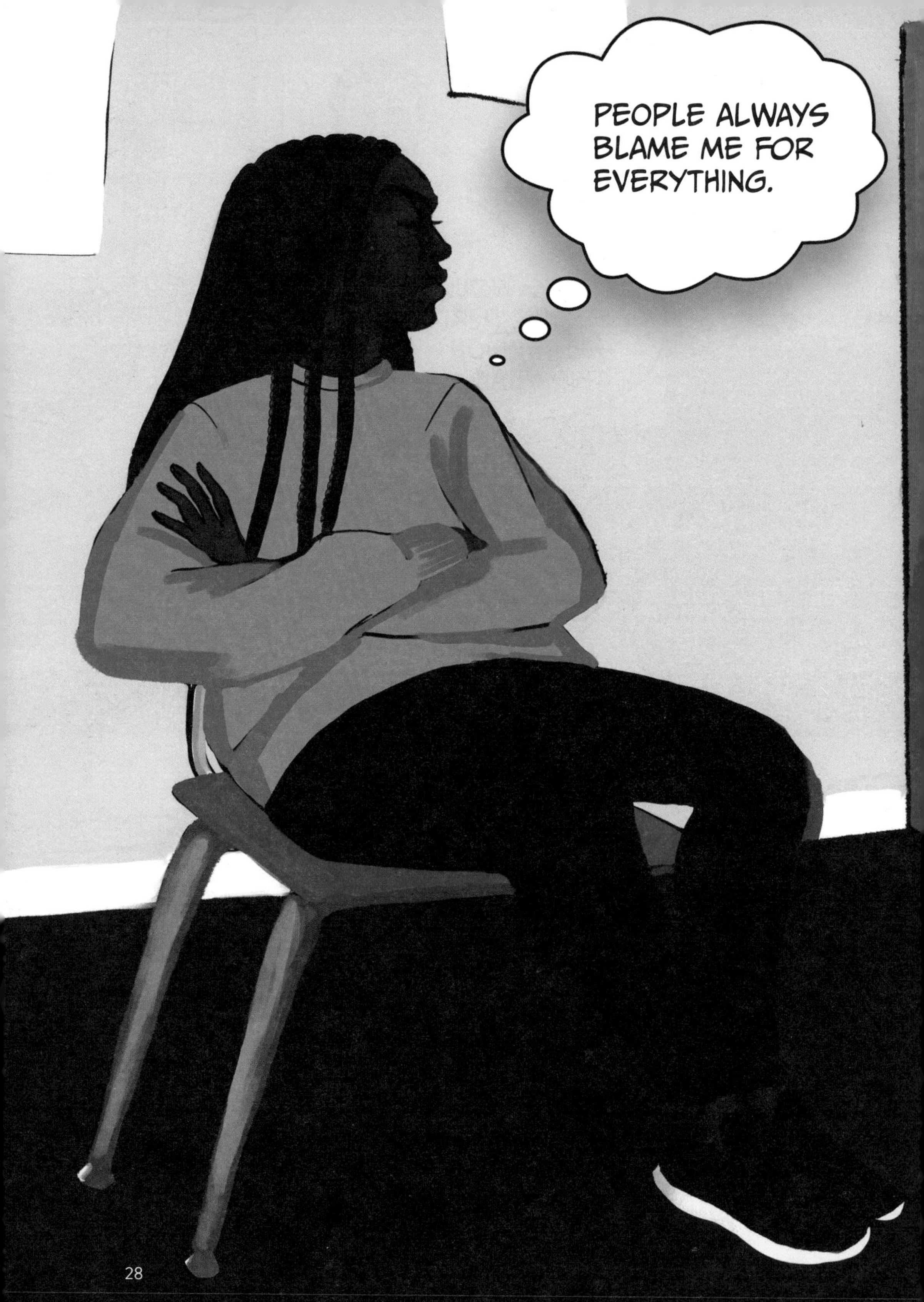
PEOPLE ALWAYS BLAME ME FOR EVERYTHING.

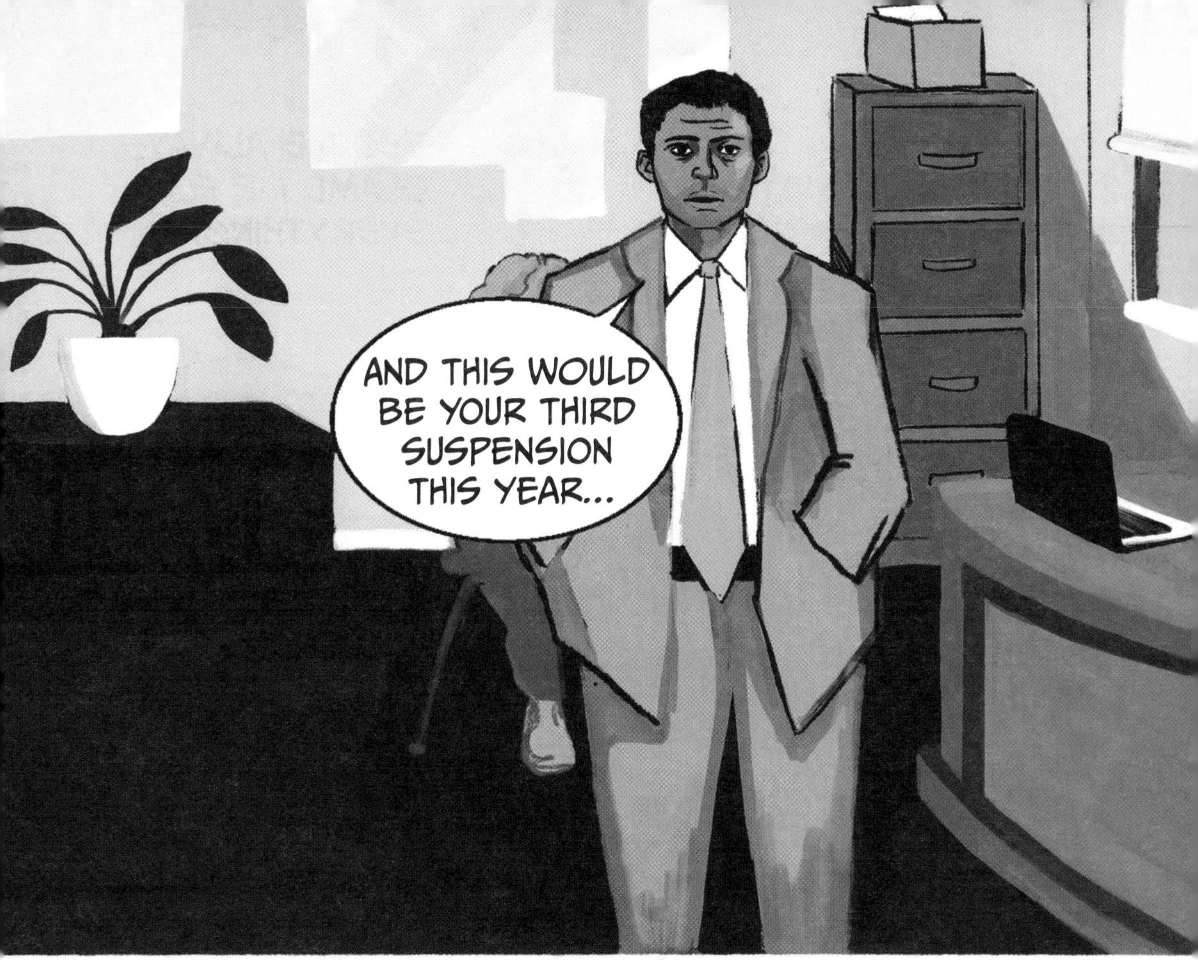
AND THIS WOULD BE YOUR THIRD SUSPENSION THIS YEAR...

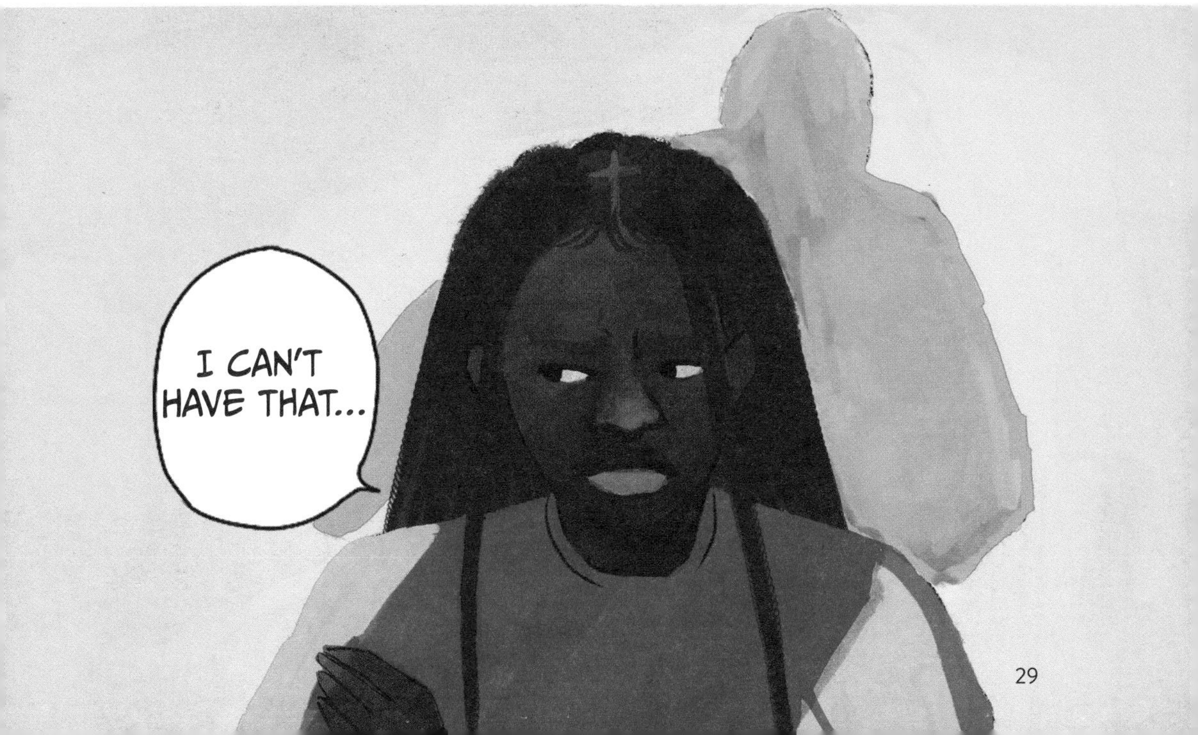
I CAN'T HAVE THAT...

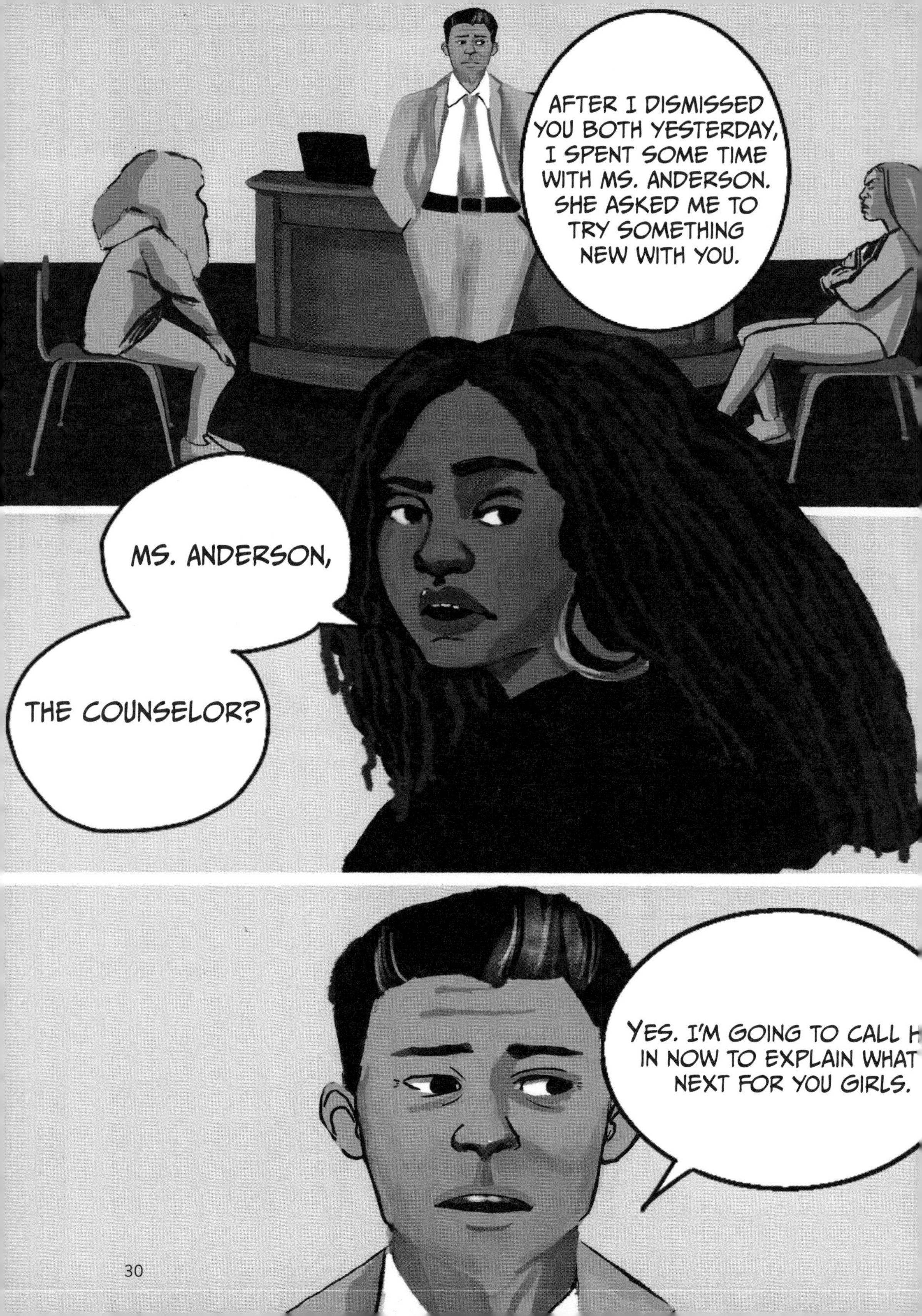
AFTER I DISMISSED YOU BOTH YESTERDAY, I SPENT SOME TIME WITH MS. ANDERSON. SHE ASKED ME TO TRY SOMETHING NEW WITH YOU.
MS. ANDERSON,
THE COUNSELOR?
YES. I'M GOING TO CALL H
IN NOW TO EXPLAIN WHAT
NEXT FOR YOU GIRLS.

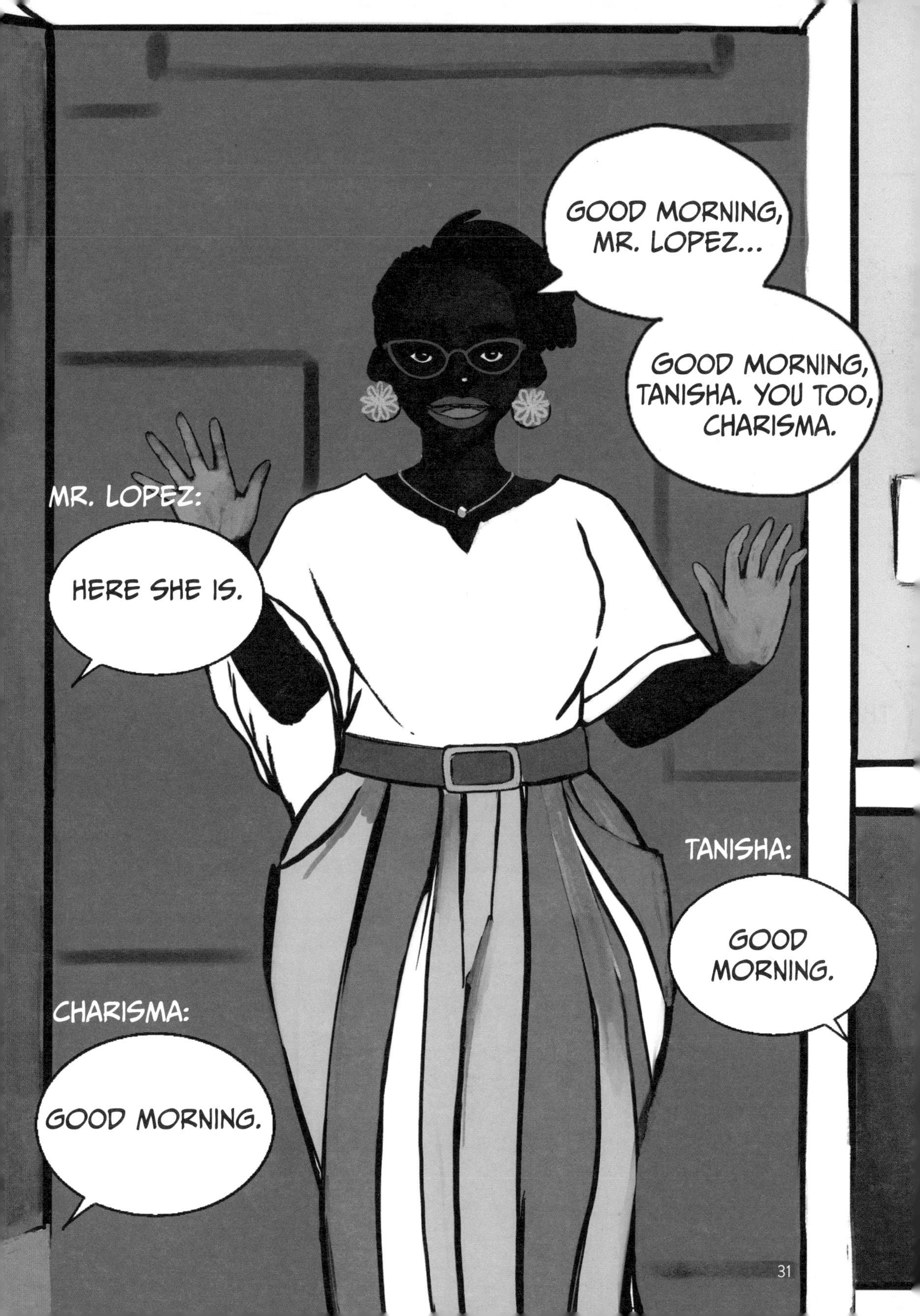
MR. LOPEZ:
HERE SHE IS.
GOOD MORNING, MR. LOPEZ...
GOOD MORNING, TANISHA. YOU TOO, CHARISMA.
TANISHA:
GOOD MORNING.
CHARISMA:
GOOD MORNING.

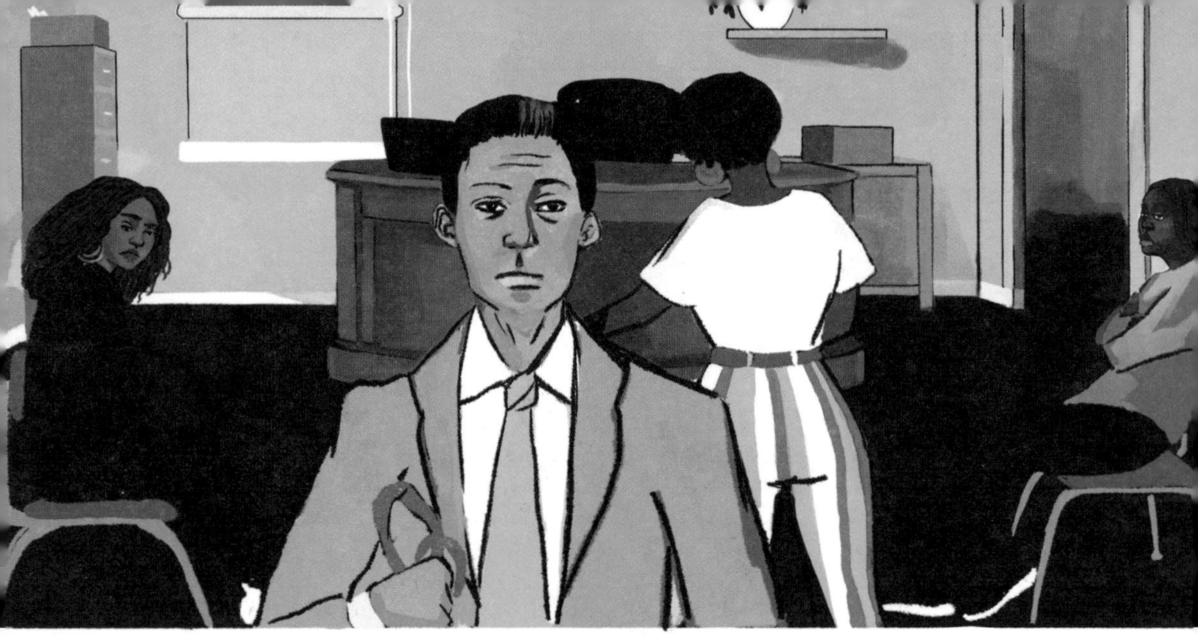

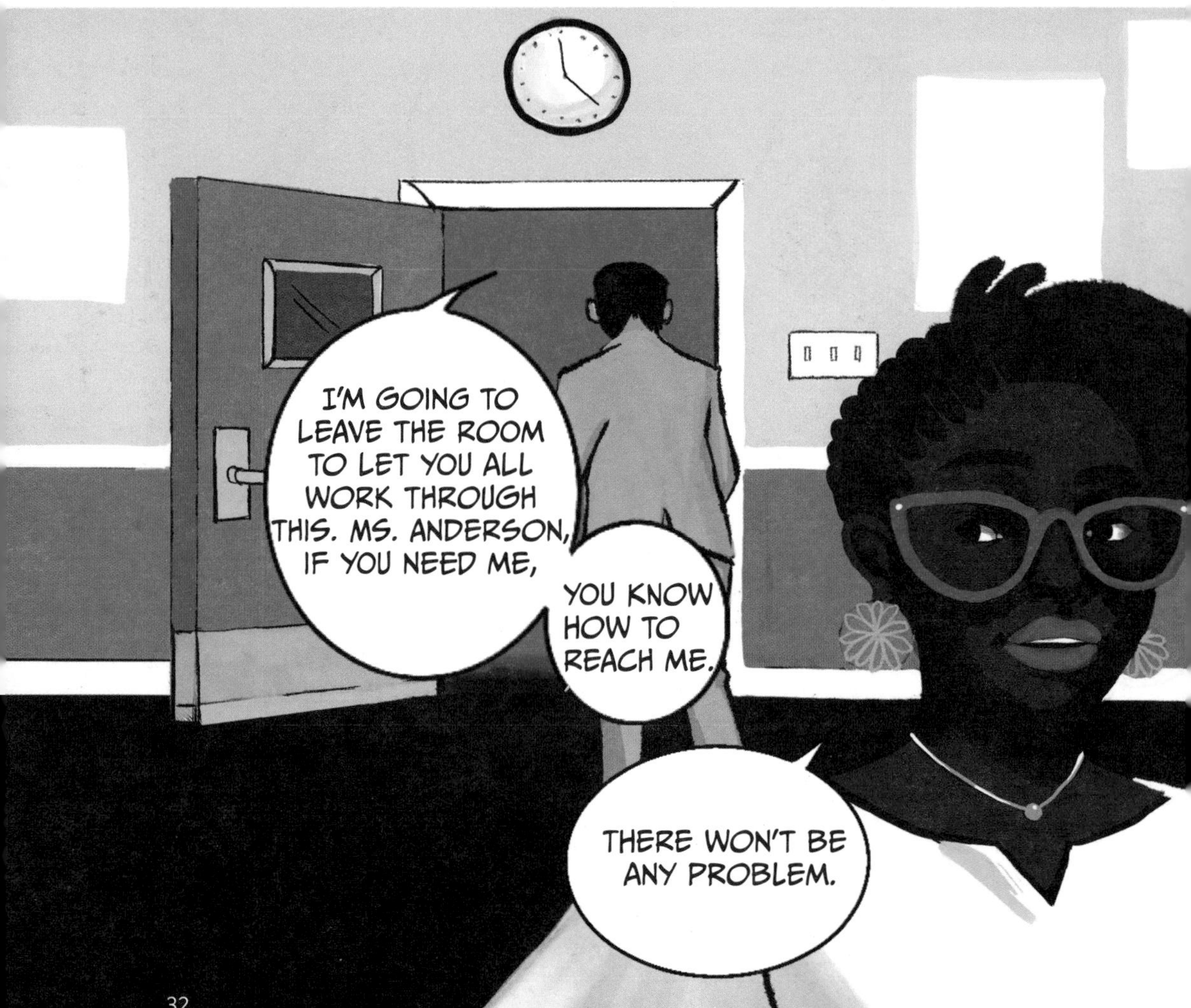
I'M GOING TO LEAVE THE ROOM TO LET YOU ALL WORK THROUGH THIS. MS. ANDERSON, IF YOU NEED ME,
YOU KNOW HOW TO REACH ME.
THERE WON'T BE ANY PROBLEM.

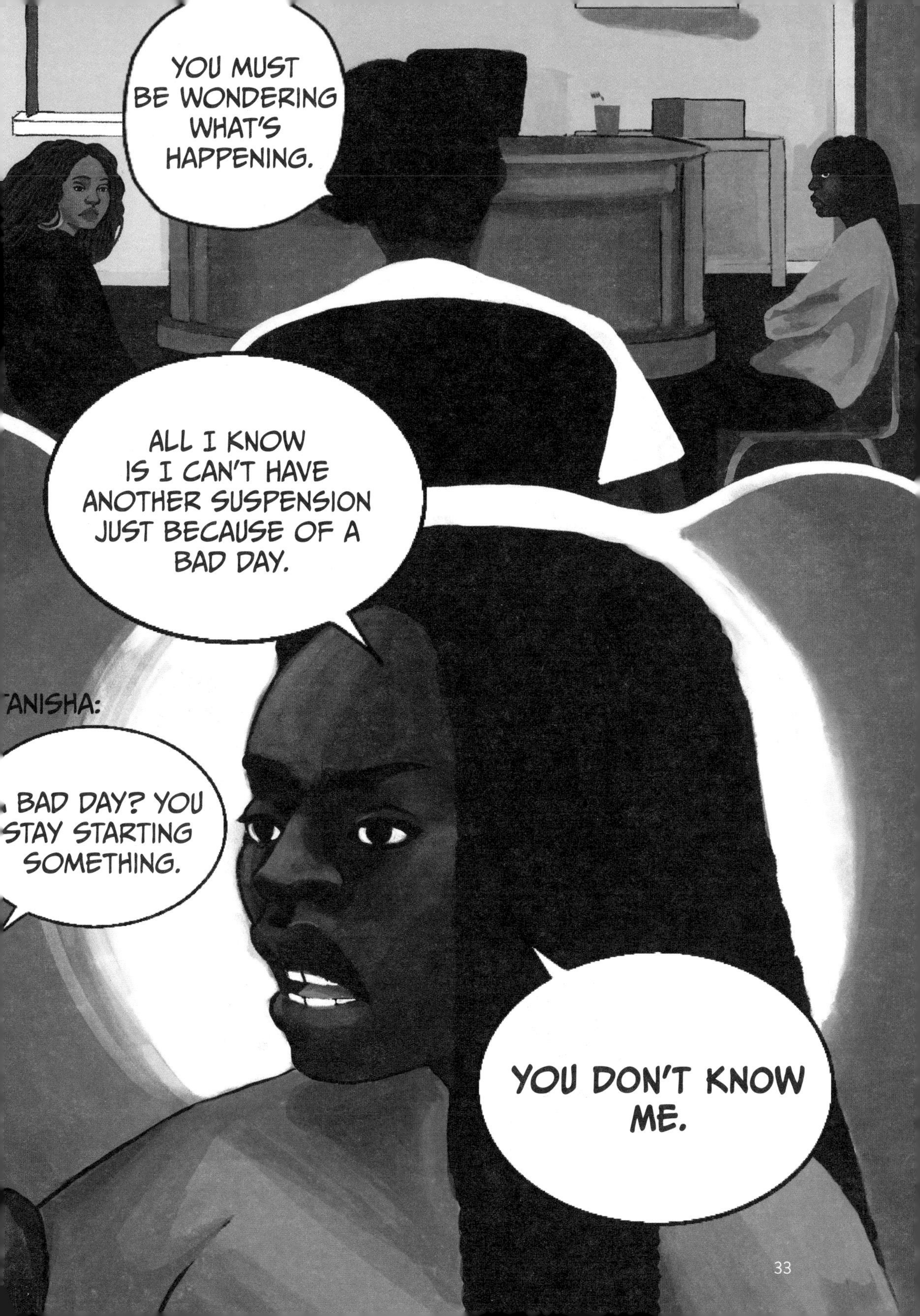
YOU MUST BE WONDERING WHAT'S HAPPENING.
ALL I KNOW IS I CAN'T HAVE ANOTHER SUSPENSION JUST BECAUSE OF A BAD DAY.
ANISHA:
BAD DAY? YOU STAY STARTING SOMETHING.
YOU DON'T KNOW ME.

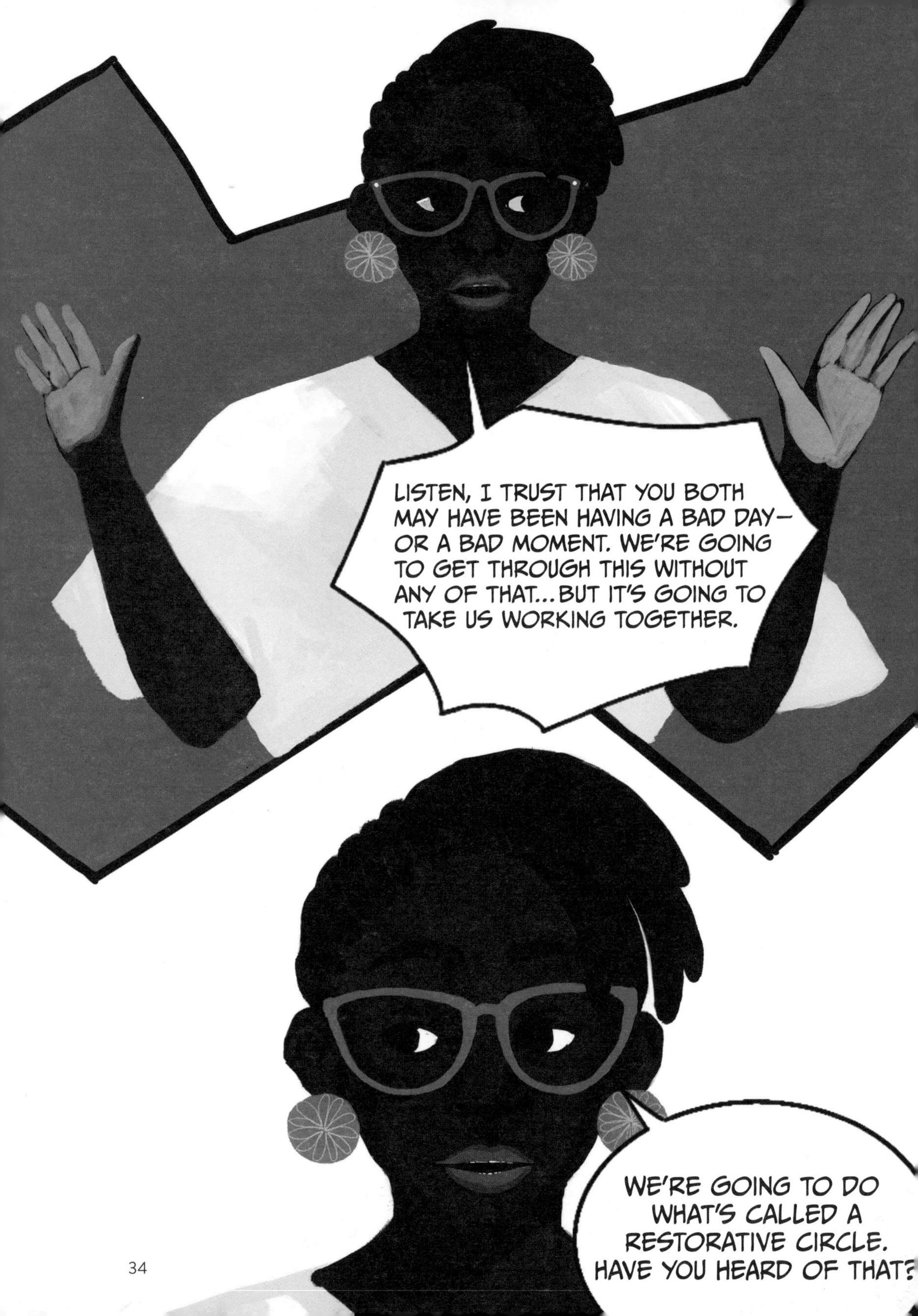
LISTEN, I TRUST THAT YOU BOTH MAY HAVE BEEN HAVING A BAD DAY— OR A BAD MOMENT. WE'RE GOING TO GET THROUGH THIS WITHOUT ANY OF THAT...BUT IT'S GOING TO TAKE US WORKING TOGETHER.
WE'RE GOING TO DO WHAT'S CALLED A RESTORATIVE CIRCLE. HAVE YOU HEARD OF THAT?

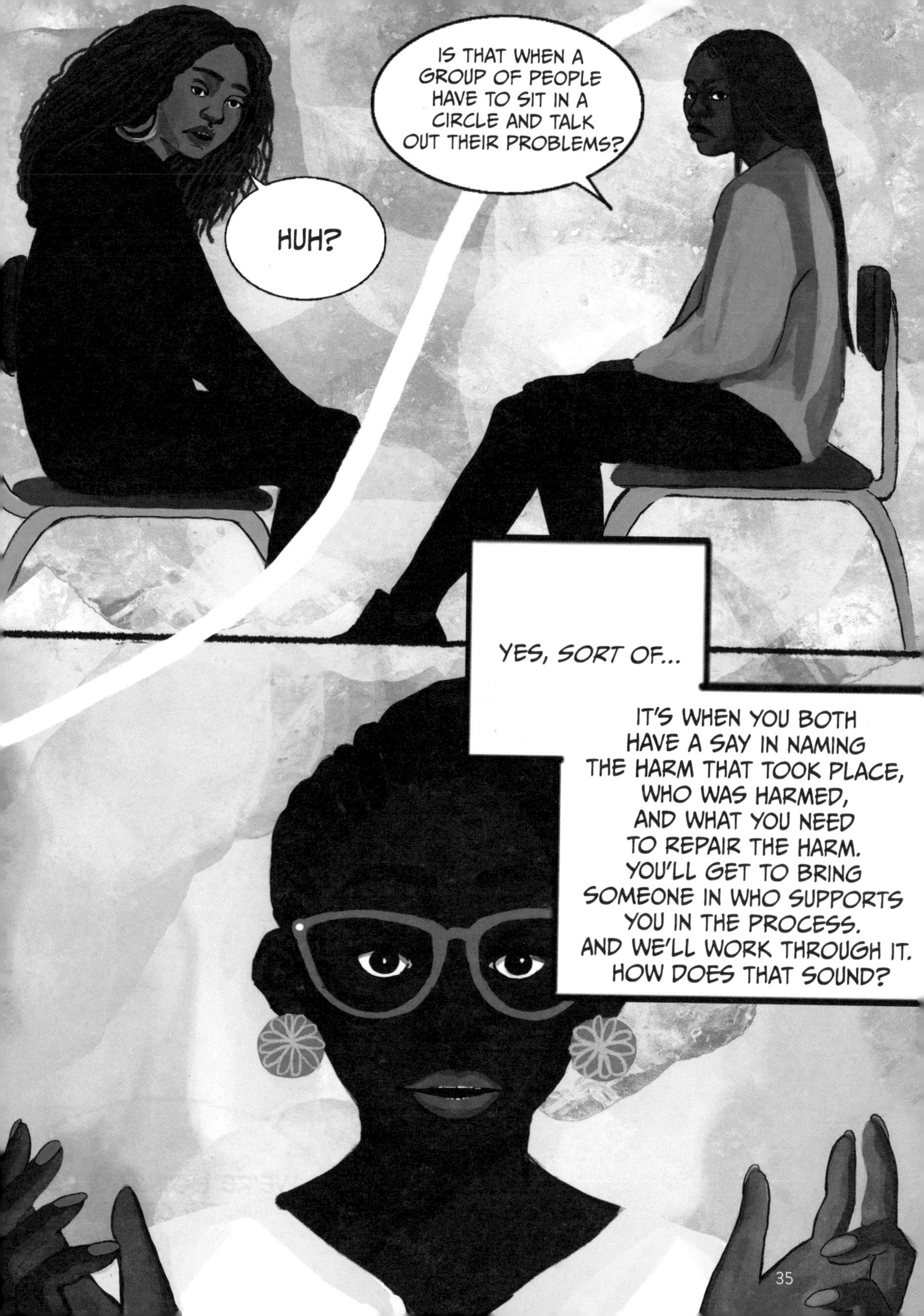
IS THAT WHEN A GROUP OF PEOPLE HAVE TO SIT IN A CIRCLE AND TALK OUT THEIR PROBLEMS?
HUH?
YES, SORT OF...
IT'S WHEN YOU BOTH HAVE A SAY IN NAMING THE HARM THAT TOOK PLACE, WHO WAS HARMED, AND WHAT YOU NEED TO REPAIR THE HARM. YOU'LL GET TO BRING SOMEONE IN WHO SUPPORTS YOU IN THE PROCESS. AND WE'LL WORK THROUGH IT. HOW DOES THAT SOUND?

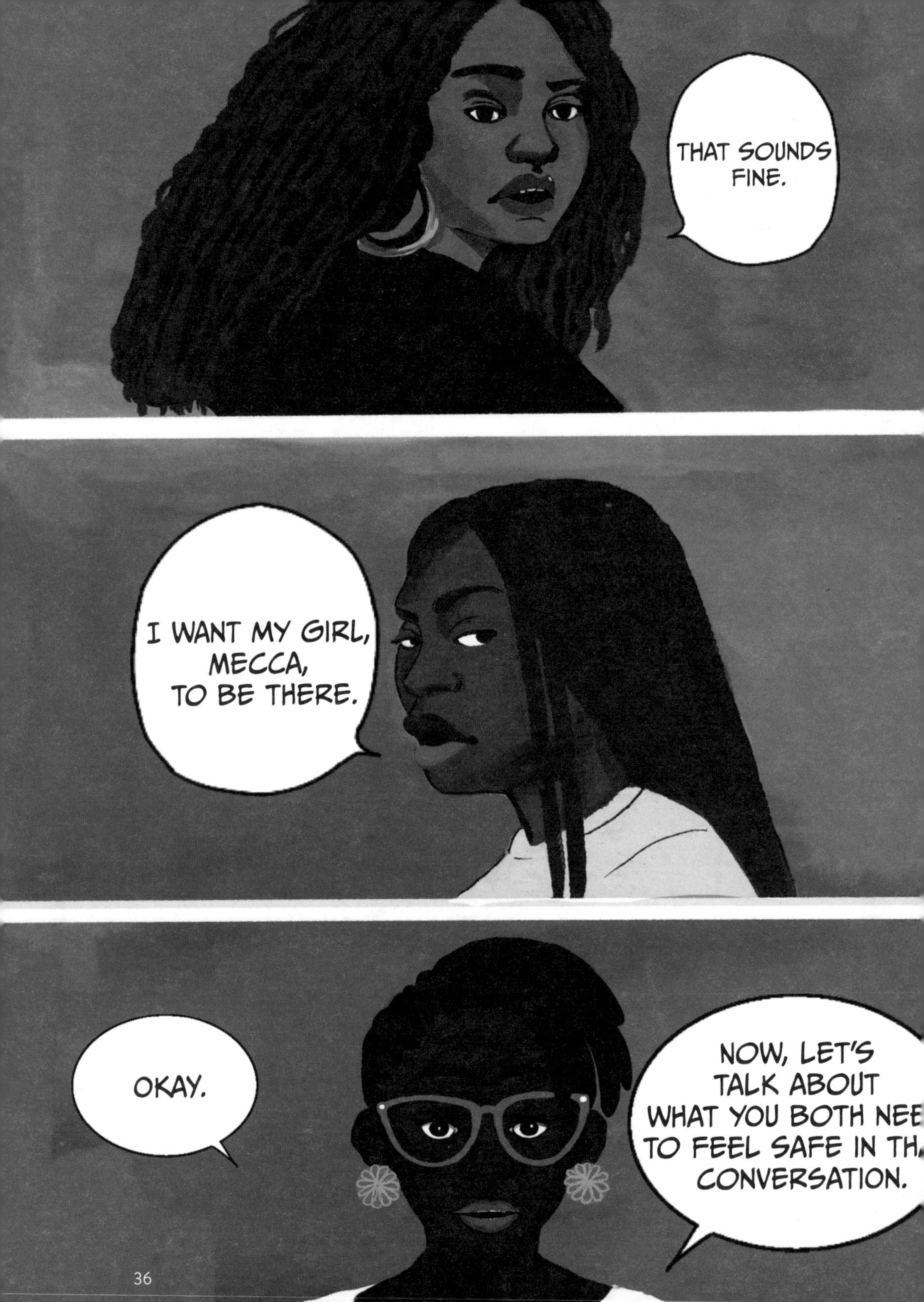
THAT SOUNDS FINE.
I WANT MY GIRL, MECCA, TO BE THERE.
OKAY.
NOW, LET'S TALK ABOUT WHAT YOU BOTH NEE TO FEEL SAFE IN TH CONVERSATION.

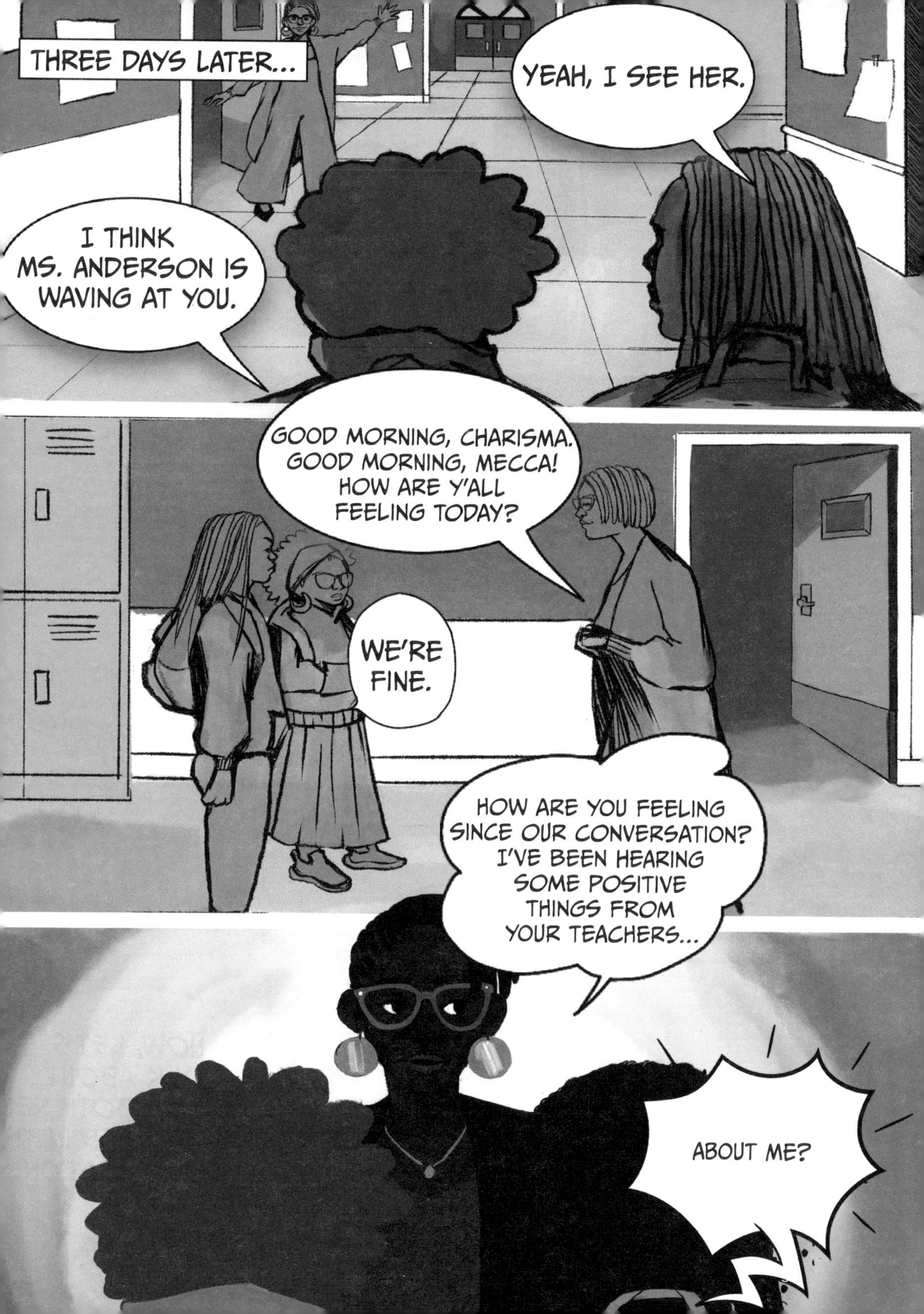
THREE DAYS LATER...
YEAH, I SEE HER.
I THINK MS. ANDERSON IS WAVING AT YOU.
GOOD MORNING, CHARISMA. GOOD MORNING, MECCA! HOW ARE Y'ALL FEELING TODAY?
WE'RE FINE.
HOW ARE YOU FEELING SINCE OUR CONVERSATION? I'VE BEEN HEARING SOME POSITIVE THINGS FROM YOUR TEACHERS...
ABOUT ME?

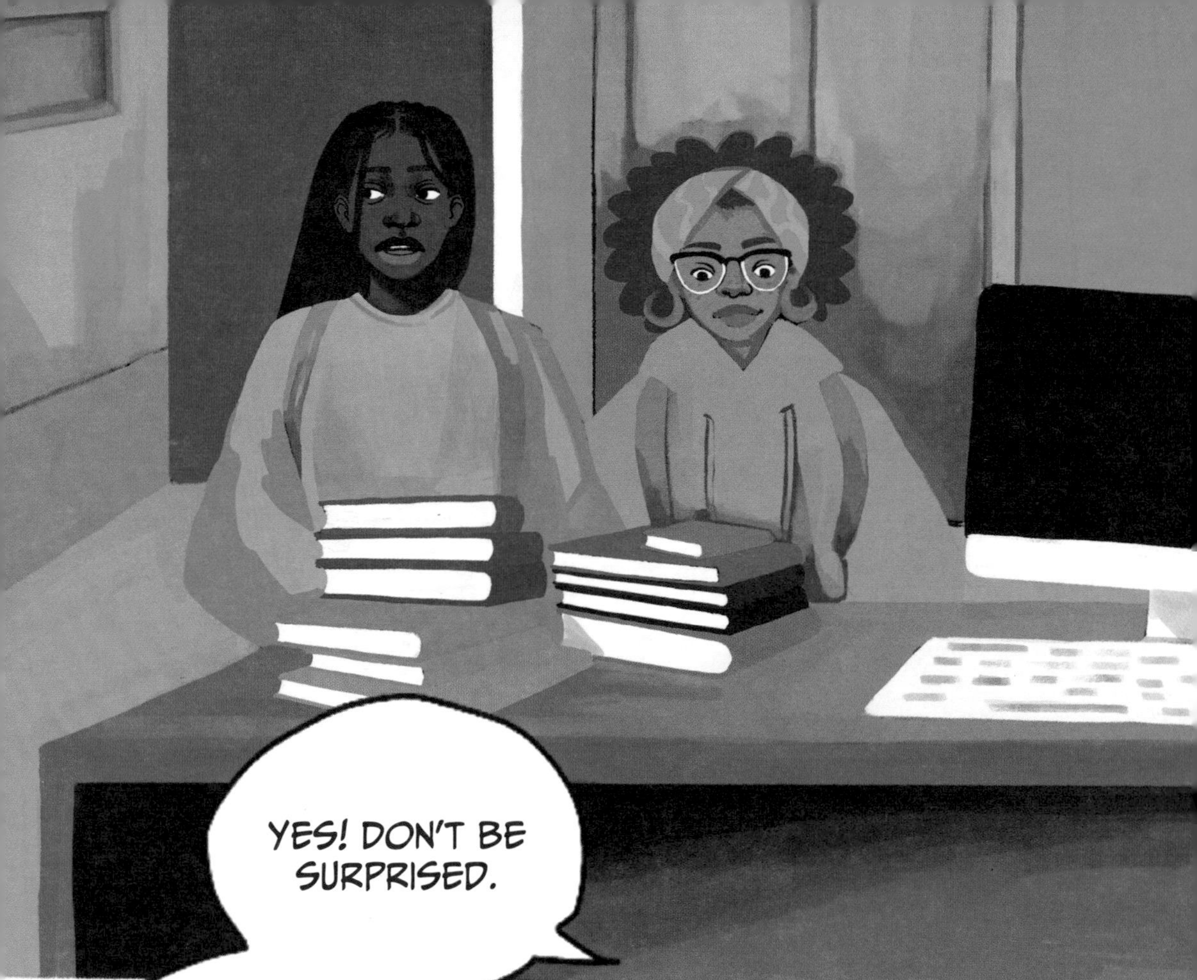
YES! DON'T BE SURPRISED.

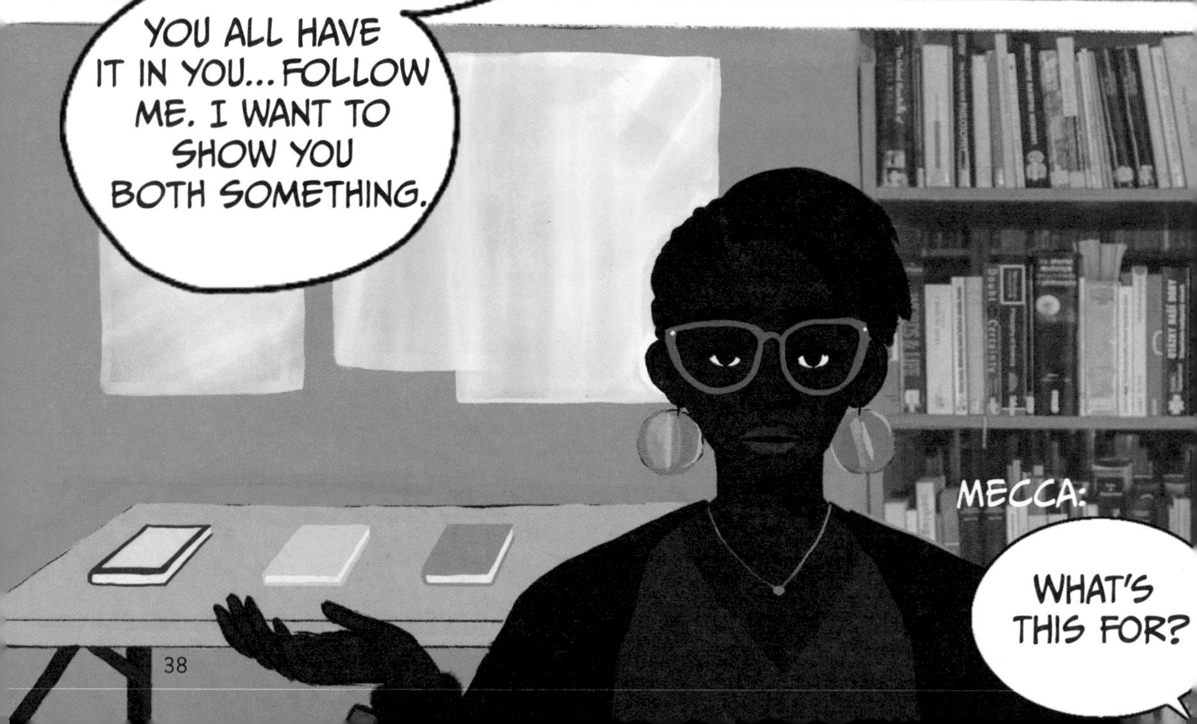
YOU ALL HAVE IT IN YOU...FOLLOW ME. I WANT TO SHOW YOU BOTH SOMETHING.
MECCA:
WHAT'S THIS FOR?

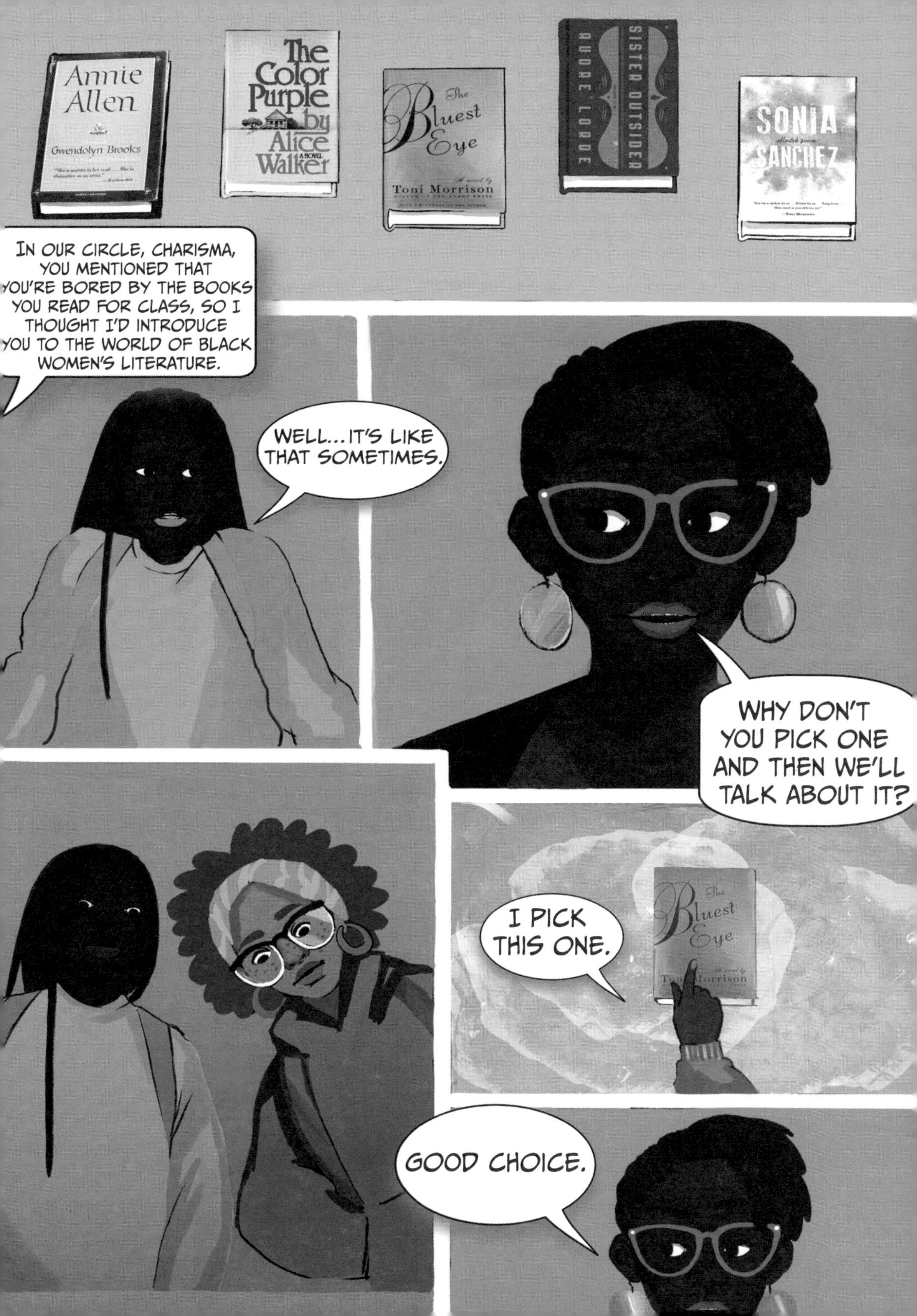
Annie Allen
Gwendolyn Brooks
The Color Purple by Alice Walker
The Bluest Eye
Toni Morrison
SISTER OUTSIDER
AUDRE LORDE
SONIA SANCHEZ
IN OUR CIRCLE, CHARISMA, YOU MENTIONED THAT YOU'RE BORED BY THE BOOKS YOU READ FOR CLASS, SO I THOUGHT I'D INTRODUCE YOU TO THE WORLD OF BLACK WOMEN'S LITERATURE.
WELL... IT'S LIKE THAT SOMETIMES.
WHY DON'T YOU PICK ONE AND THEN WE'LL TALK ABOUT IT?
I PICK THIS ONE.
GOOD CHOICE.

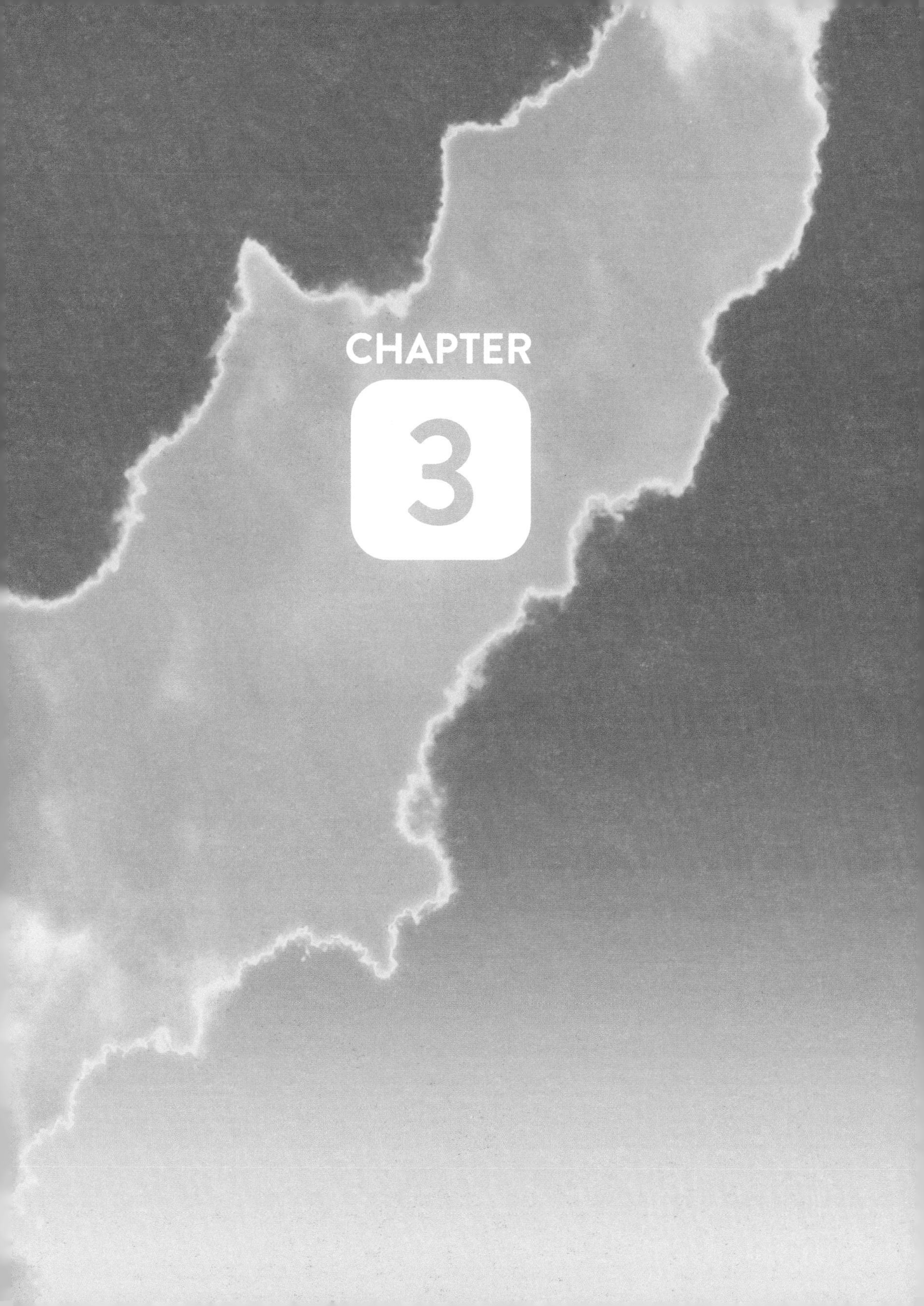

CHAPTER 3

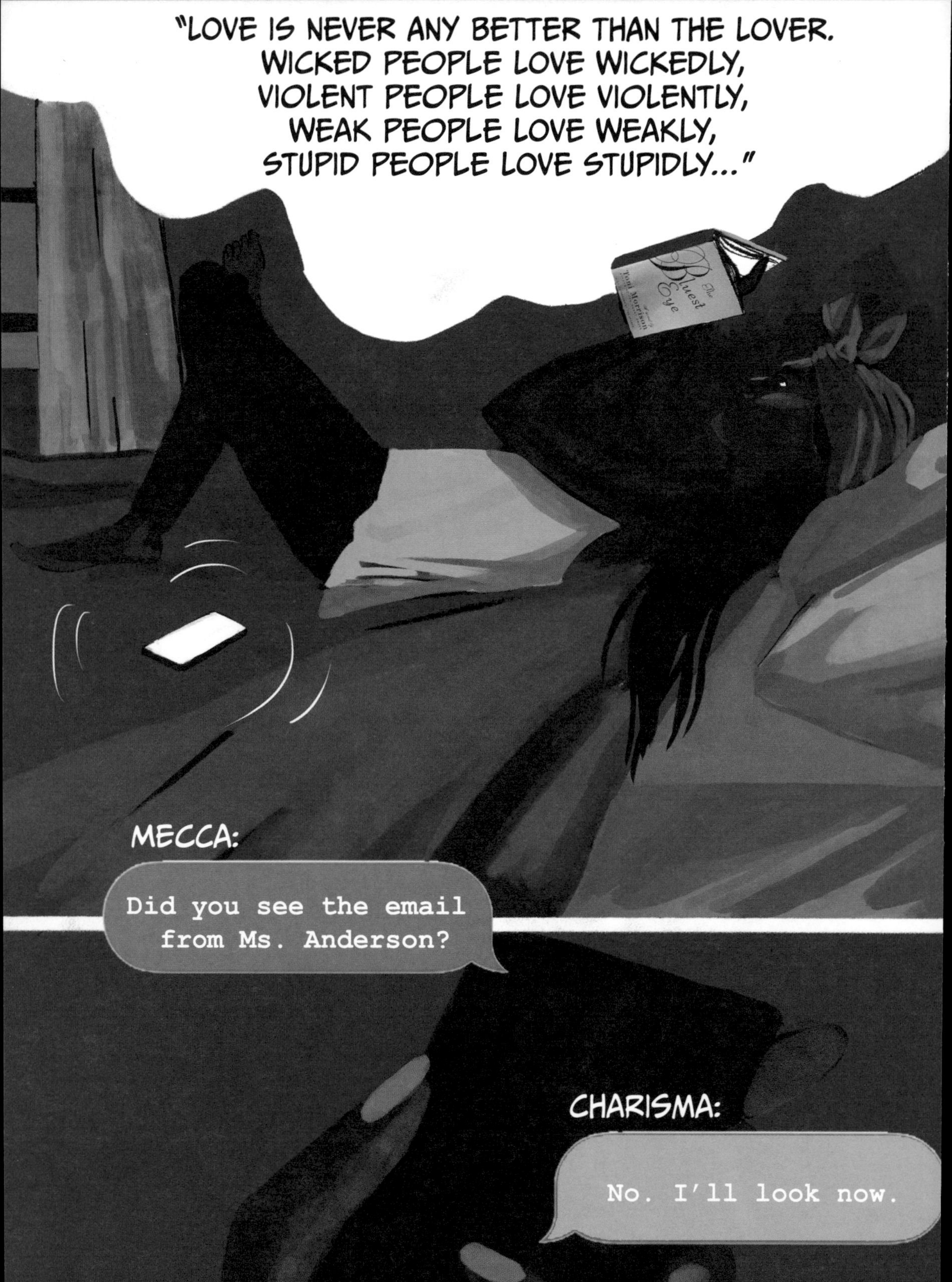
"LOVE IS NEVER ANY BETTER THAN THE LOVER. WICKED PEOPLE LOVE WICKEDLY, VIOLENT PEOPLE LOVE VIOLENTLY, WEAK PEOPLE LOVE WEAKLY, STUPID PEOPLE LOVE STUPIDLY..."
The Bluest Eye
Toni Morrison
MECCA:
Did you see the email from Ms. Anderson?
CHARISMA:
No. I'll look now.

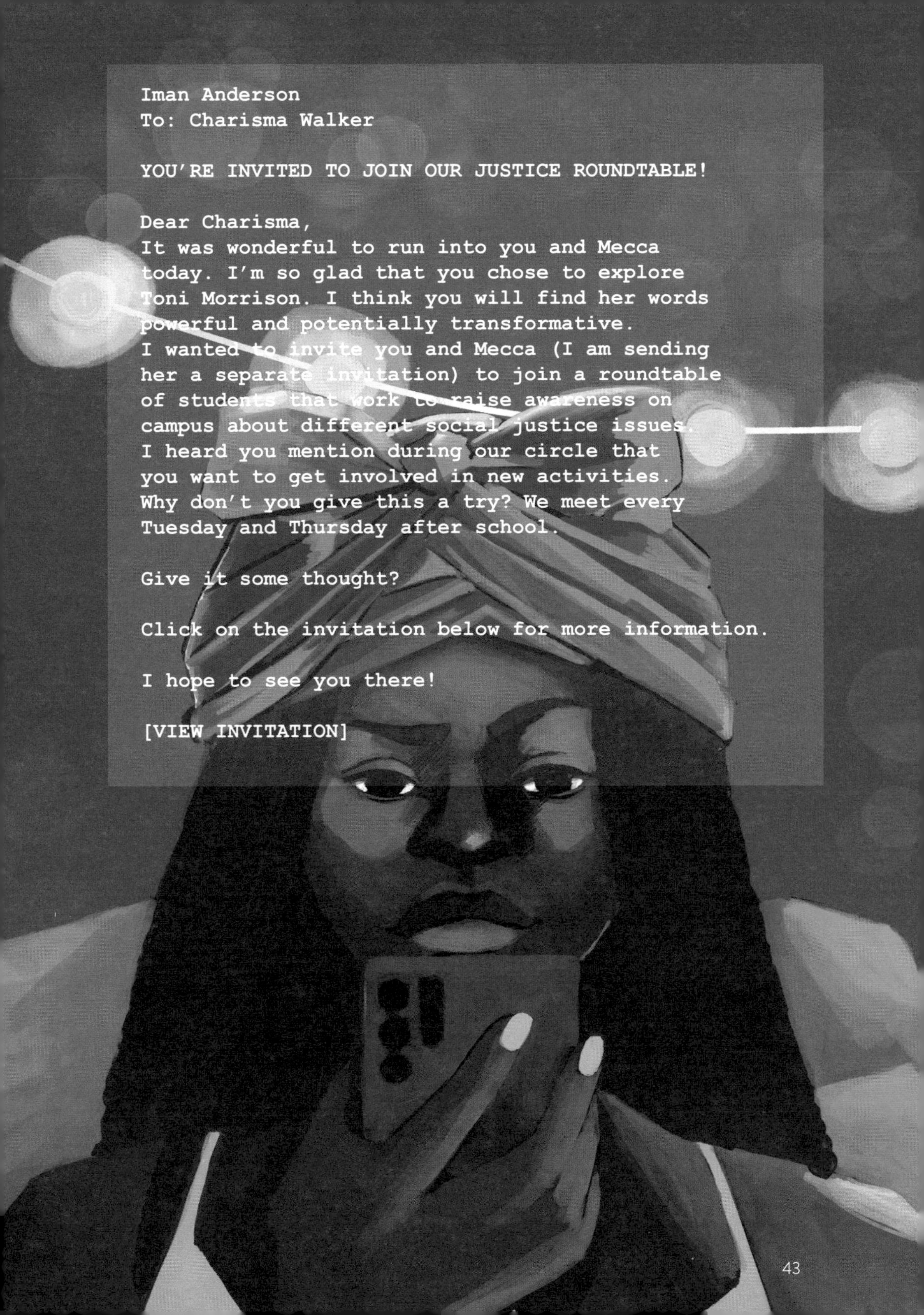

Iman Anderson
To: Charisma Walker

YOU'RE INVITED TO JOIN OUR JUSTICE ROUNDTABLE!

Dear Charisma,
It was wonderful to run into you and Mecca today. I'm so glad that you chose to explore Toni Morrison. I think you will find her words powerful and potentially transformative.
I wanted to invite you and Mecca (I am sending her a separate invitation) to join a roundtable of students that work to raise awareness on campus about different social justice issues. I heard you mention during our circle that you want to get involved in new activities. Why don't you give this a try? We meet every Tuesday and Thursday after school.

Give it some thought?

Click on the invitation below for more information.

I hope to see you there!

[VIEW INVITATION]

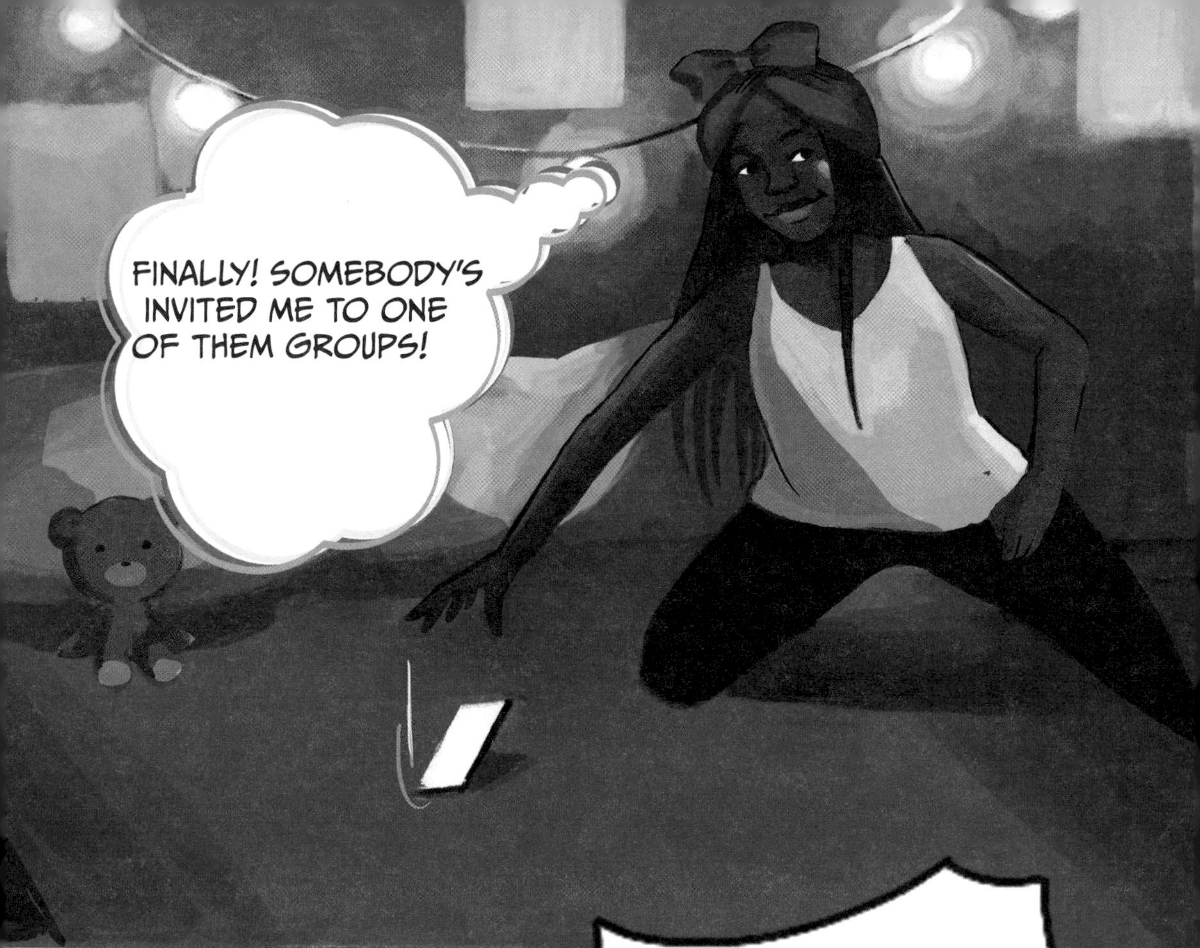
FINALLY! SOMEBODY'S INVITED ME TO ONE OF THEM GROUPS!
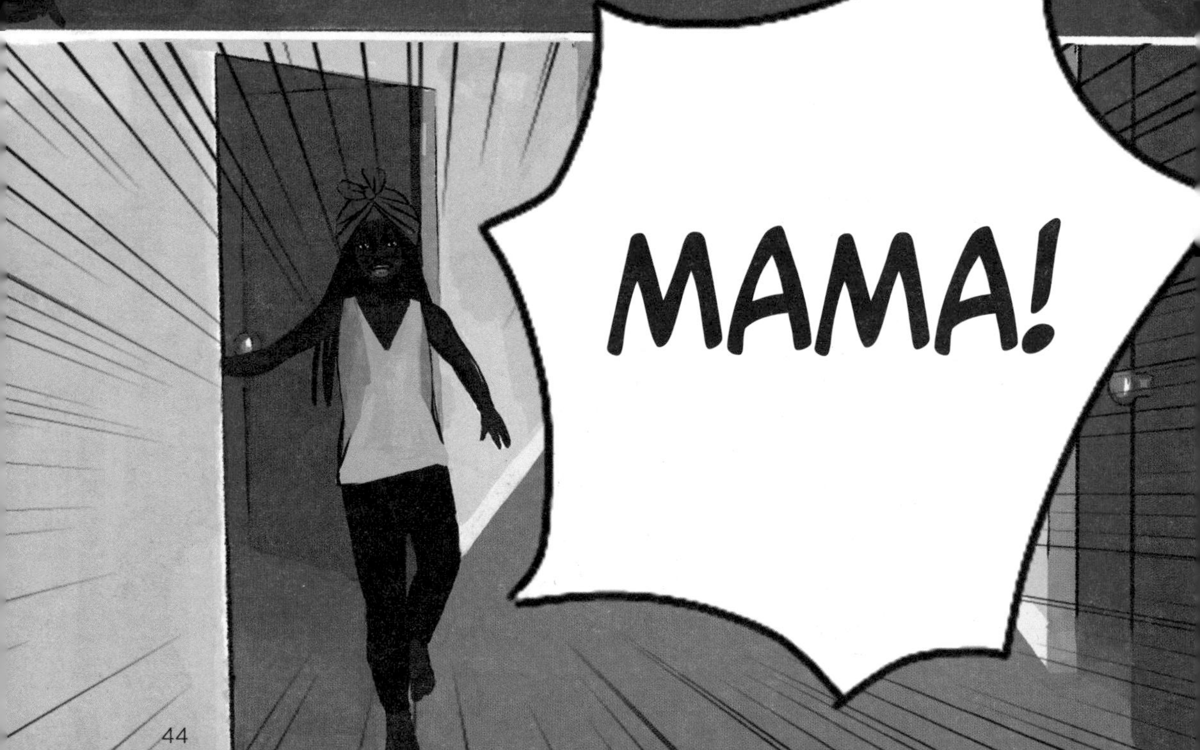
MAMA!

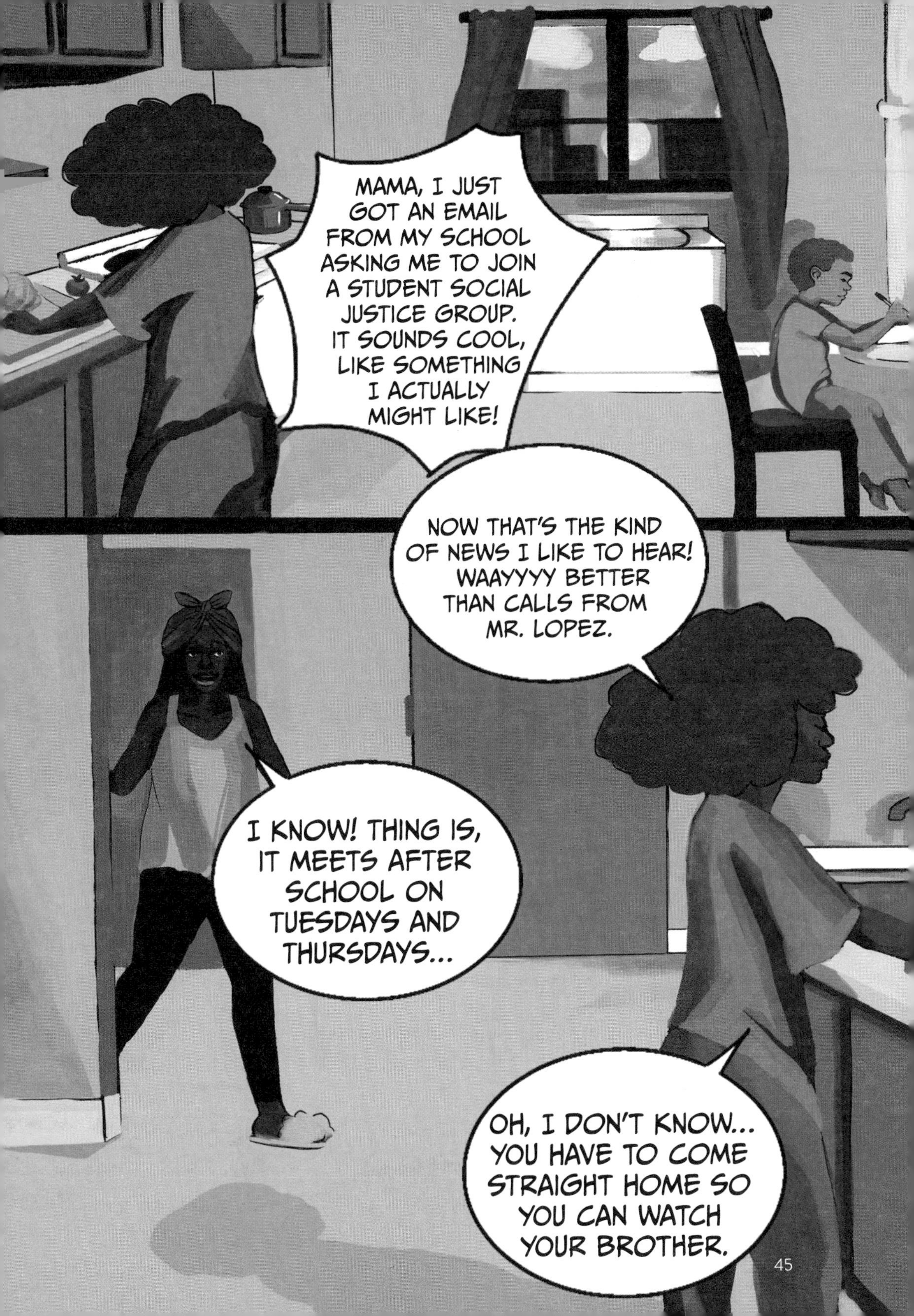
MAMA, I JUST GOT AN EMAIL FROM MY SCHOOL ASKING ME TO JOIN A STUDENT SOCIAL JUSTICE GROUP. IT SOUNDS COOL, LIKE SOMETHING I ACTUALLY MIGHT LIKE!
NOW THAT'S THE KIND OF NEWS I LIKE TO HEAR! WAAYYYY BETTER THAN CALLS FROM MR. LOPEZ.
I KNOW! THING IS, IT MEETS AFTER SCHOOL ON TUESDAYS AND THURSDAYS...
OH, I DON'T KNOW... YOU HAVE TO COME STRAIGHT HOME SO YOU CAN WATCH YOUR BROTHER.

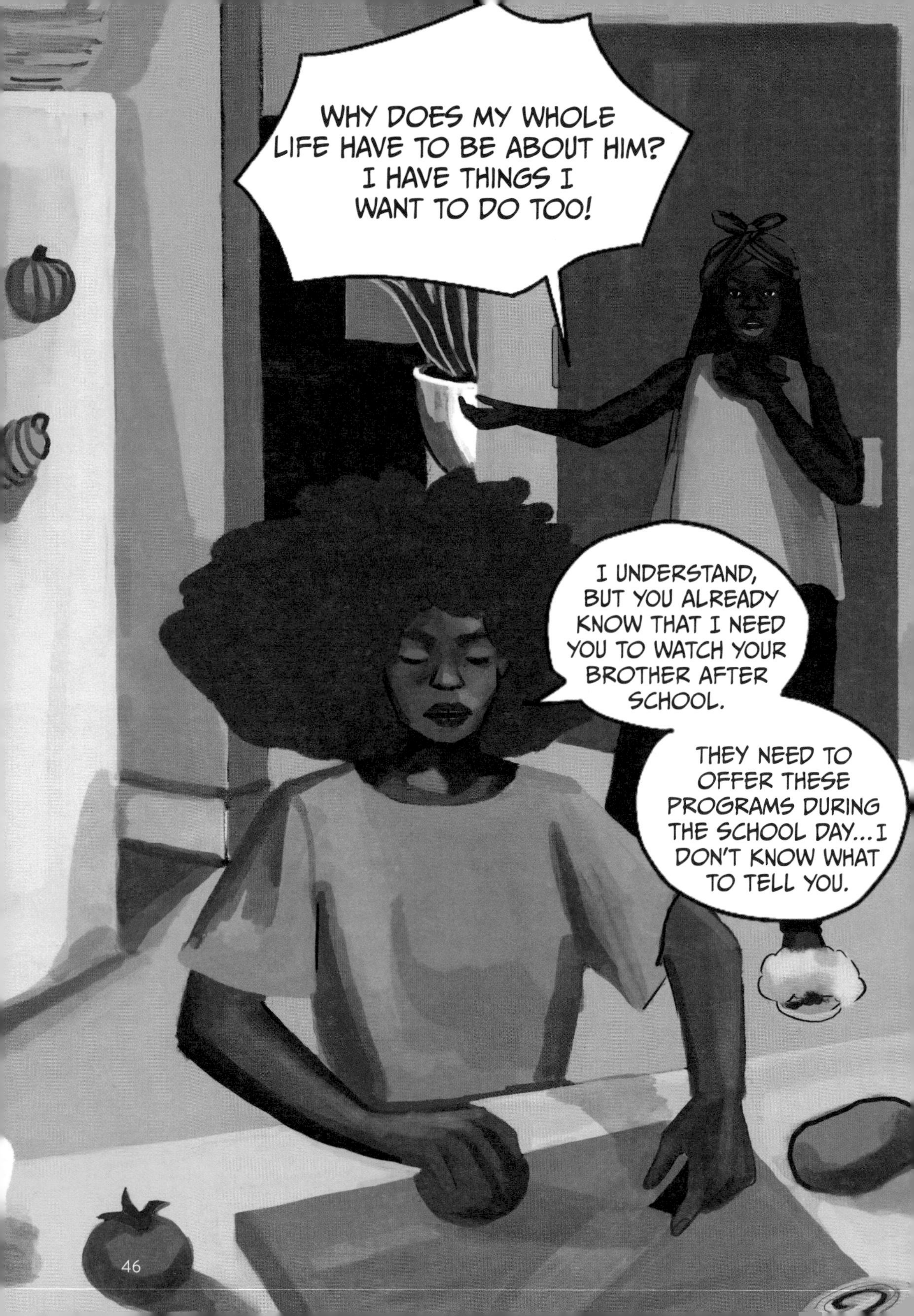
WHY DOES MY WHOLE LIFE HAVE TO BE ABOUT HIM? I HAVE THINGS I WANT TO DO TOO!
I UNDERSTAND, BUT YOU ALREADY KNOW THAT I NEED YOU TO WATCH YOUR BROTHER AFTER SCHOOL.
THEY NEED TO OFFER THESE PROGRAMS DURING THE SCHOOL DAY...I DON'T KNOW WHAT TO TELL YOU.

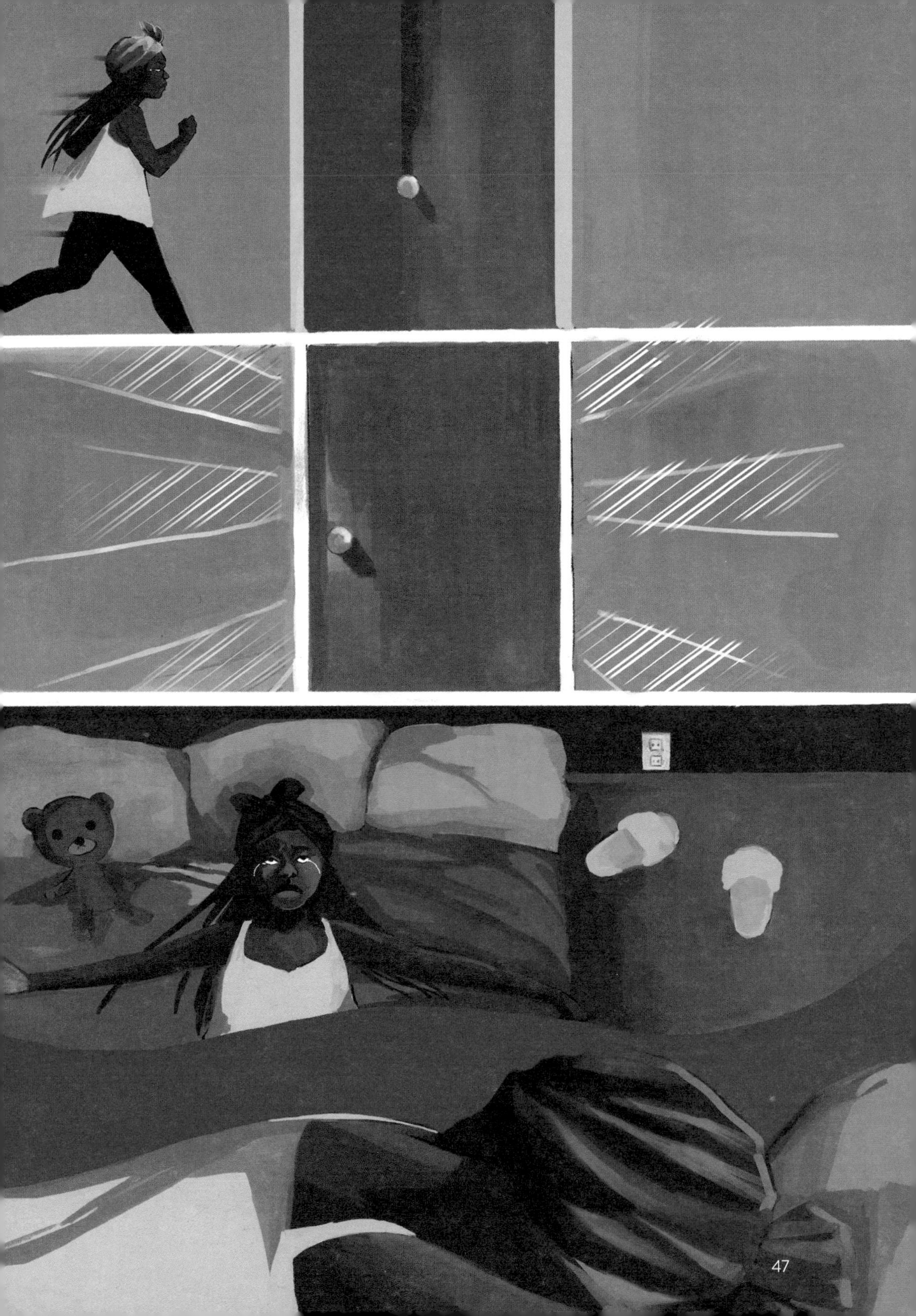

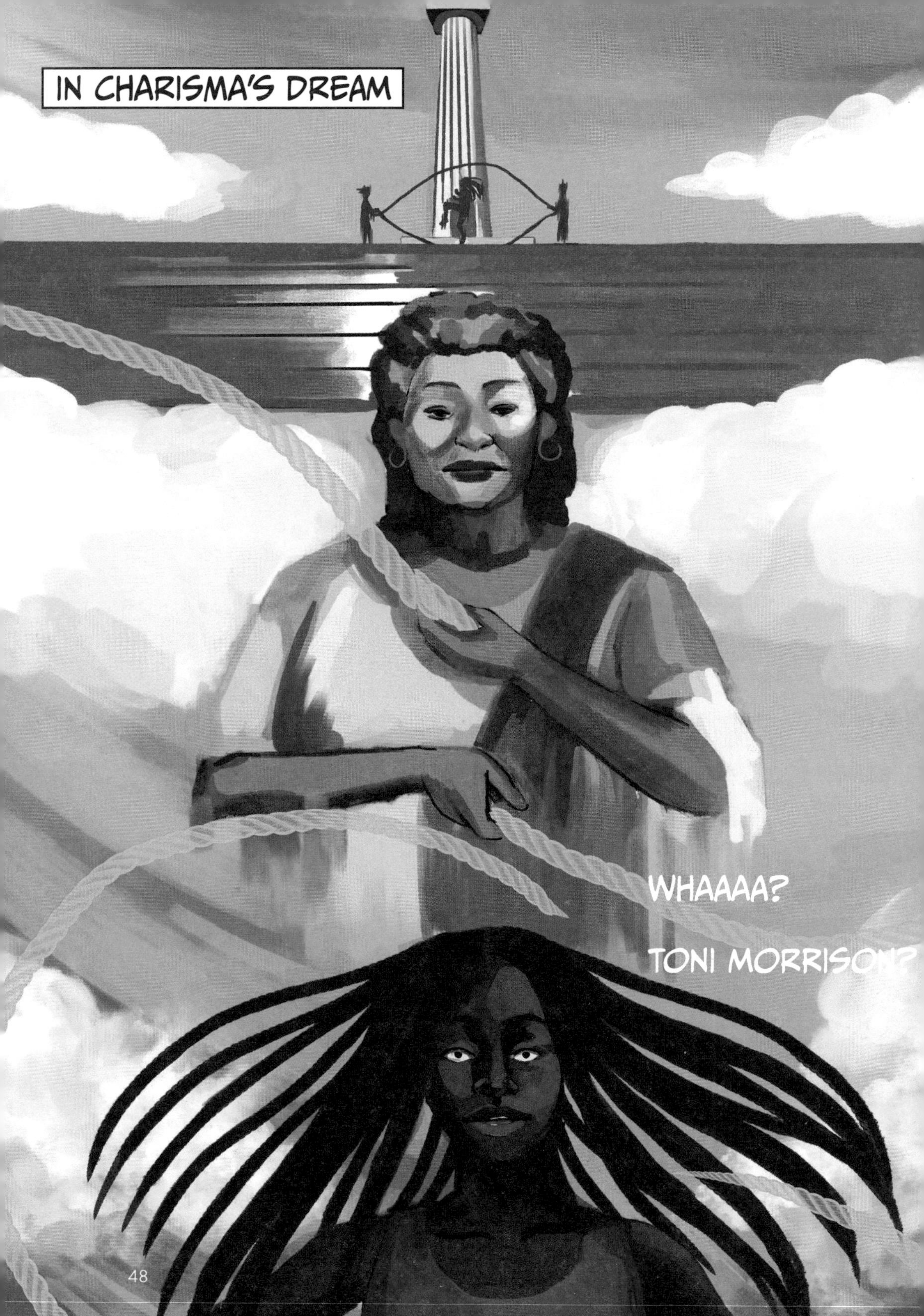
IN CHARISMA'S DREAM
WHAAAA?
TONI MORRISON?

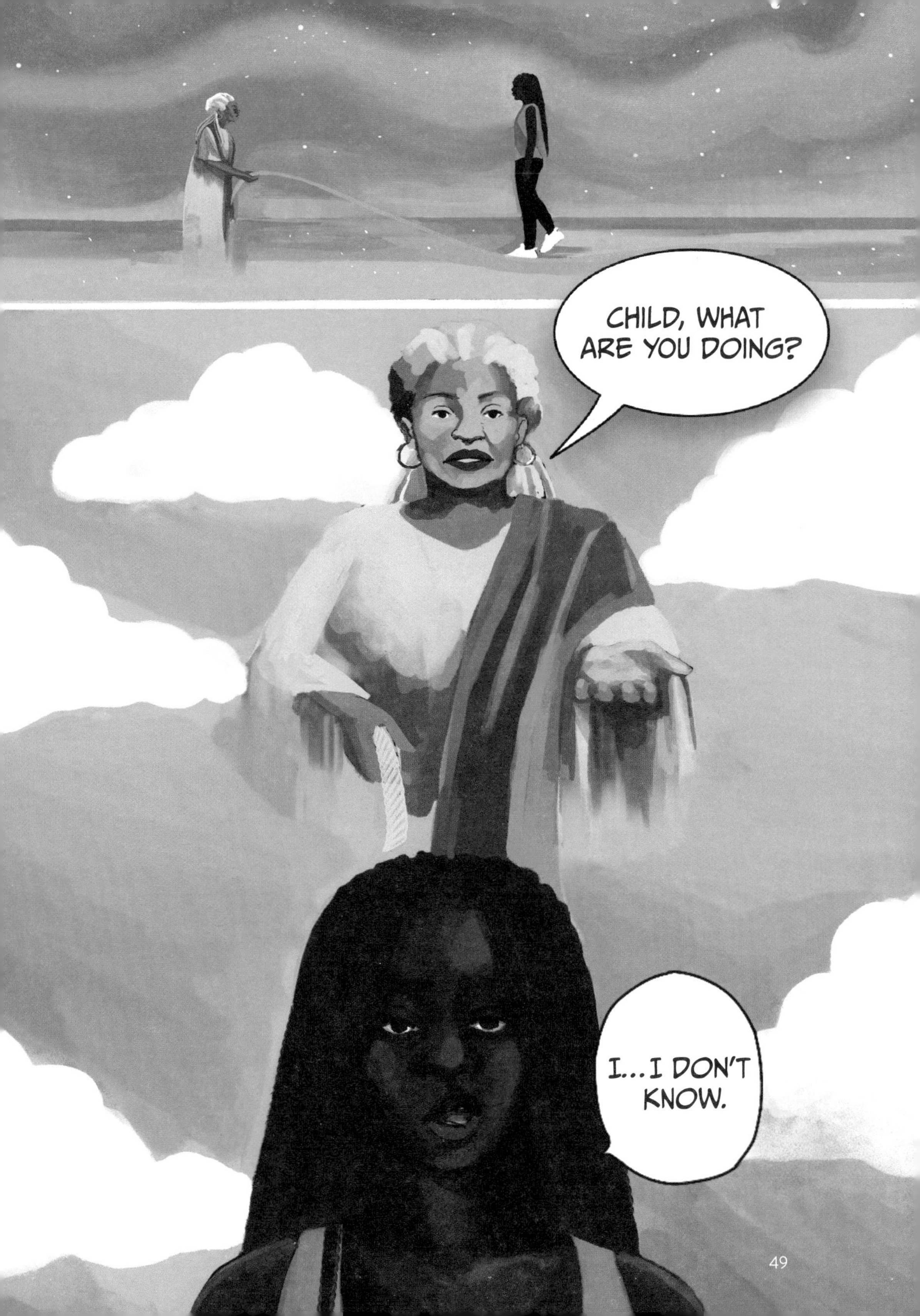
CHILD, WHAT ARE YOU DOING?
I...I DON'T KNOW.

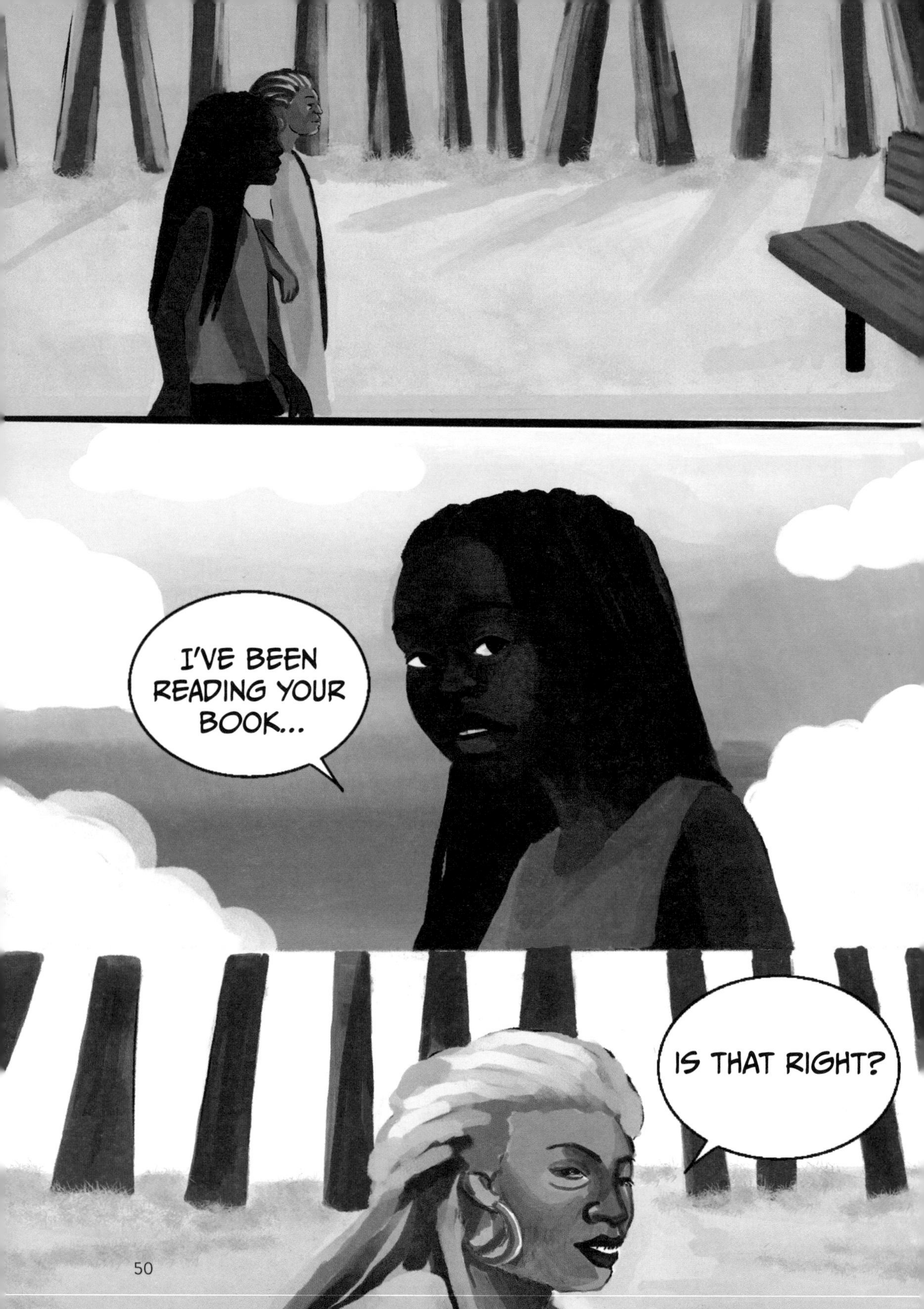
I'VE BEEN READING YOUR BOOK...
IS THAT RIGHT?

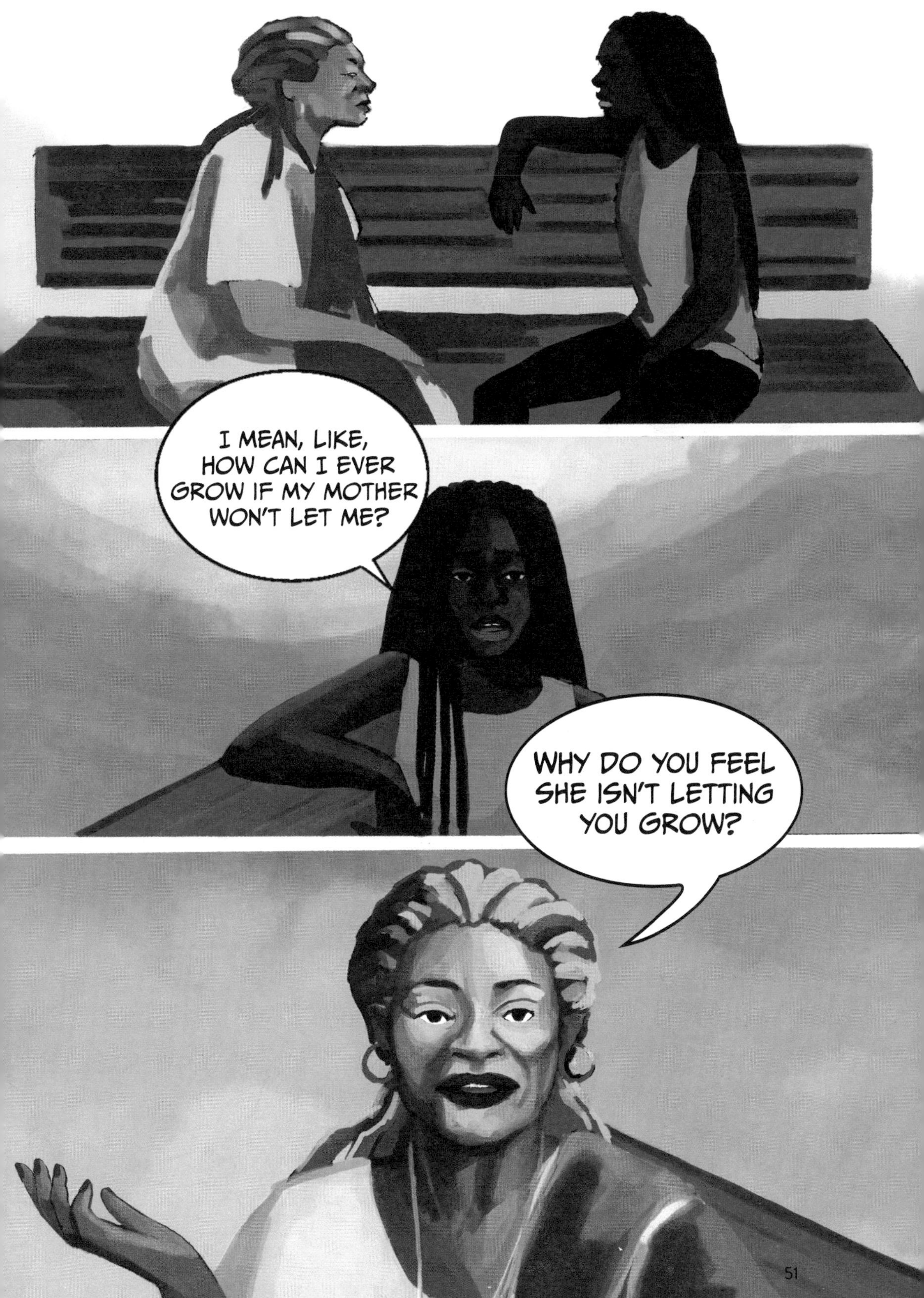
I MEAN, LIKE, HOW CAN I EVER GROW IF MY MOTHER WON'T LET ME?
WHY DO YOU FEEL SHE ISN'T LETTING YOU GROW?

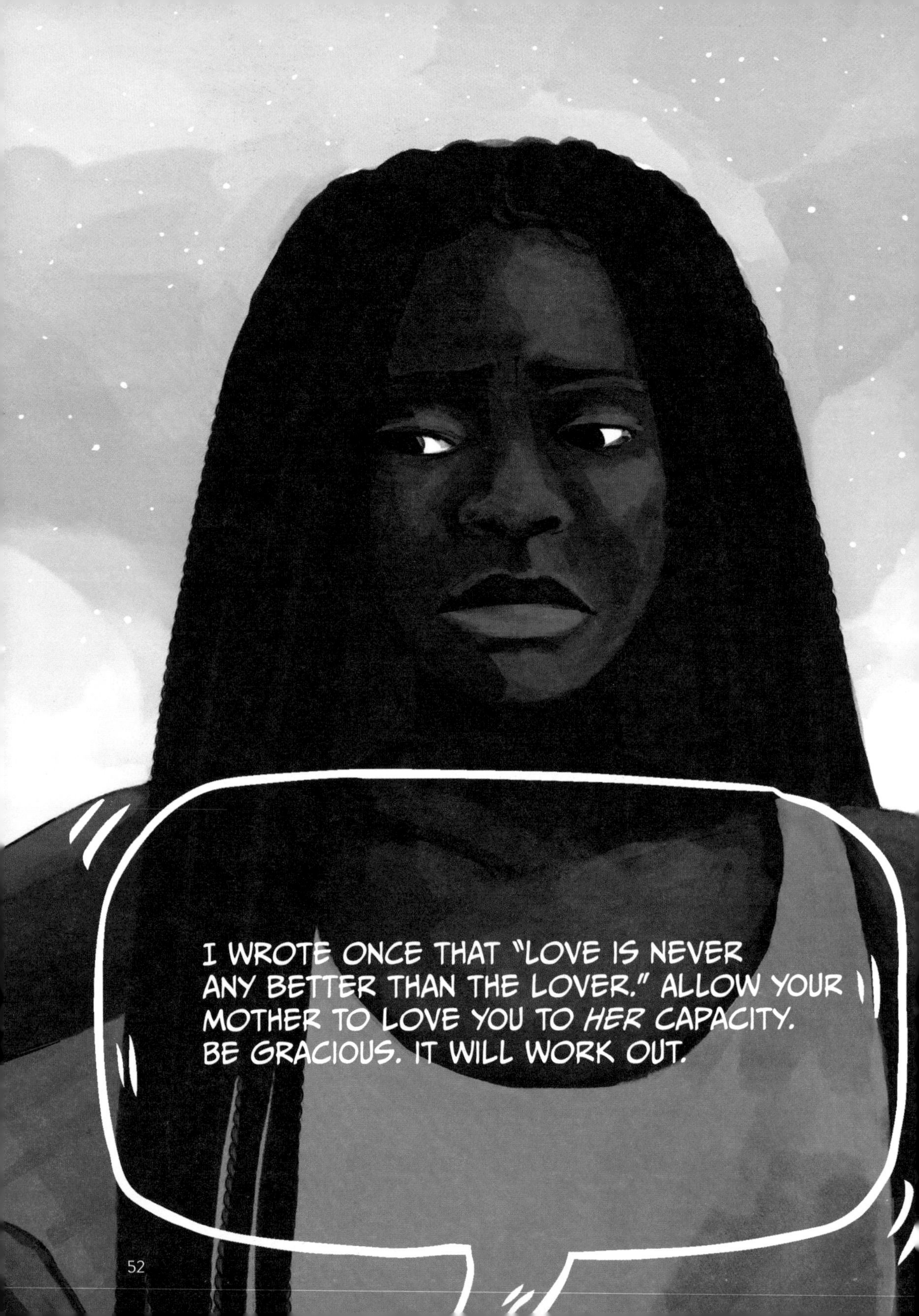
I WROTE ONCE THAT "LOVE IS NEVER ANY BETTER THAN THE LOVER." ALLOW YOUR MOTHER TO LOVE YOU TO *HER* CAPACITY. BE GRACIOUS. IT WILL WORK OUT.

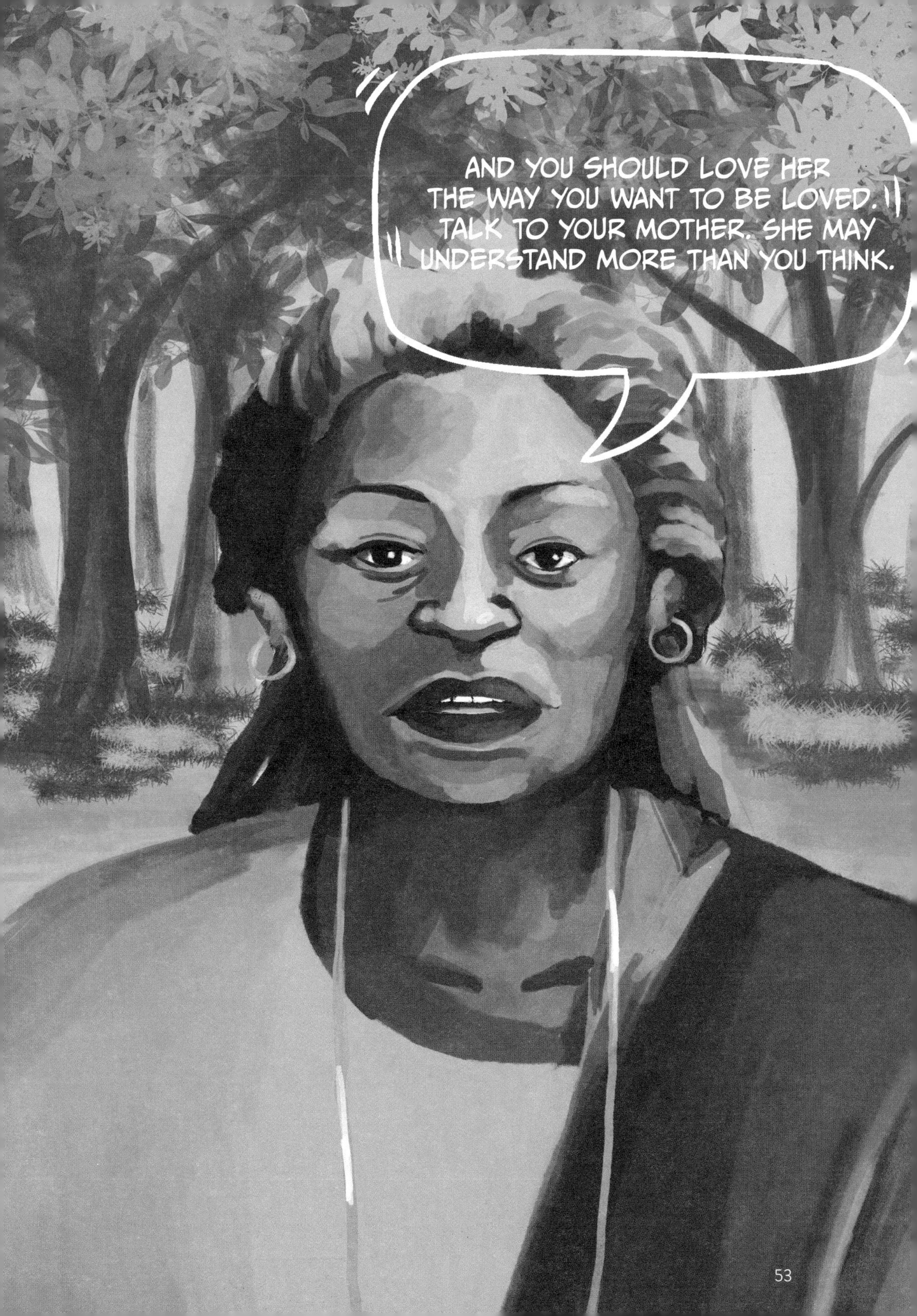
AND YOU SHOULD LOVE HER THE WAY YOU WANT TO BE LOVED. TALK TO YOUR MOTHER. SHE MAY UNDERSTAND MORE THAN YOU THINK.

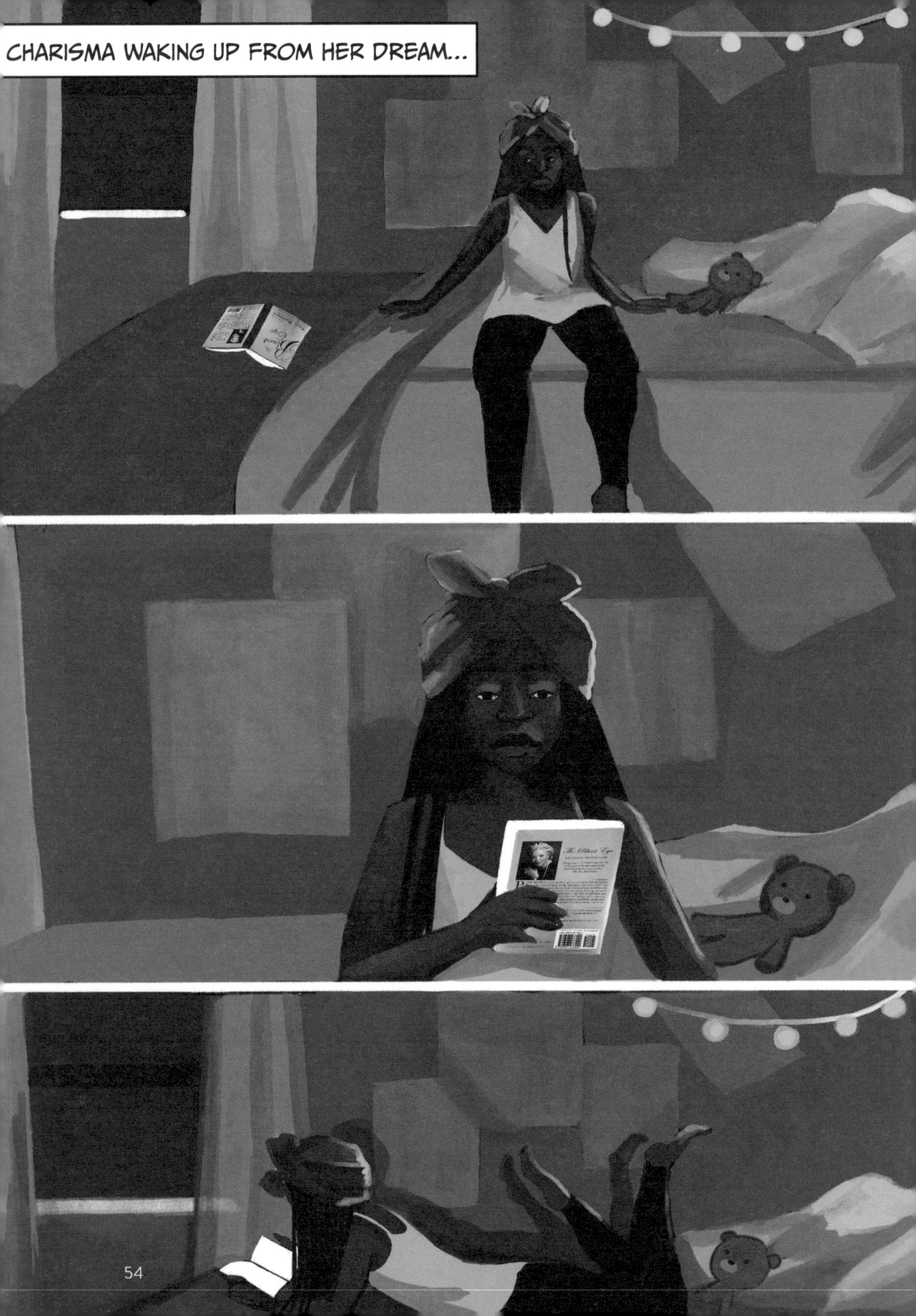
CHARISMA WAKING UP FROM HER DREAM...

CHAPTER 4

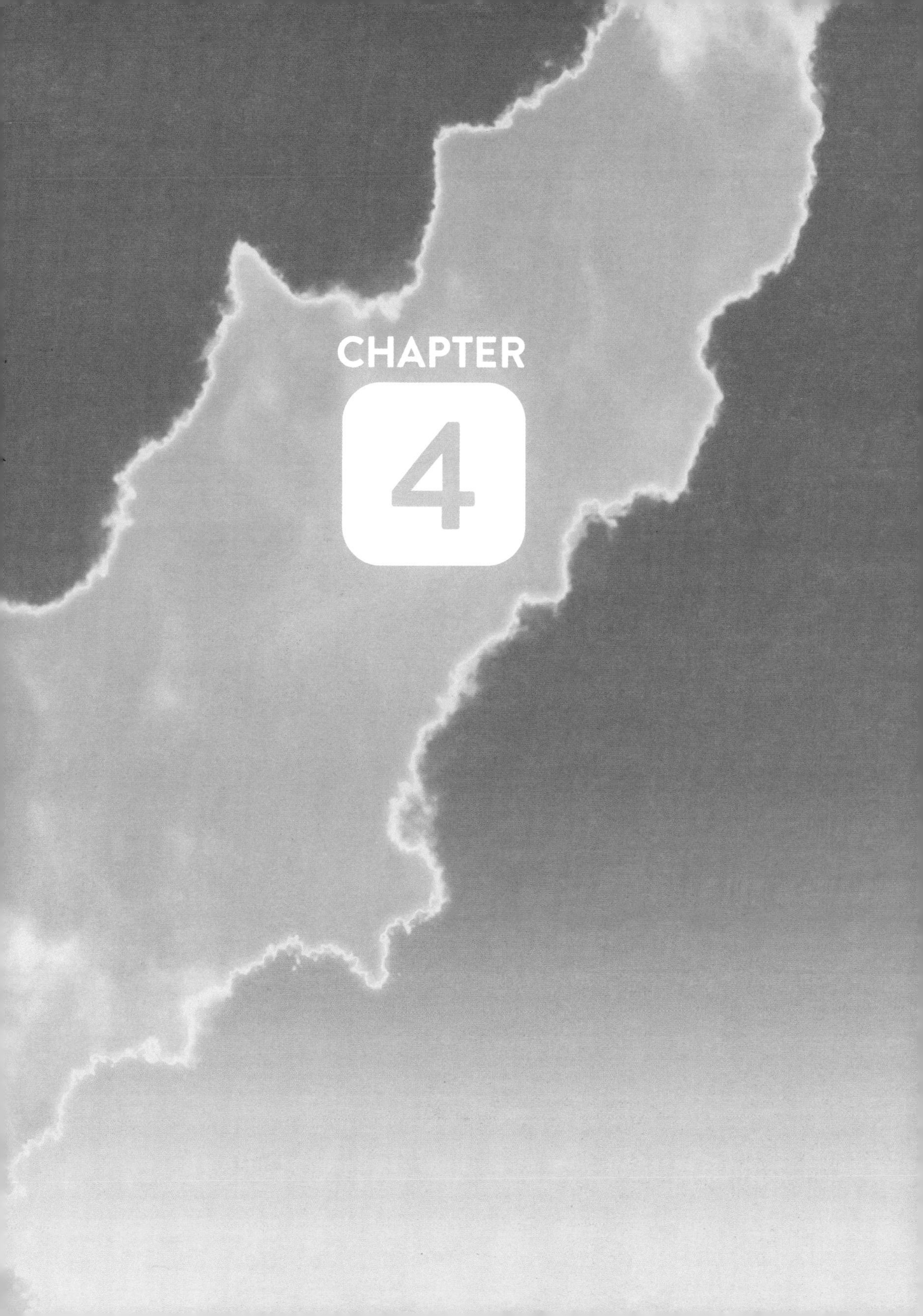

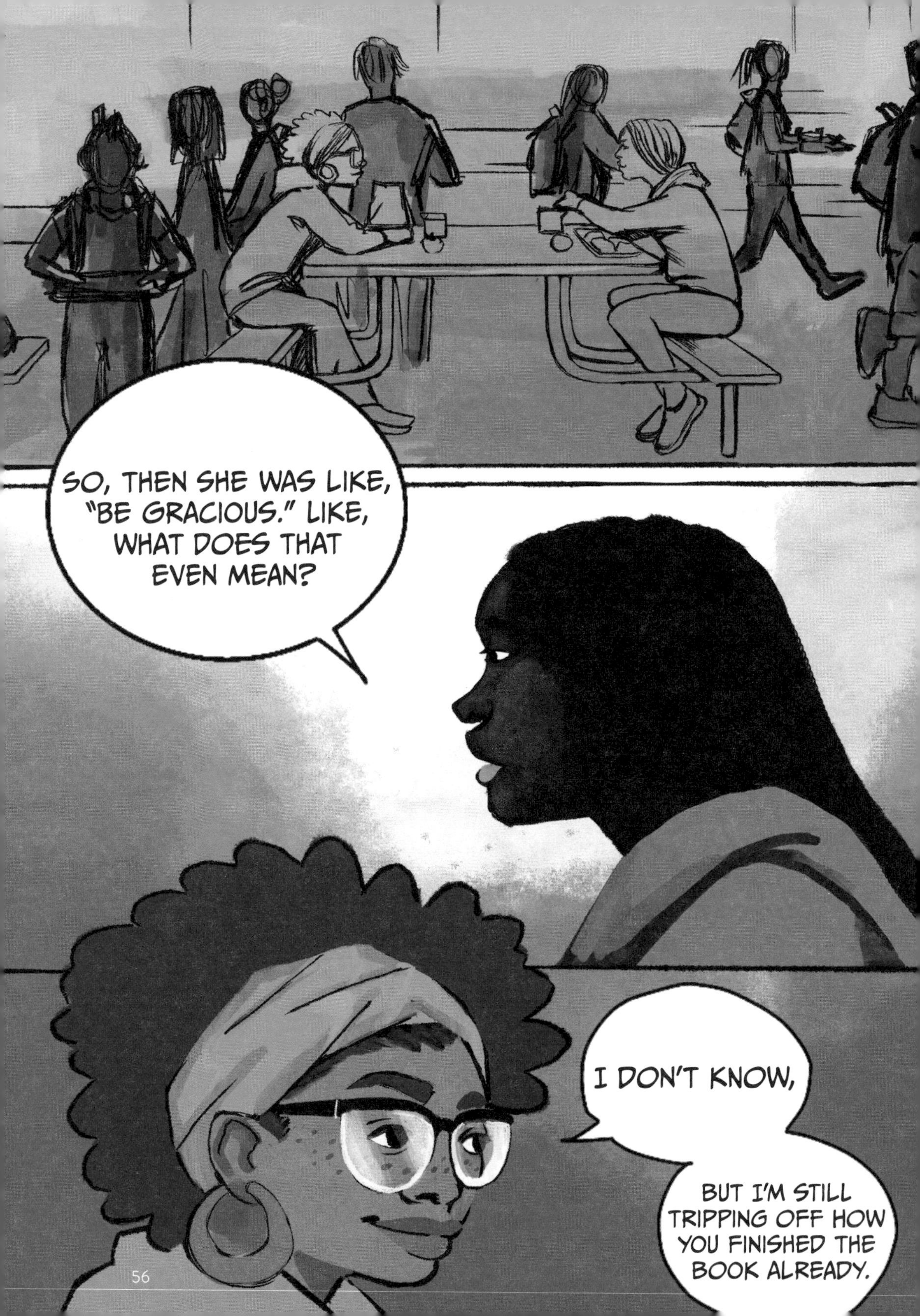
SO, THEN SHE WAS LIKE, "BE GRACIOUS." LIKE, WHAT DOES THAT EVEN MEAN?
I DON'T KNOW,
BUT I'M STILL TRIPPING OFF HOW YOU FINISHED THE BOOK ALREADY.

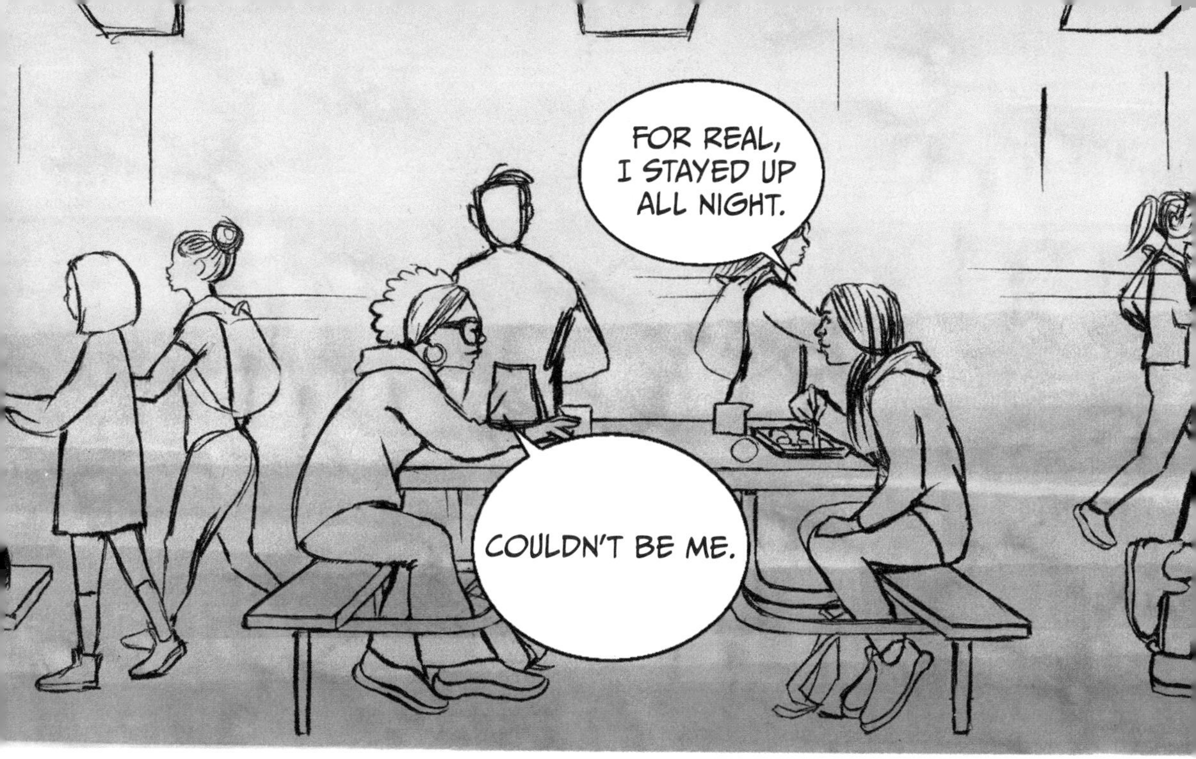
FOR REAL, I STAYED UP ALL NIGHT.
COULDN'T BE ME.

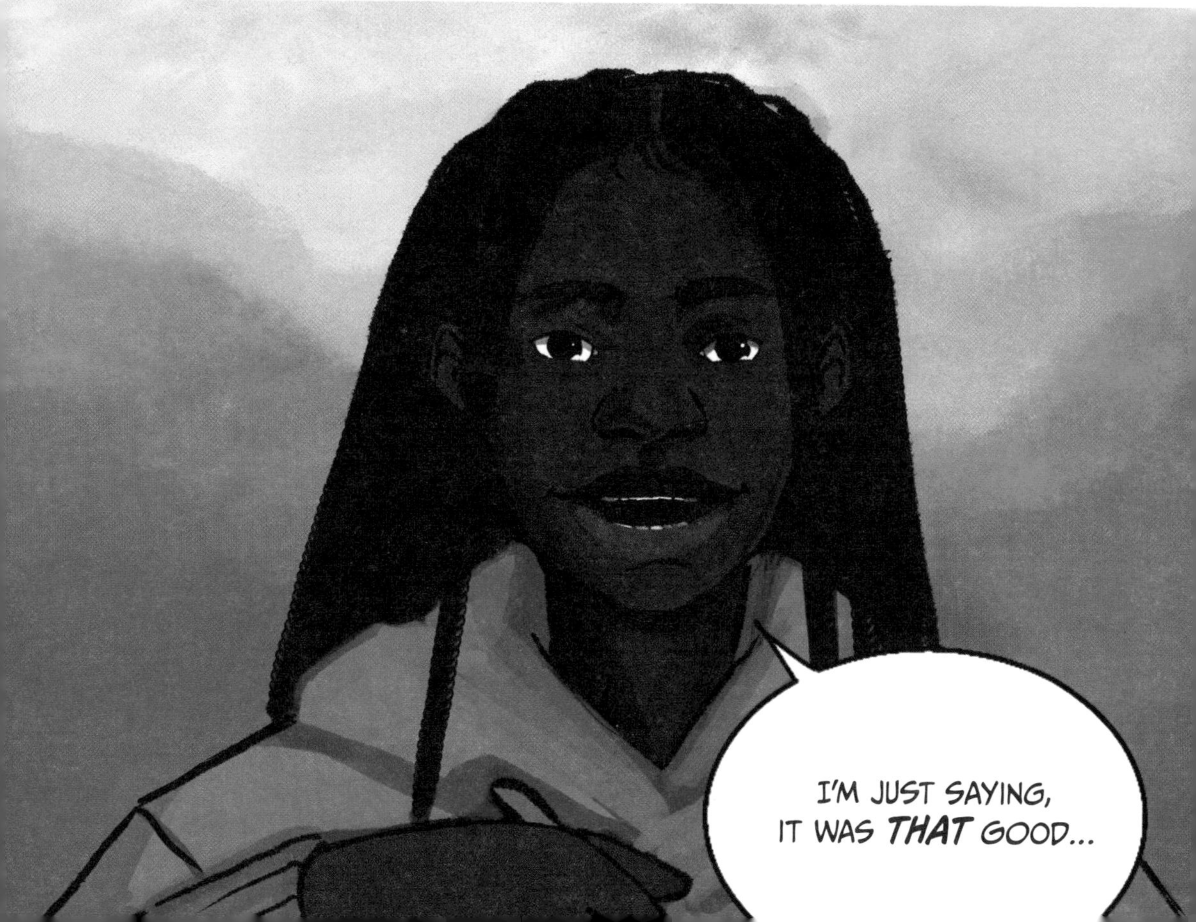
I'M JUST SAYING, IT WAS THAT GOOD...

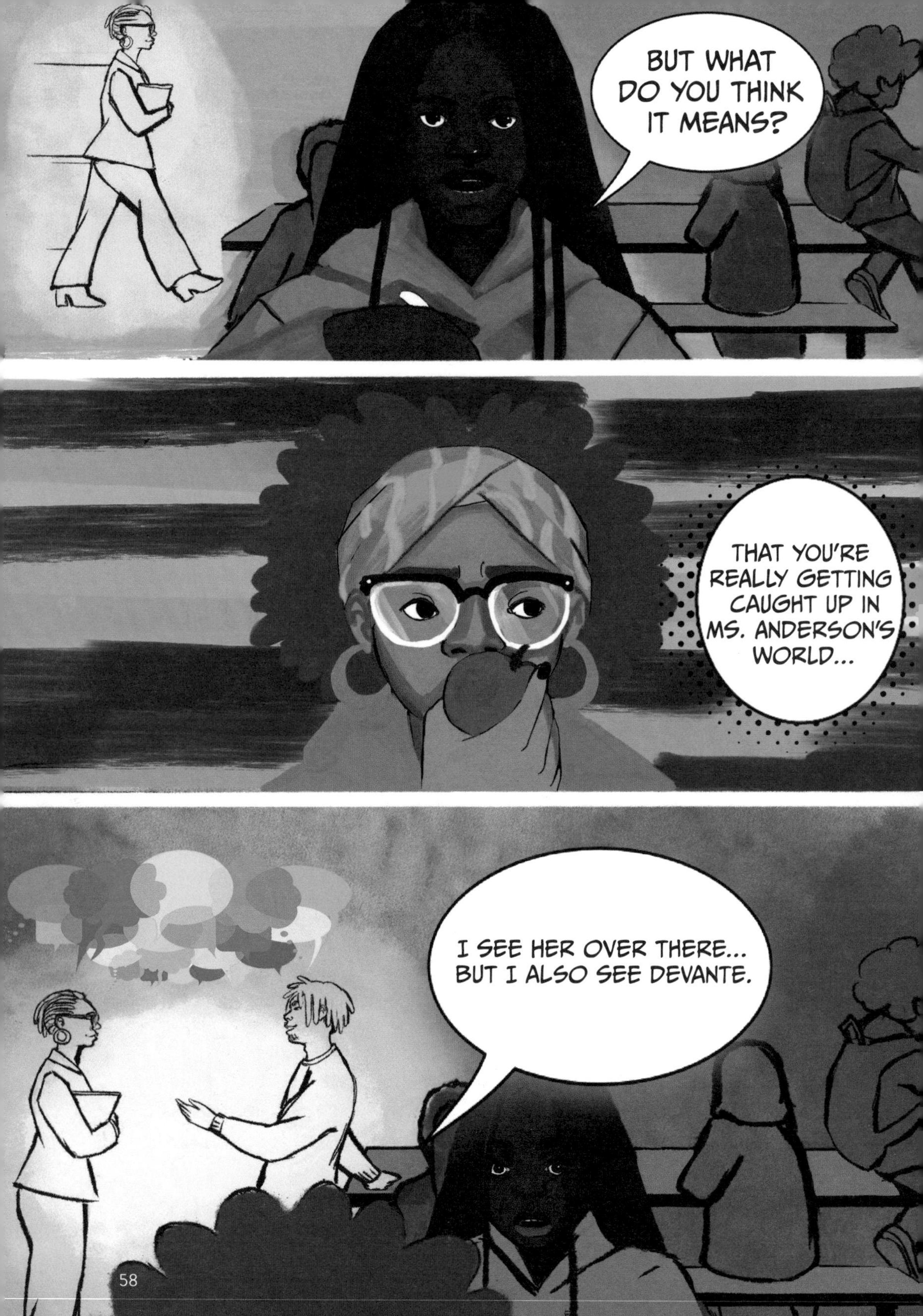
BUT WHAT DO YOU THINK IT MEANS?
THAT YOU'RE REALLY GETTING CAUGHT UP IN MS. ANDERSON'S WORLD...
I SEE HER OVER THERE... BUT I ALSO SEE DEVANTE.

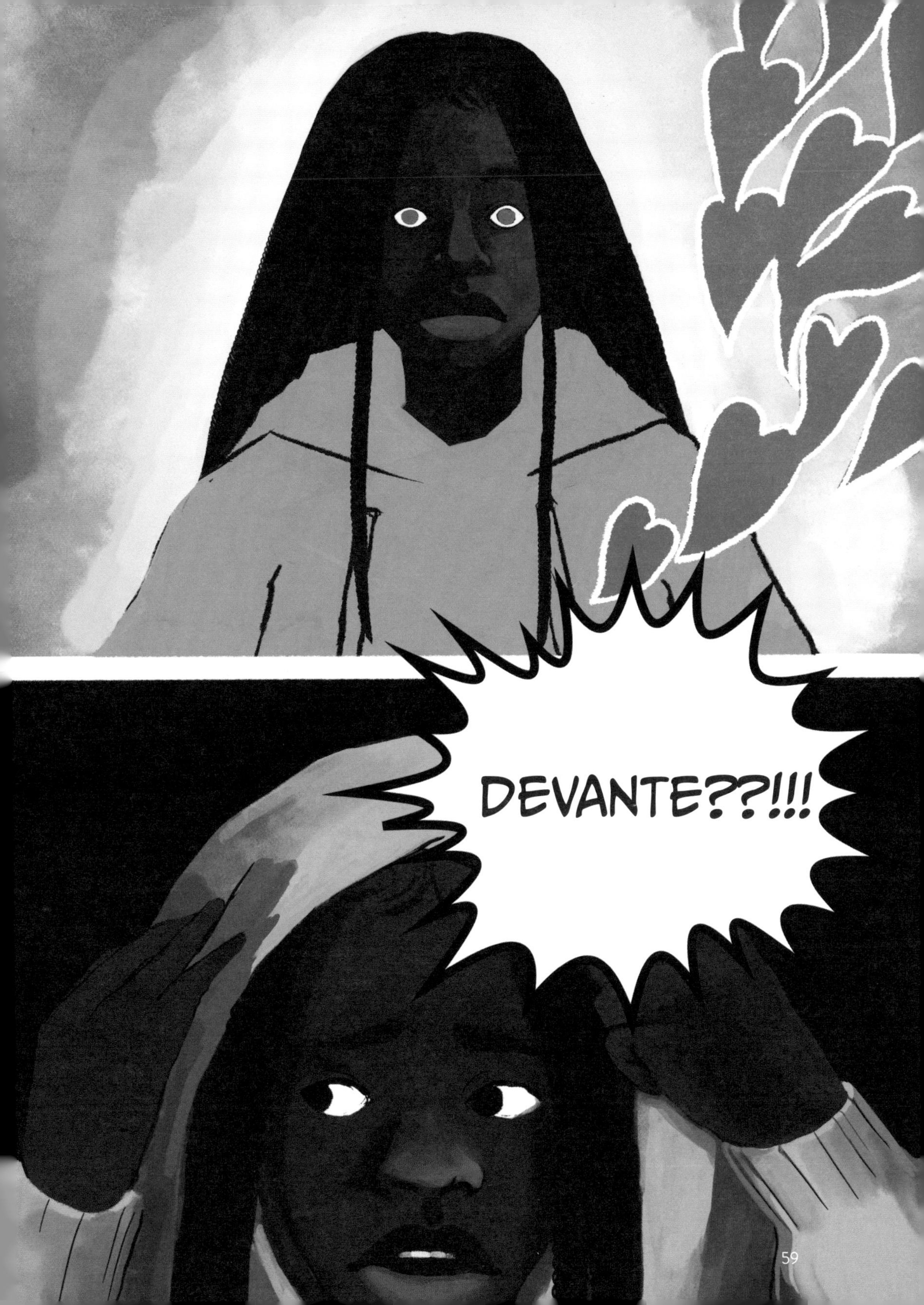
DEVANTE??!!!

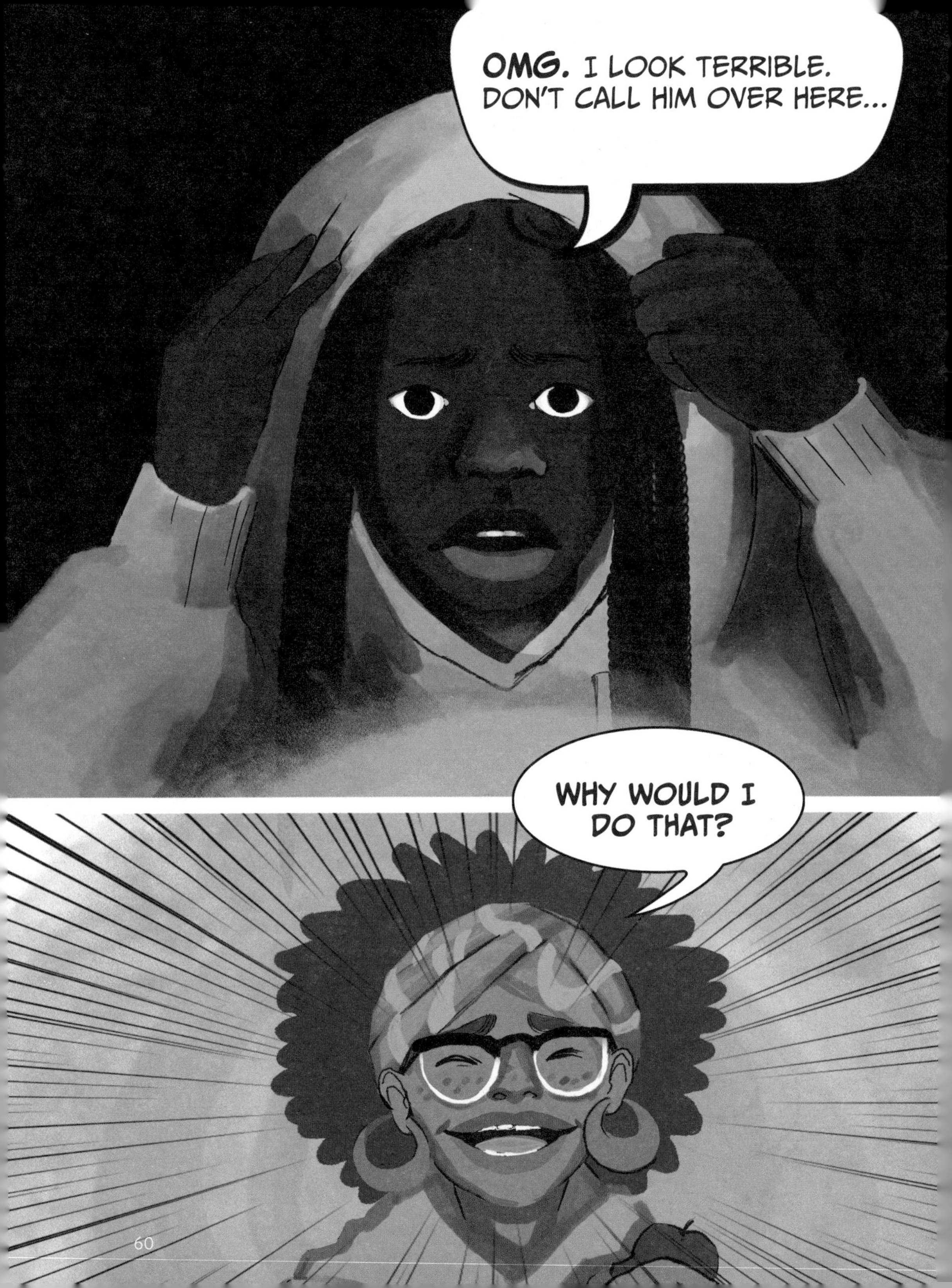
OMG. I LOOK TERRIBLE. DON'T CALL HIM OVER HERE...
WHY WOULD I DO THAT?

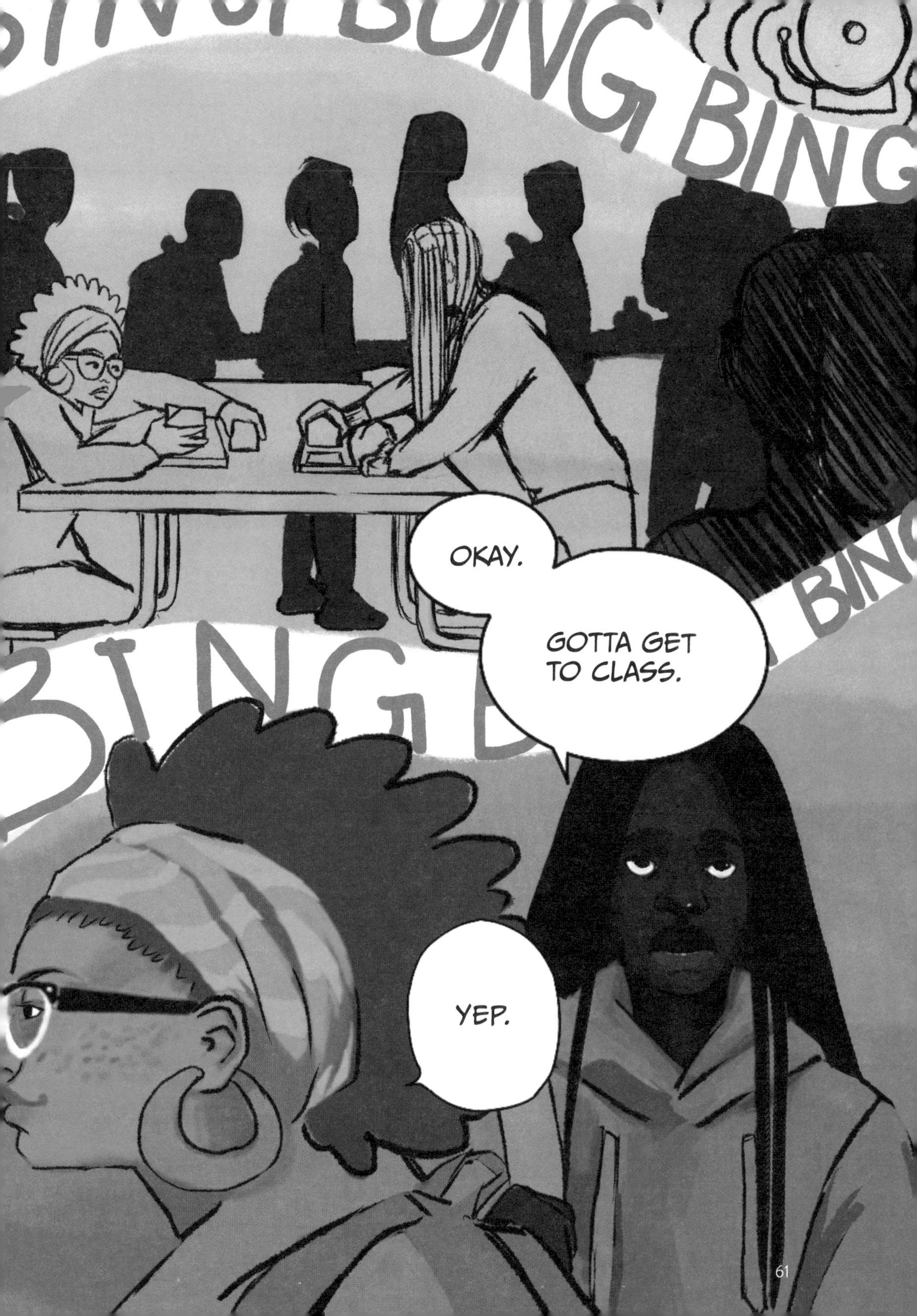
BONG
BING
OKAY.
BING
BING
GOTTA GET TO CLASS.
YEP.

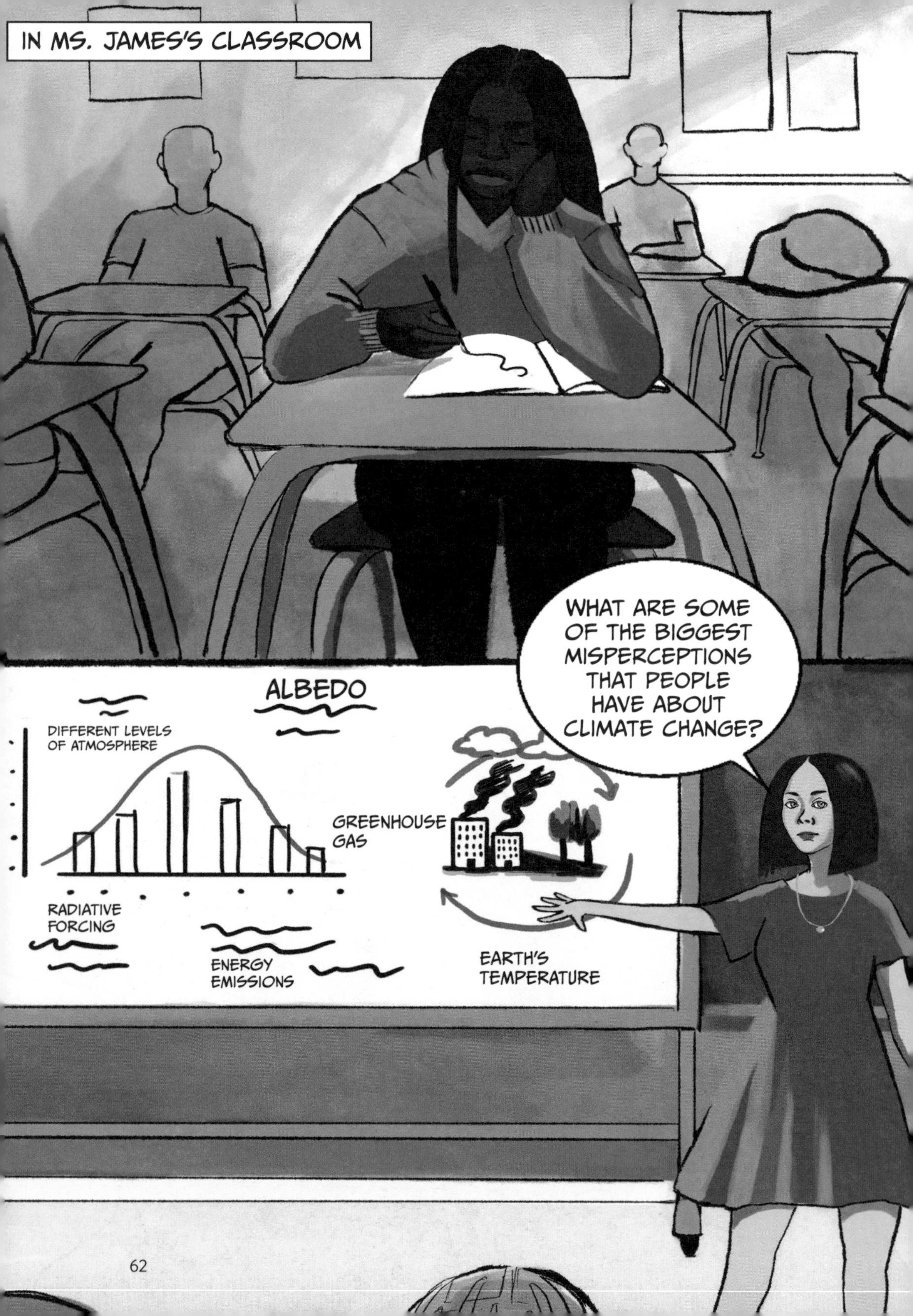
IN MS. JAMES'S CLASSROOM
ALBEDO
DIFFERENT LEVELS OF ATMOSPHERE
GREENHOUSE GAS
RADIATIVE FORCING
ENERGY EMISSIONS
EARTH'S TEMPERATURE
WHAT ARE SOME OF THE BIGGEST MISPERCEPTIONS THAT PEOPLE HAVE ABOUT CLIMATE CHANGE?

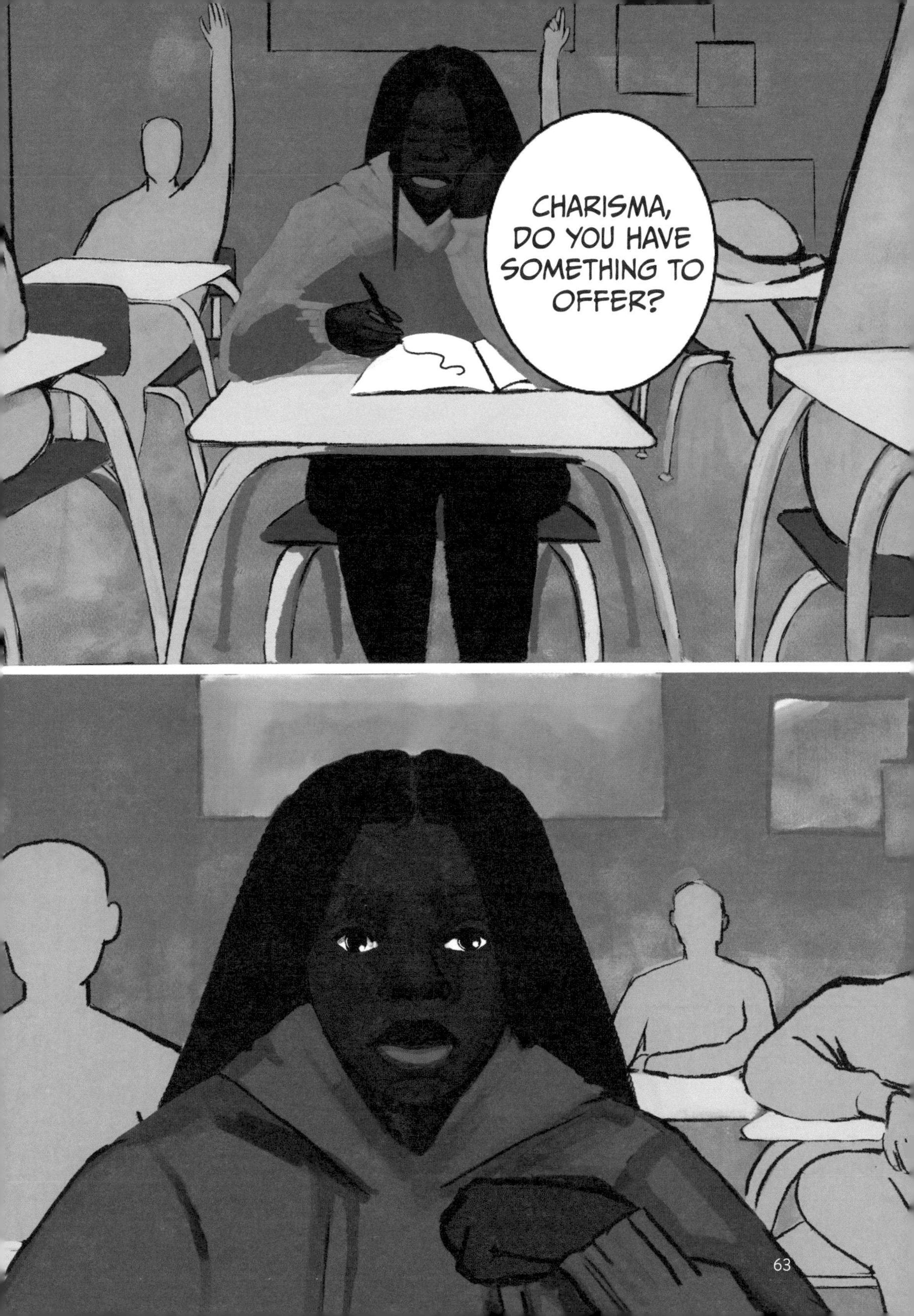
CHARISMA, DO YOU HAVE SOMETHING TO OFFER?

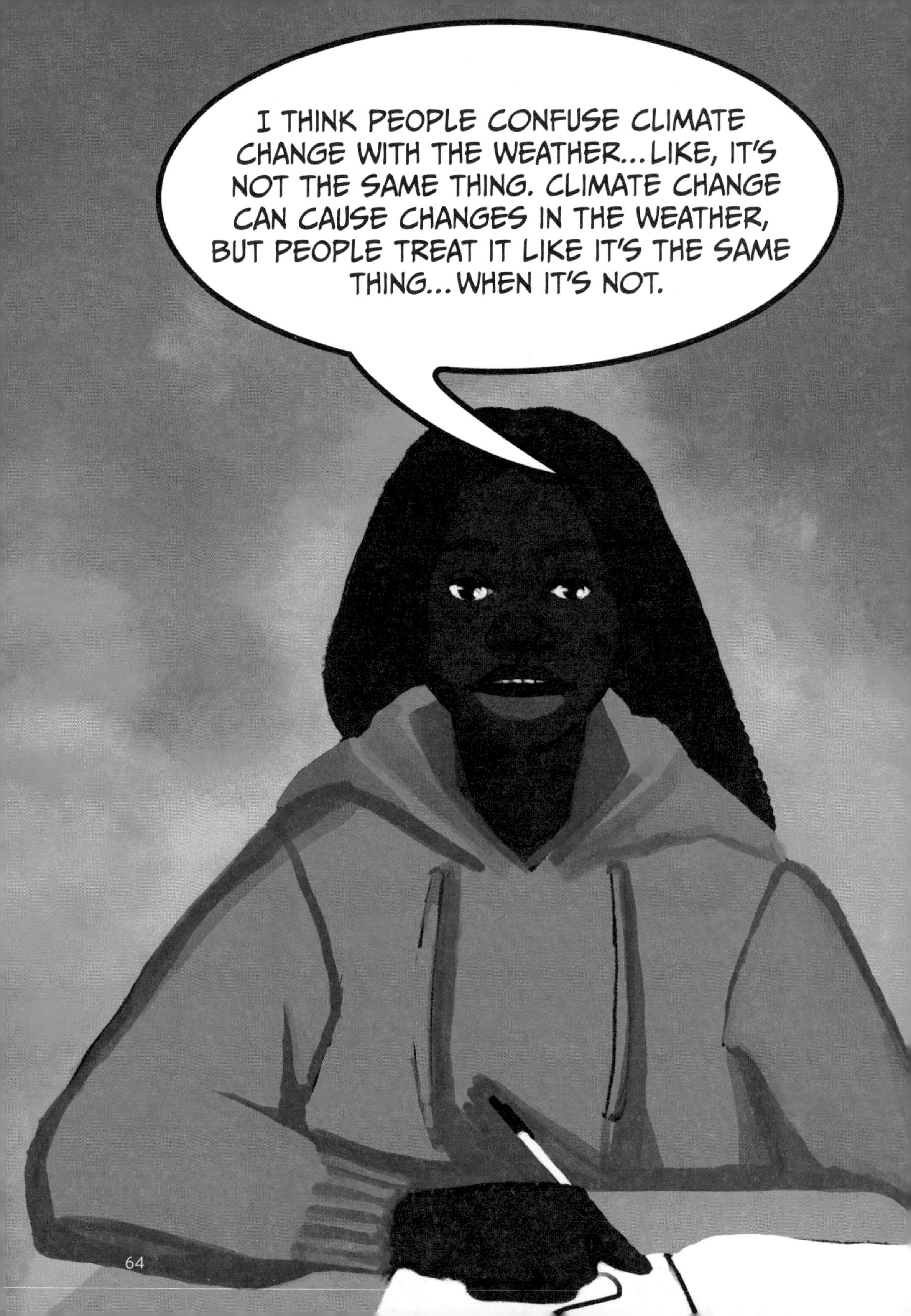
I THINK PEOPLE CONFUSE CLIMATE CHANGE WITH THE WEATHER...LIKE, IT'S NOT THE SAME THING. CLIMATE CHANGE CAN CAUSE CHANGES IN THE WEATHER, BUT PEOPLE TREAT IT LIKE IT'S THE SAME THING...WHEN IT'S NOT.

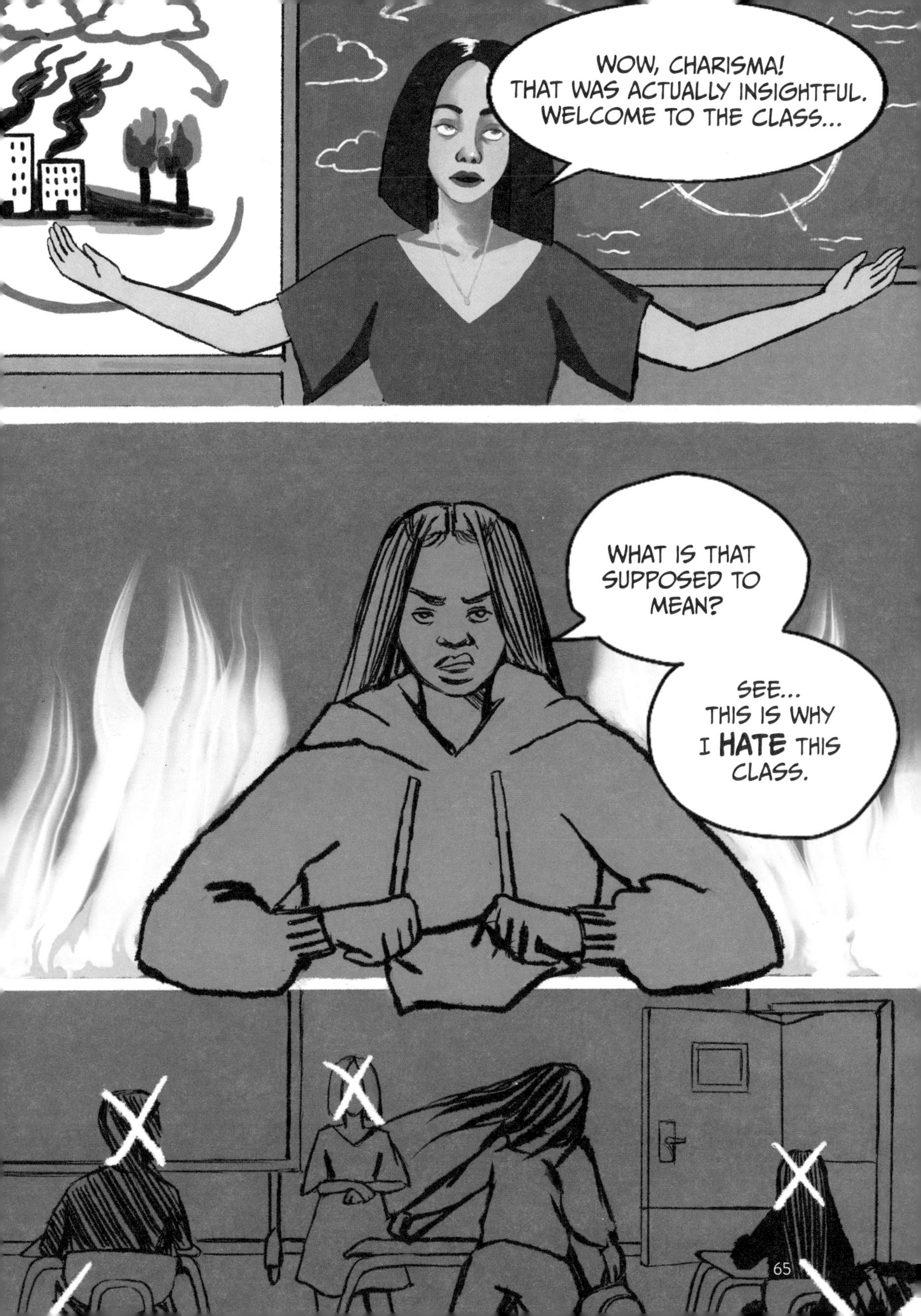
WOW, CHARISMA! THAT WAS ACTUALLY INSIGHTFUL. WELCOME TO THE CLASS...
WHAT IS THAT SUPPOSED TO MEAN?
SEE... THIS IS WHY I **HATE** THIS CLASS.

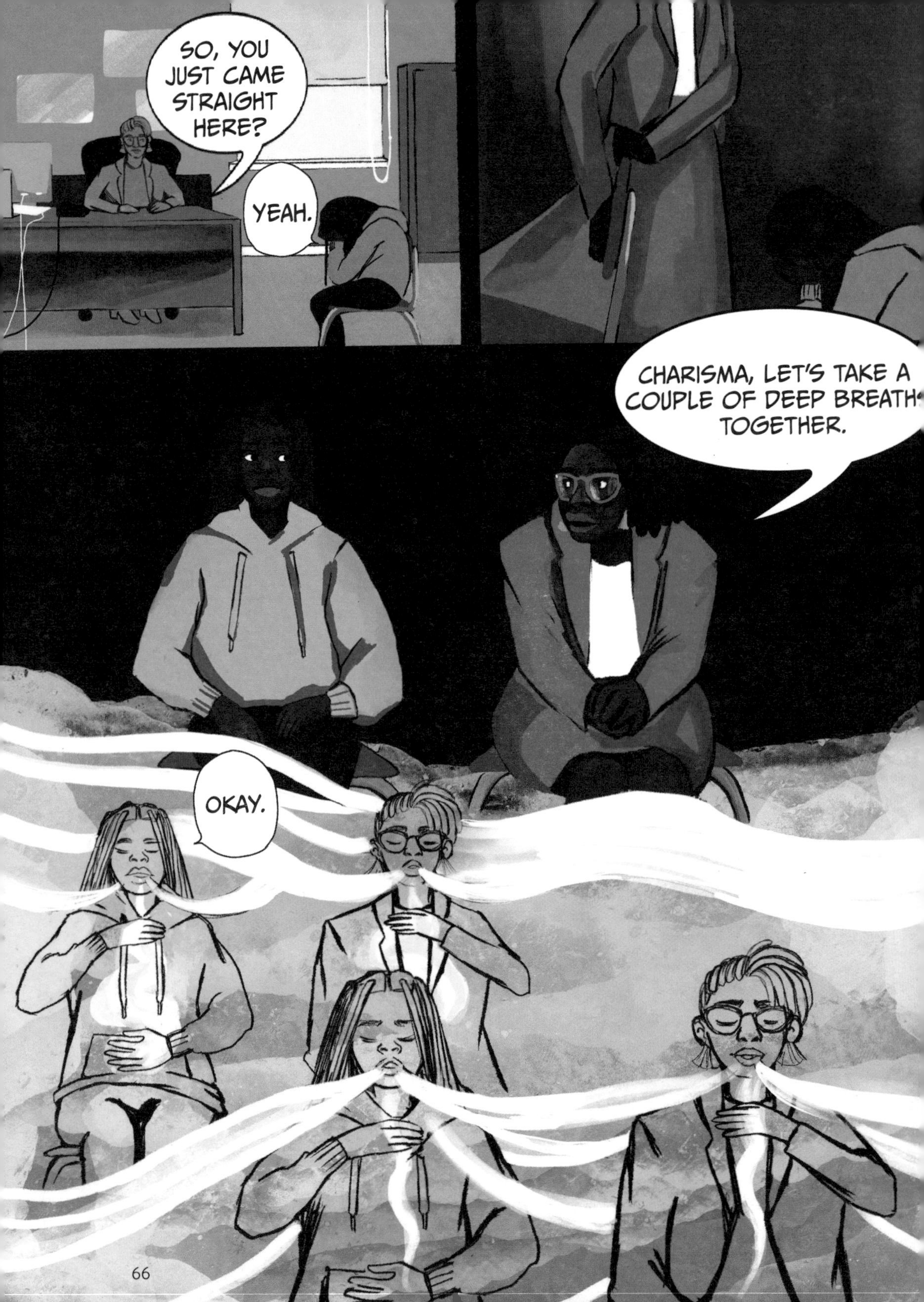
SO, YOU JUST CAME STRAIGHT HERE?
YEAH.
CHARISMA, LET'S TAKE A COUPLE OF DEEP BREATHS TOGETHER.
OKAY.

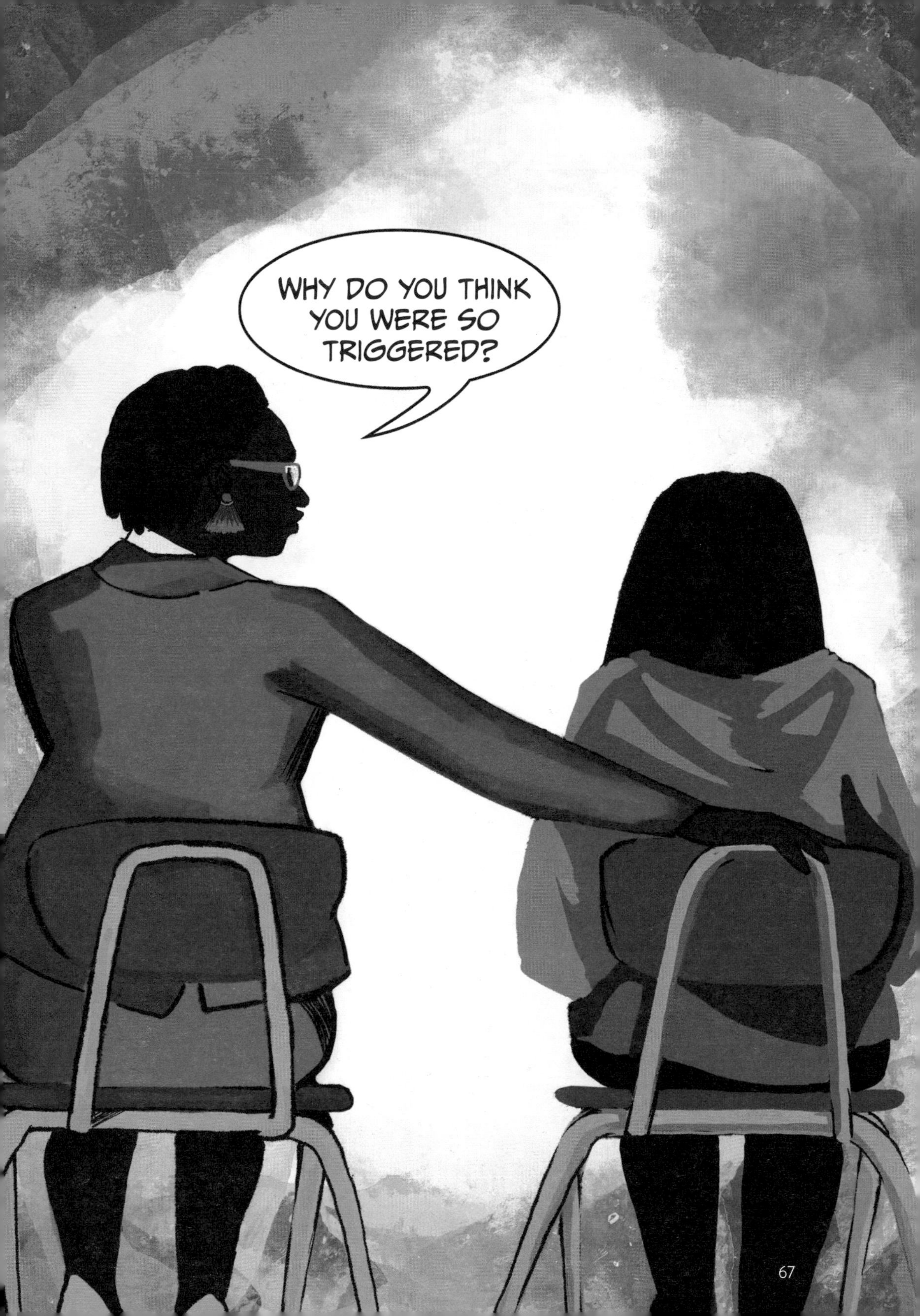
WHY DO YOU THINK YOU WERE SO TRIGGERED?

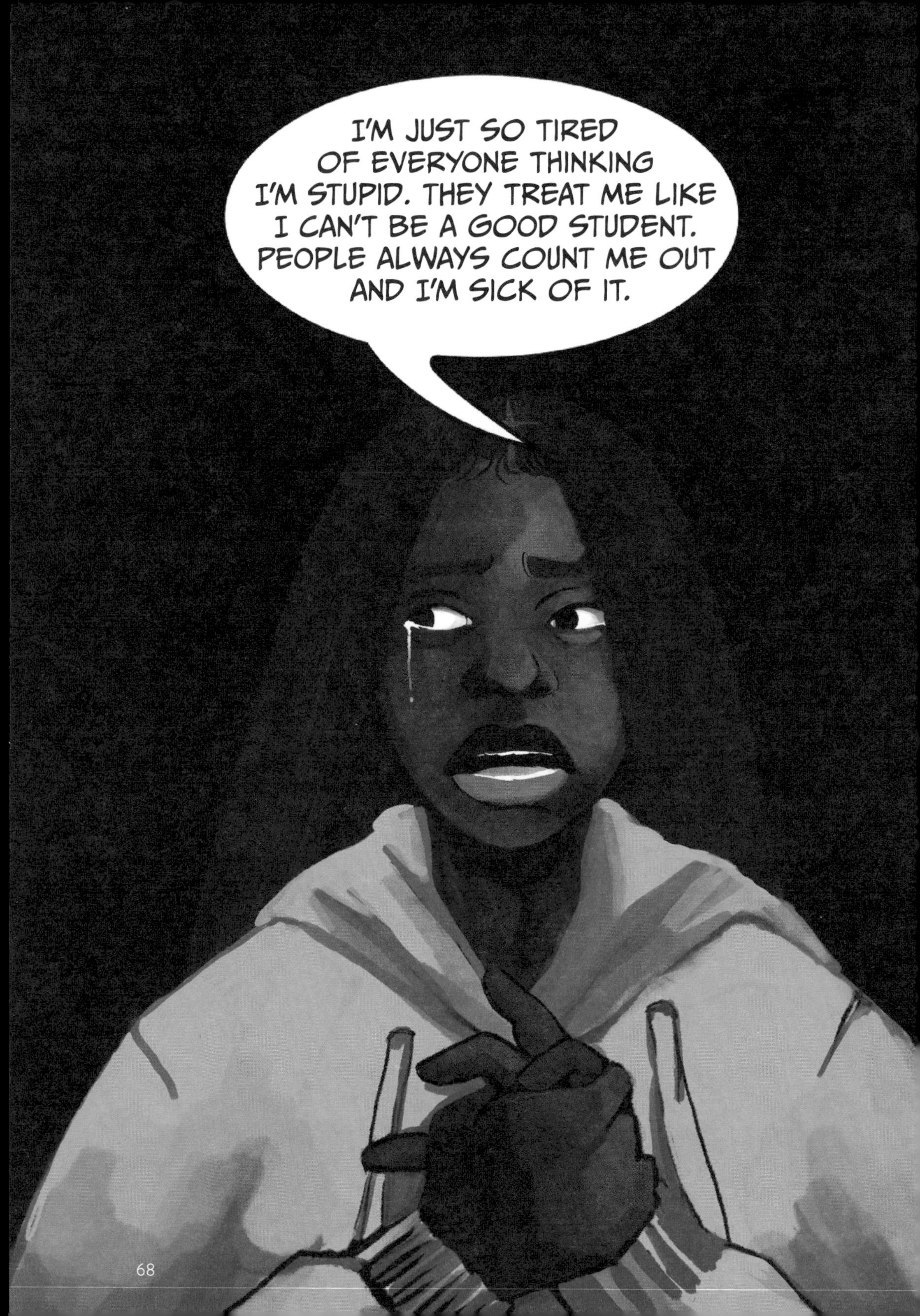
I'M JUST SO TIRED OF EVERYONE THINKING I'M STUPID. THEY TREAT ME LIKE I CAN'T BE A GOOD STUDENT. PEOPLE ALWAYS COUNT ME OUT AND I'M SICK OF IT.

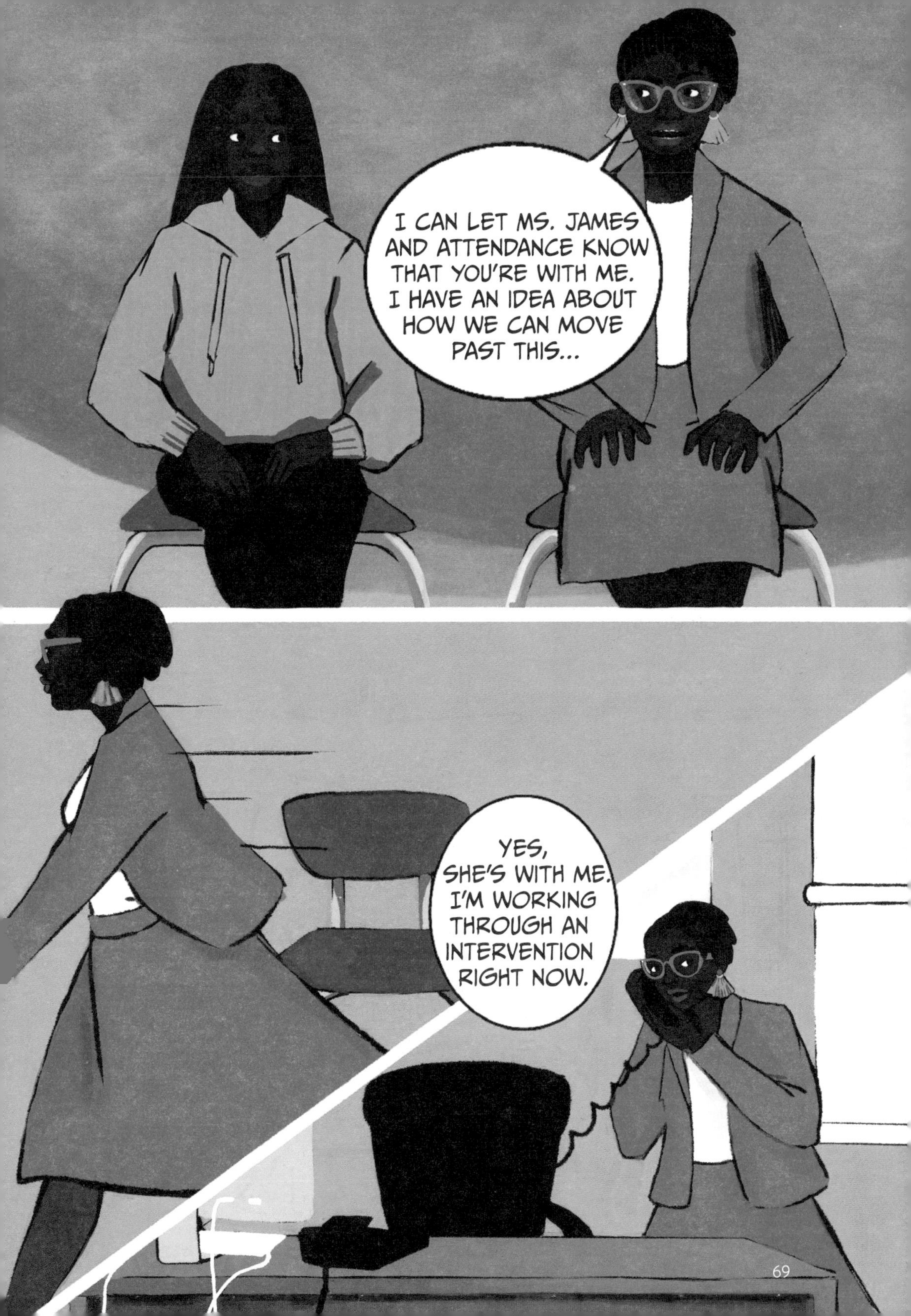
I CAN LET MS. JAMES AND ATTENDANCE KNOW THAT YOU'RE WITH ME. I HAVE AN IDEA ABOUT HOW WE CAN MOVE PAST THIS...
YES, SHE'S WITH ME. I'M WORKING THROUGH AN INTERVENTION RIGHT NOW.

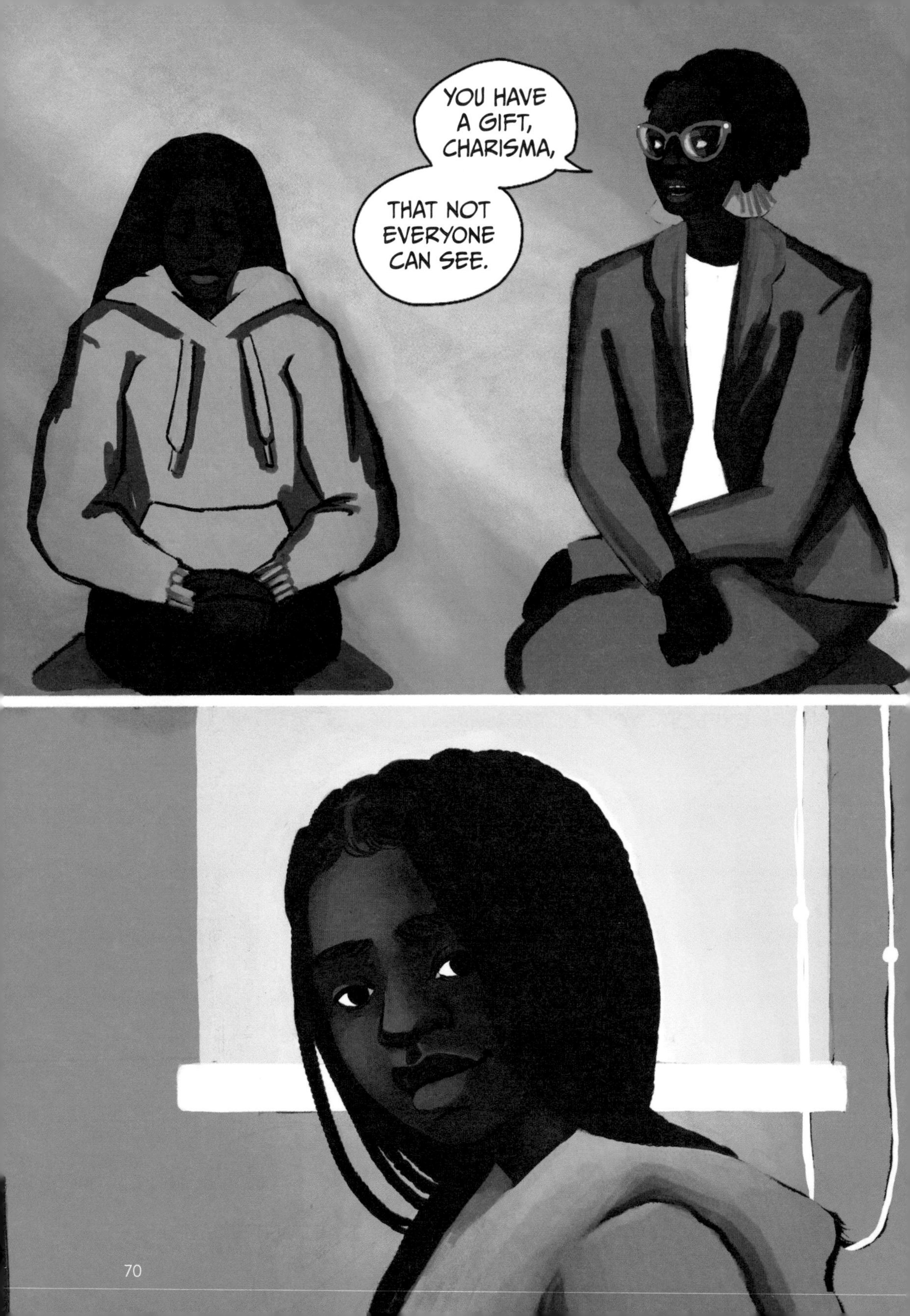
YOU HAVE A GIFT, CHARISMA,
THAT NOT EVERYONE CAN SEE.

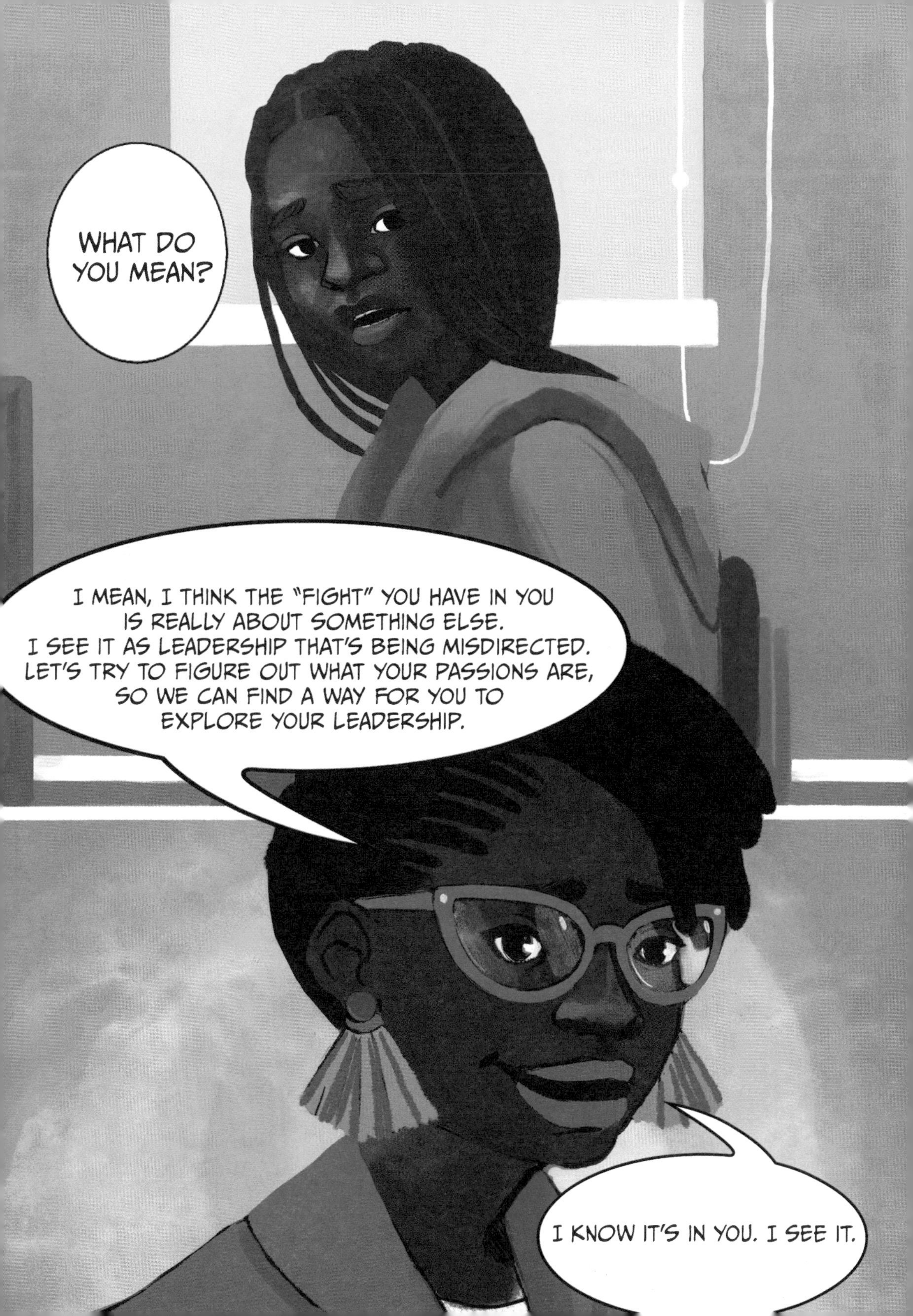
WHAT DO YOU MEAN?
I MEAN, I THINK THE "FIGHT" YOU HAVE IN YOU IS REALLY ABOUT SOMETHING ELSE. I SEE IT AS LEADERSHIP THAT'S BEING MISDIRECTED. LET'S TRY TO FIGURE OUT WHAT YOUR PASSIONS ARE, SO WE CAN FIND A WAY FOR YOU TO EXPLORE YOUR LEADERSHIP.
I KNOW IT'S IN YOU. I SEE IT.

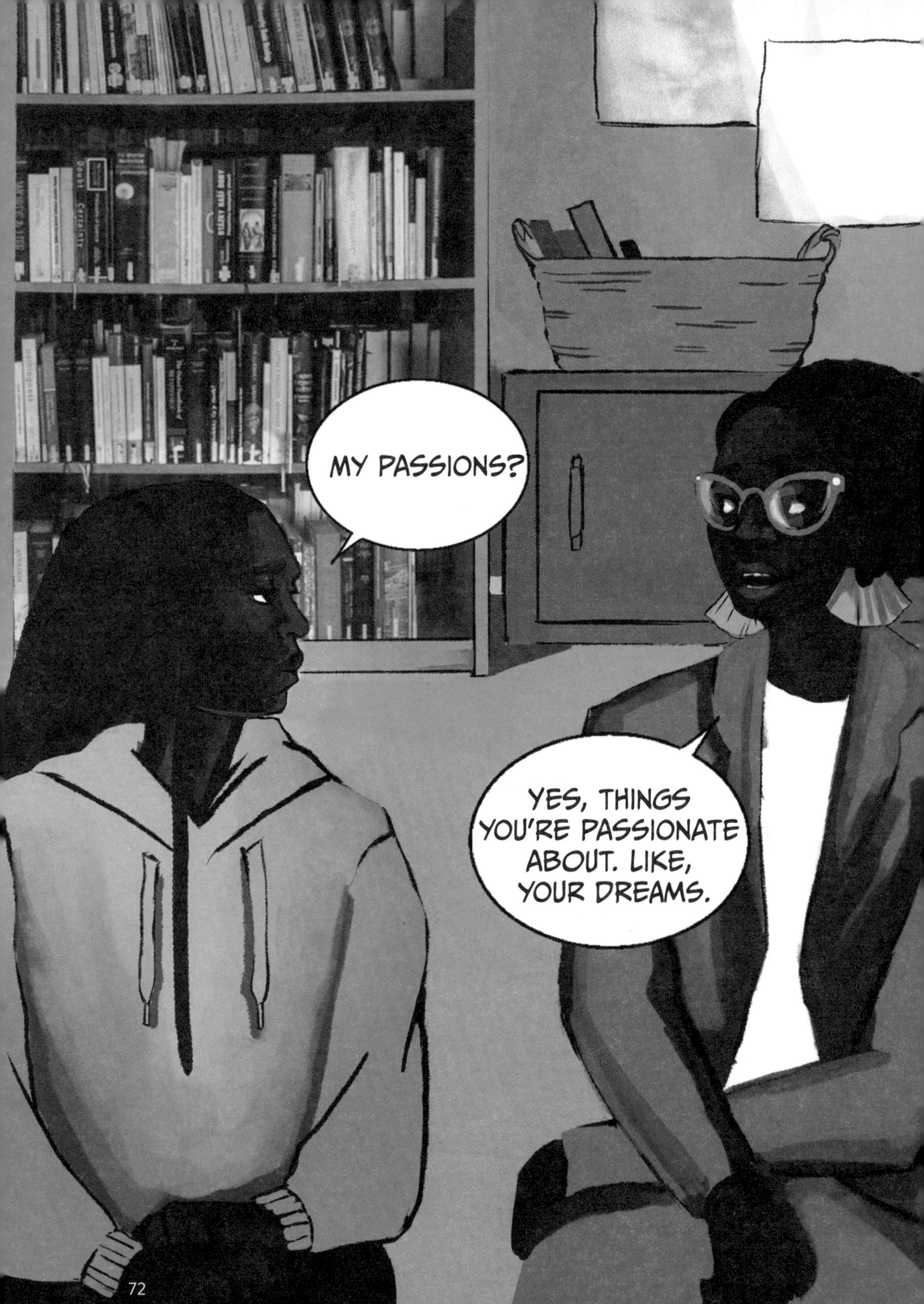
MY PASSIONS?
YES, THINGS YOU'RE PASSIONATE ABOUT. LIKE, YOUR DREAMS.

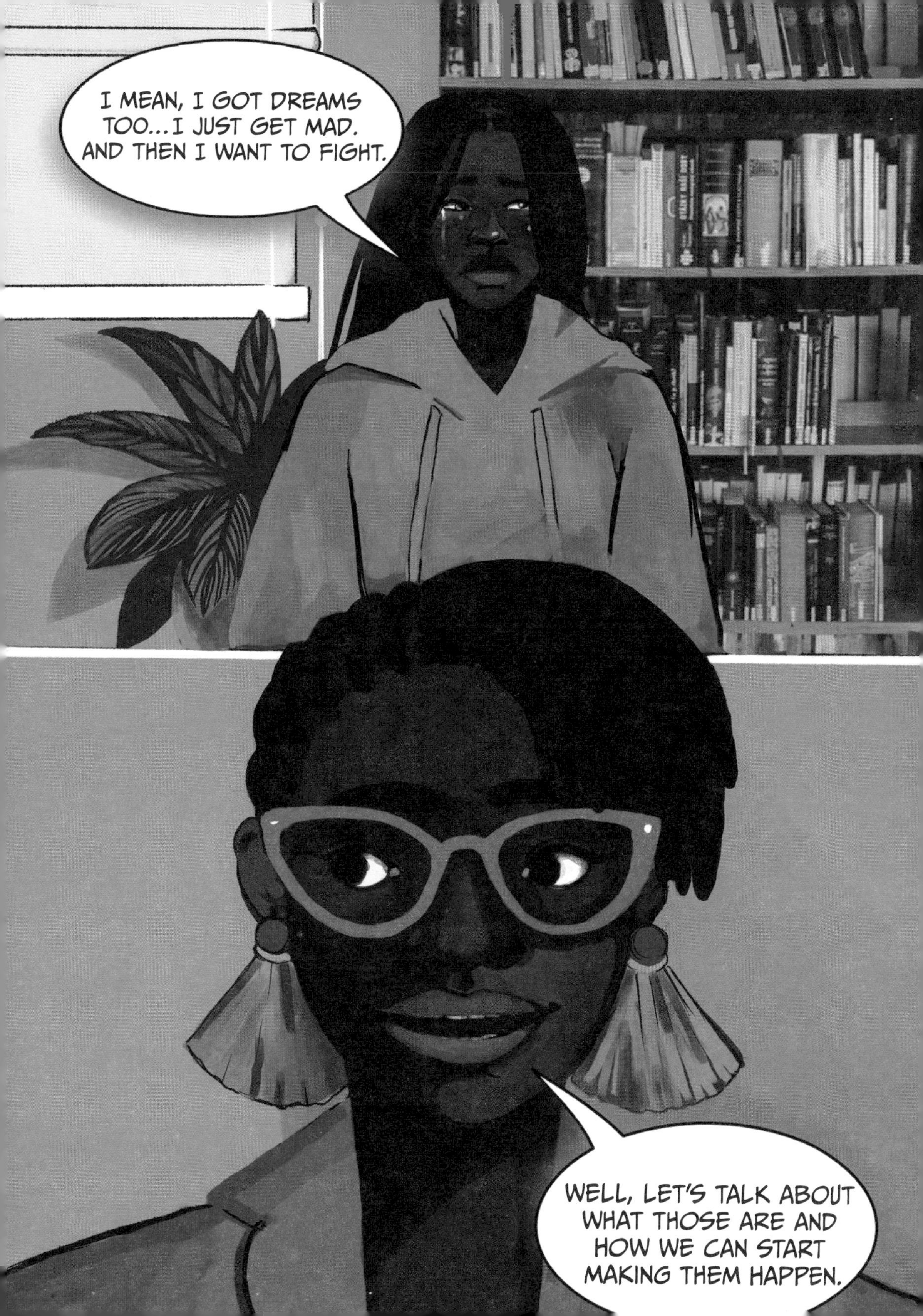
I MEAN, I GOT DREAMS TOO...I JUST GET MAD. AND THEN I WANT TO FIGHT.
WELL, LET'S TALK ABOUT WHAT THOSE ARE AND HOW WE CAN START MAKING THEM HAPPEN.

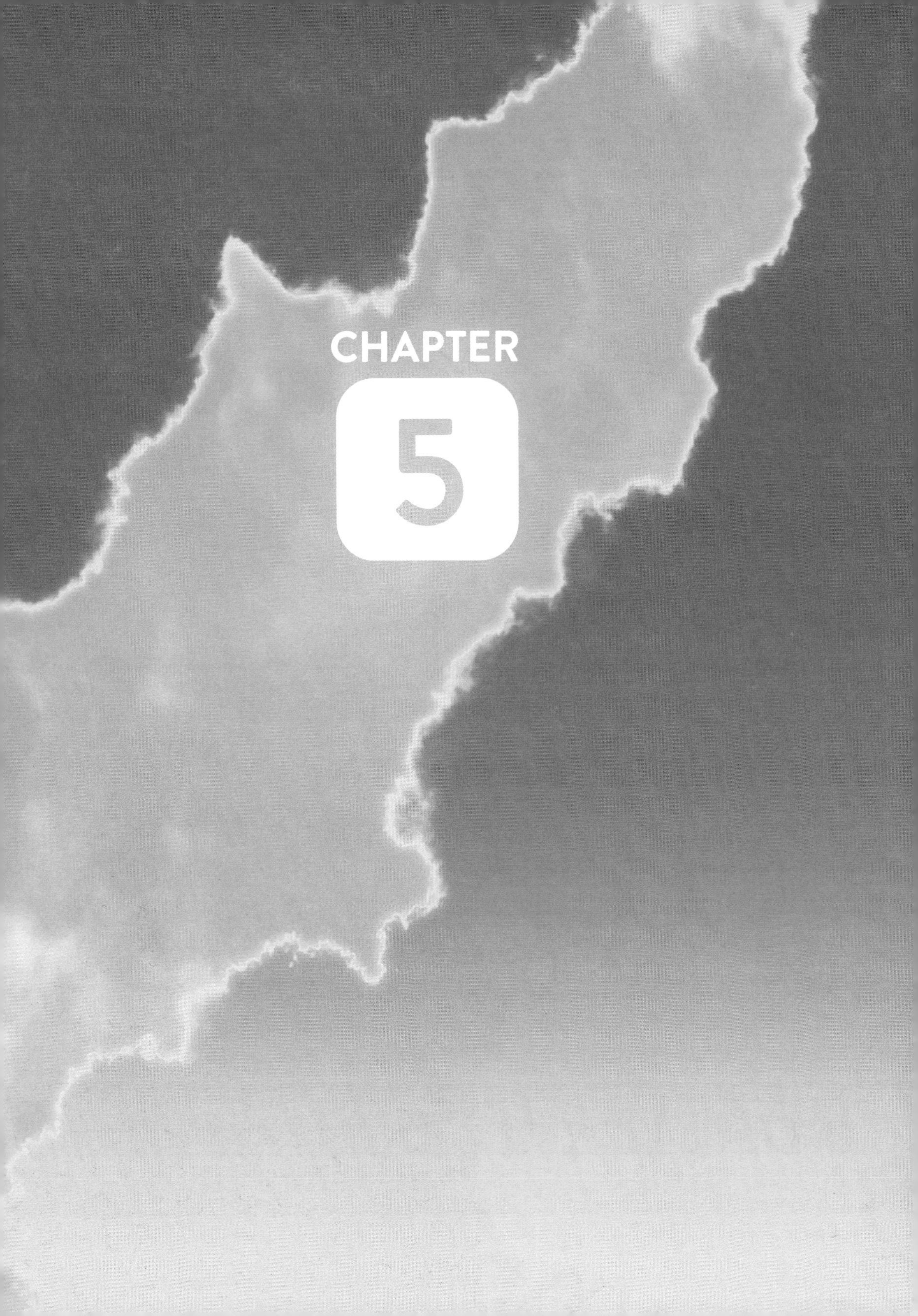

CHAPTER 5

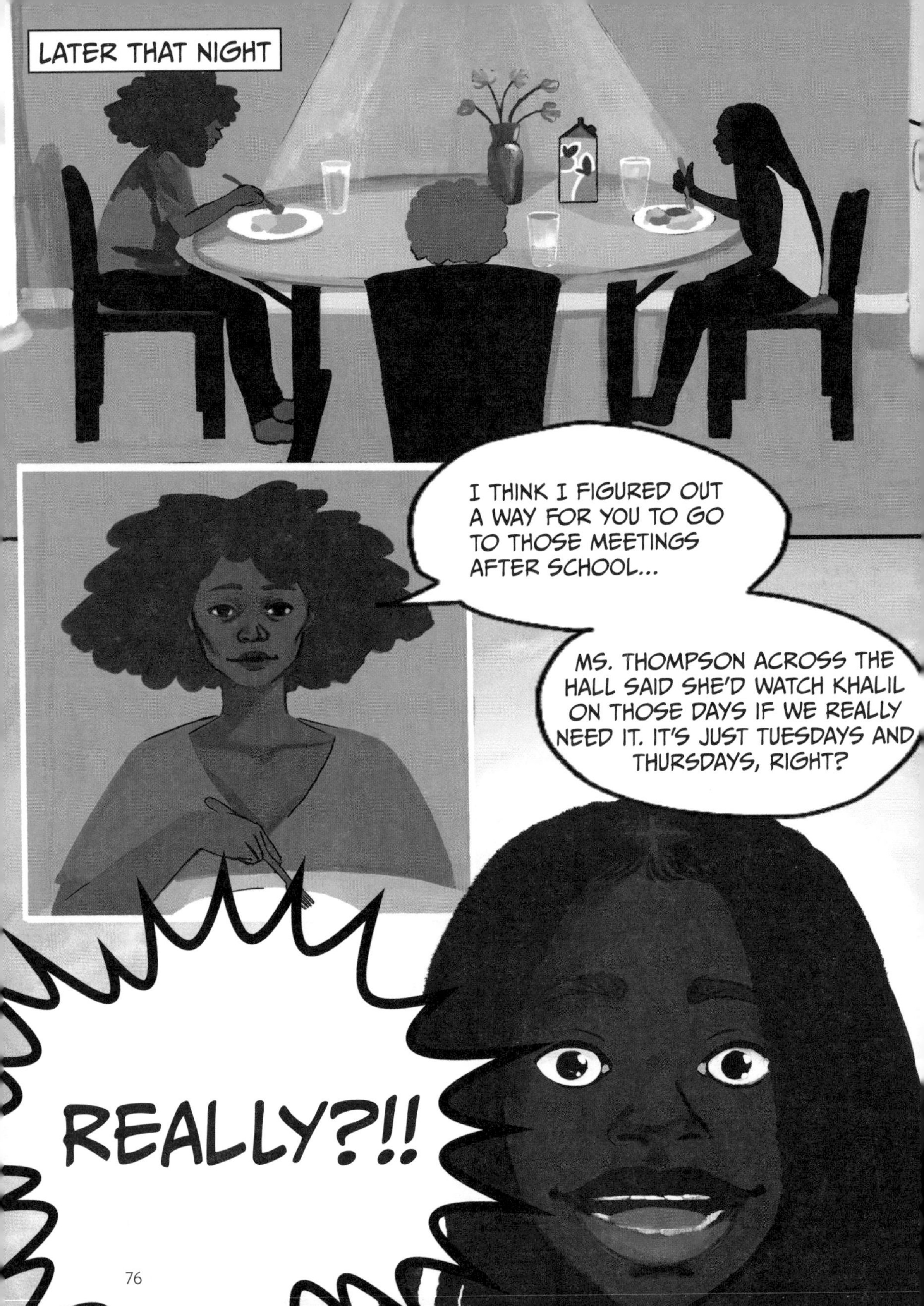
LATER THAT NIGHT
I THINK I FIGURED OUT A WAY FOR YOU TO GO TO THOSE MEETINGS AFTER SCHOOL...
MS. THOMPSON ACROSS THE HALL SAID SHE'D WATCH KHALIL ON THOSE DAYS IF WE REALLY NEED IT. IT'S JUST TUESDAYS AND THURSDAYS, RIGHT?
REALLY?!!

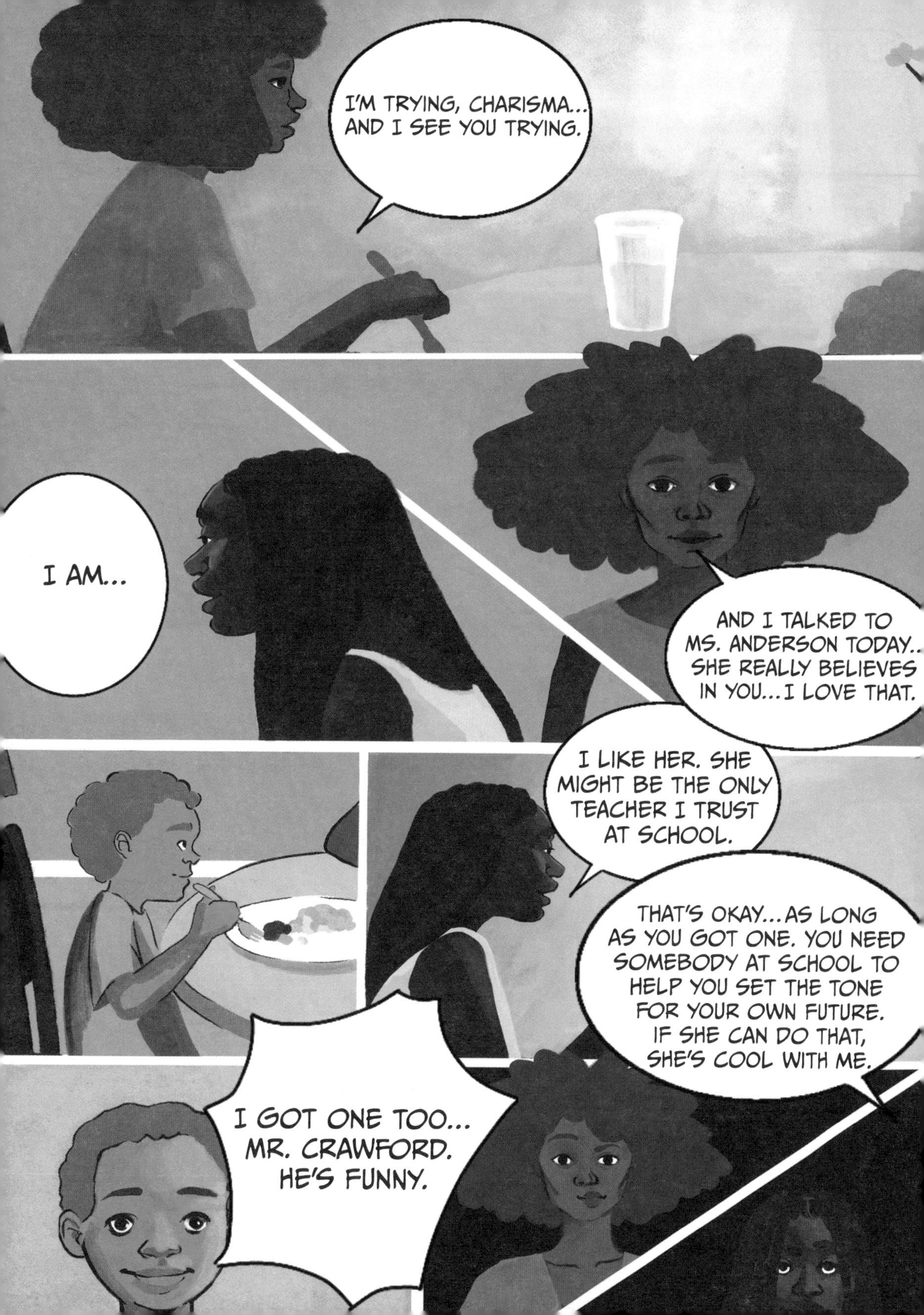
I'M TRYING, CHARISMA... AND I SEE YOU TRYING.
I AM...
AND I TALKED TO MS. ANDERSON TODAY... SHE REALLY BELIEVES IN YOU... I LOVE THAT.
I LIKE HER. SHE MIGHT BE THE ONLY TEACHER I TRUST AT SCHOOL.
THAT'S OKAY... AS LONG AS YOU GOT ONE. YOU NEED SOMEBODY AT SCHOOL TO HELP YOU SET THE TONE FOR YOUR OWN FUTURE. IF SHE CAN DO THAT, SHE'S COOL WITH ME.
I GOT ONE TOO... MR. CRAWFORD. HE'S FUNNY.

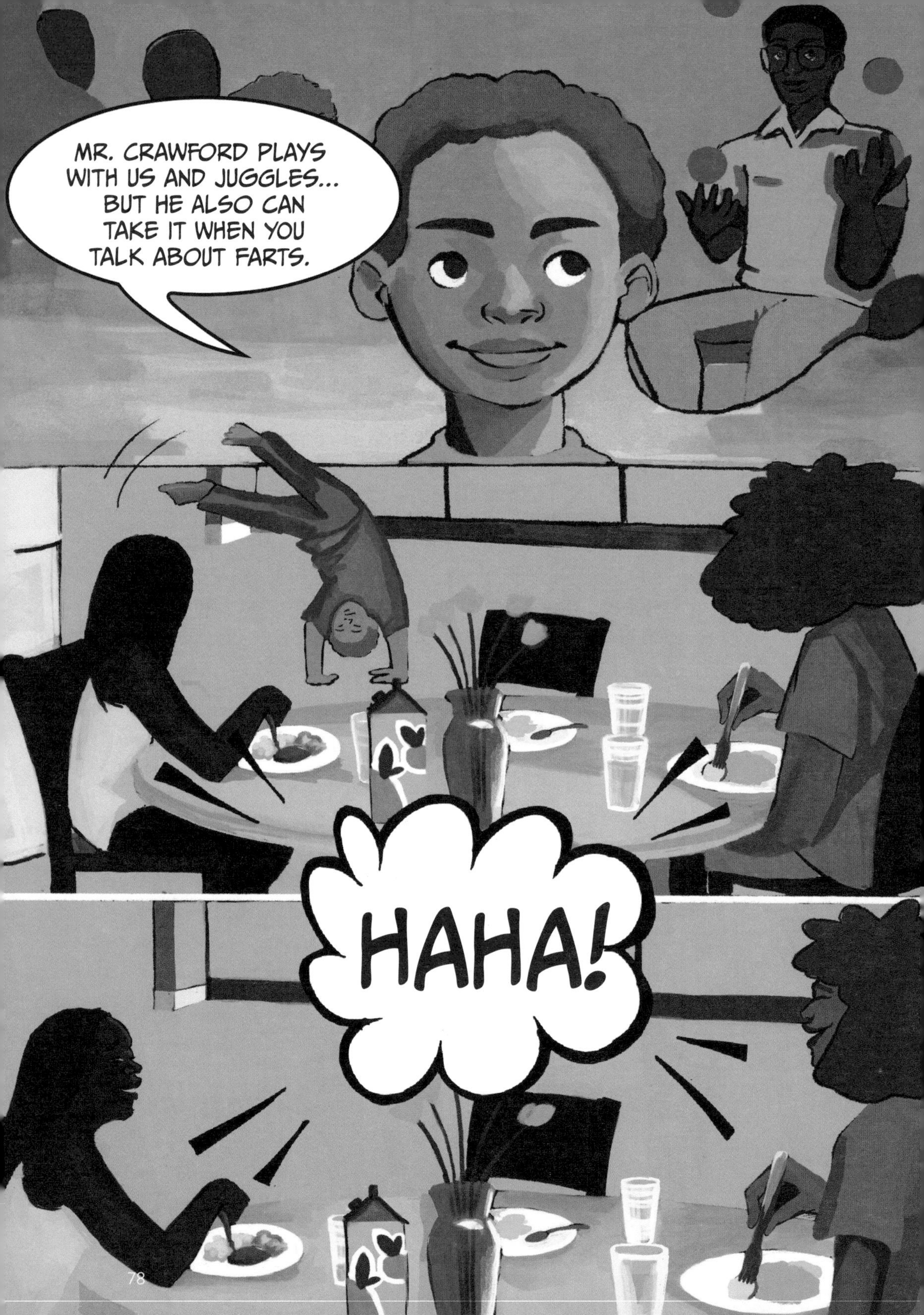
MR. CRAWFORD PLAYS WITH US AND JUGGLES... BUT HE ALSO CAN TAKE IT WHEN YOU TALK ABOUT FARTS.
HAHA!

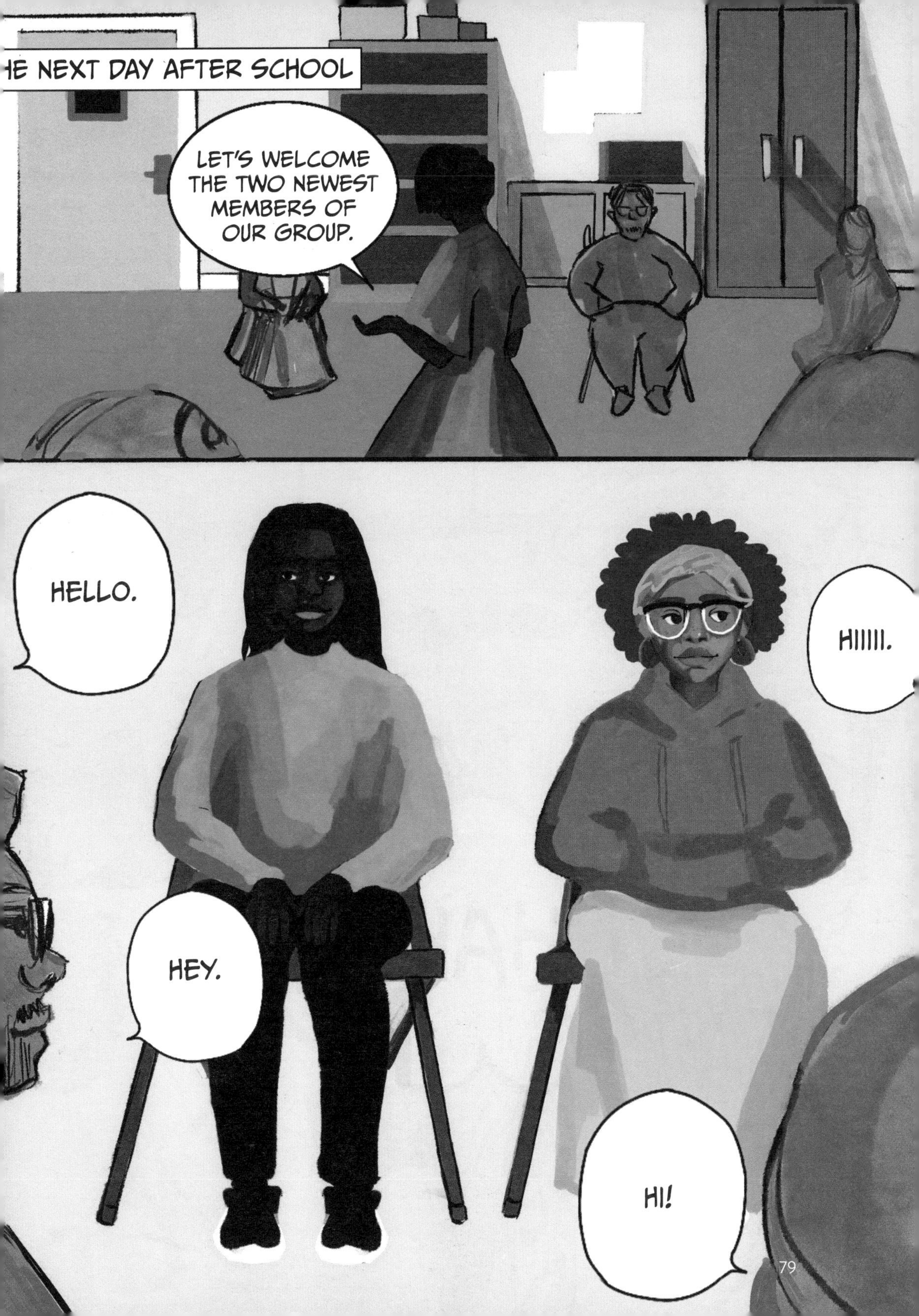

HE NEXT DAY AFTER SCHOOL
LET'S WELCOME THE TWO NEWEST MEMBERS OF OUR GROUP.
HELLO.
HIIIII.
HEY.
HI!

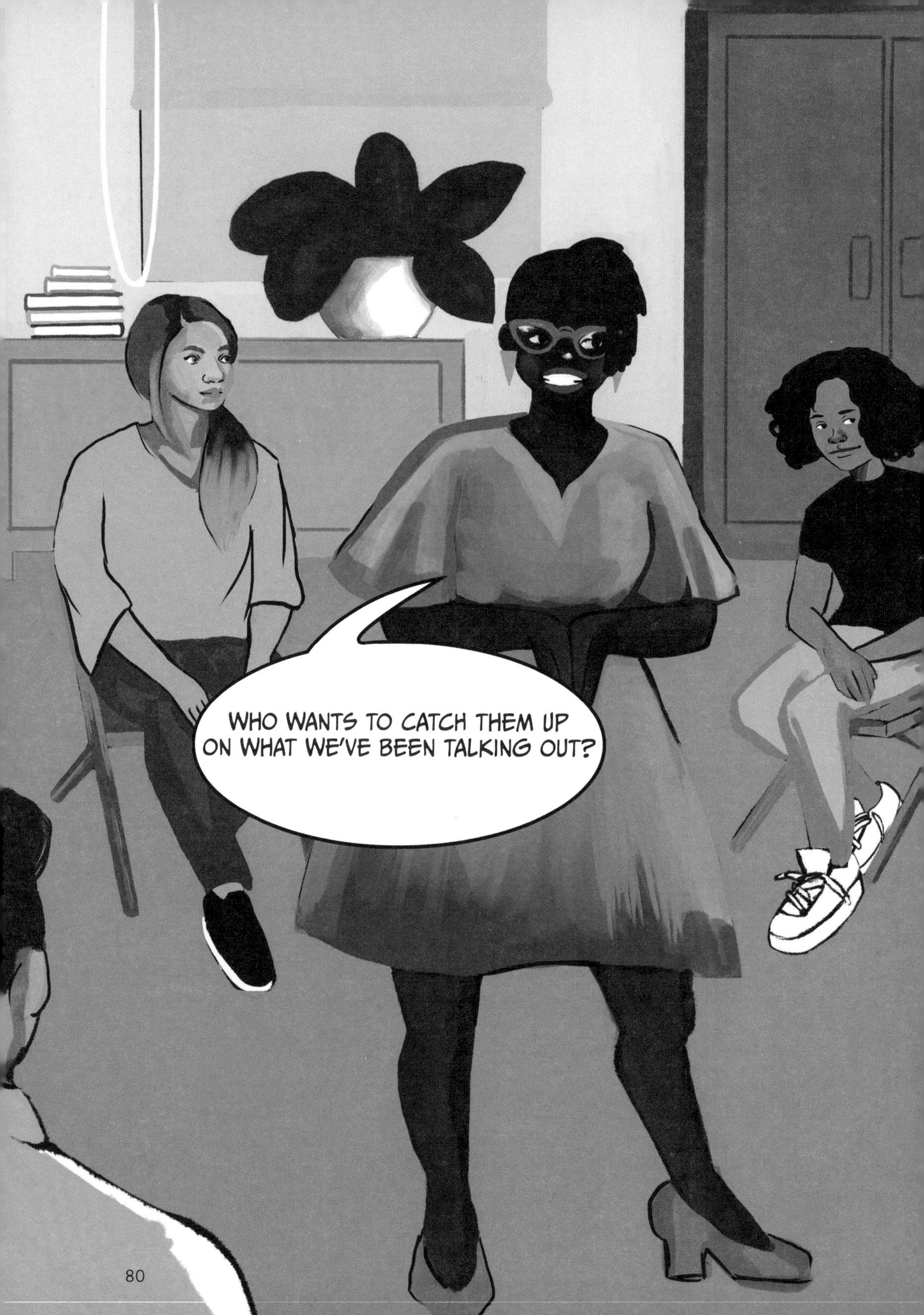
WHO WANTS TO CATCH THEM UP ON WHAT WE'VE BEEN TALKING OUT?

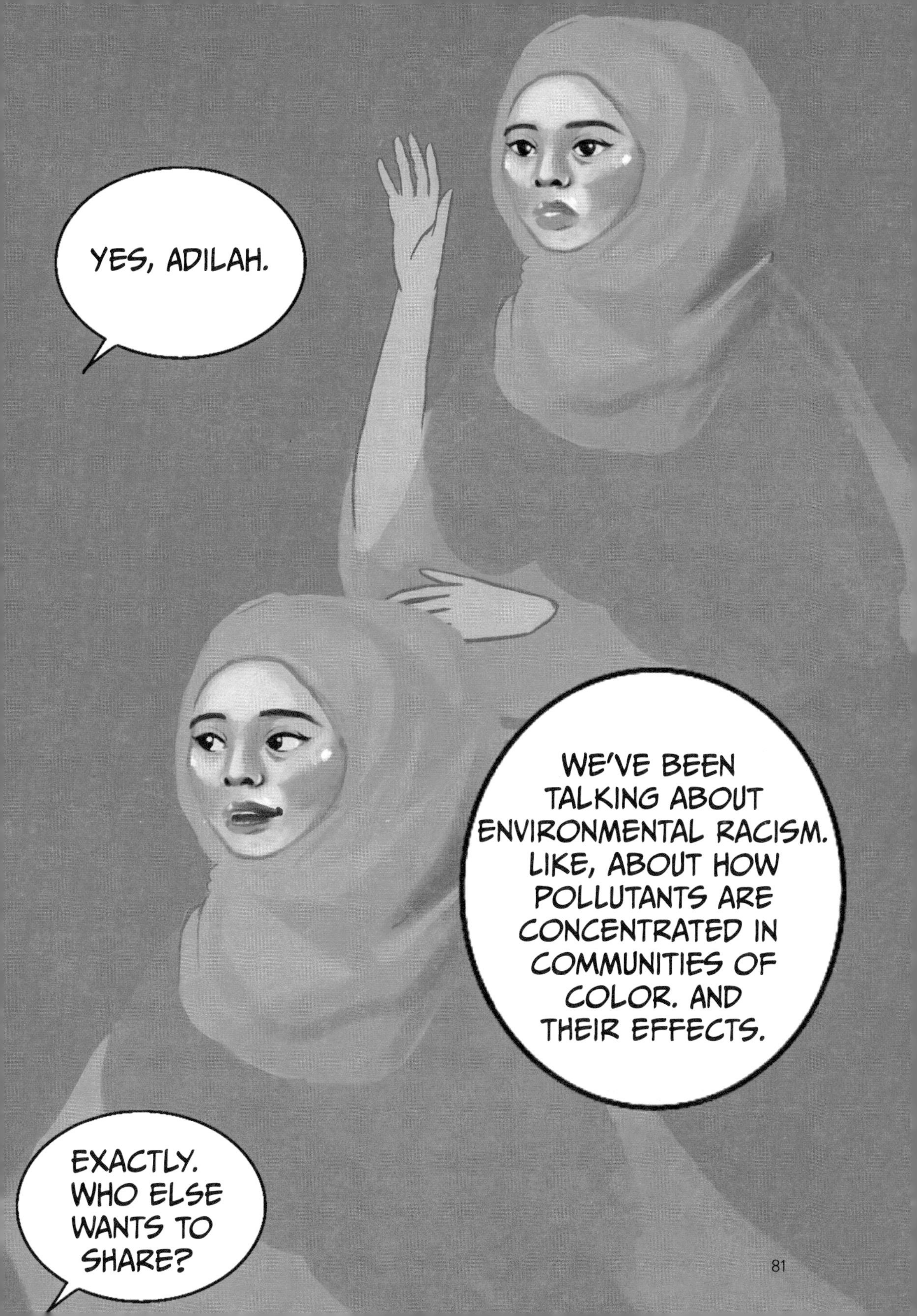
YES, ADILAH.
WE'VE BEEN TALKING ABOUT ENVIRONMENTAL RACISM. LIKE, ABOUT HOW POLLUTANTS ARE CONCENTRATED IN COMMUNITIES OF COLOR. AND THEIR EFFECTS.
EXACTLY. WHO ELSE WANTS TO SHARE?

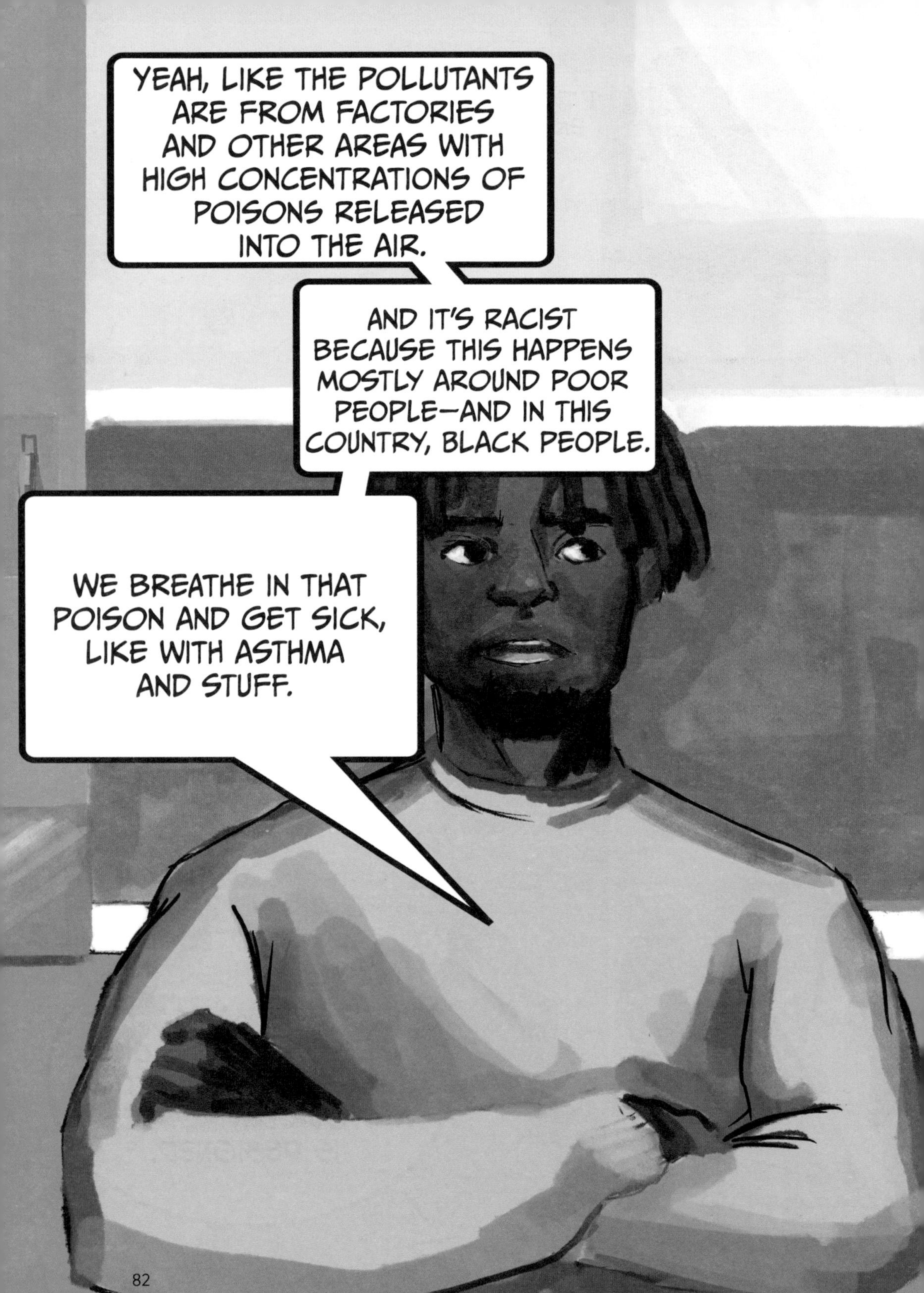
YEAH, LIKE THE POLLUTANTS ARE FROM FACTORIES AND OTHER AREAS WITH HIGH CONCENTRATIONS OF POISONS RELEASED INTO THE AIR.
AND IT'S RACIST BECAUSE THIS HAPPENS MOSTLY AROUND POOR PEOPLE—AND IN THIS COUNTRY, BLACK PEOPLE.
WE BREATHE IN THAT POISON AND GET SICK, LIKE WITH ASTHMA AND STUFF.

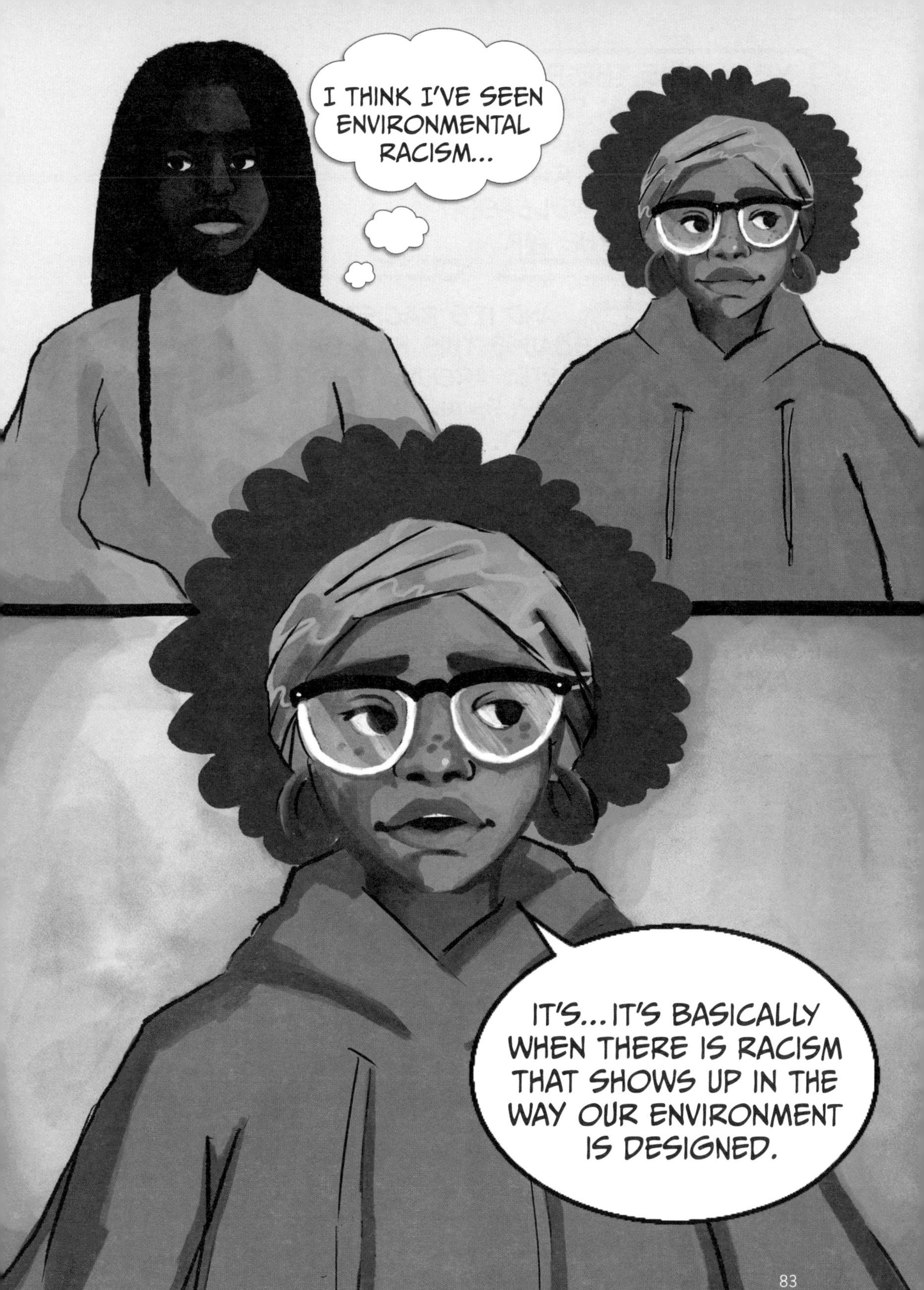
I THINK I'VE SEEN ENVIRONMENTAL RACISM...
IT'S...IT'S BASICALLY WHEN THERE IS RACISM THAT SHOWS UP IN THE WAY OUR ENVIRONMENT IS DESIGNED.

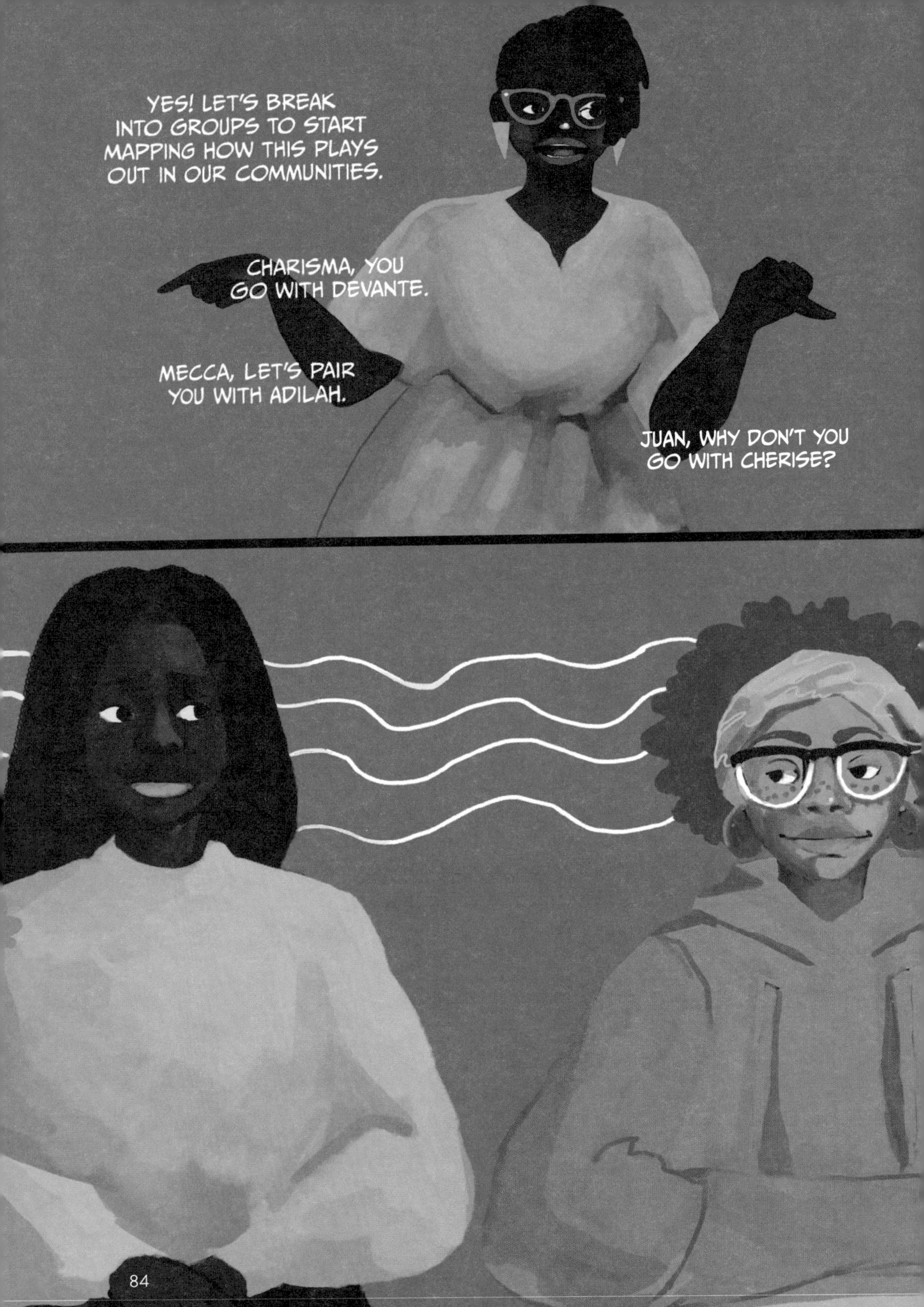
YES! LET'S BREAK INTO GROUPS TO START MAPPING HOW THIS PLAYS OUT IN OUR COMMUNITIES.
CHARISMA, YOU GO WITH DEVANTE.
MECCA, LET'S PAIR YOU WITH ADILAH.
JUAN, WHY DON'T YOU GO WITH CHERISE?

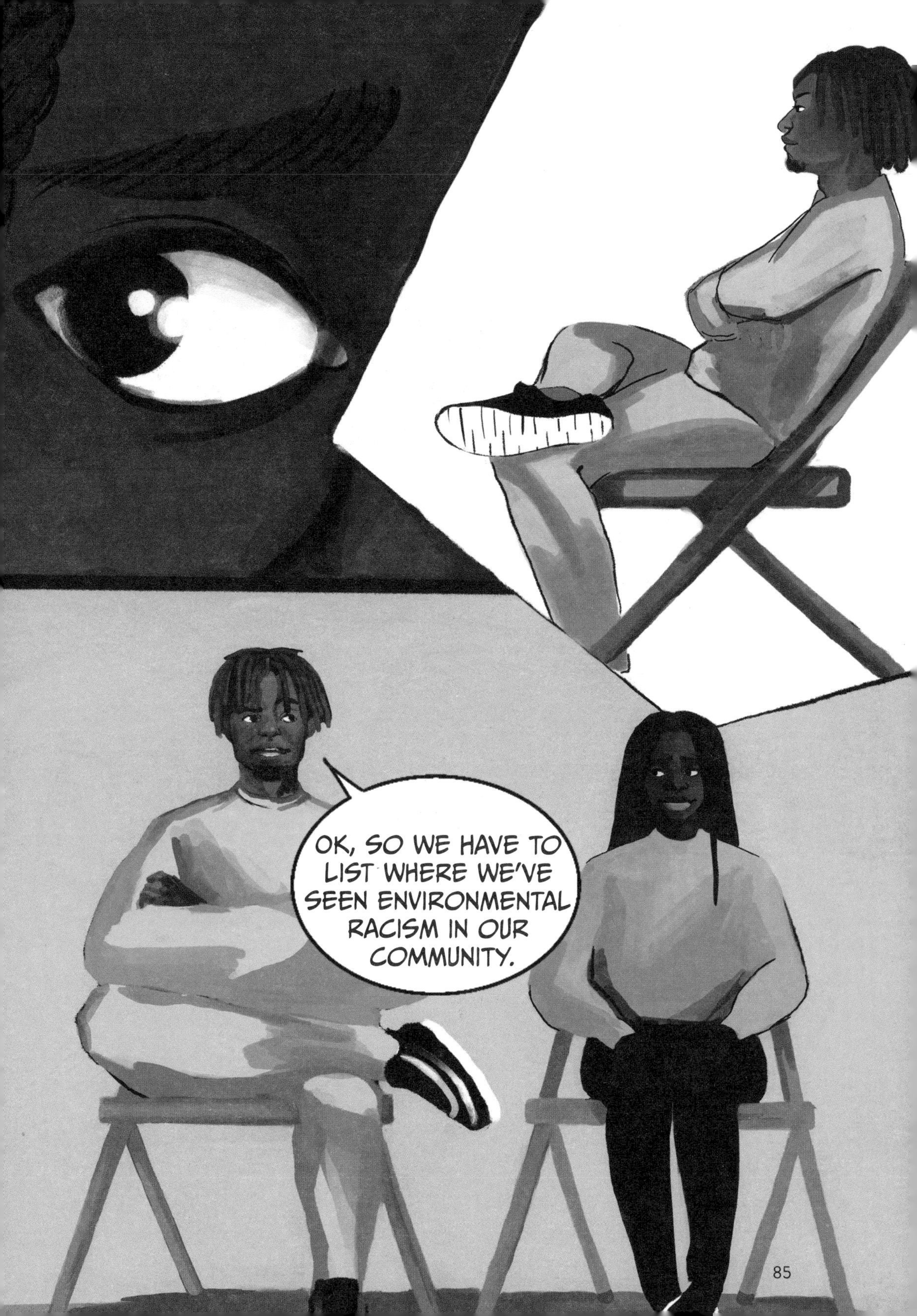
OK, SO WE HAVE TO LIST WHERE WE'VE SEEN ENVIRONMENTAL RACISM IN OUR COMMUNITY.

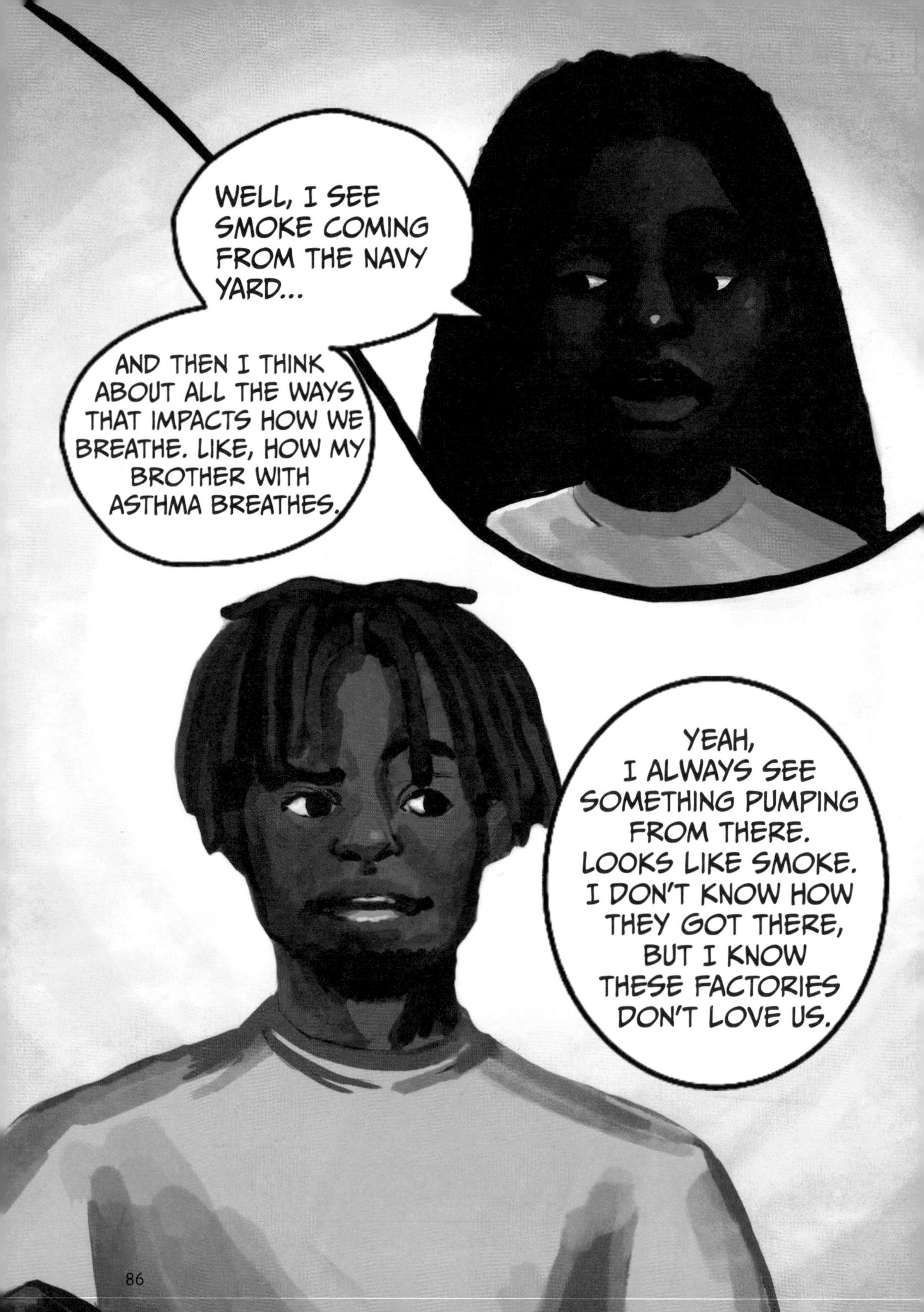
WELL, I SEE SMOKE COMING FROM THE NAVY YARD...
AND THEN I THINK ABOUT ALL THE WAYS THAT IMPACTS HOW WE BREATHE. LIKE, HOW MY BROTHER WITH ASTHMA BREATHES.
YEAH, I ALWAYS SEE SOMETHING PUMPING FROM THERE. LOOKS LIKE SMOKE. I DON'T KNOW HOW THEY GOT THERE, BUT I KNOW THESE FACTORIES DON'T LOVE US.

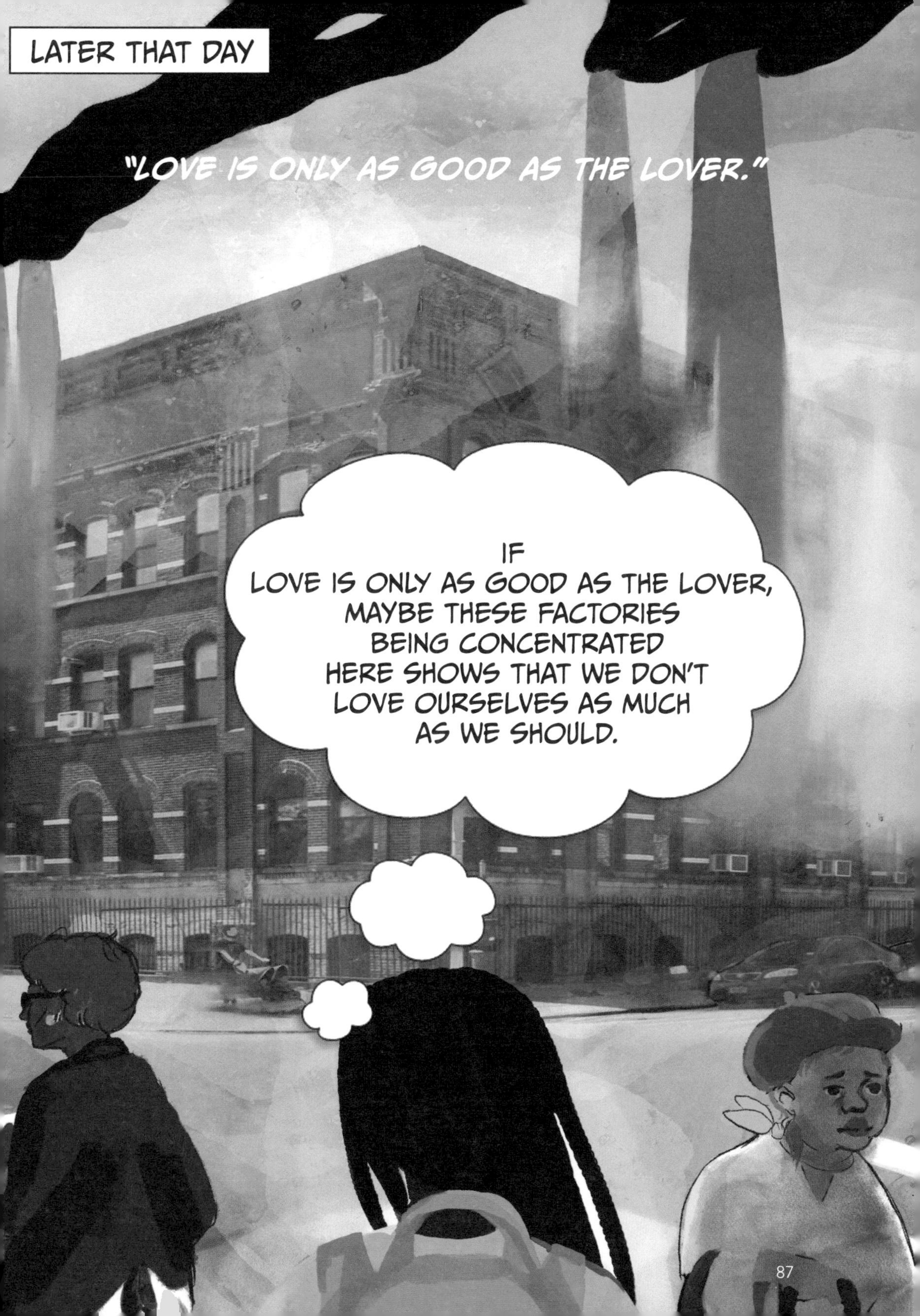
LATER THAT DAY
"LOVE IS ONLY AS GOOD AS THE LOVER."
IF LOVE IS ONLY AS GOOD AS THE LOVER, MAYBE THESE FACTORIES BEING CONCENTRATED HERE SHOWS THAT WE DON'T LOVE OURSELVES AS MUCH AS WE SHOULD.

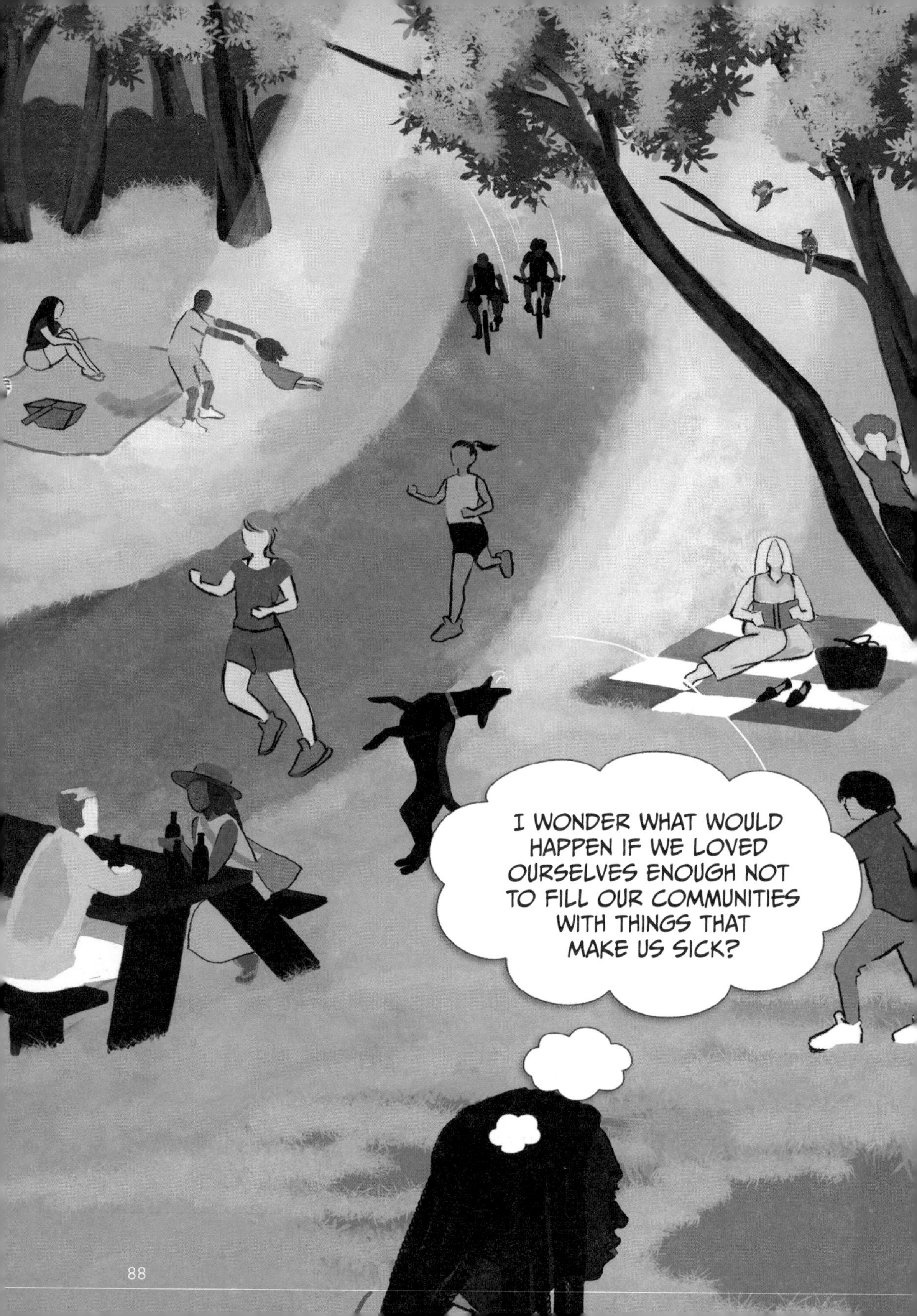
I WONDER WHAT WOULD HAPPEN IF WE LOVED OURSELVES ENOUGH NOT TO FILL OUR COMMUNITIES WITH THINGS THAT MAKE US SICK?

CHAPTER 6

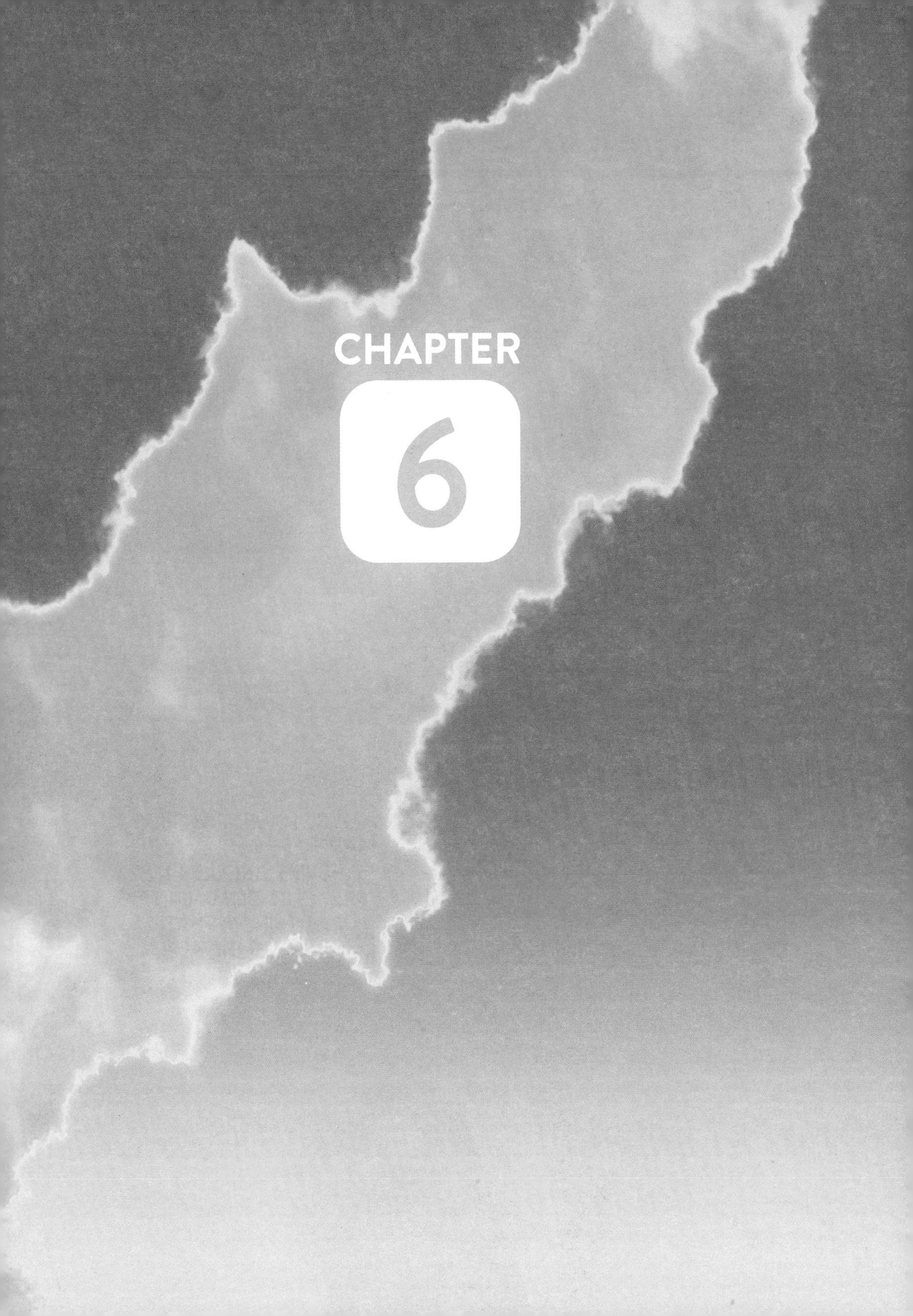

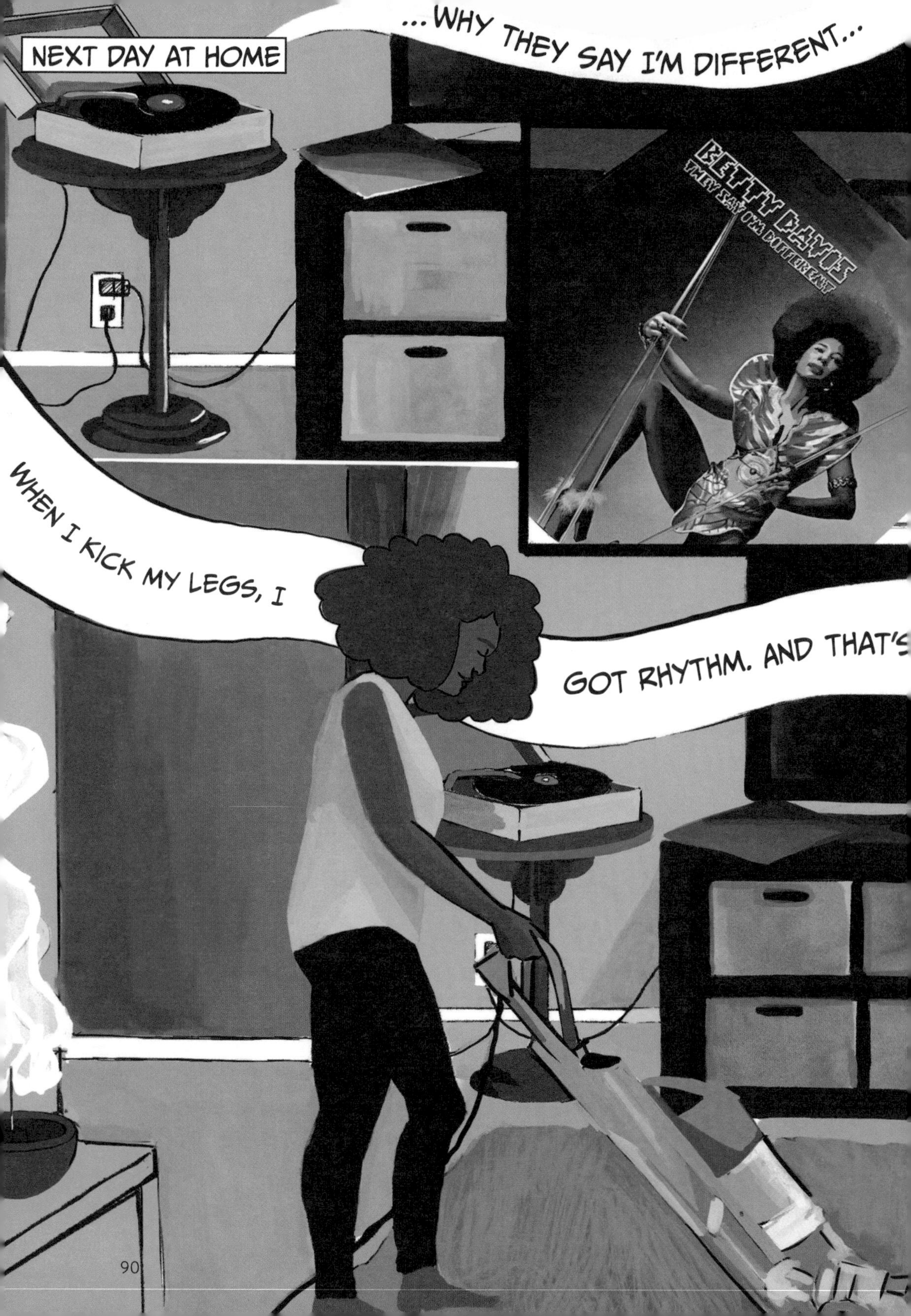
NEXT DAY AT HOME
...WHY THEY SAY I'M DIFFERENT...
BETTY DAVIS
THEY SAY I'M DIFFERENT
WHEN I KICK MY LEGS, I
GOT RHYTHM. AND THAT'S

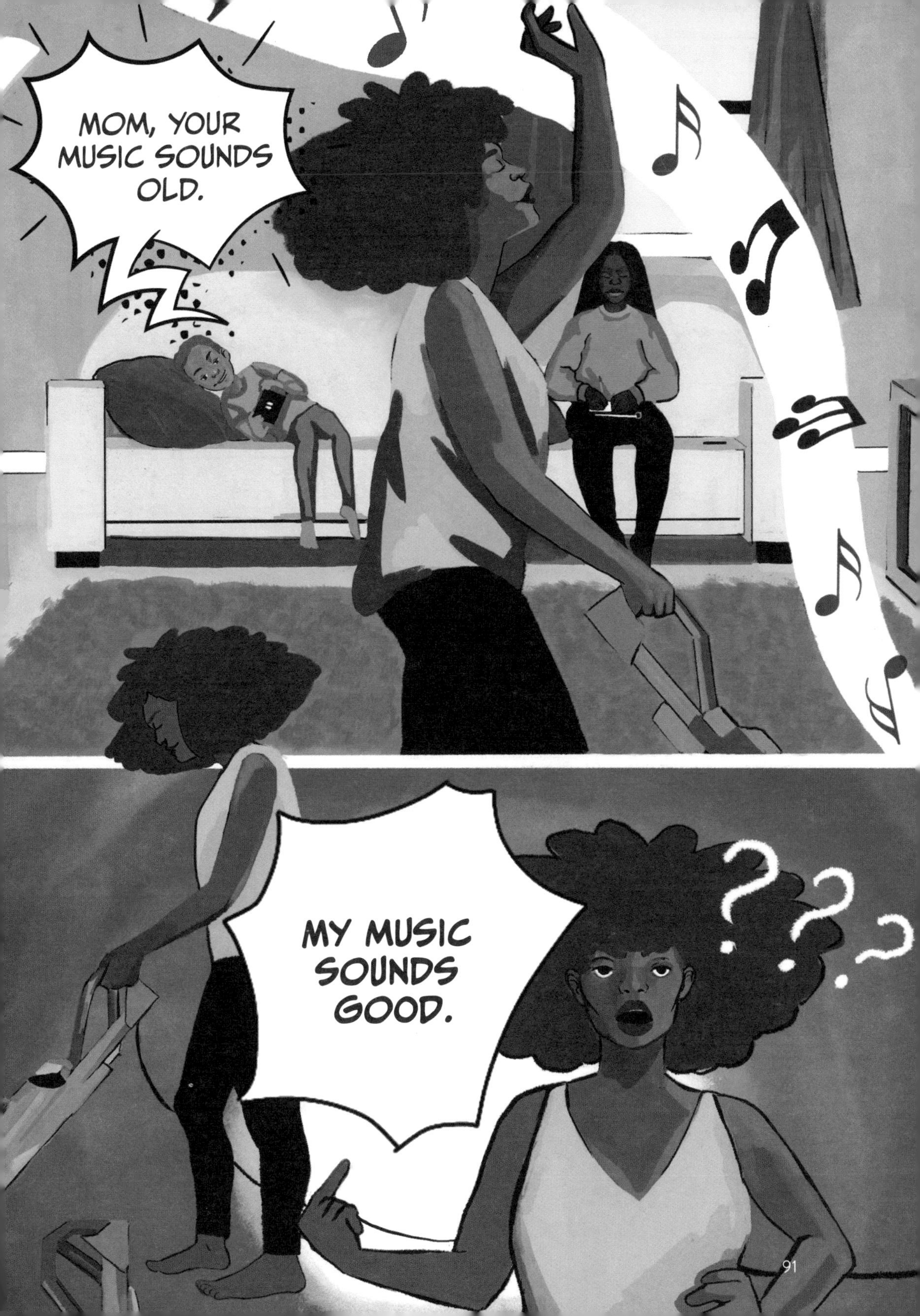
MOM, YOUR MUSIC SOUNDS OLD.
MY MUSIC SOUNDS GOOD.

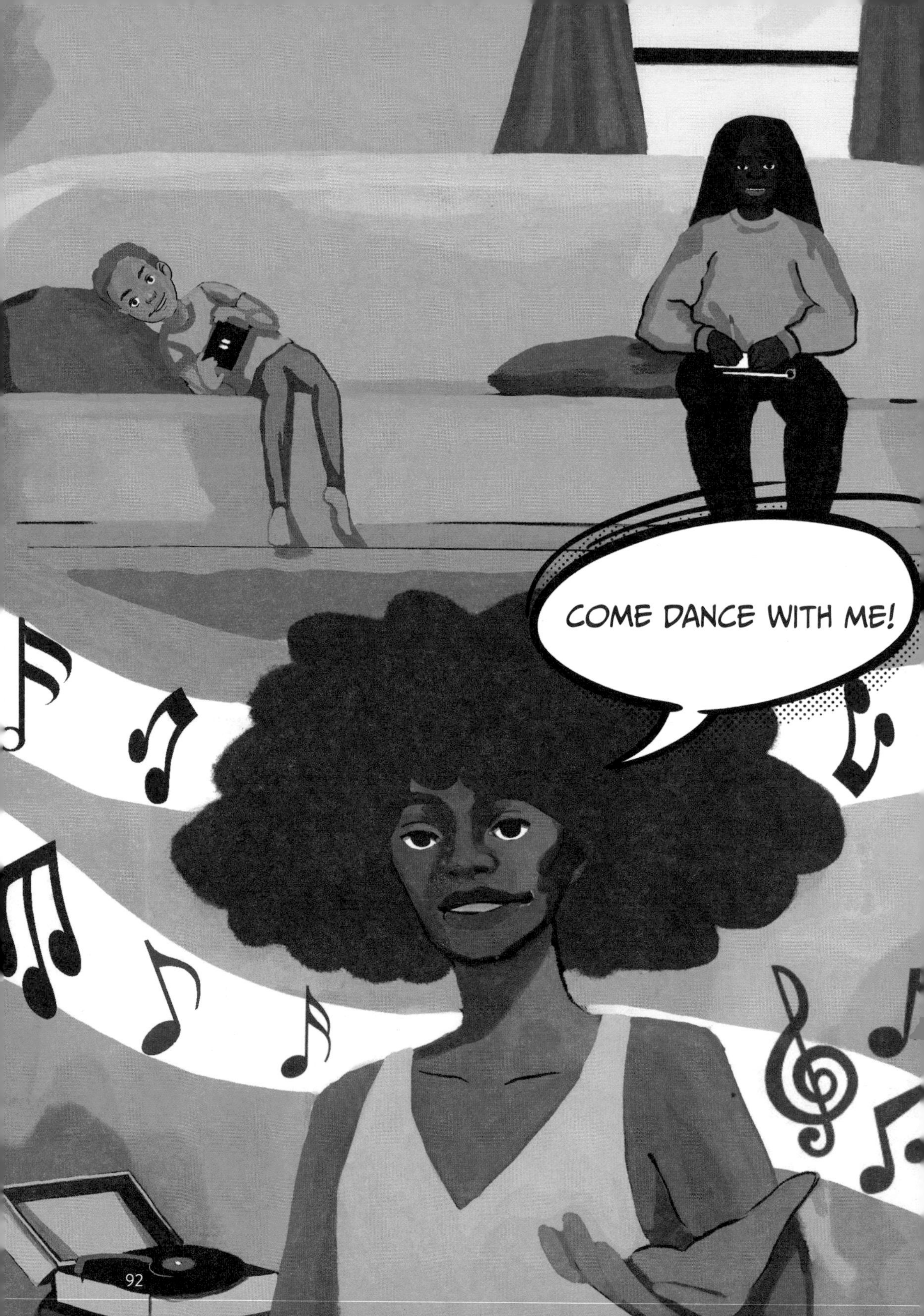
COME DANCE WITH ME!

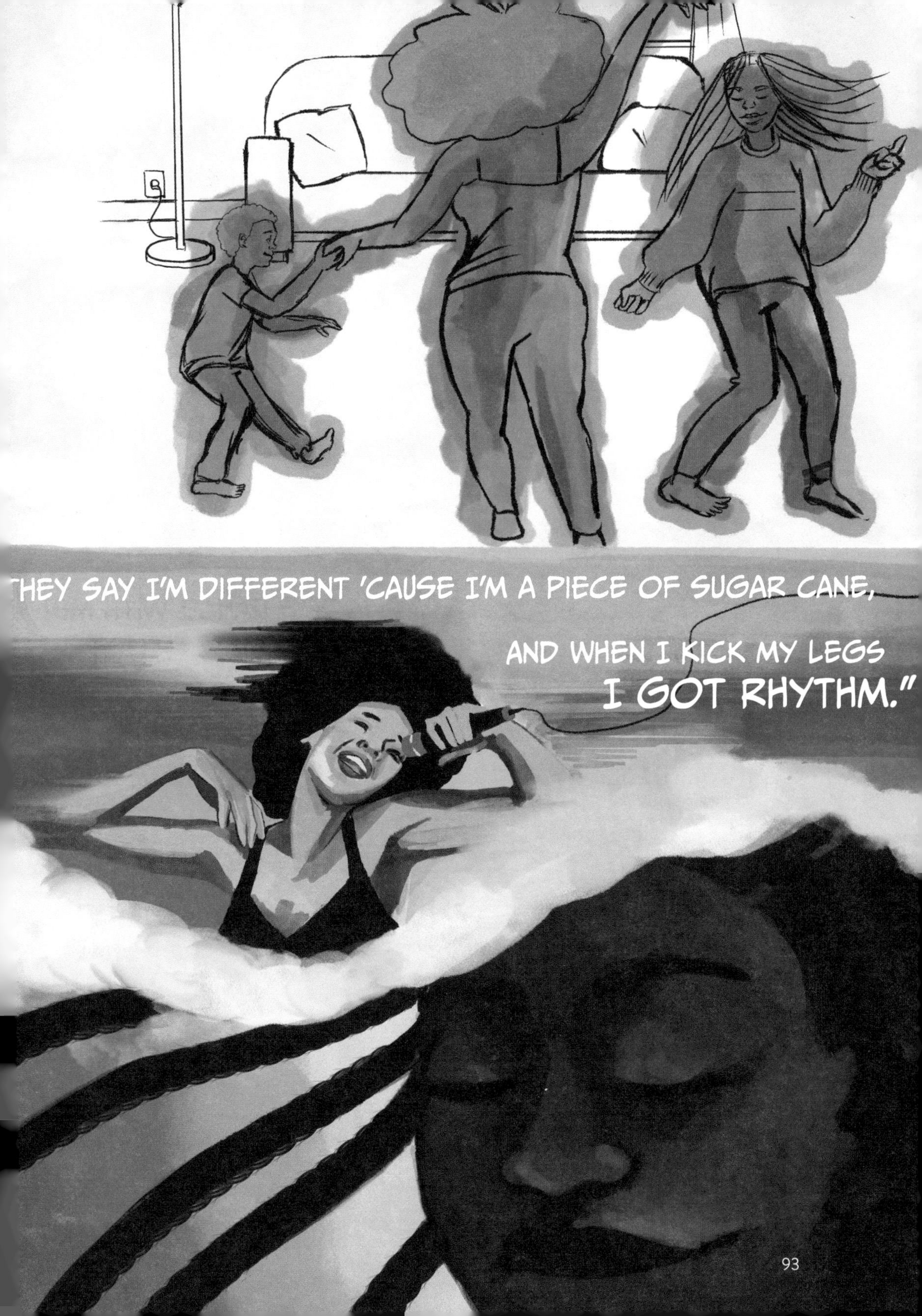
THEY SAY I'M DIFFERENT 'CAUSE I'M A PIECE OF SUGAR CANE,
AND WHEN I KICK MY LEGS
I GOT RHYTHM."

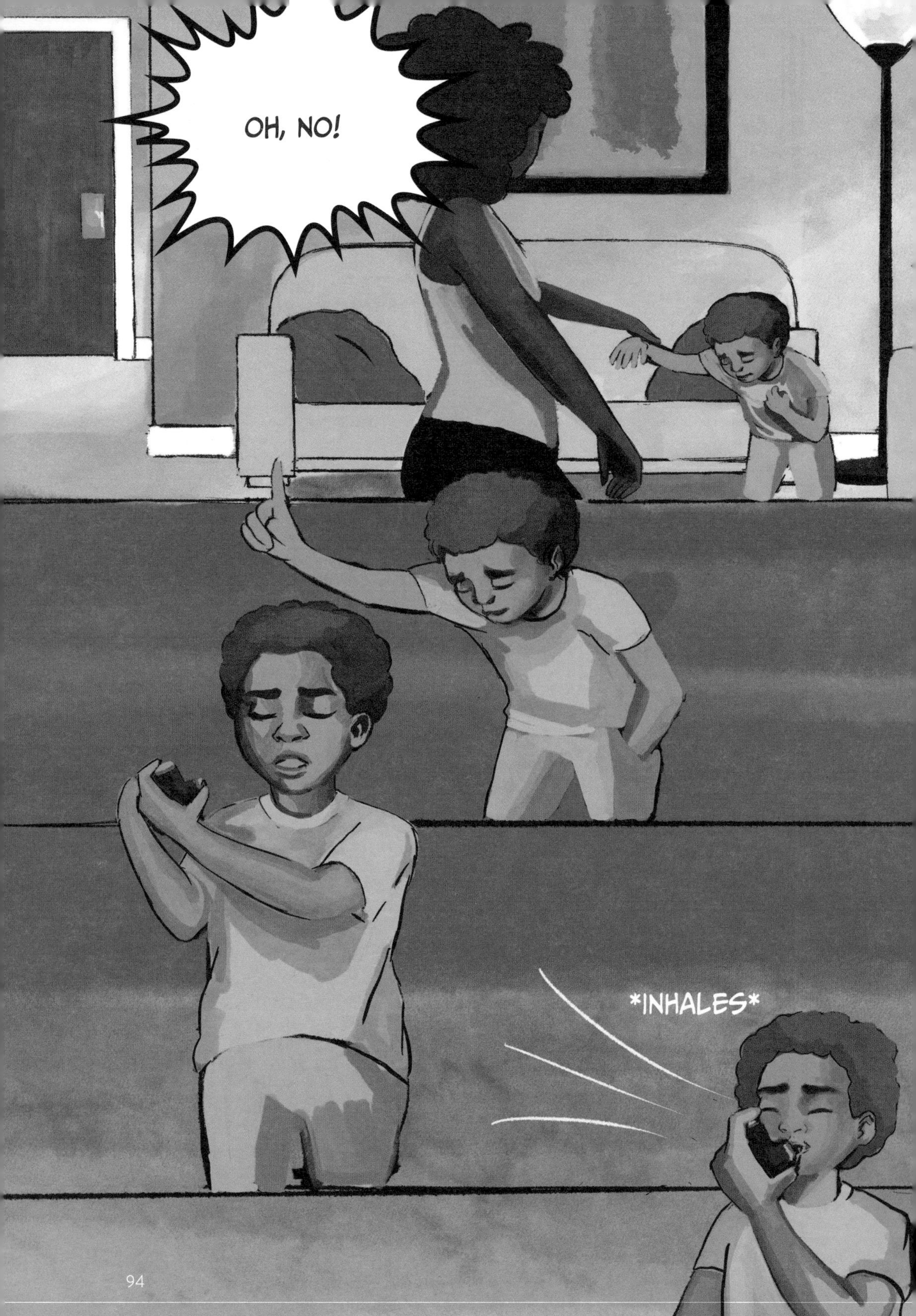
OH, NO!
INHALES

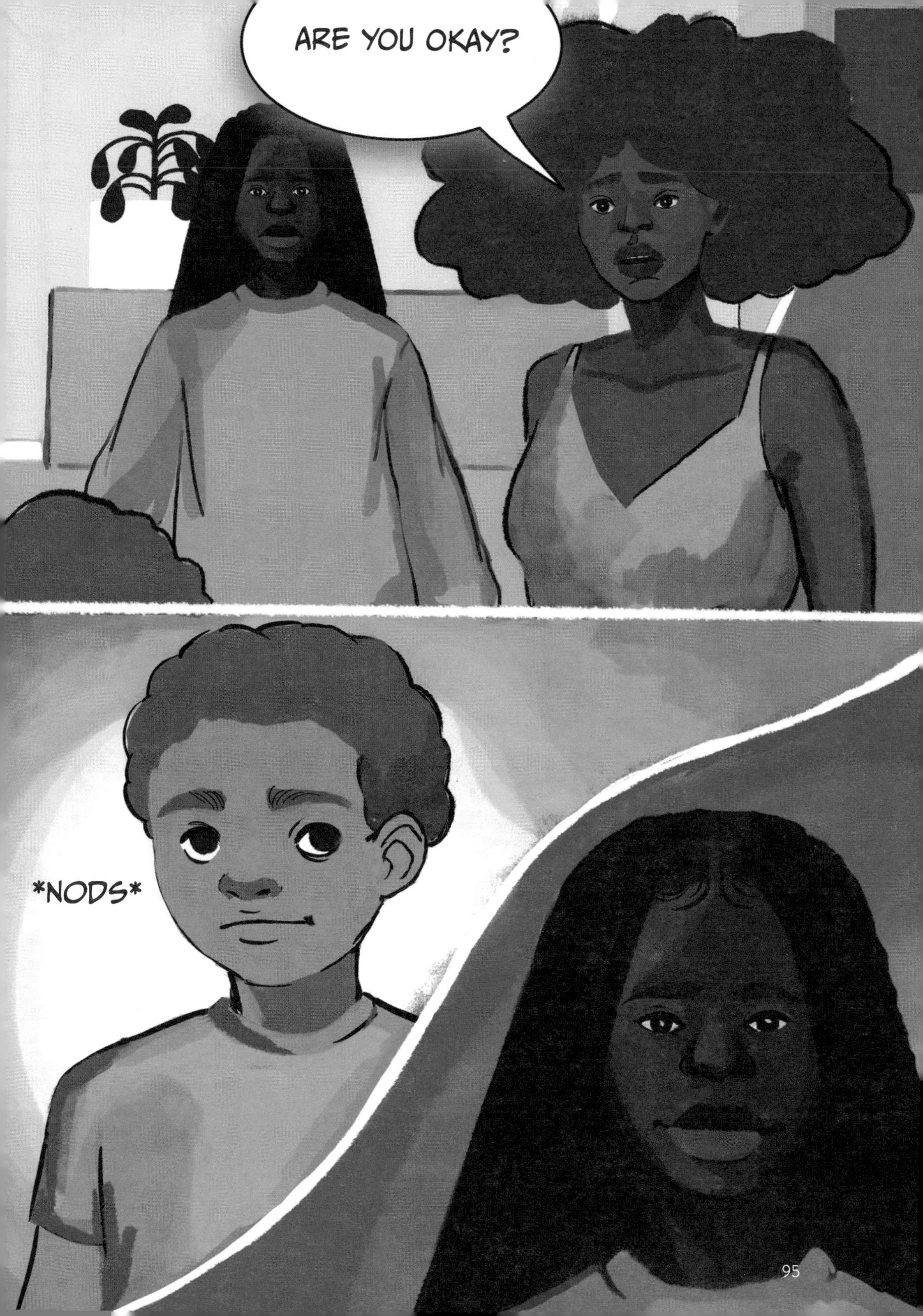
ARE YOU OKAY?
NODS

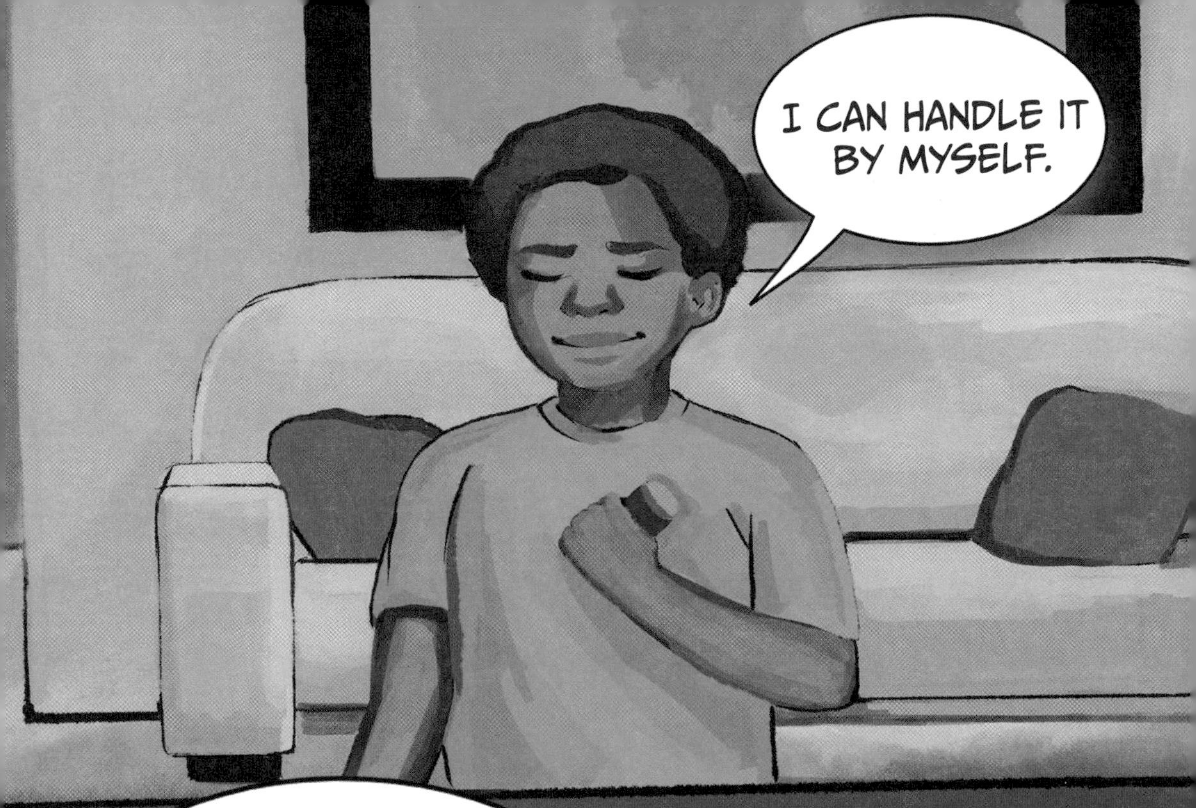
I CAN HANDLE IT BY MYSELF.

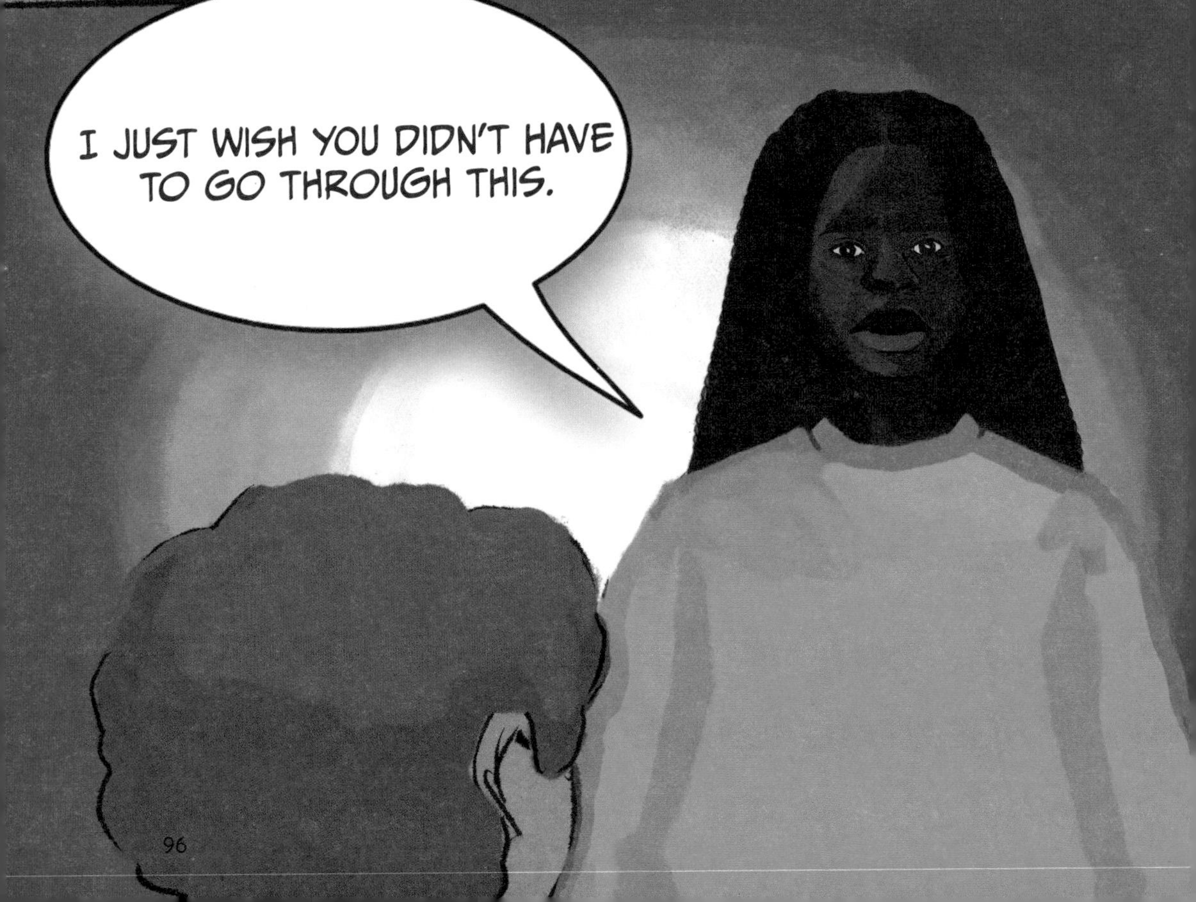
I JUST WISH YOU DIDN'T HAVE TO GO THROUGH THIS.

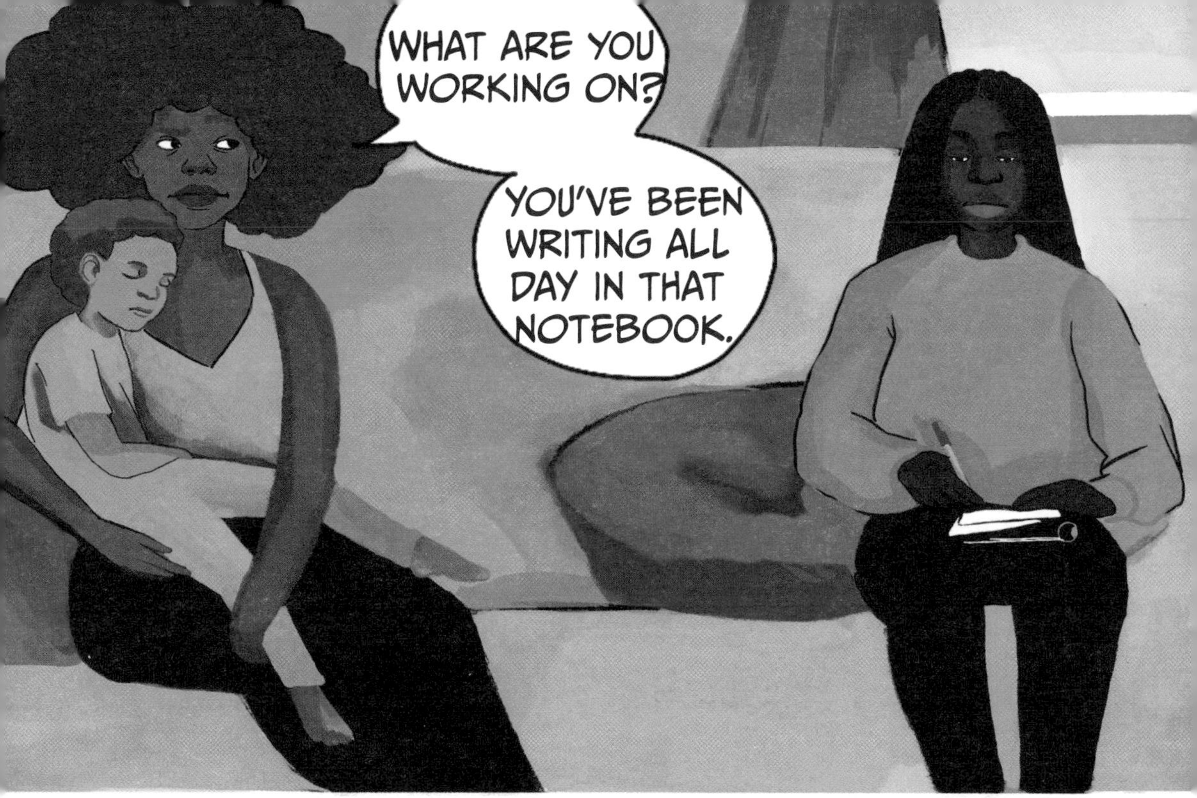
WHAT ARE YOU WORKING ON?
YOU'VE BEEN WRITING ALL DAY IN THAT NOTEBOOK.

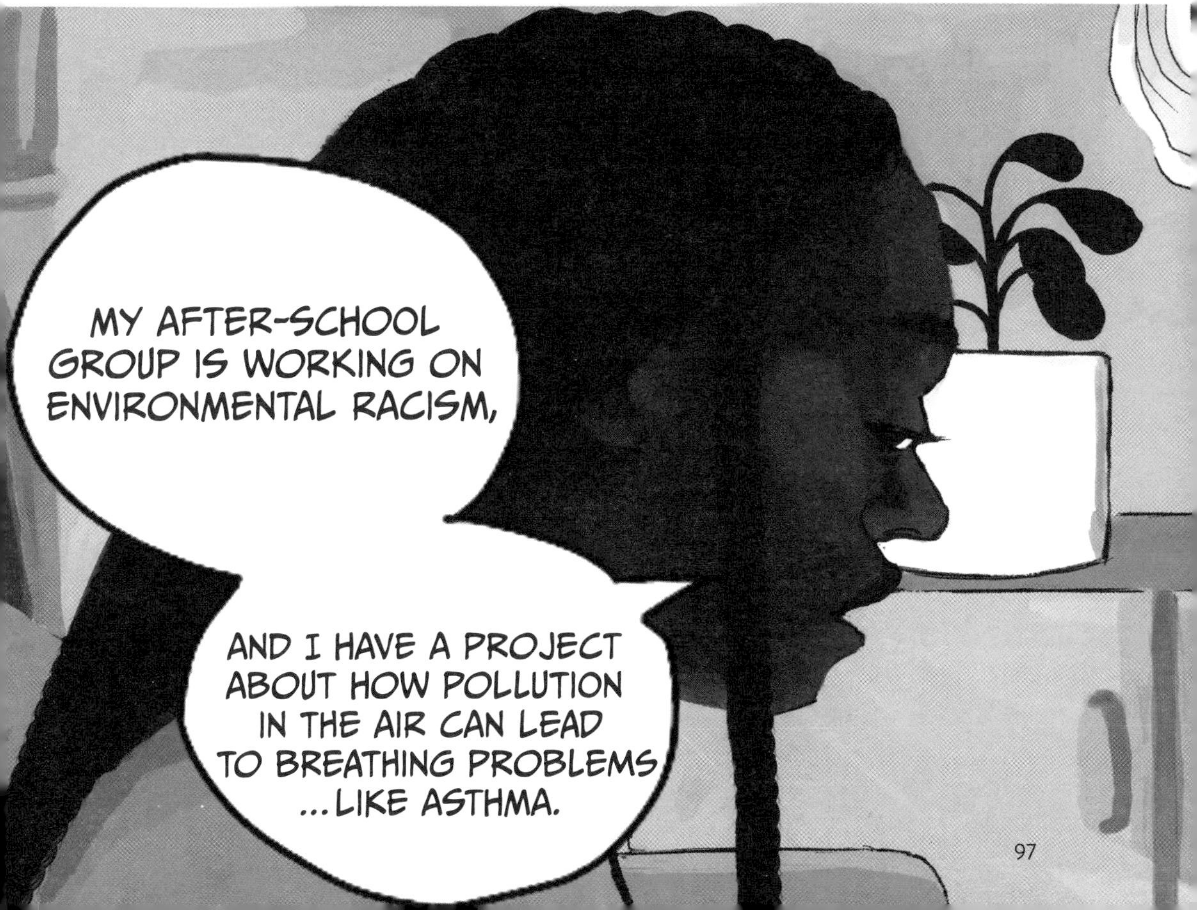
MY AFTER-SCHOOL GROUP IS WORKING ON ENVIRONMENTAL RACISM,
AND I HAVE A PROJECT ABOUT HOW POLLUTION IN THE AIR CAN LEAD TO BREATHING PROBLEMS ...LIKE ASTHMA.

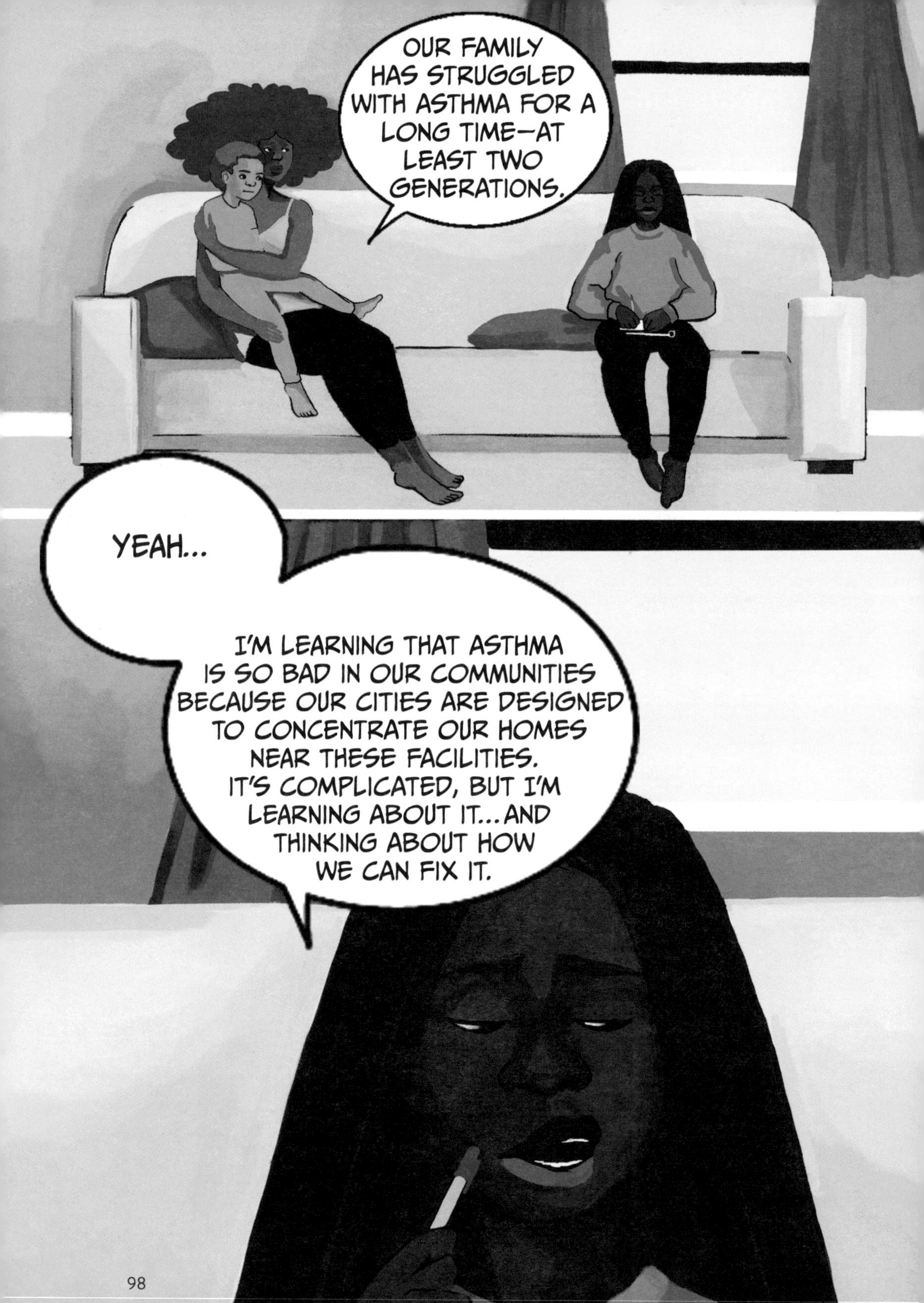
OUR FAMILY HAS STRUGGLED WITH ASTHMA FOR A LONG TIME—AT LEAST TWO GENERATIONS.
YEAH...
I'M LEARNING THAT ASTHMA IS SO BAD IN OUR COMMUNITIES BECAUSE OUR CITIES ARE DESIGNED TO CONCENTRATE OUR HOMES NEAR THESE FACILITIES. IT'S COMPLICATED, BUT I'M LEARNING ABOUT IT...AND THINKING ABOUT HOW WE CAN FIX IT.

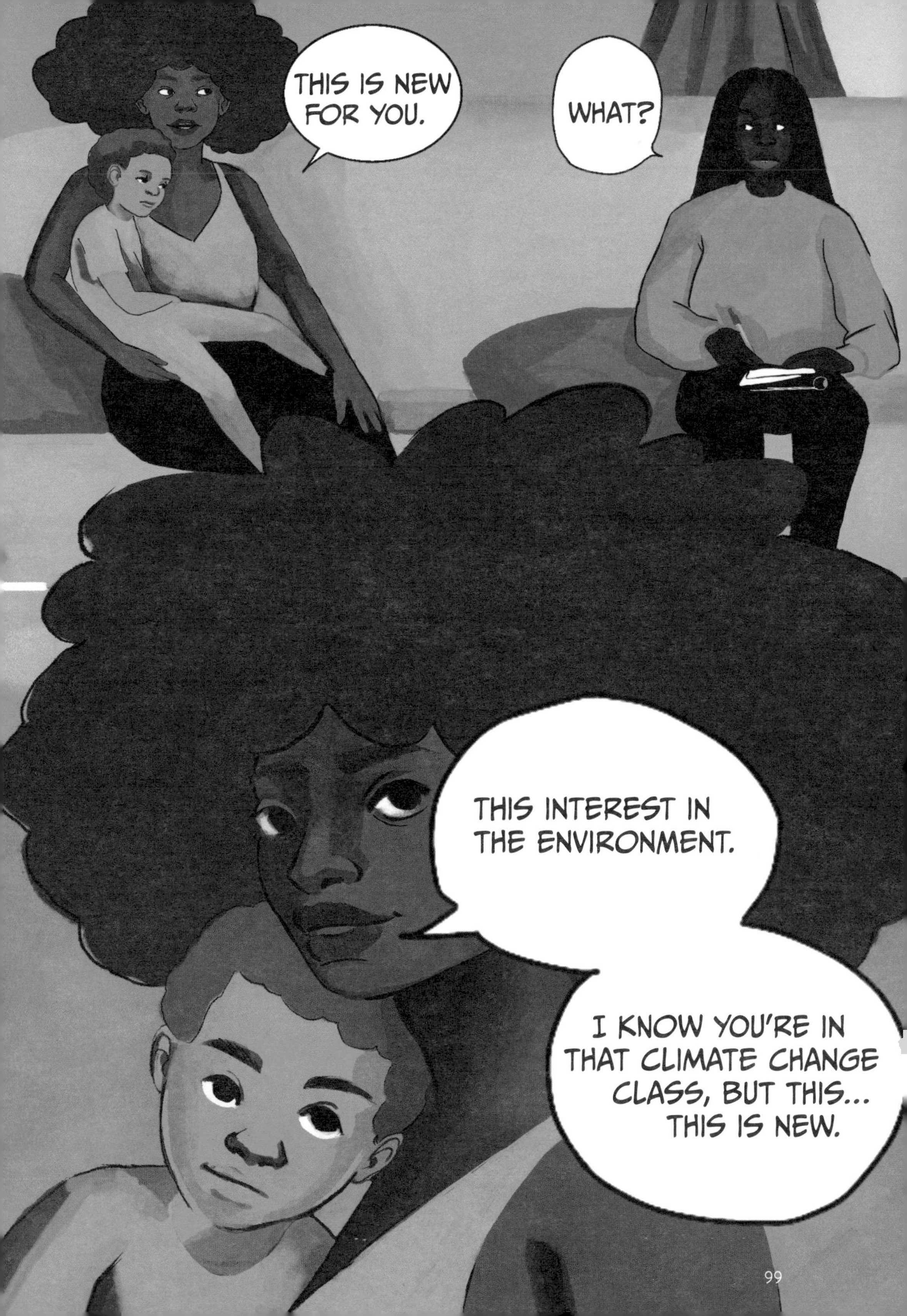
THIS IS NEW FOR YOU.
WHAT?
THIS INTEREST IN THE ENVIRONMENT.
I KNOW YOU'RE IN THAT CLIMATE CHANGE CLASS, BUT THIS... THIS IS NEW.

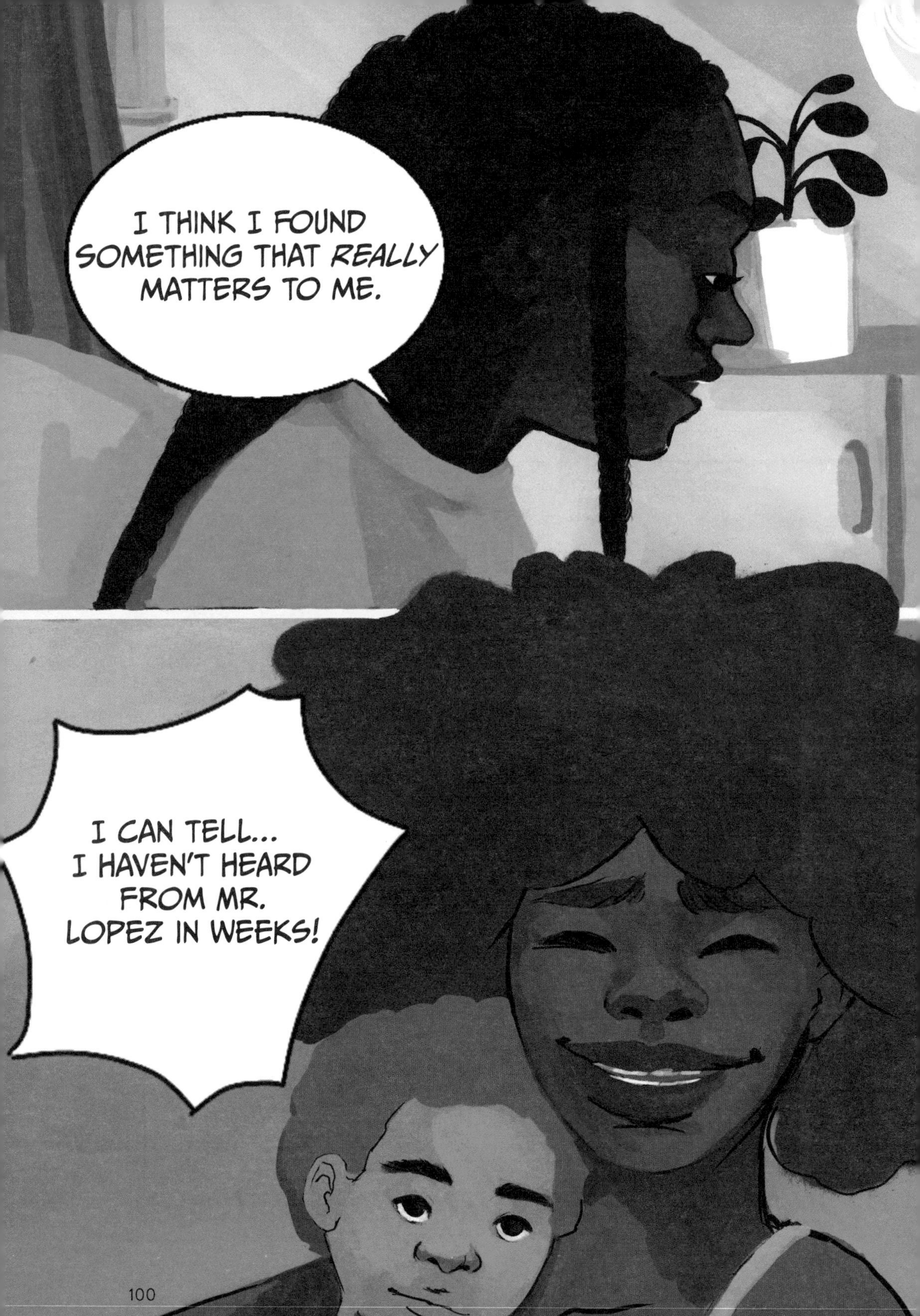
I THINK I FOUND SOMETHING THAT *REALLY* MATTERS TO ME.
I CAN TELL... I HAVEN'T HEARD FROM MR. LOPEZ IN WEEKS!

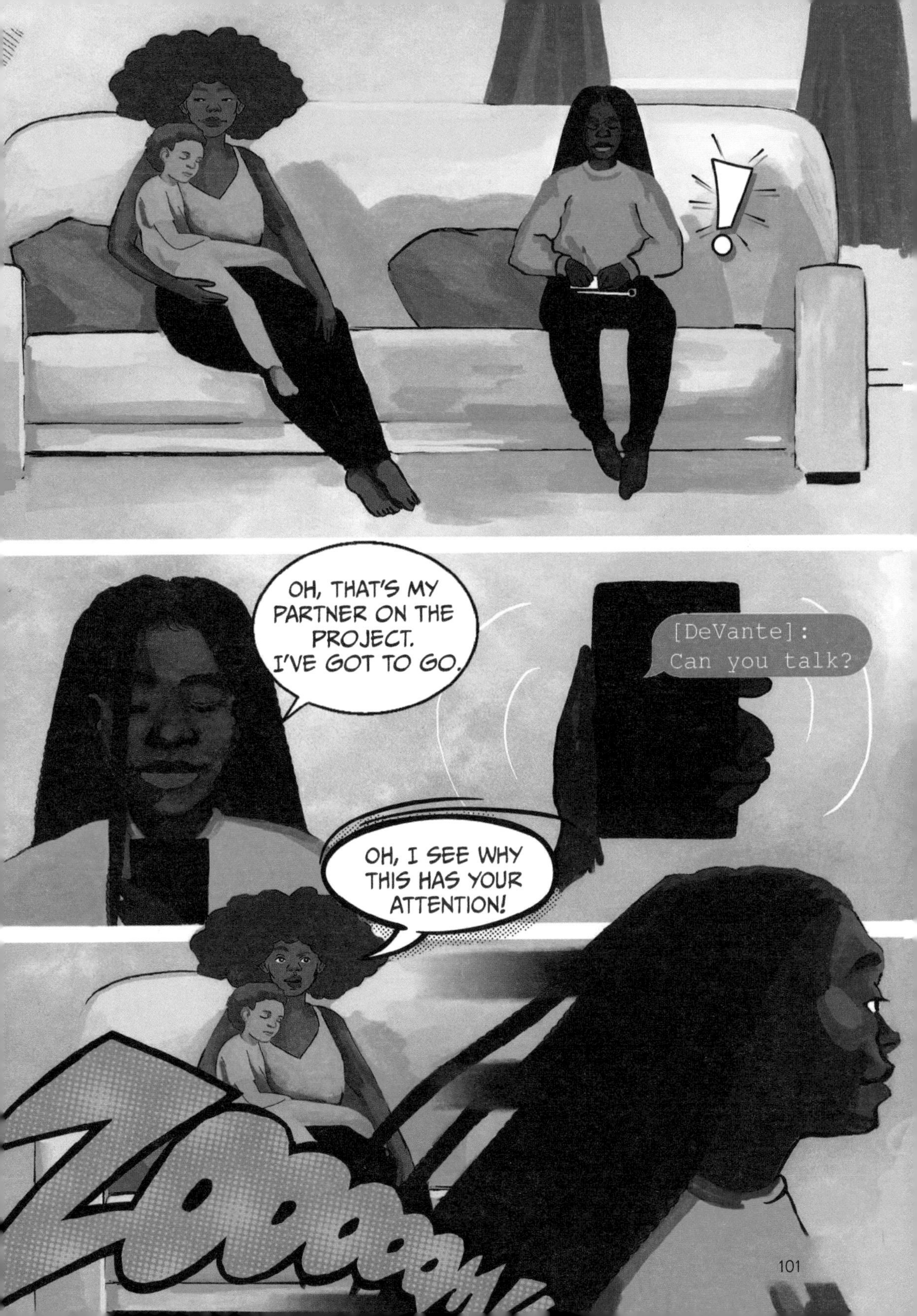
OH, THAT'S MY PARTNER ON THE PROJECT. I'VE GOT TO GO.
[DeVante]: Can you talk?
OH, I SEE WHY THIS HAS YOUR ATTENTION!

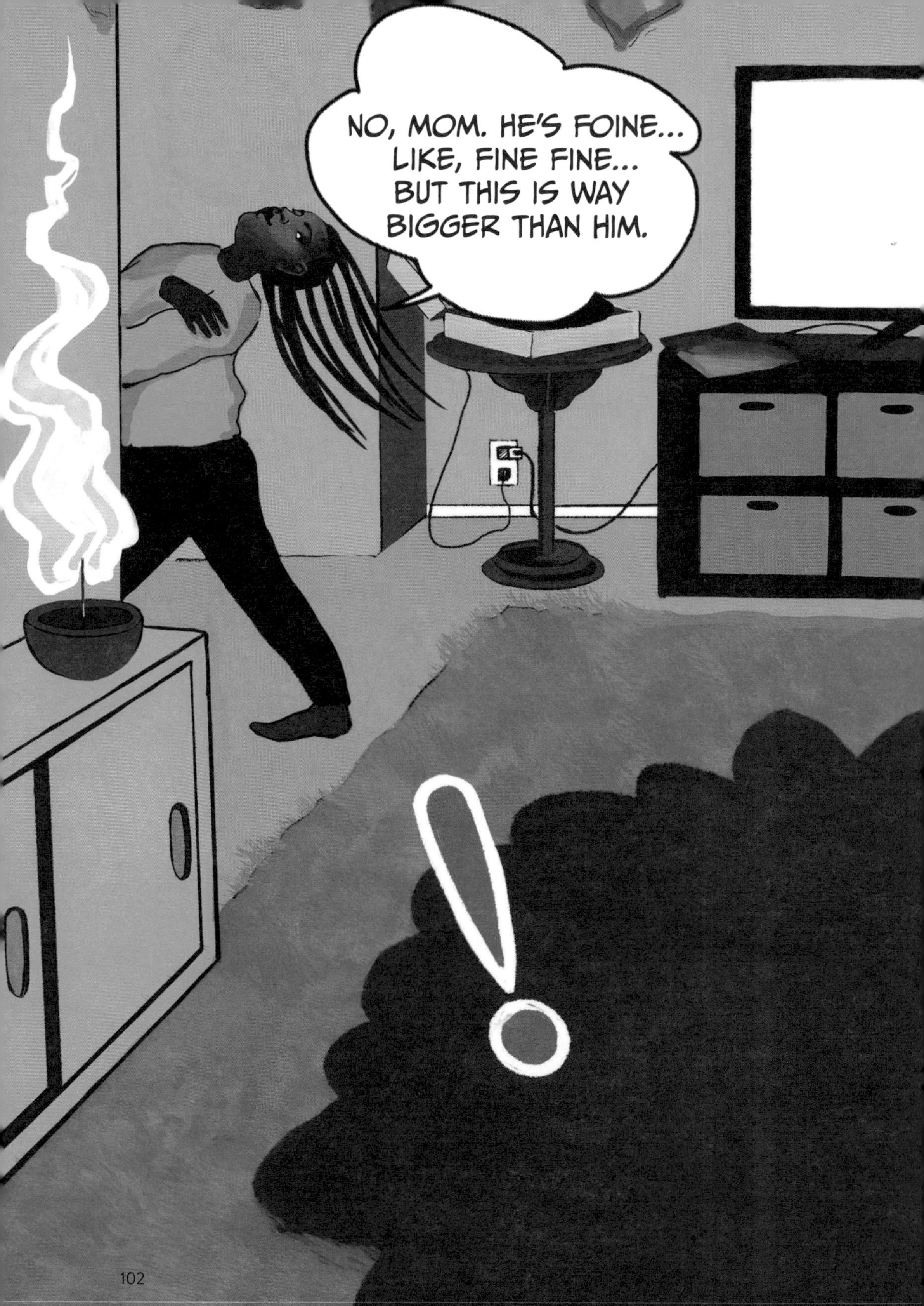
NO, MOM. HE'S FOINE... LIKE, FINE FINE... BUT THIS IS WAY BIGGER THAN HIM.

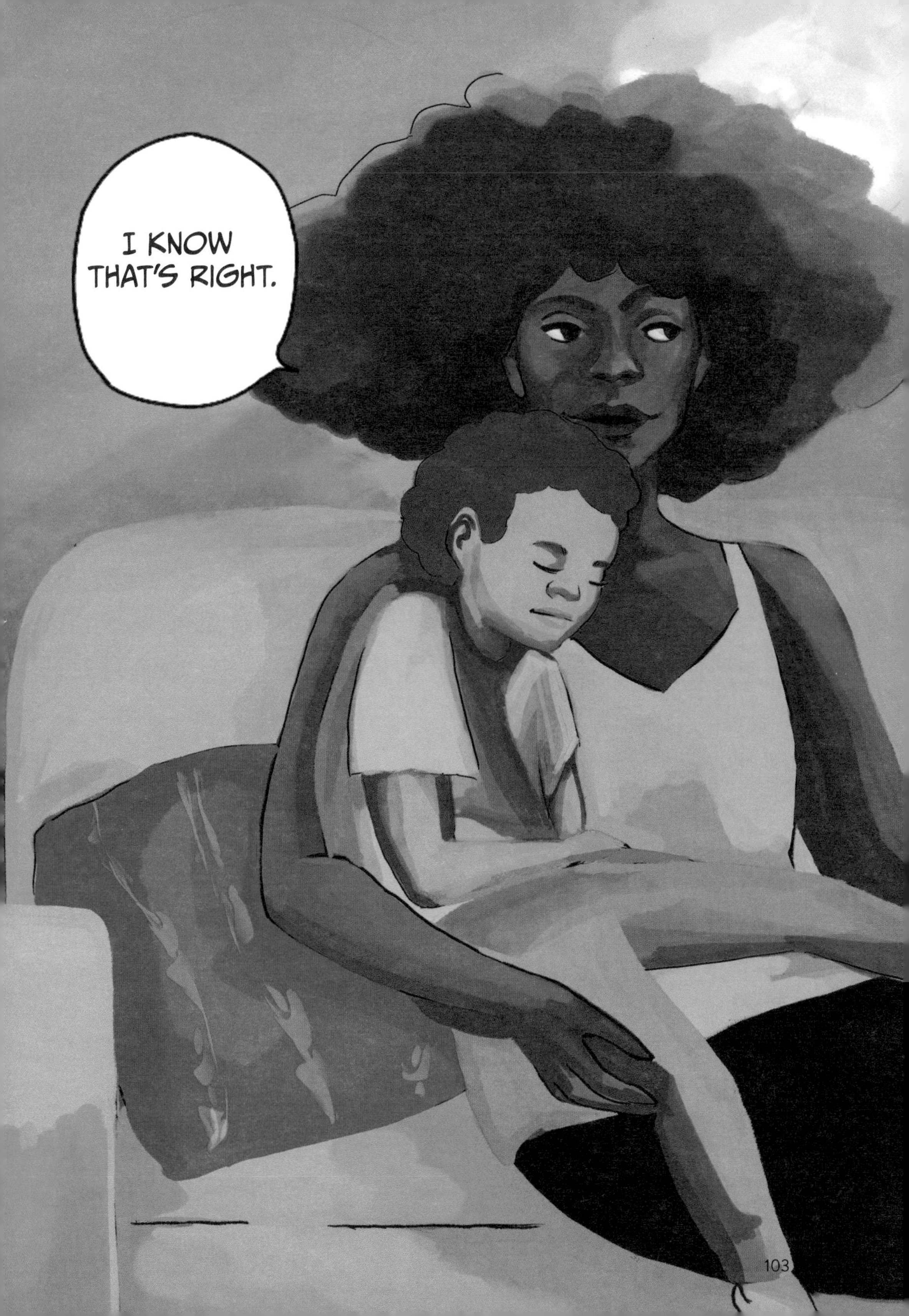
I KNOW THAT'S RIGHT.

CHAPTER 7

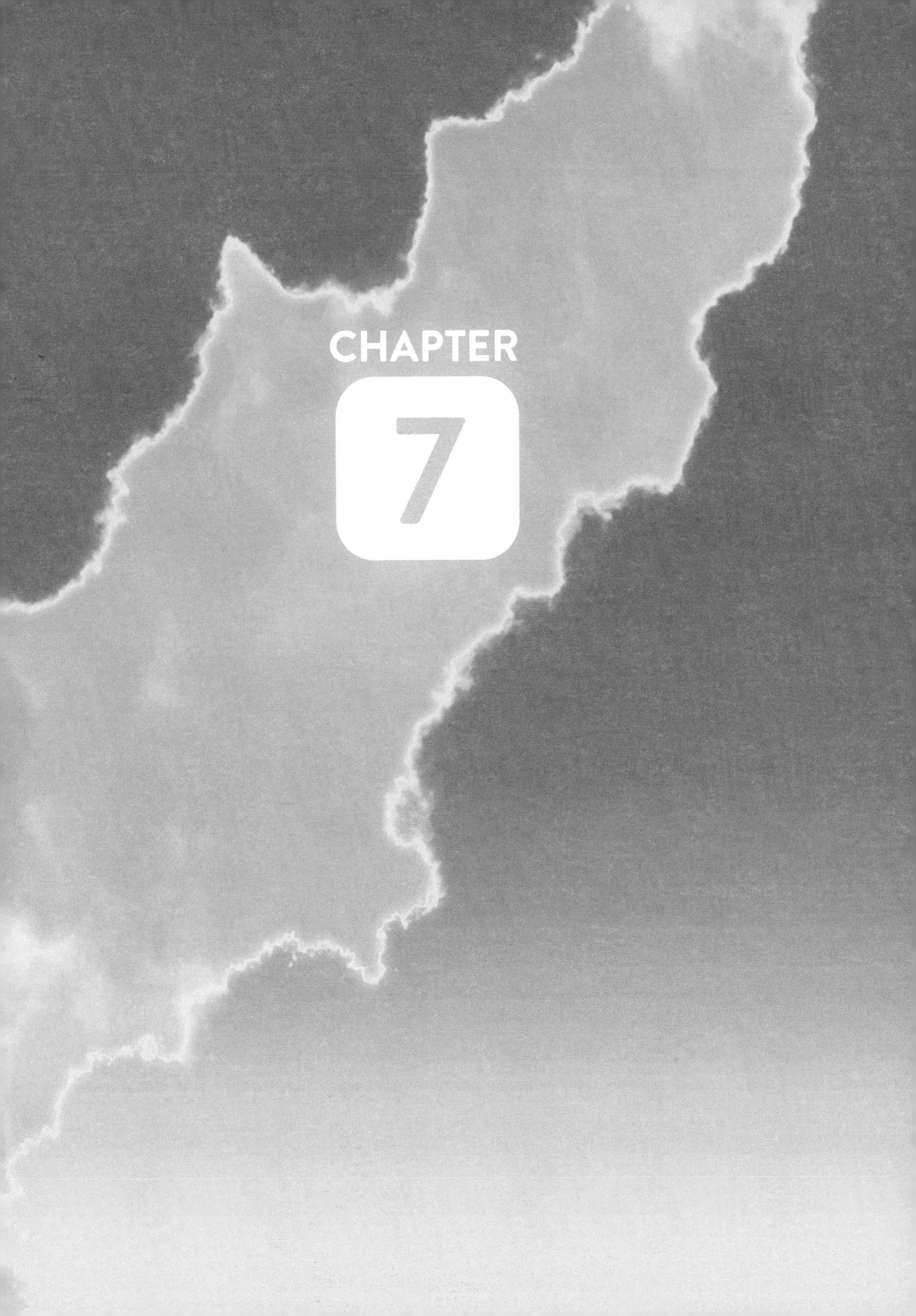

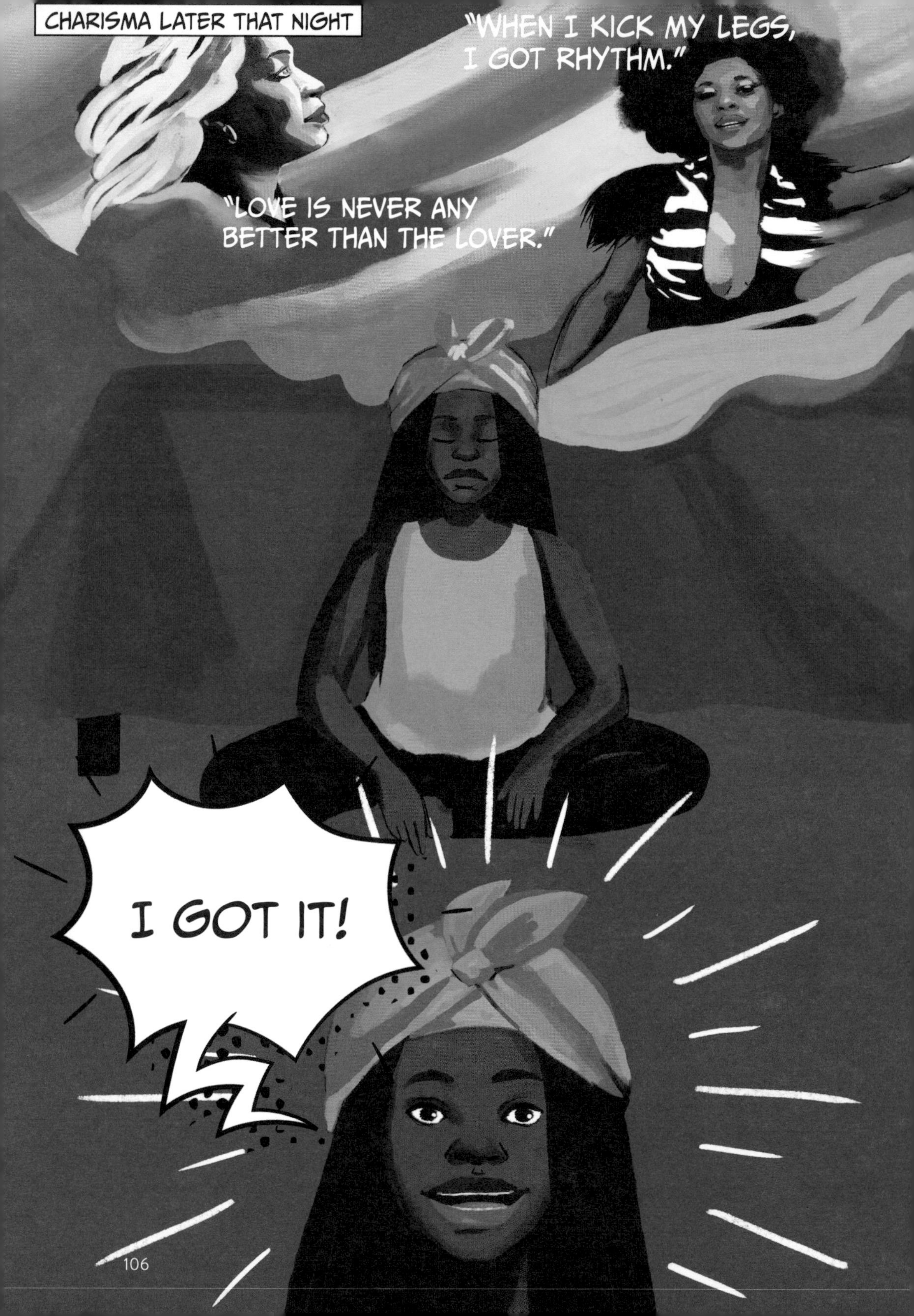
CHARISMA LATER THAT NIGHT
"WHEN I KICK MY LEGS, I GOT RHYTHM."
"LOVE IS NEVER ANY BETTER THAN THE LOVER."
I GOT IT!

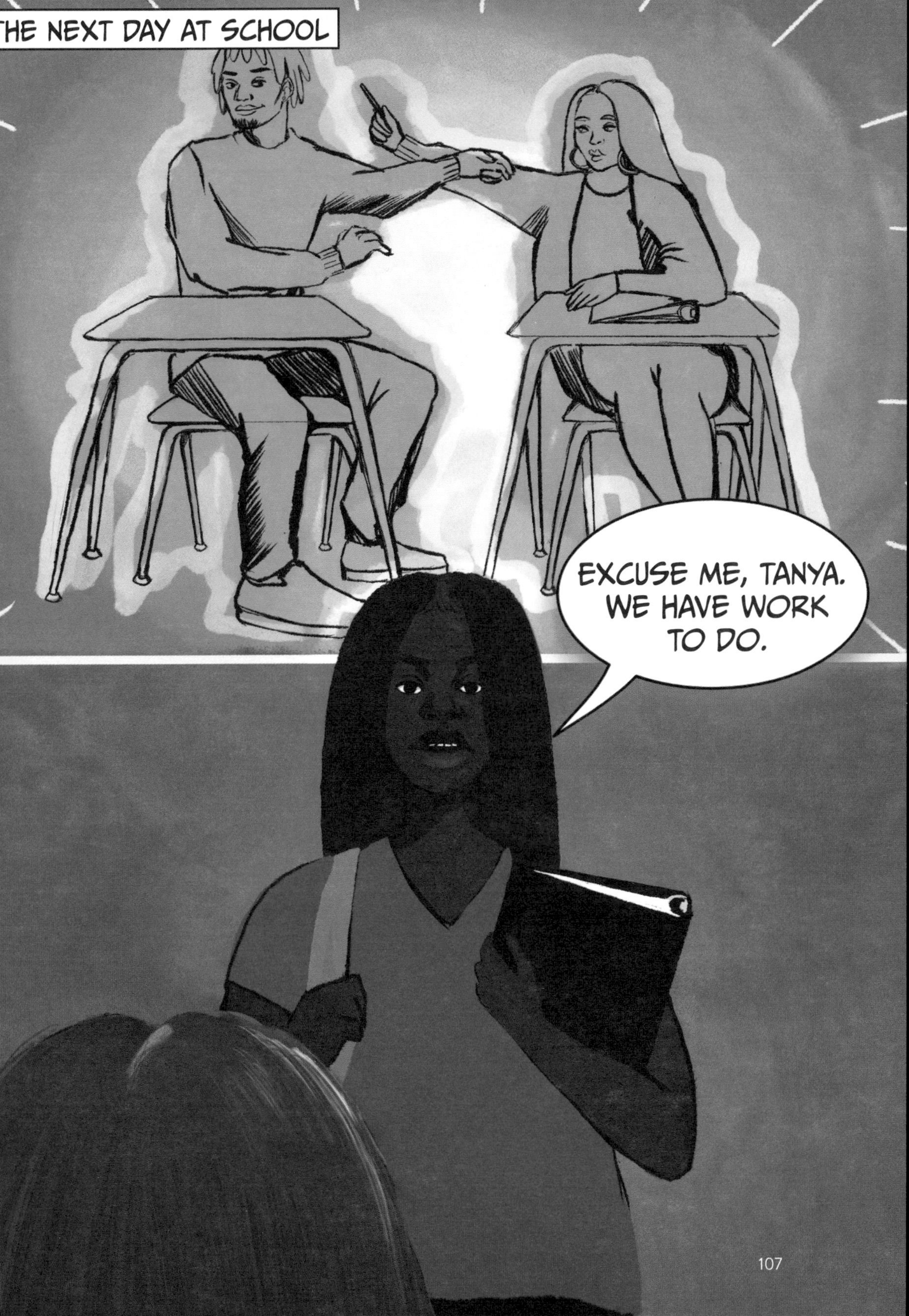
THE NEXT DAY AT SCHOOL
EXCUSE ME, TANYA. WE HAVE WORK TO DO.

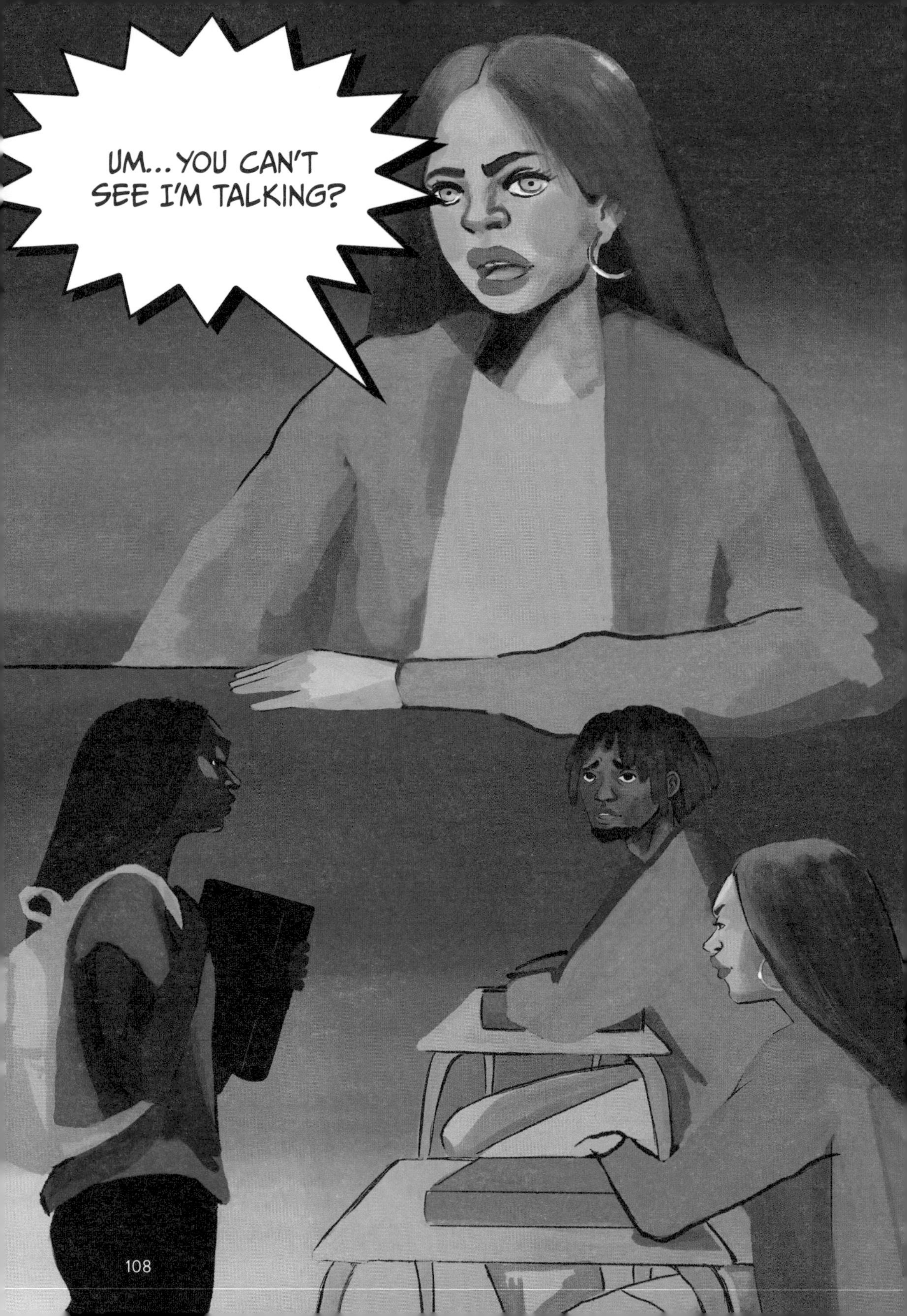
UM...YOU CAN'T SEE I'M TALKING?

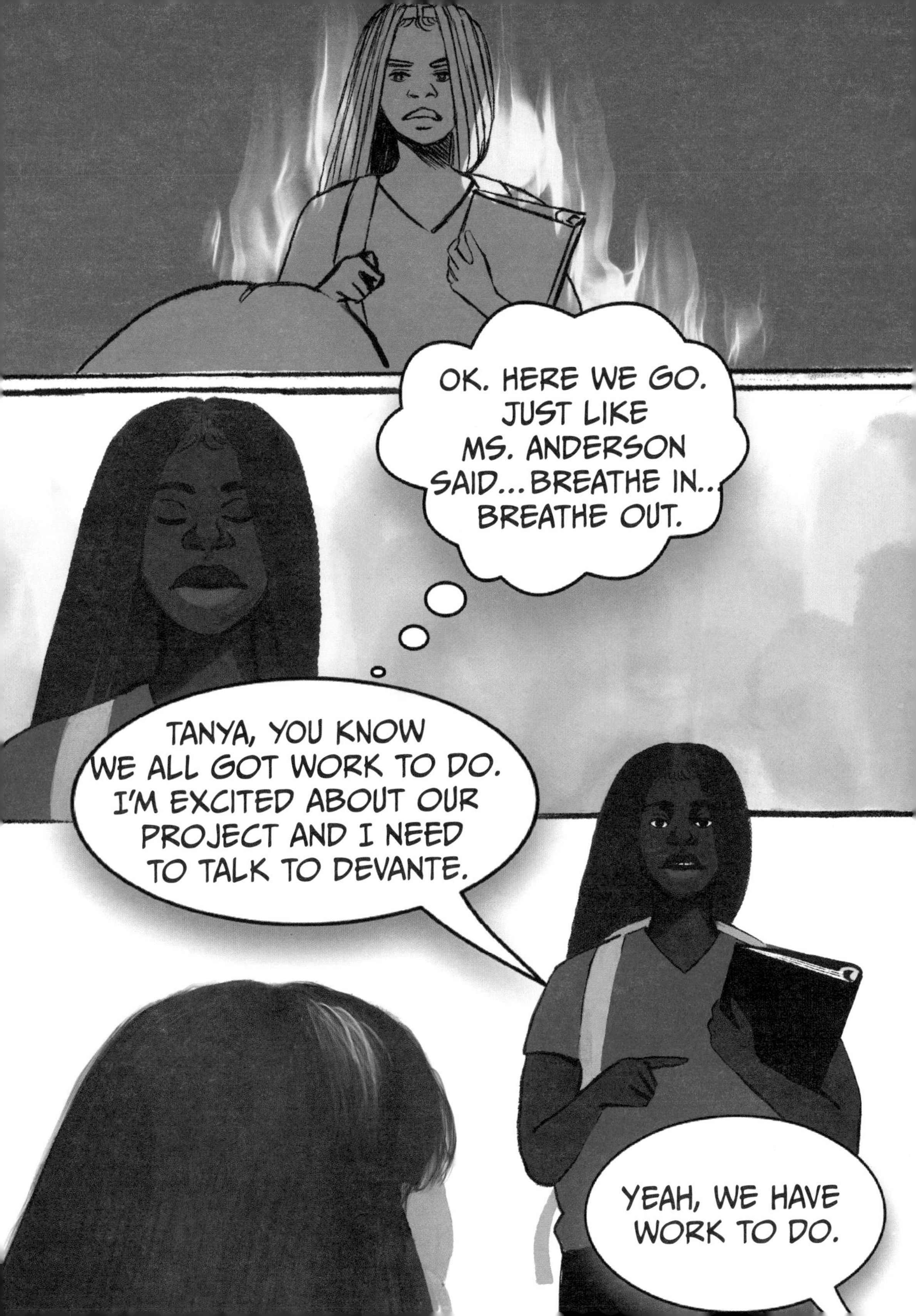
OK. HERE WE GO. JUST LIKE MS. ANDERSON SAID...BREATHE IN... BREATHE OUT.
TANYA, YOU KNOW WE ALL GOT WORK TO DO. I'M EXCITED ABOUT OUR PROJECT AND I NEED TO TALK TO DEVANTE.
YEAH, WE HAVE WORK TO DO.

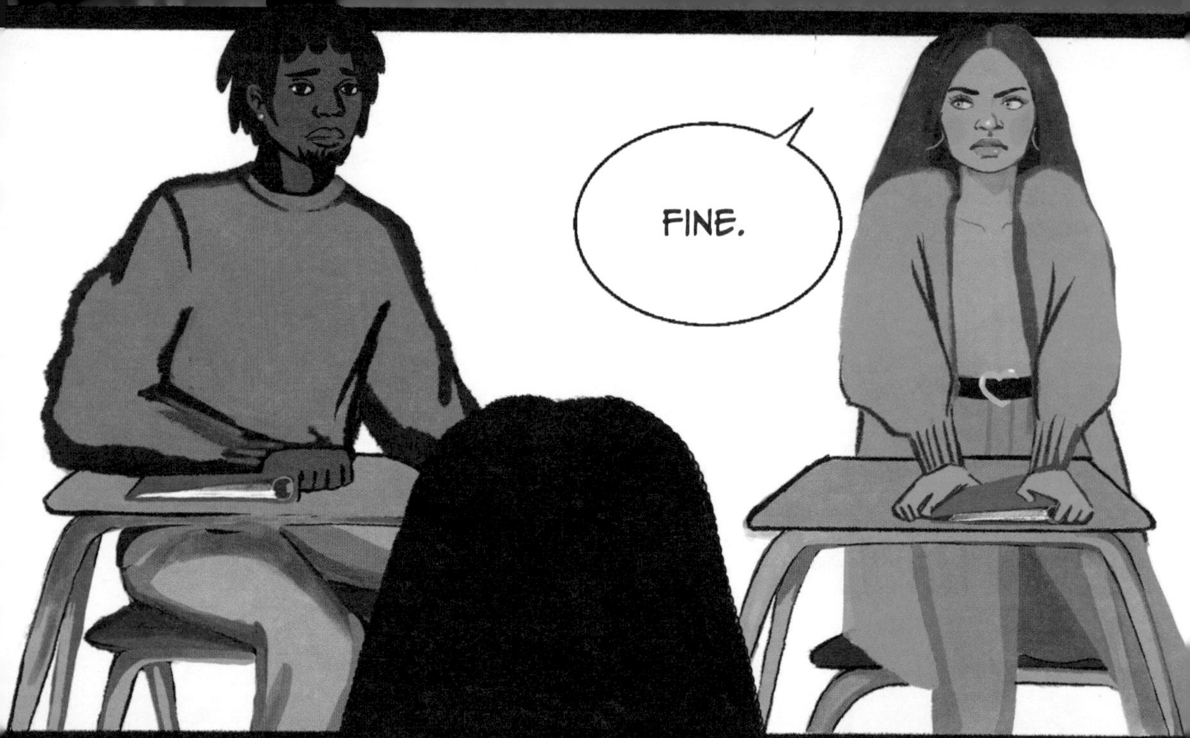
FINE.

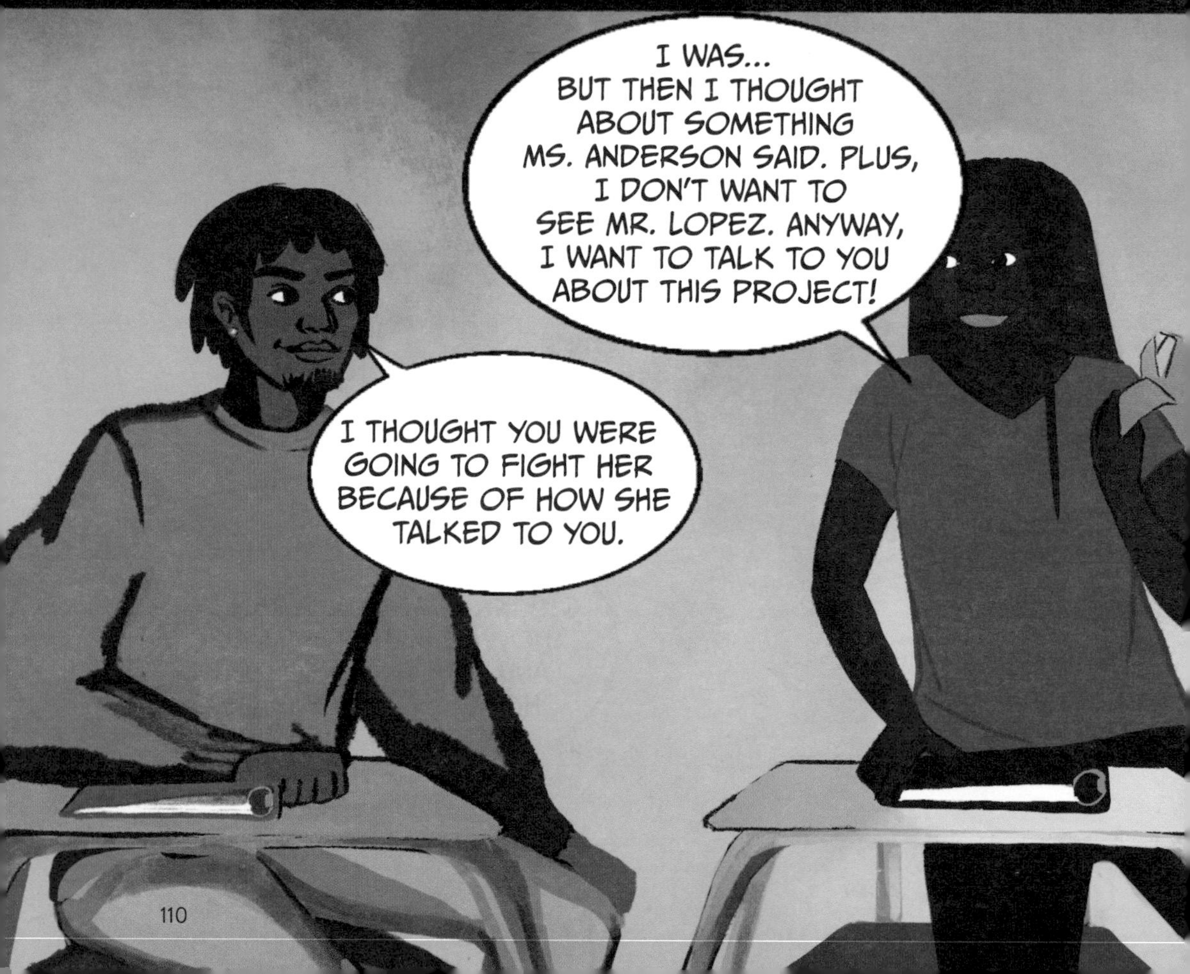
I THOUGHT YOU WERE GOING TO FIGHT HER BECAUSE OF HOW SHE TALKED TO YOU.
I WAS... BUT THEN I THOUGHT ABOUT SOMETHING MS. ANDERSON SAID. PLUS, I DON'T WANT TO SEE MR. LOPEZ. ANYWAY, I WANT TO TALK TO YOU ABOUT THIS PROJECT!

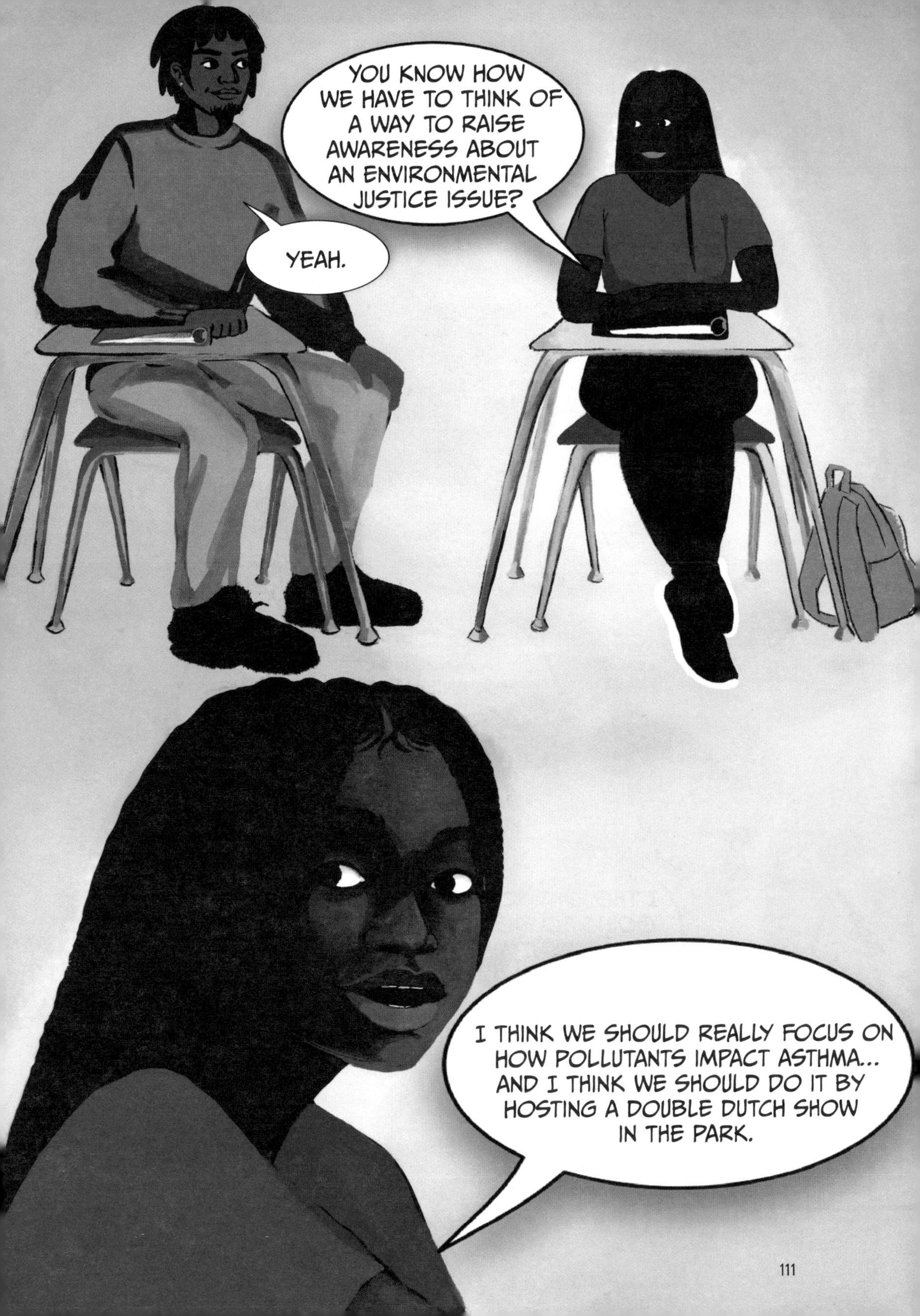
YOU KNOW HOW WE HAVE TO THINK OF A WAY TO RAISE AWARENESS ABOUT AN ENVIRONMENTAL JUSTICE ISSUE?
YEAH.
I THINK WE SHOULD REALLY FOCUS ON HOW POLLUTANTS IMPACT ASTHMA... AND I THINK WE SHOULD DO IT BY HOSTING A DOUBLE DUTCH SHOW IN THE PARK.

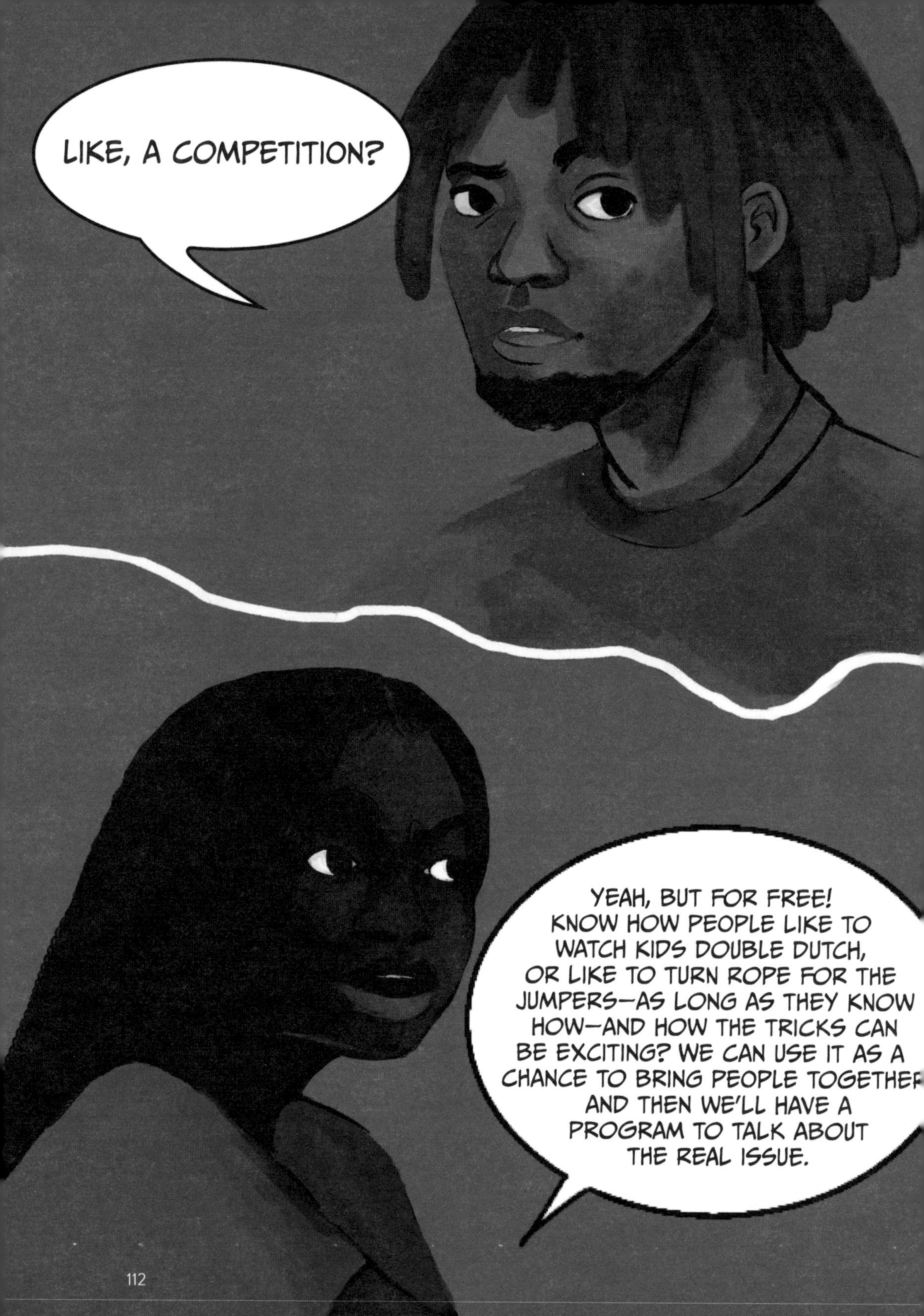
LIKE, A COMPETITION?
YEAH, BUT FOR FREE! KNOW HOW PEOPLE LIKE TO WATCH KIDS DOUBLE DUTCH, OR LIKE TO TURN ROPE FOR THE JUMPERS—AS LONG AS THEY KNOW HOW—AND HOW THE TRICKS CAN BE EXCITING? WE CAN USE IT AS A CHANCE TO BRING PEOPLE TOGETHER AND THEN WE'LL HAVE A PROGRAM TO TALK ABOUT THE REAL ISSUE.

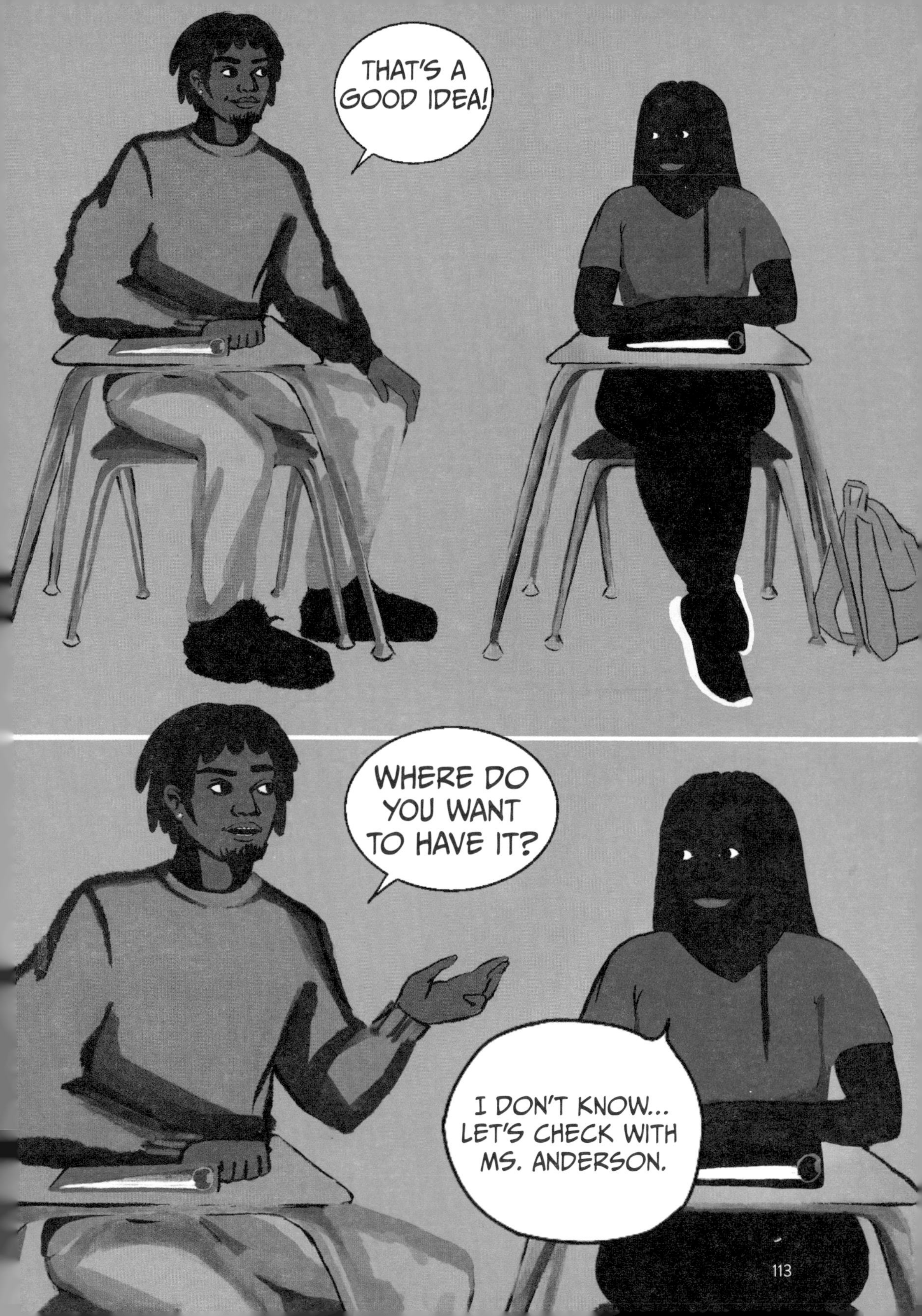
THAT'S A GOOD IDEA!
WHERE DO YOU WANT TO HAVE IT?
I DON'T KNOW... LET'S CHECK WITH MS. ANDERSON.

PRINCIPAL LOPEZ'S OFFICE
I WANTED TO TALK TO YOU ABOUT CHARISMA. SHE'S REALLY SHOWN LEADERSHIP ON THIS PROJECT FOR MY AFTER-SCHOOL CLASS.
I'VE NOTICED THAT SHE'S BEEN DOING QUITE WELL LATELY!

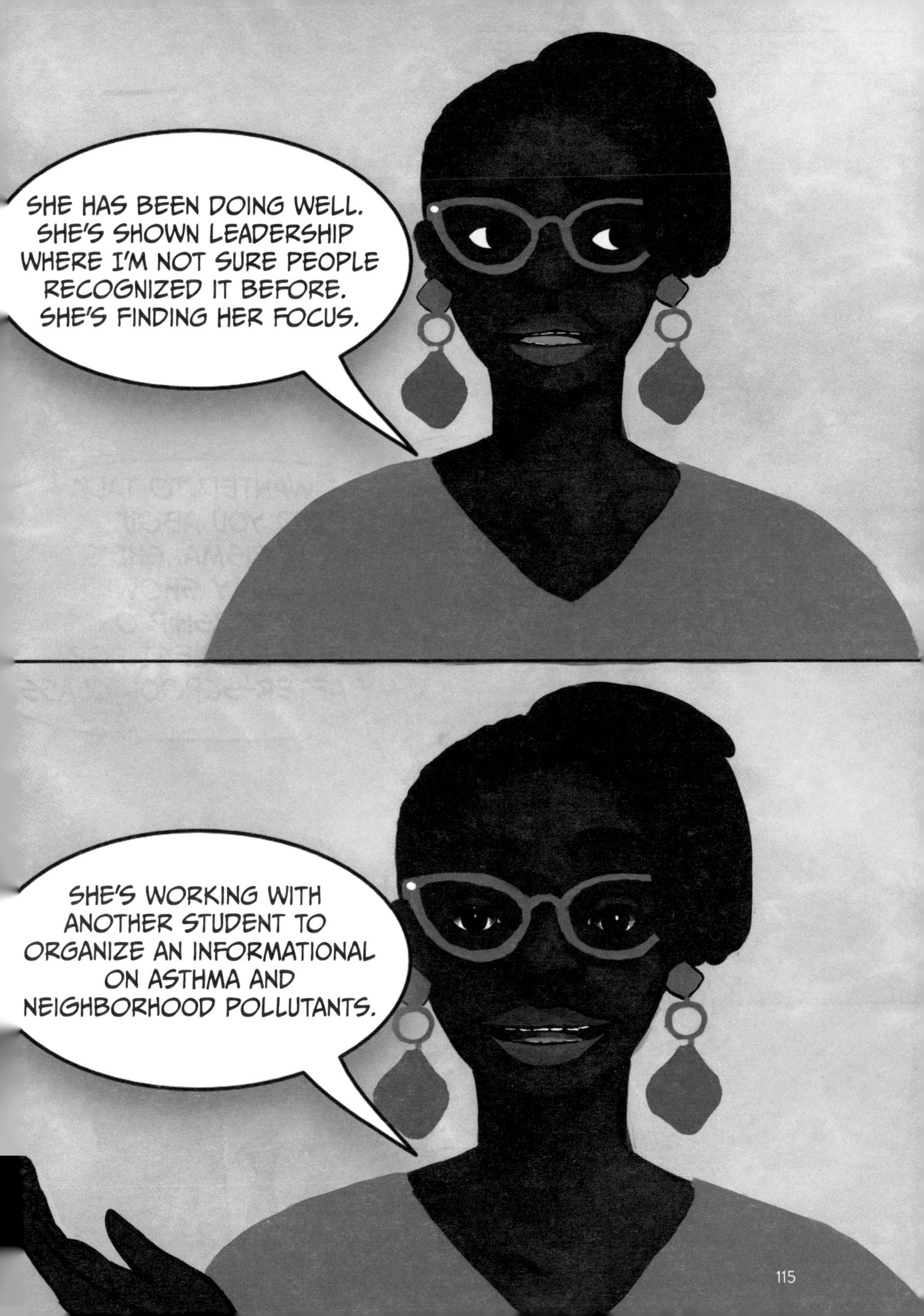
SHE HAS BEEN DOING WELL. SHE'S SHOWN LEADERSHIP WHERE I'M NOT SURE PEOPLE RECOGNIZED IT BEFORE. SHE'S FINDING HER FOCUS.
SHE'S WORKING WITH ANOTHER STUDENT TO ORGANIZE AN INFORMATIONAL ON ASTHMA AND NEIGHBORHOOD POLLUTANTS.

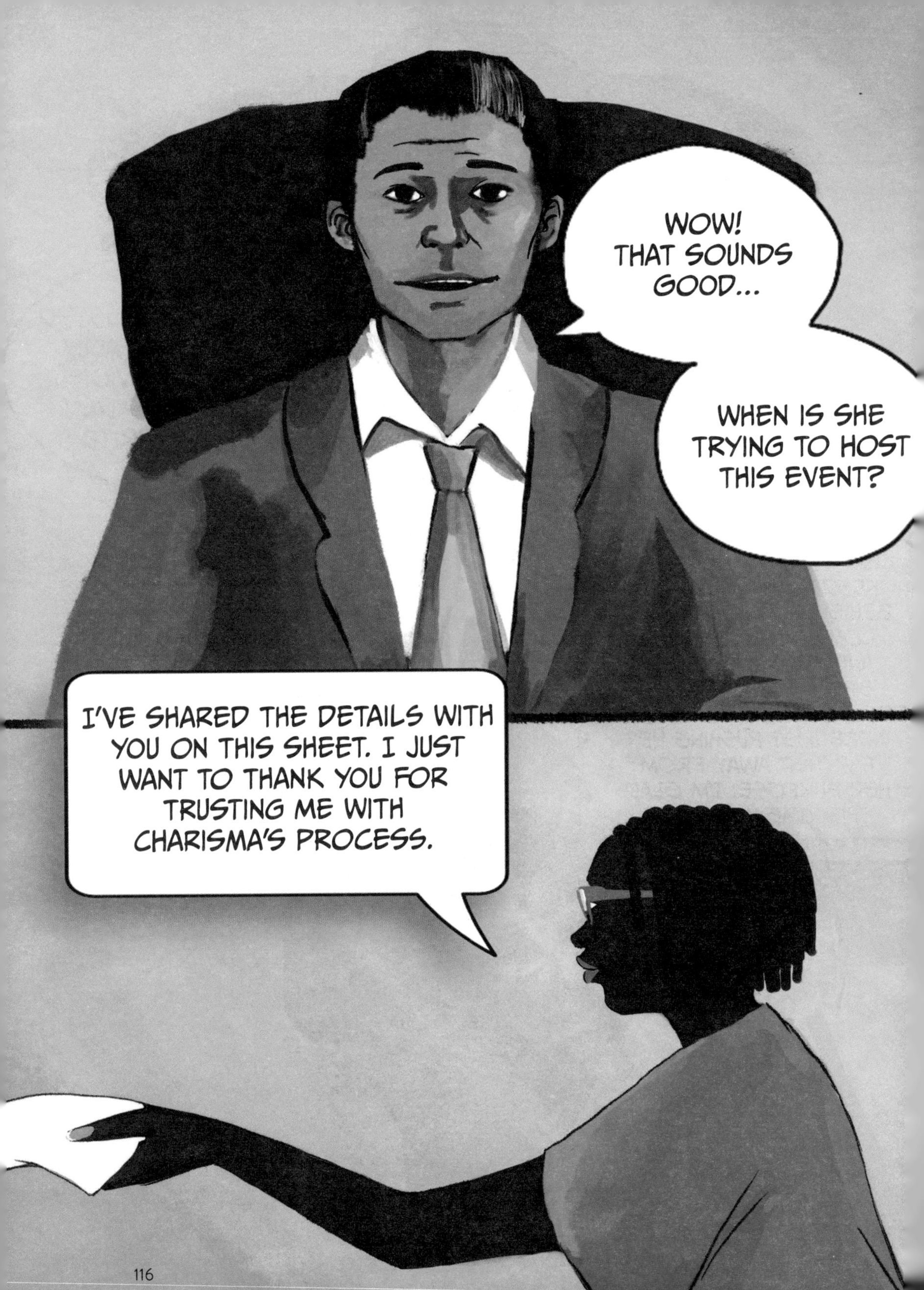
WOW! THAT SOUNDS GOOD...
WHEN IS SHE TRYING TO HOST THIS EVENT?
I'VE SHARED THE DETAILS WITH YOU ON THIS SHEET. I JUST WANT TO THANK YOU FOR TRUSTING ME WITH CHARISMA'S PROCESS.

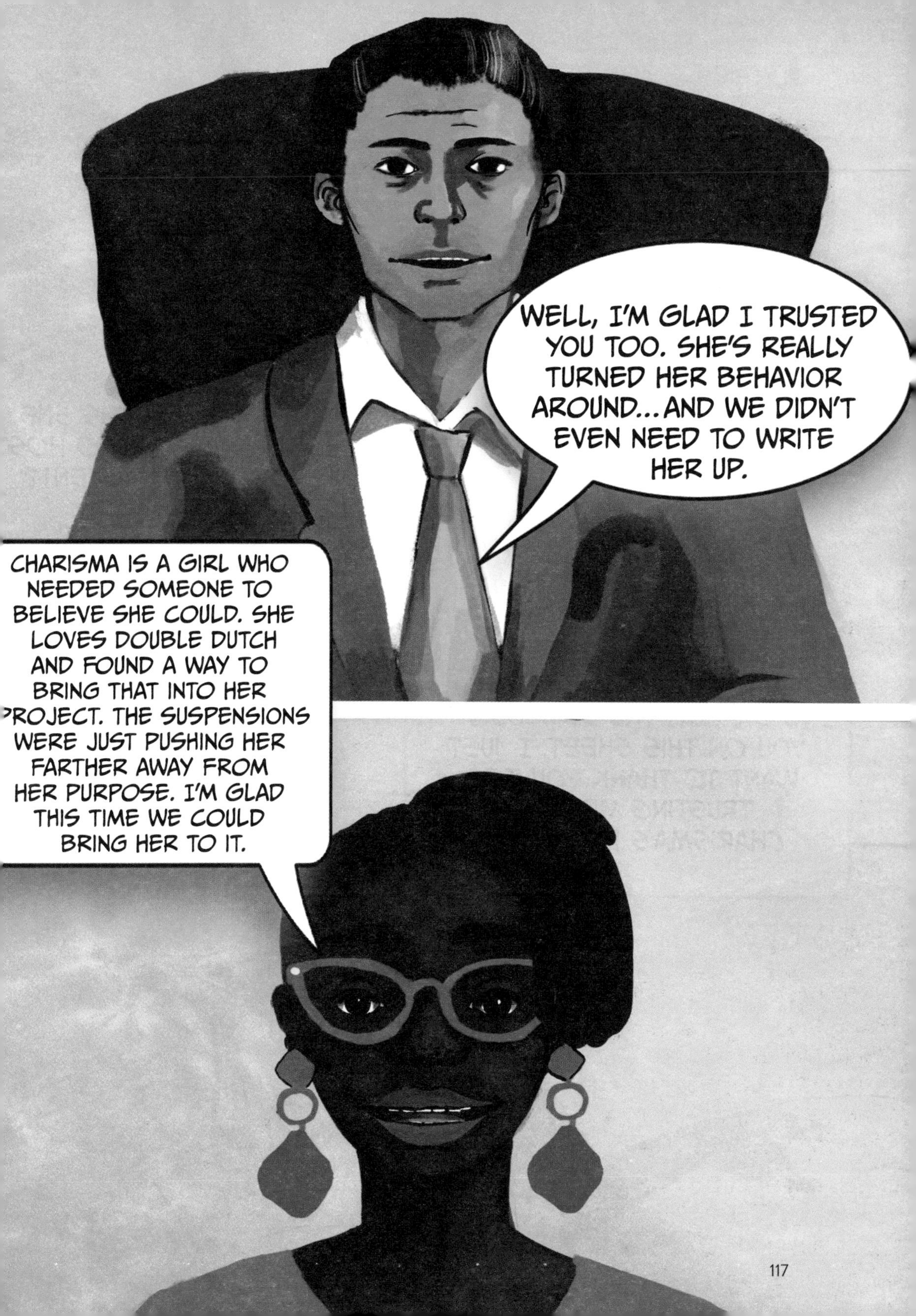
WELL, I'M GLAD I TRUSTED YOU TOO. SHE'S REALLY TURNED HER BEHAVIOR AROUND...AND WE DIDN'T EVEN NEED TO WRITE HER UP.
CHARISMA IS A GIRL WHO NEEDED SOMEONE TO BELIEVE SHE COULD. SHE LOVES DOUBLE DUTCH AND FOUND A WAY TO BRING THAT INTO HER PROJECT. THE SUSPENSIONS WERE JUST PUSHING HER FARTHER AWAY FROM HER PURPOSE. I'M GLAD THIS TIME WE COULD BRING HER TO IT.

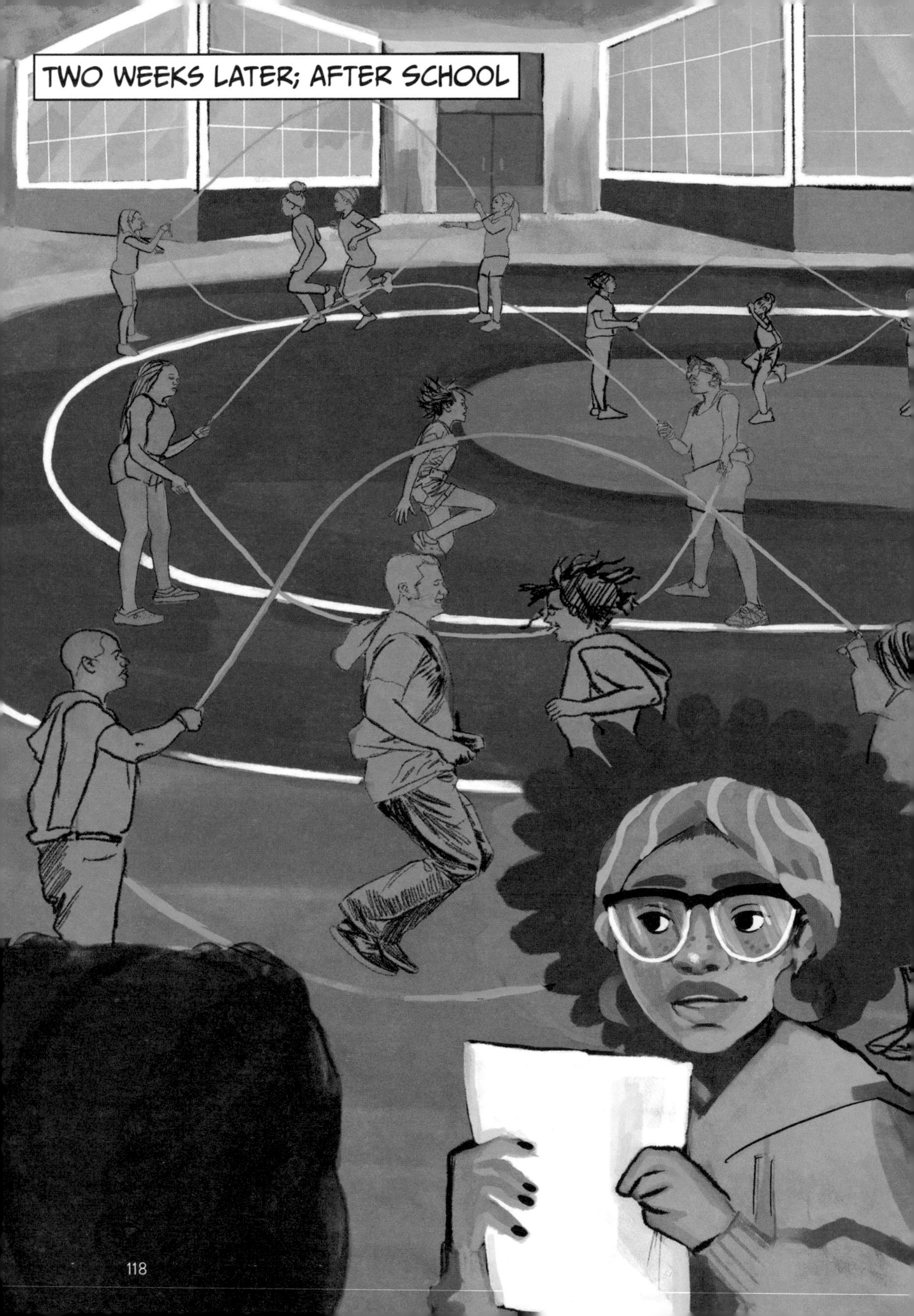
TWO WEEKS LATER; AFTER SCHOOL

TAKE CONTROL

People talk about air pon and climate change, but we
sometimes ignore how pollution impacts everyday life, especially
if you have asthma.

According to the American Lung Association, asthma affects
24.8 million Americans (5.5 million children).

Did you know?

Air pollution is defined as "any visible or invisible particle or gas
found in the air that is not part of the natural composition of air."
Air pollution makes asthma conditions worse, especially in high
pollution summer days.
Ozone, a gas, is one of the most common air pollutants.
It irritates the lungs and airways and triggers asthma.
Small particles in the air, found in haze, smoke, and airborne dust,
present a serious air quality problem.

Black, Latino, and Asian people are more likely to die prematurely
from particle pollution.
Black and Indigenous/Native peoples have the highest overall rates of
asthma in the U.S. In 2018, African American people (10.9%) were 42 percent
more likely than white people (7.7%) to also have asthma.

Puerto Ricans have among the highest asthma rates (14%) in the U.S.

(American Lung Association).

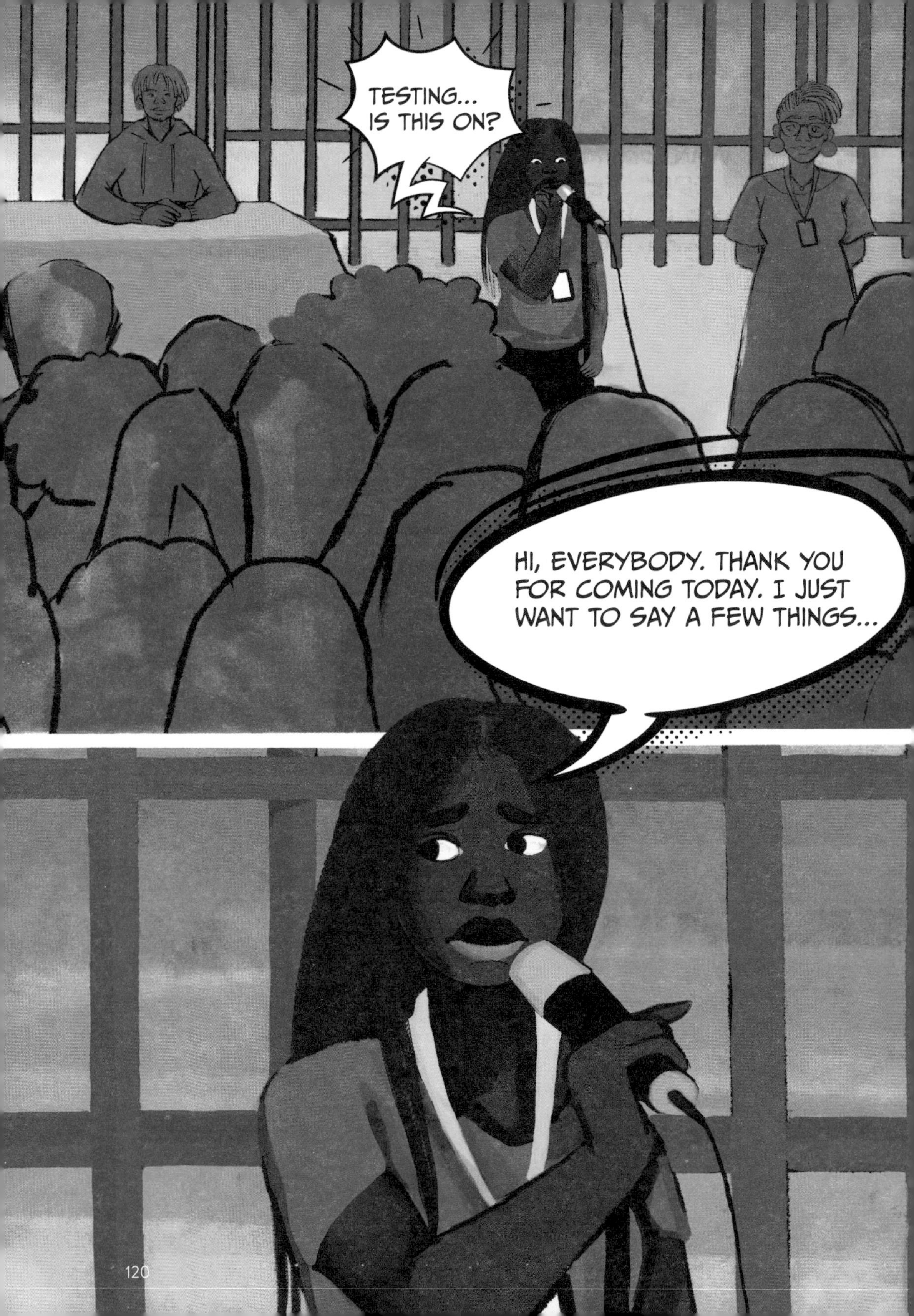
TESTING... IS THIS ON?
HI, EVERYBODY. THANK YOU FOR COMING TODAY. I JUST WANT TO SAY A FEW THINGS...

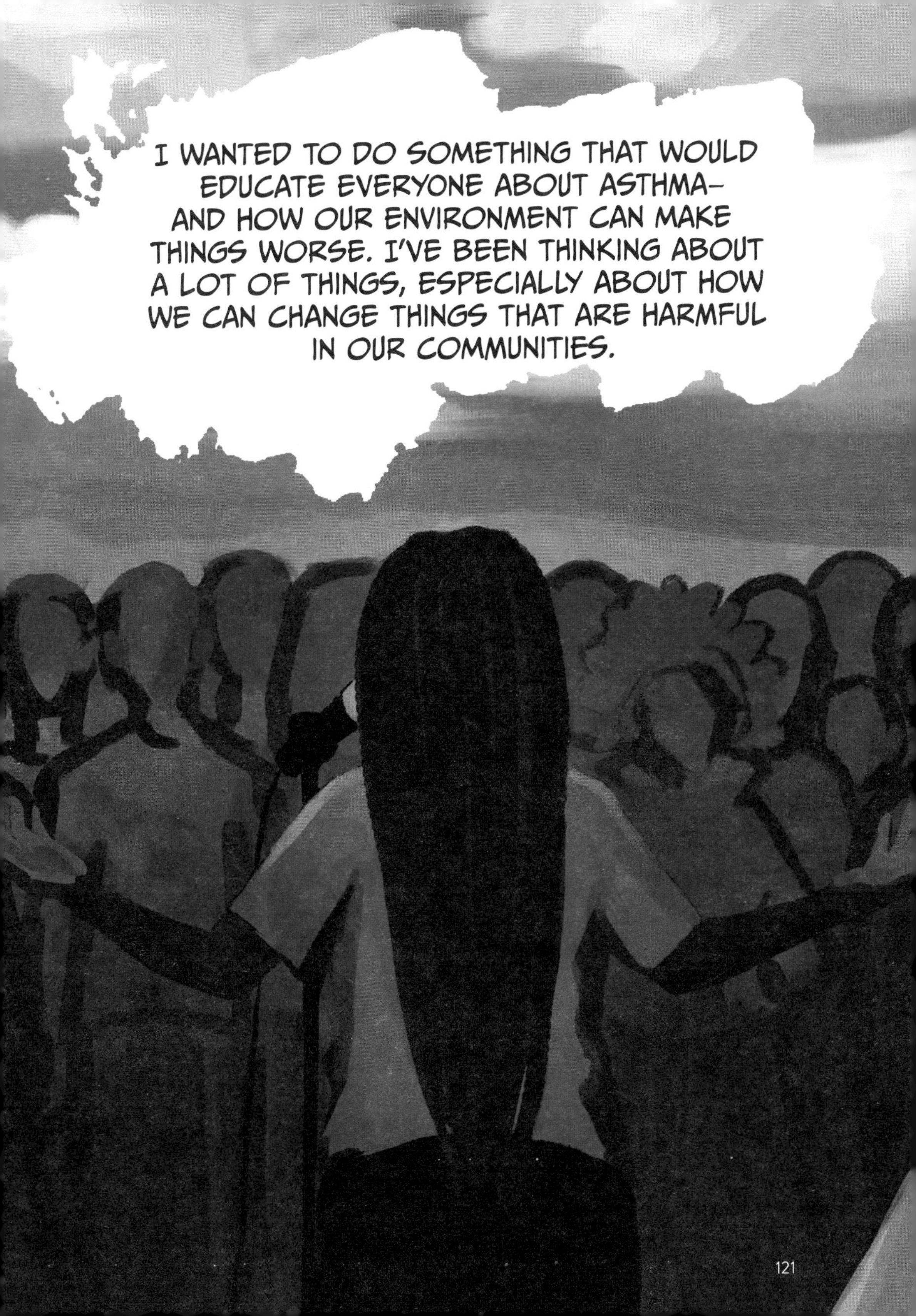
I WANTED TO DO SOMETHING THAT WOULD EDUCATE EVERYONE ABOUT ASTHMA– AND HOW OUR ENVIRONMENT CAN MAKE THINGS WORSE. I'VE BEEN THINKING ABOUT A LOT OF THINGS, ESPECIALLY ABOUT HOW WE CAN CHANGE THINGS THAT ARE HARMFUL IN OUR COMMUNITIES.

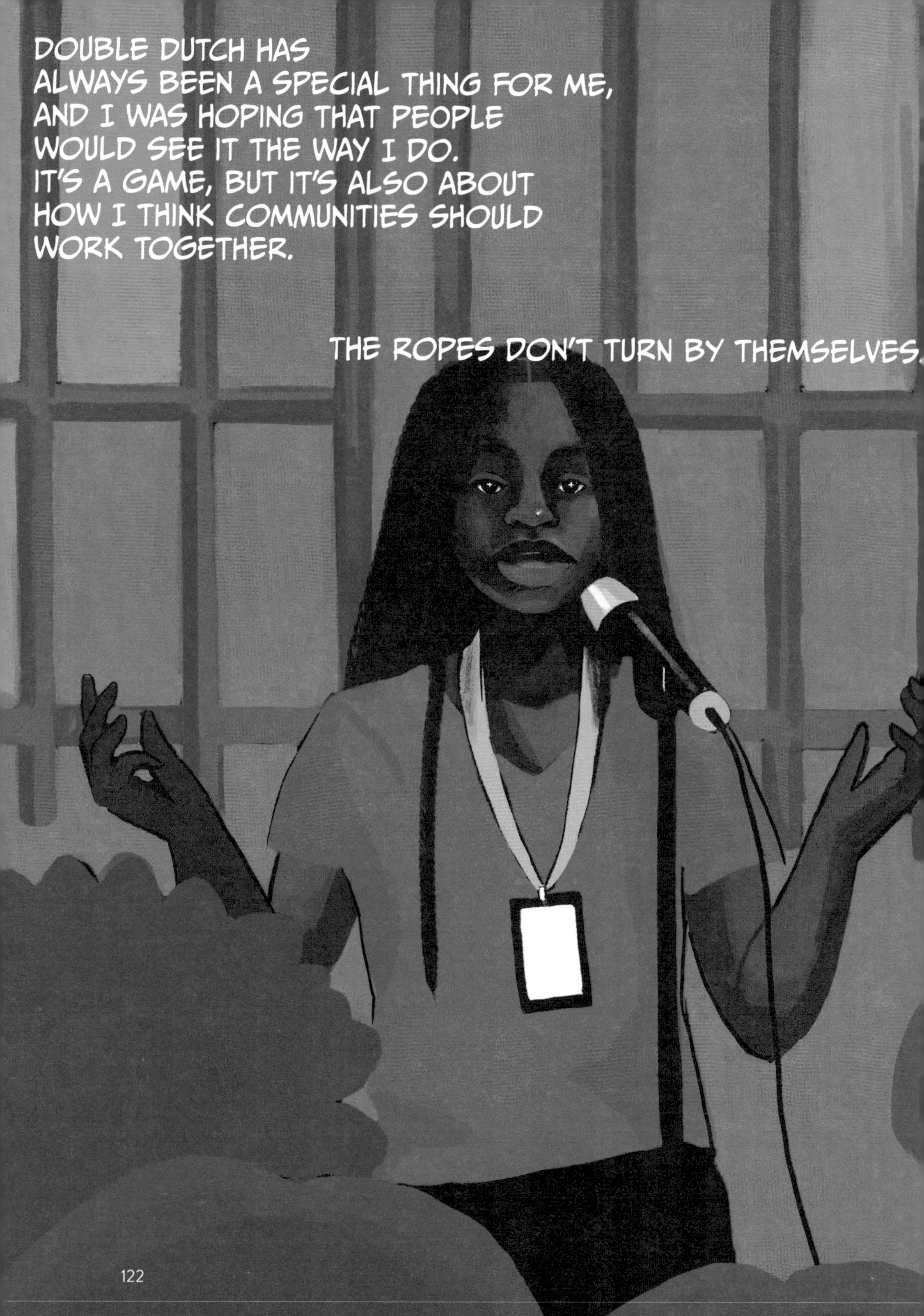
DOUBLE DUTCH HAS
ALWAYS BEEN A SPECIAL THING FOR ME,
AND I WAS HOPING THAT PEOPLE
WOULD SEE IT THE WAY I DO.
IT'S A GAME, BUT IT'S ALSO ABOUT
HOW I THINK COMMUNITIES SHOULD
WORK TOGETHER.
THE ROPES DON'T TURN BY THEMSELVES.

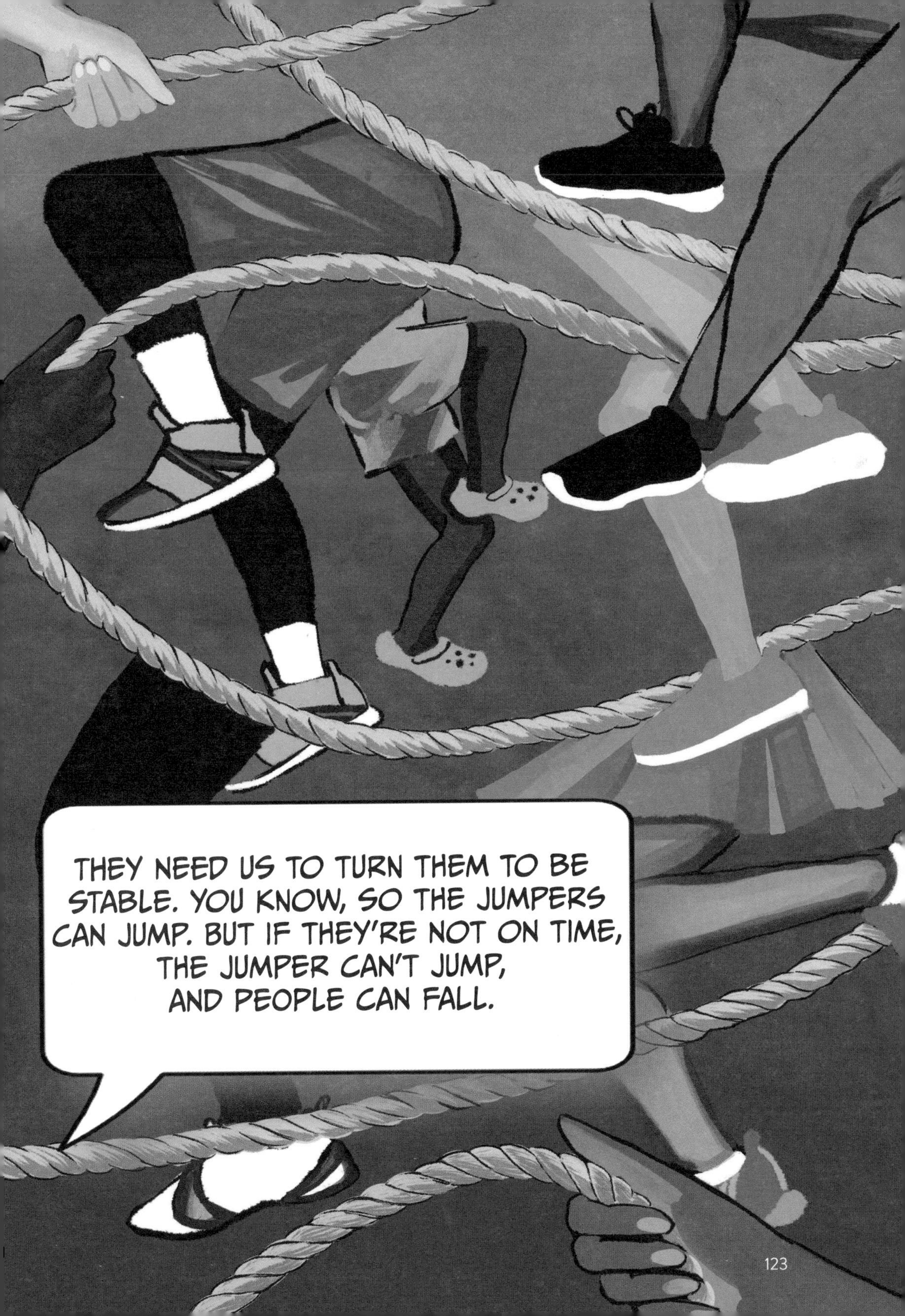
THEY NEED US TO TURN THEM TO BE STABLE. YOU KNOW, SO THE JUMPERS CAN JUMP. BUT IF THEY'RE NOT ON TIME, THE JUMPER CAN'T JUMP, AND PEOPLE CAN FALL.

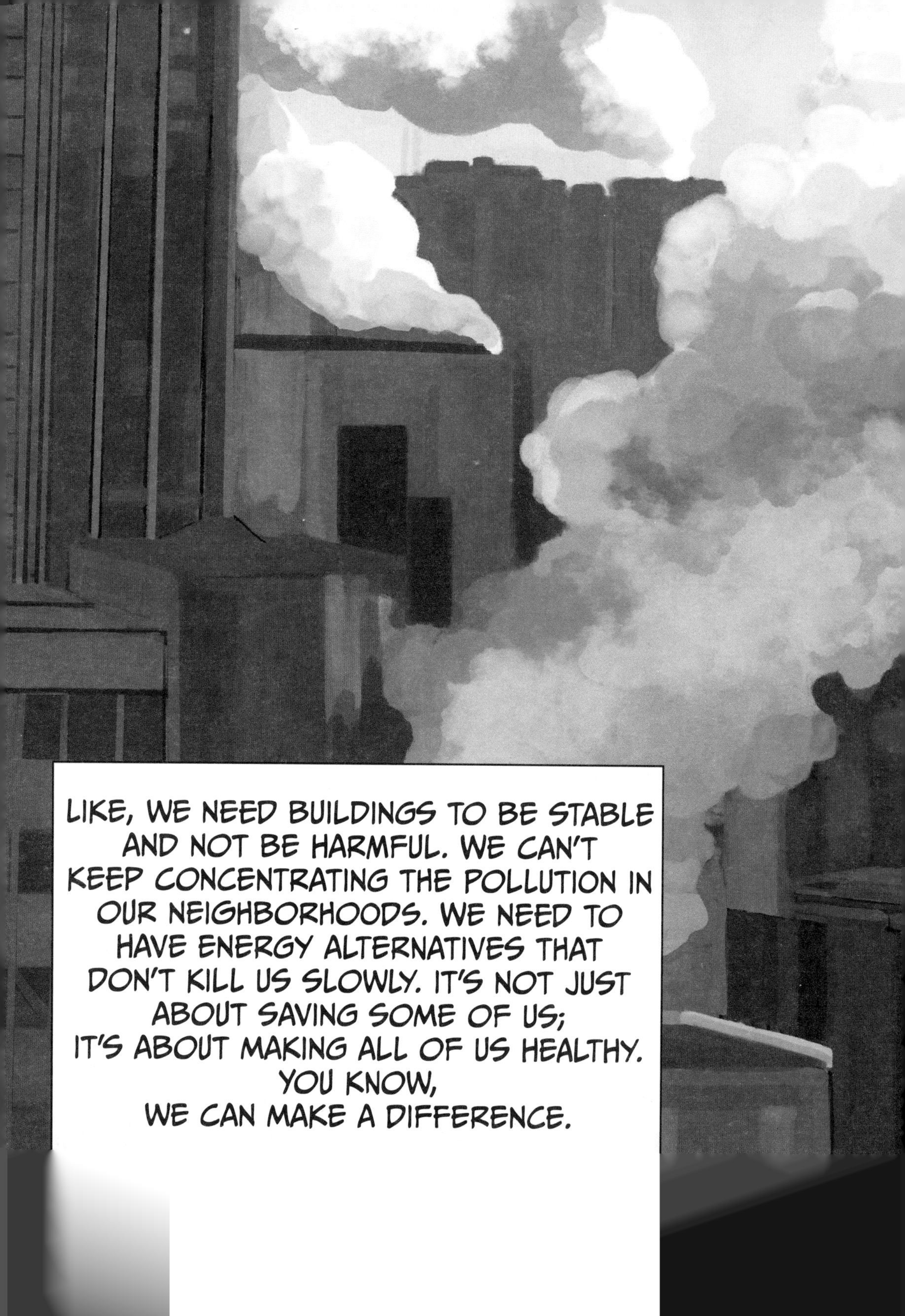
LIKE, WE NEED BUILDINGS TO BE STABLE AND NOT BE HARMFUL. WE CAN'T KEEP CONCENTRATING THE POLLUTION IN OUR NEIGHBORHOODS. WE NEED TO HAVE ENERGY ALTERNATIVES THAT DON'T KILL US SLOWLY. IT'S NOT JUST ABOUT SAVING SOME OF US; IT'S ABOUT MAKING ALL OF US HEALTHY. YOU KNOW, WE CAN MAKE A DIFFERENCE.

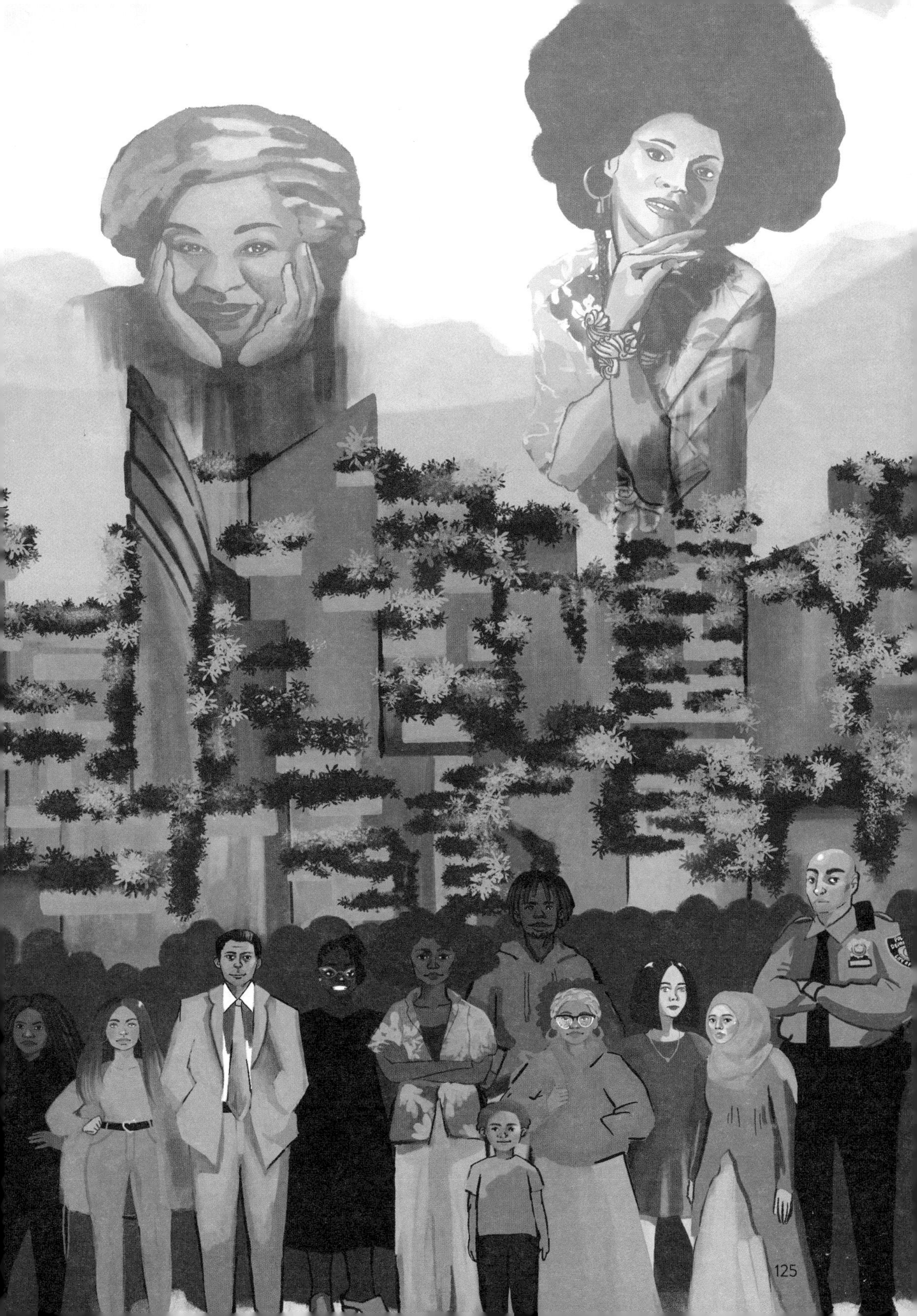

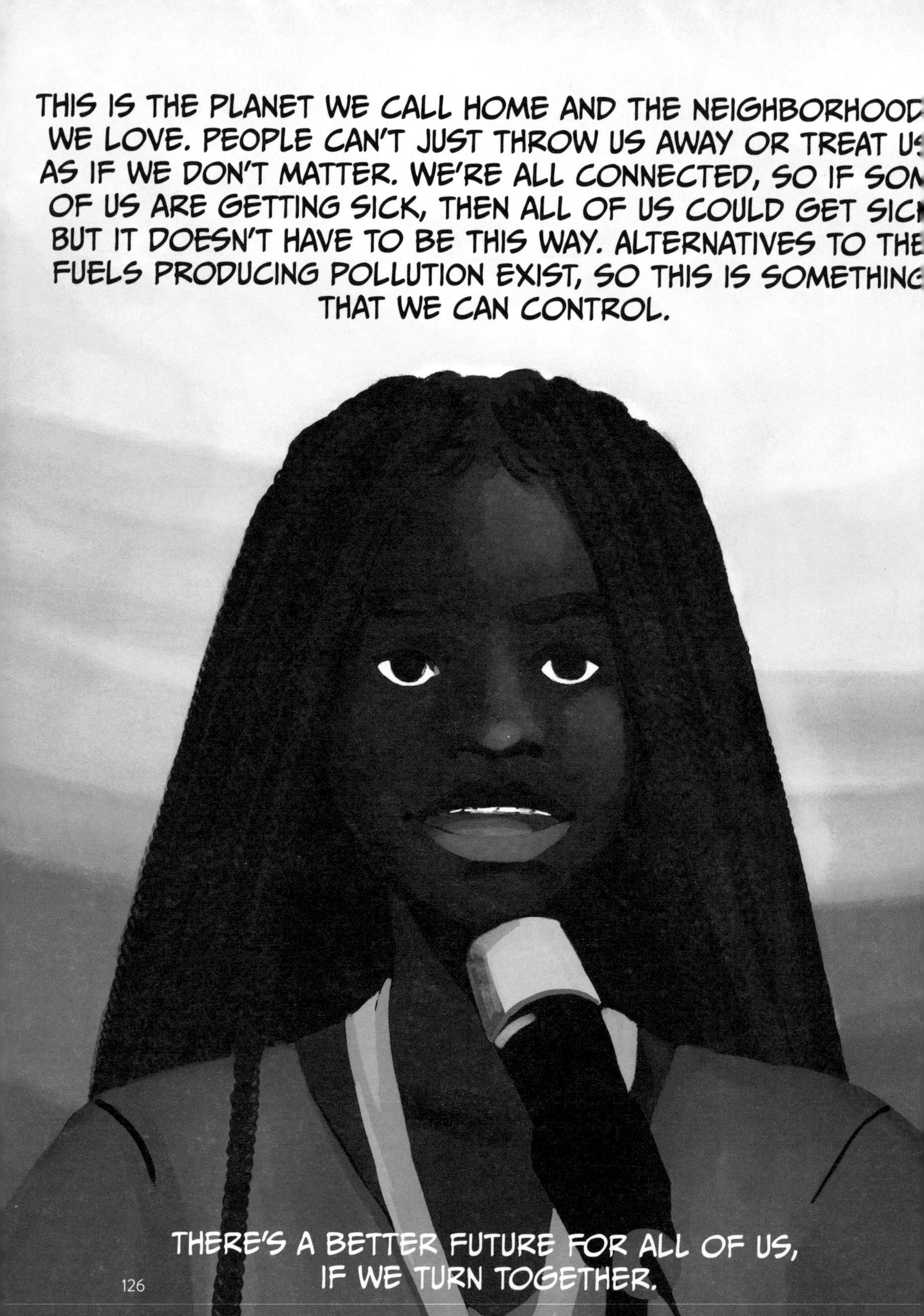
THIS IS THE PLANET WE CALL HOME AND THE NEIGHBORHOOD
WE LOVE. PEOPLE CAN'T JUST THROW US AWAY OR TREAT U
AS IF WE DON'T MATTER. WE'RE ALL CONNECTED, SO IF SO
OF US ARE GETTING SICK, THEN ALL OF US COULD GET SIC
BUT IT DOESN'T HAVE TO BE THIS WAY. ALTERNATIVES TO THE
FUELS PRODUCING POLLUTION EXIST, SO THIS IS SOMETHIN
THAT WE CAN CONTROL.
THERE'S A BETTER FUTURE FOR ALL OF US,
IF WE TURN TOGETHER.

Monique Couvson (formerly Monique W. Morris) is president / CEO of Grantmakers for Girls of Color and co-founder of the National Black Women's Justice Institute. Her books include *Pushout*, *Black Stats*, and *Sing a Rhythm, Dance a Blues* (all from The New Press). She lives in New York.

Amanda Jones is a freelance illustrator based in Manhattan. She dedicates her time to exploring her individuality through artistic concepts while having a never-ending dedication to helping others achieve their creative visions through her artistic skills. She has a deep and devoted passion for all things beautiful.

Susan Arauz Barnes is a multitalented master teacher and educator trainer with over twenty-five years of experience designing culturally responsive curriculum. She currently teaches at the Ron Clark Academy, a highly acclaimed, nonprofit middle school located in Atlanta, Georgia.

Publishing in the Public Interest

Thank you for reading this book published by The New Press; we hope you enjoyed it. New Press books and authors play a crucial role in sparking conversations about the key political and social issues of our day.

We hope that you will stay in touch with us. Here are a few ways to keep up to date with our books, events, and the issues we cover:

- Sign up at www.thenewpress.com/subscribe to receive updates on New Press authors and issues and to be notified about local events
- www.facebook.com/newpressbooks
- www.twitter.com/thenewpress
- www.instagram.com/thenewpress

Please consider buying New Press books not only for yourself, but also for friends and family and to donate to schools, libraries, community centers, prison libraries, and other organizations involved with the issues our authors write about.

The New Press is a 501(c)(3) nonprofit organization; please consider supporting our work with a tax-deductible gift by visiting www.thenewpress.com/donate or by using the QR code below.